A Lady's Gift for Seduction

Copyright © 2019 by Jess Michaels

A Lady's Gift for Scandal

Copyright © 2019 by Elizabeth Essex

All rights reserved.

No part of this book may be reproduced in any form or by any electronic or mechanical means, including information storage and retrieval systems, without written permission from the author, except for the use of brief quotations in a book review.

BETROTHED BY CHRISTMAS
A HOLIDAY DUET

JESS MICHAELS
ELIZABETH ESSEX

A LADY'S GIFT FOR SEDUCTION

JESS MICHAELS

This project would not have been possible at all without the wonderful Elizabeth Essex. Your enthusiasm and wonderful writing helped me take this story to the next level. And your friendship makes me love our new city all the more. Thank you and love you!

Also for Michael, my own smart hero.

CHAPTER 1

London, December 1814

"Lady Evangeline, you should smile more! There is peace!"
Lady Evangeline lifted the corners of her lips in only the barest sense as one of the diamonds of the previous season spun by her on the arm of some duke or earl or one of their sons. What did it matter? The lot of them were the same, they even dressed in identical style.

She sighed as she turned back to the table and drew another ladle of wassail into her cup. It seemed her enthusiasm for the season would not be found until she had drunk some more. And she supposed she *did* need to find that enthusiasm. After all, it was true—for the first time in over a decade, the world teetered on *peace*. There had been a terrible cost, which hadn't seemed to occur to most of the titled, rich fops around her.

Of course, it was a cost most of them had not paid. They and their sons and grandsons were too important to fight in wars. They only benefitted from them.

She sighed and shook her head. No, this sour mood would not do. She couldn't even place the cause of it. Normally she didn't hate a party. She was often the center of them. But tonight it all felt so very...stale. Like this year that was circling the drain with 1815 looming large behind it.

Would the next year be any different for her? She feared the answer was no. And perhaps *that* was the cause of the dreary malaise she couldn't seem to shake.

The noise of the crowd behind her lifted, and she turned in time to see a group of men bringing out a bowl brimming with brandy. She let her eyes come shut as someone shouted out, "Ah yes, it's about time we played Snapdragon! Dim the candles there!"

She folded her arms as the silver bowl was placed on a low table that had been dragged to the center of the room. The lights went down and, with great pomp and circumstance, one of the men brought over a candle and laughed as he lowered it to the liquor. Flames leapt from the brew, nearly singeing off the man's hair as he yelped in surprise.

"I suppose a game of Snapdragon can't be counted a success until at least one idiot has lost an eyebrow."

Evangeline jerked her head to her right. She had been so caught up in the foolishness going on around her, she hadn't noticed that another lady had stepped up near her. She recognized her. Miss Thomasina Lesley, eldest daughter of Colonel Lesley. She was a pretty enough girl, with an air of reserve that was put down to modest country manners. But with her wide blue eyes, fair hair and petite features, she had been proclaimed a diamond just as Evangeline was.

And right now she had as judgmental an expression on her face as Evangeline felt down to her soul.

"Sometimes two," Evangeline added.

Miss Lesley jumped and pink lifted to her cheeks, as if she hadn't realized Evangeline could hear her. "I do beg your pardon," she said. "I fear I should not be so critical of the fun, especially at this time of year."

Evangeline snorted out what could only be described as a very unladylike laugh. "Do not go back now, I need an ally. You are utterly correct that they are all idiots. They're not the sort of fellows one wants for a husband, are they?"

"Heavens, no."

They watched in silence as those very idiots now stood around the flames, faces dancing in shadow and light as they tossed raisins into the cauldron. Evangeline had never liked this game. Her older brothers had made her play as a little girl and she'd always known it was foolish. Who thought it fun to toss perfectly good fruit into a flaming bowl of hell, then snatch them out with bare fingers and toss them into one's mouth? Her tongue had never fully recovered, she was certain of that.

And yet here was a group of adults—titled, supposedly respectable men—doing just that. One by one they reached into the fire, forever shocked that they were getting burned.

"Lord, grant me the confidence of a man of supposed education who knows absolutely nothing in truth," Evangeline sighed.

"Indeed. If this is what's on offer, I don't think I want any sort of a husband at all. It seems a devil's bargain at best."

"True, but what sort of life can one have without one?" She asked the question sarcastically, for that was the established mode of thinking, after all. That a lady could have no future without a man to bind herself to.

"An independent life," Miss Lesley said. "I had rather entertain myself, not with silly parties with flaming punch bowls, but with intelligent salons where ideas and ideals might be exchanged. Where books might be discussed or poetry recited."

Evangeline turned to face her a bit more directly, and her smile went wide and very true. "*You're* a secret bluestocking."

"It's no great secret. I would be a true bluestocking if I were allowed, like my aunt Dahlia—she has her own establishment here in London and has the most elegant salons, full of the most interesting people." Miss Lesley's face was lit up with a passion that only increased her beauty. Still, her smile fell as she continued,

"But the sad truth is that if I don't marry one of *them*, I'll only be married off to my odious cousin who is to be a baronet someday but cares nothing for books or ideas, unless they're to do with beef cattle or crop rotation."

Evangeline shook her head with a shudder that wracked her entire body. "Great God."

She could sympathize with the woman beside her. After all, such had been the lot of many a lady she'd known in her life. Including her mother, including her sister and her sister-in-law. Marrying well was what one did when one was a woman of a certain stature, whether or not one wished for it.

Even Evangeline, who had what anyone would describe as a preposterous level of independence, was not immune to the possibility in her own future. Her father mentioned it from time to time, that she would be married off to some gentleman who was nearly his same rank. He spoke of it more often than ever, truth be told.

Just that morning, actually.

"Might you be able to manage him into thinking better?" Evangeline pressed, seeking any kind of solace, not just for her new friend, but for herself. "A good woman can often make a mediocre man into something more."

"I doubt it."

Evangeline shivered despite the heat of the close room. What Miss Lesley was facing was not so very far from her own worst fear.

"Lady Evangeline?"

"Yes?"

Miss Lesley shifted. "I was only saying I wish we were truly allowed to choose, don't you?"

She forced herself to attend and ignored the question. "I'm sorry, Miss Lesley, I was just woolgathering. Thinking of your situation. So you do not wish to marry this dreadful cousin?"

Miss Lesley shook her head, faint tears glistening in her eyes.

"What is it you *do* want, then?"

The other woman drew a long breath, and from her expression Evangeline could tell this was not a question she was often asked. But it was one she had an immediate answer to.

"I'd rather be a spinster, like my aunt Dahlia. My mama does say she ruined herself coming to London on her own, but she's left to live in peace with books and cats and no men. It's heavenly."

It did sound the stuff of dreams. And for a lady like Thomasina Lesley, Evangeline could see how that might work. For herself... her father would never allow it. He was too important a man, too important a *duke* to have his daughter adopt an eccentric lifestyle of cats and Gothic novels. Ruined or not.

"That is what I want. But my mama will never approve," Miss Lesley continued. "I must choose, and by the end of this little Christmas season. The very thought of Cousin Edward makes me want to ruin myself like Aunt Dahlia, so he'll have nothing to do with me."

Evangeline lifted her chin. Perhaps this gauzy dream life of spinsterhood wasn't something *she* could have, but that didn't mean Miss Lesley should be trapped. If Evangeline could help her...

"Why not do it then?"

Miss Lesley shook her head. "Do what?"

"Ruin yourself," Evangeline repeated. She looked around the room as her mind spun on the problem. "It would have to be light ruination. To maintain your standing on some level. It all has to be done very carefully, in a controlled fashion." She rubbed her chin. "A bespoke ruination, if you like."

Miss Lesley stared at her. "Do you really think so?"

"Absolutely."

Miss Leslie drew her away from the edge of the ballroom floor and the crowd still engaged in the game of Snapdragon. "Pray, tell me more."

Evangeline shrugged, for it all seemed rather obvious to her as the entire scenario played out in her mind. "If you truly do not want to fall victim to the machinations of your parents, you must do a little *machinating* of your own."

"How?" Miss Leslie asked, her eyes wide.

Evangeline drew a long breath as she pondered the question. Then the answer hit her like a punch to the chest, and she smiled. "We must simply think like the men, mustn't we, when they want to find a biddable bride." She clapped her hands together as the plan snapped in place, easy as a child's wooden puzzle. "And who is a biddable bride, at least in their minds? A wallflower."

"A wallflower," Miss Leslie repeated. "A *masculine* wallflower."

"Exactly," Evangeline insisted with a grin, and reached out to catch Thomasina's arm. "And I know just where they are."

Miss Leslie didn't resist as Evangeline drew her from the ballroom and down through the long, twisting halls of the manor. At last they reached a door that was partially ajar, and Evangeline pushed it wider so they could see inside.

"The library," Miss Leslie said in the hushed tones of reverence such a place afforded.

Evangeline looked up at the massive bookshelves that reached almost to the high ceiling of the room. She gave a contented sigh and then shook off her reaction to focus on matters at hand. "And just as I promised, here are the wallflowers."

There were three gentlemen in the room at present. Two sat on opposite ends of a long settee, reading. The third stood at the window, staring out of a telescope into the night sky. As he turned toward the door and the intruders who had invaded the privacy of the men, Evangeline caught her breath. Lost it entirely as he smiled at her.

Miss Leslie's gaze followed Evangeline's and her grip tightened on her arm. "Who is that?"

Evangeline glanced at her new friend from the corner of her

eye. "Do you not know Henry Killam?" she said, her tone a bit sharper than she'd meant to make it.

"Might he do? He seems quite a bluestocking sort himself," Miss Lesley said, her tone now full of regard of Evangeline's plan. A plan that suddenly felt a little ill-thought.

"Well..." Evangeline hesitated. "He is a thorough, scientific sort of fellow, who never does anything by halves, so that would be an advantage in your predicament, specifically..."

Evangeline swallowed as her attention shifted back to Henry at the window. Miss Lesley spoke of his obvious intellect, but she must have also noticed how handsome Henry was. Not as showy as the dukes, perhaps, more plainly dressed. Not as puffed out like a peacock. But his figure spoke of a lean strength. A grace. He had a very nice face with interesting angles.

His hair was a bit too long, of course, and always looked as though he'd just run his hand through it. And then there were his eyes. Hidden behind spectacles, but still lovely green depths that reminded one of pale fields in the spring and...

Her teeth were clenched and she had to force herself to unclench them. "Do you know, I don't think Henry will do at all for your purposes, not at all," she heard herself say.

"No?" Thomasina said with a bit of disappointment lacing her tone.

"No. Because he's...because he's not..." Evangeline stammered and stuttered as she tried to think of one reason Henry Killam was not a good choice for her new friend's endeavor. Before she could, her gaze was caught by a fourth person she hadn't realized was in the room with them. A handsome gentleman, fast asleep on another settee across the room.

"Simon!" she burst out as she all but leapt toward him, crossing halfway to the alcove in that one long step and drawing the brief attention of the other men before they went back to reading almost as if she wasn't there at all. She motioned to him with one hand. "Oh, yes. Simon Cathcart ought to do quite nicely."

Miss Lesley stared at him and her face twisted in disbelief. "Really? He looks rather too indolent. And too…too everything."

She thought she saw Miss Lesley's gaze flicker back toward Henry, and she motioned her closer to Cathcart instead.

"Hmmm, yes," she said, fighting for as many reasons as she could to turn her new friend's attention to the sleeping man before her. She ticked them off on her fingers, waxing poetic about his days as a soldier, his lack of opinions, anything that jumped to mind about him just so that the attention would stay where it belonged.

And if she embellished, well, what harm was there? The more she thought about it, the more Cathcart seemed the better fit for Miss Lesley! Better than Henry, for heaven's sake. Evangeline was doing her a favor turning her away toward a far more appropriate match for the job she wanted done.

Miss Lesley looked down at Cathcart over the edge of the spectacles she had pulled from her pocket at some point during Evangeline's poetic recitation of the gentleman's better qualities.

"I *suppose* if I were going to all the ugly trouble of being ruined, I might want something beautiful to look at," Miss Lesley said at last.

Relief flooded Evangeline. "*Exactly*, he is imminently suitable for the purpose. Uncomplicated, simple Simon." She glared at the man still sleeping on the couch. He was not helping. She closed the remaining distance to him and nudged him with her foot. "Aren't you, Simon?"

Cathcart opened his eyes with a grin that had probably melted a dozen hearts, but had never done a thing for Evangeline. "Of course I am. Is that you, then, Evie, old girl?"

Evangeline let out her breath and glared at him. God's teeth, she'd forgotten what a shameless tease the man could be. Of course, Miss Lesley might like that about him. Cathcart was fun, in his own way. "It is. Good evening, Simon. Do get up, dear man. Miss Lesley has a proposition for you."

She glanced away as she said it, her interest brought again to Henry at the window. He was frowning now as he gazed up at the stars. Like something had troubled him. She found herself wondering what it was.

To her left, Simon said something and she forced her attention back to her friends. Miss Lesley looked a bit uncomfortable. She was shifting, in fact, and Simon just looked confused. She started as she realized the man had been lamenting *treaties*, of all things. Gracious, did she have to do everything? "Miss Lesley desires to be ruined," she said bluntly.

She saw Simon's eyes go wide and Miss Lesley gasped as she tried to explain that shocking statement. As she did so, Evangeline took another peek at Henry. He was looking at her now. No, not at her. At Simon Cathcart.

His frown was deeper than ever.

Miss Lesley was speaking again. "And I give you my word that no other young lady will hear it from my lips."

Evangeline smiled, for it seemed they had come to terms of some kind. "Nor mine," she said. "And to make sure I know nothing of the affair, I shall leave you to arrange it as you will."

With that, Evangeline swept toward the study door. There she paused and looked back at Henry. He had returned to his telescope and was leaning over it intently, giving her a very nice view of a shapely backside beneath his trousers. She cleared her throat gently as she stepped away from the view and the confusing thoughts it made her think.

Thoughts of a biddable groom. One who would thwart her own father's potential interference and give her a lasting independence that few ladies of her sphere ever enjoyed. Certainly that was all she was thinking about. There was nothing else to consider.

CHAPTER 2

Henry Killam stared out the carriage window as his father's London estate loomed large just past the parted curtain. It was intimidating, as always. That was by design, of course. The Viscount Killam had always wanted everyone to be aware of his station, and of the station he aspired to by toadying about for men higher than himself.

Something Henry had never given a fiddler's damn about. There was so much more to life than rank and inheritance and ill-gotten gains from world domination. There was science and stars and steam to be explored. But not today. Today he had been called here with a curt note that did not speak well of what he would find inside these cold, familiar walls.

And so he sighed as he stepped down from the carriage.

"I'll walk home after my meeting, so you may take the carriage back to the little house," he directed his driver.

The little house. That was the nickname his father and brother had given his townhouse across the park years ago, and somehow Henry had taken to calling it the same, despite how dismissive it was.

"Of course, Mr. Killam," Adams said with a tip of his head

before he encouraged the horses to jog on, and turned the vehicle back up the drive and to the street.

Henry looked up the long stair to the red door above. Subtle, his father was not. Nor was his butler, Morley, who was already waiting for him at the entrance to the foyer. Apparently, Henry was late, for Morley's expression was tight and irritated, which meant his father's would likely be the same.

He moved up the stairs, ignoring how Morley sniffed up and down at his lack of hat, which he had forgotten in his hurry to leave the Society of London Astronomical Studies an hour earlier. He did take Henry's heavy coat and his gloves, then directed him to the blue parlor.

Henry made his way there swiftly, wiping off his spectacles, which had steamed up when he entered the warm house out of the frigid afternoon temperatures. He had high hopes he could quickly finish whatever business his father had in store for him. He needed to return to the little house for but a moment to fetch some notes, and he hoped to be back to the Society meeting hall before supper. He had other things to occupy his time.

He set his glasses back on the bridge of his nose and stepped into the room with a false smile. "Good afternoon, Fa—"

He interrupted his greeting as he took in the room. His father stood at the fireplace, dressed like he was in mourning, his clothing was so dark and his expression so dour. Henry's eldest brother, Philip, stood beside him, with an equally hangdog expression, though Henry knew that was from waiting for what he considered his "due".

Their middle brother, Robert, lounged on his back on the settee to his right, bored of it all, as usual. Henry glared, for that reminded him of another recumbent gentleman. Another parlor. He dismissed the thoughts with a sigh.

"Ah," Henry drawled. "It is an ambush, then."

"You are late," Lord Killam barked without any other preamble.

Henry glanced at the clock on the mantel. "Three minutes late," he said softly.

Philip's eyes went wide and Robert lifted his head slightly from the settee pillow to give him a small shake of his head. Henry would see the warning in his middle brother's stare, and his own defenses rose exponentially as he tried to recall whatever he could have done to deserve the rage that lit his father's expression.

"When the Viscount Killam says two, you come at one forty-five," his father snapped, and stormed across the room to the sideboard, where he poured himself a drink. He didn't offer anyone else in the room the same boon.

"My apologies," Henry said, shifting tactics as the mood of the room and its inhabitants truly sank in. A good scientist adapted—he was certainly capable of doing that with his father. He pushed at his spectacles, although they were perfectly in place, and continued, "I should have been early, you are correct. You are clearly upset and I must assume it is with me. So tell me, Father, what have I done to cause this? For I cannot think of what it could be."

"Can't you?" the viscount asked with an angry bark of laughter. "My supposedly brilliant son cannot ferret out what it is that could upset me? Allow me to enlighten you. You were at the ball two nights ago, yes?"

Henry tensed. Normally he did not love a ball, but he attended them regularly. Two nights ago, he had been at the gathering his father had referred to. The most memorable part of the night was when Lady Evangeline, the daughter of one of the dukes his father had toadied to Henry's entire life, had come into the library. Evangeline, with her shiny black locks and impossibly blue eyes.

He shook his head. That supposedly brilliant mind his father had just mocked knew one thing for certain, even if nothing else. Although he could admire Evangeline from a distance and sometimes she would grace him with a smile or a laugh or a brief chat...she was out of his reach by far. Like a star that looked so bright and close on a clear night in the countryside, but was really eons out of reach.

That had been proven by all the attention she'd shown to Simon Cathcart in the parlor that night. Cathcart was smooth when he chose to speak, and women seemed to find him handsome. Henry had watched them talk. And though Evangeline had left the other man with her friend eventually, the sensation their interaction had caused on Henry's chest was...unpleasant. And foolish.

"Yes, I was at the ball," Henry said, shaking off his uncontrolled thoughts and focusing on his purple-faced father. "What of it? I did not dance, nor cause a scene. I sat in the library with a few other chaps that night. Nothing that could have inspired this reaction."

"Your brother had a report from several people there that night. One I could scarcely believe except it has proven itself to be true." The viscount folded his arms as if that was supposed to explain everything, but there was hardly enough evidence yet for a hypothesis on Henry's part.

He glanced at Philip for an explanation and his brother shifted with a guilty air. "What was reported to you?" Henry asked.

"The paper, Henry," Philip said at last, his tone soft.

Henry wrinkled his brow and then understanding dawned. The paper. "You mean...you mean my piece on the equations I have used to track the possibility of a new planet?"

His father's eyes went wide. "He admits it!" he burst out, finishing his drink in one slug.

"It was published three weeks ago," Henry said.

He shifted. He had written the paper for the Society and it had been published in a small monthly they produced for the scientific community and those interested in the research. Sometimes those papers were picked up by larger journals that were published quarterly and more widely disseminated, but he had yet to hear if his had been chosen.

His father glared at him. "You said nothing to us of this *great honor*."

"I did not think you would care," Henry said, the politeness of his tone at last fraying. "Perhaps not even understand."

Philip recoiled slightly as their father took a step closer.

"That's right, you got your mind from your poor, dead mother, didn't you?" the viscount spat. "She never should have encouraged you with the comets and stars."

Jaw setting at the dismissiveness of his father's tone, Henry fought to meter his reaction. His late mother had been the one to first introduce him to a telescope. He'd been but nine years old and seen his first comet that night. A memory seared into his mind, as was the weight of his mother's hand on his shoulder, the warmth of it as they shared that brilliant flash of light. She had died a few months after, gone far too soon, just like the comet. It had been a devastating loss to their entire family, including his father, despite the viscount's current attitude.

Henry thrust his shoulders back slightly. "You ask if I admit that I wrote the piece. I do, with pride. The search for a new celestial body is no small thing, Father. It has been predicted to exist by equation for decades. A new star—or by my theory, even a planet. Can you imagine being part of that?"

He asked the question but already knew the answer. His father's bland expression told him he cared not one fig about that kind of thrill of discovery. The viscount turned away and Henry continued to speak, as if he could find words that might change his father's hard heart.

"If I could be a part of solving such an astronomical mystery... if the equations I have developed could help even a fraction—"

The viscount slammed his drink down on the sideboard hard enough that the wood shivered. He spun back. "Enough! You can sputter at me all you like about the importance of this foolishness and perhaps you are right that what you are doing is vastly significant. You did it under your real name, Henry. Your *real name*." He moved forward, now deceptively calm. "*My* name. It is one thing to have a hobby, boy. And one I have indulged, clearly to my detriment."

"This is not a hobby!" Henry burst out, hating that his emotions flooded to the surface. "You have dismissed it as such for years, but it is much more. This is a *life's work*, Father. A new *planet*!"

Philip shook his head with a snort of laughter. "That sounds like a children's tale every time you say it." Henry glared at him briefly.

"This is a trade," his father said, soft and deadly as a blade to the chest. "As much as if you worked in a shop."

Henry shut his eyes, trying to find calm, trying to find reason. "And what is wrong with a trade? Would you prefer I be a layabout like Robert?"

His middle brother lifted his head from the cushion. "What's that?"

"Shut up, Robert," their father said. Robert rolled his eyes and put his head back on the pillow. The viscount caught Henry's arms none-too-gently and shook him slightly. "You will cease this foolishness, Henry."

Panic rose in Henry's chest, overwhelming wisdom for a moment. He jerked from his father's grip and staggered back a few steps. "Cease *what*?"

The viscount crossed his arms. "It seems you must be cut away from all of it. The stars, the planets, the...*science*." He said the last like it was a curse. Something disgusting to be scraped off his boot heel.

"You cannot be serious," Henry said, somehow managing to speak even though the rush of blood in his ears made hearing close to impossible.

"I am *entirely* serious."

Henry shook his head. He was trembling and he hated himself for this emotional display. It was not his nature, nor his desire to let his heart rule him like some fool. And yet he couldn't seem to control himself. "No," he said at last. "No, I won't."

There was a stunned silence from all in the room. Henry understood it. He felt its weight as much as the rest. No one refused their father. Certainly none of them ever had. Now Philip stood gape-mouthed, and Robert had sat up from the settee and was staring at Henry with wide eyes. Their father's jaw was set.

Slowly the viscount moved closer, invading Henry's space once more. His face was less than an inch from Henry's now. All the anger still burned in his eyes, but his voice was dangerously cool as he said, "I will cut you off."

The viscount had enunciated each word carefully, but Henry still gasped. "What?"

"If you want to act like a commoner, you can live like one," his father said. "You will be penniless. The little house? That will return to me. You will be roofless and bedless. Do I make myself clear enough for your sharp mind to understand?"

"But then I would not be able to—"

"You would not be able to do a great many things," his father said, voice still soft. "I will end this nonsense one way or another."

Henry's stomach roiled, what was left of his breakfast rising to his throat as he stared into his father's eyes and tried to find a tiny kernel of hope. There was none. The viscount meant this threat. It was not empty.

"Father, please," he said softly.

Silence greeted him. Stony and cold. "Think on it, as you like to do," the viscount said after what felt like an eternity. "I expect to hear from you within a week's time about your decision."

He pointed at the door, dismissing Henry as abruptly as he had been summoned. Henry had no choice but to do as he had been directed. He stumbled out into the hall and toward the foyer. He had almost made it there, almost with unseeing eyes, when he heard footfalls behind him.

He pivoted to find Philip there. His older brother's face was lined with guilt. "I didn't know he would threaten this," he said.

Henry stared at him, hating him and understanding him with equal power in this charged, painful moment. "It wouldn't have stopped you from showing him the journal, would it?" His brother's darting gaze told the answer to that. Henry sighed. "You just wanted his approval, at any cost. Just as you always have."

The barb seemed to hit its mark, for Philip recoiled ever so slightly. Then he pushed his shoulders back and said, "Don't be a fool. Do as he asks. You have no other choice now. Your life comes at his pleasure."

Henry shifted with discomfort. How he wished that there was a clever retort he could give, but there wasn't because his brother was entirely correct. Henry was a third son, one who depended on the allowance the viscount allowed. He didn't live extravagantly, but had little saved. When he had it, extra money went to the Society and their needs. A new telescope lens here, an abacus there. It had never occurred to him that those indulgences would be his downfall.

He didn't reply to his brother's suggestion, but turned and made the rest of his way down the hall. Morley was waiting, his expression now concerned as Henry silently took his coat and gloves and exited the house without even putting them on.

What was the cold when everything he'd ever cared about was about to be taken away? What was anything when compared to that?

CHAPTER 3

A brisk breeze blew through the park from time to time, and Evangeline tightened her coat around herself as she stared through the stripped tree branches toward the manor of Lord Killam. It was outrageous that she was here, spying on the house of her father's old friend. And yet she could not help herself. Since two nights before at the ball, the seed of an idea had been planted in her mind and troubled her ceaselessly as it took root.

And so she was here, pursuing it. What use was life if you did not manage it?

"I must strenuously object to this foolishness once again, Lady Evangeline."

Evangeline turned toward her lady's companion. Hester Tibbins was only a decade older than her. She had been let go by another house five years ago after a horrible experience with a duke who had been visiting. It had created quite the stir, with a shouting match between the duke and duchess that had rang through Society for months. It had been too interesting a piece of gossip for Evangeline not to ferret out more details and realize that the true victim in all the mess was the maid.

Tibby would have been out on the street had Evangeline not

interceded on her behalf. Tibby had been her maid and companion ever since. Her confidante. Her friend, or as close to it as Evangeline ever allowed. If that made Tibby a bit more familiar in private than she perhaps ought to have been, well...what was one to do?

"I'm only feeling it out, Tibby." She rolled her eyes in a most unladylike fashion, which she knew Tibby hated. "Gracious, you act as though I'm going to strip down naked right here."

Tibby shivered. "You'd catch your death if you did that, and deserve it. Spying on a gentleman is *not* for a lady to do. Following him? It's unseemly."

"I'm two and twenty, Tibby, and have been a lady all my life. I do not need a reminder."

"Don't you?" Tibby tried to sound stern, but there was a lilt of laughter to her tone.

Evangeline fought the urge to stick her tongue out and shook her head. "Oh, hush. Men do this and worse all the time when they are in pursuit of a lady. Now look lively, I see Henry leaving his father's house. Since his carriage was seen at his home, that means he'll have to walk through the park to get there. It will be the perfect opportunity."

"To make a fool of yourself," Tibby muttered.

Evangeline did stick her tongue out this time and then focused her attention back on Henry. He was still standing at the top of the stairs at his father's house. From this distance, she couldn't read his expression, but his posture seemed...odd. His shoulders were rolled and his hands tight against his sides. He was holding his coat in his hand, despite the frigid temperatures.

Then he started to walk. It was brisk and businesslike, and he moved across the lane without even looking for carriages in the way. She caught her breath as he entered the park and strode forward, ever closer to her. Now she could see his face as she stepped out into the path so he would be certain to observe her. His expression was...bereft.

She tilted her head at it as he barreled closer and then careened right past her without so much as a look in her direction. Behind her, she heard Tibby snort a bit of laughter and she glared at the maid before she looked at her prey. How could he have missed her? She had practically thrown herself at him.

"I say, Mr. Killam!" she called out. He didn't slow his pace and she felt blood rush to her cheeks. An uncommon occurrence, indeed. But then again, so was being ignored. "Mr. Killam, is that you?" she called, this time louder and with more urgency. When he still didn't stop, she raised her voice even more. "*Henry!*"

He stopped in the path ten feet ahead of her and slowly turned, pushing his spectacles up as he did so. Behind the glass, his dark green gaze settled on her and she waited for him to light up as he always did when he caught a glimpse of her. But it didn't. For a moment, he didn't even seem to recognize her.

"Oh, Evangeline." He shook his head at last and began to put on his coat. "I beg your pardon, *Lady* Evangeline. I didn't see you there." His brow wrinkled. "What are you doing in the park in the dead of winter?"

"I have read a brisk walk in the cold can be good for the health." Behind her, Tibby muttered something, and Evangeline barely fought the urge to reach back and swat at her. "What luck to run into you. Were you calling on your father?"

His expression crumpled, and for a moment she saw raw emotion there. It was a rare occurrence, for Henry was almost always as controlled as she, herself, was. It was only his happiness to see her or when he talked about his projects with her that ever broke through his very calm façade. Seeing this moment's weakness made her chest hurt and a rush of empathy cascade through her.

She shook it off as best she could. *That* was not control, and in this situation, one had to have control.

"Are you well?" she asked, stepping closer and tilting her head to examine him more closely. He was very pale, his gaze distant as he darted it away from her.

"Of course, of course. I just had a—" He cut himself off and shook his head. "Well, it was not the call I expected when I went to my father's that is all."

"Perhaps I could help." She moved forward again, and now she was very close to him. Close enough to see the whiteness of his knuckles as he gripped them at his sides, and the clench of his jaw. He met her gaze and held it a moment. She felt him reading her, collecting evidence, making a decision about her.

"Certainly my troubles cannot interest you, Evangeline."

Her lips parted. He had judged that she wouldn't care. That she wasn't the sort of person he would share with. Even though they had been friends of a sort for years. Even though they'd talked at parties and danced. Even though he...liked her. She knew he liked her. Didn't he?

"You would be surprised," she said, softening her tone.

He stared at her another beat, two. She shifted under his regard, uncertain if he would completely dismiss her. "He is upset about something I wrote," he said and his tone was wistful.

Unexpected relief flowed through her at even this slight capitulation. "Are you referring to your paper on the mathematics of the new planet?"

Behind his spectacles, Henry's eyes went wide. He nodded. "Yes. Did *you* read it?"

She couldn't hide her smirk at his shock. She rather liked shocking him because it wasn't something she saw done very often. Henry was so intelligent, so careful, so certain when he spoke that being able to stymie him was actually fun.

That wasn't why she'd started seeking out the scientific journal of the Society of London Astronomical Studies he was part of over a year ago. She'd just heard about his interest in the group, and they seemed fascinating. She liked discovery as much as the next person. Why wouldn't she pursue that interest, which was separate from Henry? Completely separate.

"I did," she said. "Though I didn't understand it by half."

He arched a brow and she could see she had gone too far. His brow wrinkled. "I have a hard time believing you don't understand everything you choose to speak on."

Behind her, Tibby snorted, and Evangeline cast a quick glare over her shoulder before she put her attention back on him. "Would you care to walk with me?"

He blinked, shook his head, almost as if he remembered himself in that moment or that a spell had been broken. "I hate to be rude, but today is not a good day for it. Perhaps another time?"

"Oh." Evangeline forced a smile. "Yes, of course. No trouble at all."

He reached out and caught her hand, squeezing gently before he released it. "Thank you. It was nice to see you. Good day."

He turned and continued across the park at the same speed he had entered it, leaving Evangeline behind, staring after him in the cold.

"Good day," she muttered, for he was already out of earshot.

Tibby stepped up beside her and they watched him walk away together in silence. Evangeline felt Tibby's comments hanging in the air, unspoken but as loud as the thundering hooves of a dozen horses or the sounds of a group ice skating on the frigid lake in the distance.

"Oh, just be out with it," she muttered.

Tibby turned toward her with a half-smile. "You tried to manage him and he will not be managed."

Evangeline pursed her lips. Tibby was not wrong, though she would never admit it. She had believed she could easily turn Henry into her and obtain the response she had wanted. And yet...

"Posh," she said, waving her hand as if she had no care in the world.

Henry was almost across the park now, heading to the other entrance. She could not help but notice what a fine form he cut. She blinked at the unexpected thought.

"He is biddable enough," she proclaimed. "And he's always liked me."

"Has he now?" Tibby snorted.

She turned away now that Henry was gone from her sight. "You *know* he has. You've seen him when he comes with his father to call on my own. He always comes directly to me to talk. He always watches me even when we aren't speaking. Don't be foolish, I *know* when a man has an interest."

"That you do, with all who have circled you over the years," Tibby conceded with a tilt of her head.

Evangeline motioned toward the carriage that had been waiting for them. As they walked, she sighed. "But I do not want any of those men. Men who want my money and my influence and access to my father's title. But this...this idea of choosing a man to marry...a man who wouldn't do those things...wouldn't it solve everything?"

Tibby shot her a side glance. "Would it, though?"

A rare feeling of defensiveness shot through her, and she came to a halt on the path and faced her. "If I married a man like him, I would retain *myself*. And Henry would benefit. Whatever happened with his father, he must wish to be free."

"Would he be free?" Tibby asked.

"Yes!" Evangeline insisted, though she wondered why she felt the need to fight so strenuously to prove her point. Normally she did not feel a desire to defend herself. If someone didn't agree, who cared? She trusted her instincts. Today they felt less...instinctual.

Tibby lifted her brows.

Evangeline huffed out a breath and it crystalized before her like smoke. "I'd *like* it if he had his own pursuits. If he is busy finding planets, he would have little time to trouble me."

Now Tibby's expression fell, and Evangeline was shocked to see pity in her eyes. "My lady, that sounds positively depressing."

Evangeline pushed past her and allowed the footman to help her into the carriage. She flopped into her place, arms folded, as Tibby joined her. The carriage began to move and her maid stared at her, those last words hanging between them.

"Why?" Evangeline finally ground out through clenched teeth. "Why would that be depressing?"

The sadness on Tibby's face was so plain. "No love, Lady Evangeline. No...no passion." Her voice dropped to a whisper. "No connection at all? Is that what you really want?"

Evangeline caught her breath because when the future she imagined was laid out in that way, it did sound rather dire. And yet she had also seen the dark side of all those things Tibby extoled. The darkest side.

"Perhaps there is some value in a love match. They certainly seem in fashion at present. But we both know things like love and passion and connection don't last," she said softly. "Friendship might, though. And Henry *is* a friend, isn't he? *That* is why I would choose him for this endeavor. It's a good idea."

Tibby was quiet for a moment, then leaned forward. "Will Mr. Killam say the same when you bring this fool idea to him?"

Evangeline's lips parted at the very idea. After all, if she told Henry, he might refuse her. She didn't want that.

"I'm not going to tell him," she said. "At least not at first. I need to convince him, guide him."

"Manipulate him," Tibby said, her tone dry as dust.

"Not in a bad way," Evangeline said. "After all, he'd certainly never pursue me of his own accord. We've been friends for years and he's never been untoward. No, I'll have to catch this wallflower in true time-honored fashion."

Tibby's brow wrinkled in confusion and concern. "And how is that, my lady?"

Evangeline smiled as the doubts she had allowed herself to feel faded slightly under the weight of her renewed confidence in her plan. After all, she was the daughter of the Duke of Allingham. She was *Lady Evangeline*. She was a diamond of the first water. She was leader of the ladies. Nothing could stop her once she put her mind to something.

"It's very simple," she said, settling back more comfortably against the carriage seat. "I'll woo him."

CHAPTER 4

Henry sat at the large table in the center of the hall at the Society of London Astronomical Studies with another of his colleagues, Donovan McGilvery. It had been two days since his encounter with his father, since his strange interaction with Lady Evangeline just afterward in the park. Both had been on his mind since, which led to a level of distraction that he rarely encountered.

"Great God, man, you have just miscalculated two equations. Have it out before you compute a known planet away instead of finding a new one."

Henry stared at the equations before him and immediately saw his errors. Simple mathematical mistakes he had not made in years.

"I apologize," he said, pushing aside his papers and rising to his feet. He shoved a hand through his hair and then pushed his spectacles up his nose out of reflex rather than necessity. "I admit I am having a difficult time of it."

"Tell me about it," McGilvery said, concern lining his face. "Sometimes you need a second opinion on something if you are lost in the weeds of a problem. Is it about the equations?"

"I wish it were," Henry said with a sigh. "A simple scientific question could be debated and solved. This...well, I *would* share, but it isn't about society business and I hate to bother you with foolishness."

McGilvery raised both hands. "I asked, didn't I?"

"My father is threatening to cut me off," Henry burst out, the first time to say it out loud to another person. "Because of the paper from a few weeks ago."

McGilvery's mouth dropped open. "Oh. *Oh.*"

"Yes," Henry agreed. "Oh."

"He is that opposed to your work? My father seems pleased that I have some sort pastime that isn't drinking or whoring like my brothers do."

Henry shrugged. "You would think mine would feel the same, but he is tied up in what he believes a gentleman of even a little rank *should* do. If I participate in this work, it sullies his good name and that is that. He is not to be reasoned with." His words caught in his throat and he nearly choked on them. "I don't know what to do. He's given me a week to decide if it is to be cut off or give up my research."

"A week?" McGilvery repeated in even greater shock than before.

Hearing it repeated to him made Henry's stomach turn even more with renewed anxiety. "Five days, actually. His edict was issued two days ago, so my time slips away like sand through a damned hourglass. God's teeth, McGilvery, what am I to do?"

His friend shook his head and Henry sank back into his chair and covered his eyes. This was exactly why he had not shared his plight with anyone in his acquaintance. None of them were even as well off as he was, they couldn't help him. Even if they could, it would be unfair to ask another person to take responsibility for what he would give up.

What he would lose either way.

"Killam—" McGilvery began, but was interrupted when the society steward, Mr. Croome, stepped into the room.

"I beg your pardon, gentlemen, but a missive has arrived for you, Mr. Killam."

Henry looked up. Occasionally his household forwarded what seemed to be important letters to him here, in case he didn't come home for days on end as he worked. Now he found himself staring at a letter on fine paper, folded exquisitely and stamped in expensive wax. Immediately his thoughts went to his father. This could easily be a message from him, demanding an answer now no matter what the terms of the original mandate had been.

He took the letter reluctantly and stared at the seal. It was not the ornate K of his father's stamp, but an e. Lowercase, feminine. He wrinkled his brow as he broke it and unfolded the note.

"Who is it from?" McGilvery asked.

"Evangeline," Henry breathed, reading her words slowly.

Henry,
It truly was a pleasure running into you at the park the other day. I do hope you will come to call very soon, as I would like to continue our conversation. Perhaps this afternoon if it is not too busy for you?
Yours,
Evangeline

He did not think he had ever had the pleasure of a letter from Evangeline before. Now he stared at the words, written in a neat, feminine hand that was pure her.

"And just who is Evangeline?" McGilvery asked, drawing out her name playfully.

Henry looked up. He somehow hadn't realized he'd said her name out loud and revealed this little weakness to his friend.

"Er, an old friend," he explained.

Both of McGilvery's brows lifted. "A friend, eh? Must be some friend to make you forget your troubles with just a few lines."

Henry ducked his head. McGilvery had no idea just how close to the mark he was. Henry had always forgotten everything but Evangeline the moment she entered any room. It had been that way since she was fifteen and she'd smiled at some terrible joke he told. Since then, making her smile or laugh had been one of his greatest accomplishments. He'd made quite a study of her sense of humor. And, to be honest, just as deep an analysis of the way the light hit her face, the way her eyes changed color ever so slightly depending on what she wore.

"You like her," McGilvery said with a laugh when Henry had been silent for so long.

Henry jerked his face up and found McGilvery lounging back in his chair, grinning at him. He shook his head, pushing his distracting thoughts of Evangeline aside as he always had to in the end. "I assure you, we are nothing more than friends. Acquaintances, really. Lady Evangeline is out of my orbit," he said with a shrug.

"But she's putting herself in your orbit," McGilvery said, reaching for the letter and holding it up with a shake. "Croome!"

The steward had begun to leave the room, but hustled back. "Yes, Mr. McGilvery?"

"Was this letter forwarded from Mr. Killam's house or was it sent here directly?"

"Ah, well, it was not Mr. Killam's usual messenger," Croome said. "So I must hypothesize that it was sent directly. The man's livery was very fine, but not one I recognized as belonging to a member."

"Excellent," McGilvery said with another grin in Henry's direction. "Thank you."

As the steward left, McGilvery got up and dropped the letter back in front of Henry on the table. "You like her and she is apparently aware enough of your schedule that she is sending you notes directly to the society. Notes asking you to call on her."

"You read it?" Henry asked.

"Of course I did. So does this lady above your orbit have money?"

Henry drew back. "I—why?"

"That could solve your father problems, if you married yourself a lady with a fat dowry, couldn't it? Assuming the lady wouldn't mind if you continue your exploits here."

A brief imagine entered Henry's mind. Of marrying Evangeline. Of a wedding night with Evangeline. A ripple of awareness flowed through his body, but he stifled it.

"No one is marrying anyone," he said.

"But you will call on her, of course," McGilvery said.

Henry stared at the letter again. The words flowed one to the next, a smooth line of ups and downs like waves. They were almost peaceful. And while being with Evangeline, herself, had never been a peaceful experience, when he thought of it, it did lift his spirits.

"I would be remiss if I did not do so," he said. "Especially since I left the lady rather abruptly a two days ago."

"Good," McGilvery said with a salute as he drew papers back in front of himself. "You'll make yourself mad if you only think of figures and terrible futures. Seems a good idea to fill your head with celestial beings of a much finer kind. Off with you."

Henry sighed, but he didn't argue. In truth, he really did need a break from the riot of his mind. And spending a few hours with Evangeline couldn't do any harm. At least it would give him fodder for fantasies that came at night. Ones he would never live out, but that kept his dreams sweet indeed.

Evangeline moved down the hall, smoothing her skirts as she did so and pausing only to check her appearance in the mirror above a table in the hallway. She tucked back an errant hair and then drew a breath as she stood outside the parlor where Henry had been placed ten minutes before.

She had not fully expected him to scurry over so soon after receiving her note. But it was a good sign. One that gave her back some of her confidence after his abandoning of her in the park two days before.

"Are you going in or making him wait all day?" Tibby asked softly.

"A gentleman craves what he must wait for," Evangeline said with a shrug. "I didn't make the rules. I simply play by them."

She didn't allow Tibby a chance to argue, but opened the door to the parlor with a wide smile. Henry was standing at the fireplace that was brightly decorated with holly and ivy branches for the holiday. He turned as she entered.

"Good afternoon, Mr. Killam," she said, coming toward him.

"Lady Evangeline," he returned with a slight bow and a quick glance at Tibby. Evangeline barely kept herself from sighing. It was so very irritating to require a maid wherever one went. Made it very difficult to seduce a man.

She let her gaze flit over the very man she was trying to seduce. His hair was a little too long and he'd obviously been running his fingers through it, for it had settled in a wild manner. His spectacles were on the bridge of his nose and behind them his dark green gaze followed her as she moved to the sideboard and the tea set that had been placed there.

"You take only milk, don't you?" she asked.

His brows lifted. "You recall that detail, do you?"

"After the number of times you have joined us here, of course," she said, and turned with his cup. They moved to the settee together and sat, just a cushion between them. He sipped his tea, then set it aside on the table behind him.

"Your father is so important, he must get, what...ten to twenty callers a week? And then the suppers and other gatherings he holds...a conservative guess would be another thousand people through those front doors. Not counting balls. You must have two to three thousand guests at this house each year, at minimum. So yes, it surprises me that you would recall how I like my tea."

She laughed, and for a moment all her machinations faded and there was only Henry, making calculations in his head because he couldn't help himself. "There may be three thousand guests to this house per annum, my dear Mr. Killam, but none are you. You make an impression."

He stared at her, his gaze holding hers for a beat. Two. His pupils had dilated a fraction and she saw the hint of longing there in his stare. Wanting. She'd felt it from other men, in truth, she'd occasionally felt it *toward* other men. But this was different. This was something warmer and more specific, and she couldn't help but shift in her seat as an unexpected tingle moved through her.

"Tibby, I left my book up in my chamber," she said, glancing back over her shoulder. "And I thought Mr. Killam might have an interest. Why don't you go look for it?"

Tibby's eyes went wide and she glanced back at the door. "My lady—"

"I'm not certain where it is," Evangeline said, glaring with meaning at her servant. "Start in my bedroom. You know the one. It has a blue cover. If it's not there, try my sitting room and then the library."

Tibby's jaw set, but it was clear she'd gotten the message. She bobbed out a brief curtsey. "Yes, my lady."

Her maid left and Evangeline let out a deep sigh. "At last, we are free," she muttered.

Henry swallowed hard. "I suppose we are."

"Have I shocked you, sending away my maid?" she asked with as light a tone as she could muster when she was now surprisingly nervous. She got up and paced to the door where she turned and faced him. "Would you be even more shocked if I did…this?" She leaned against the door and slowly shut it, pressing her back to the cool surface as she stared at him.

He stood and once again his throat worked as he swallowed. "We are...friends, aren't we?" he choked out. "I suppose there is no harm in friends being alone."

"Not at all," she purred, taking a step toward him slowly. "I'm so glad you came, Henry."

She said the words, designed to make his cheeks brighten, which of course they did. But she was surprised to find she truly meant them with all her heart. She was glad he'd come. Glad he was here with her. What that meant and why it was so abjectly terrifying was not a subject she intended to explore further. Especially not when Henry had taken a long step around the settee and was now in arm's reach of her, watching her with an expression of surprise.

Her plan was working. And she couldn't stop now.

Henry had always been good at figures and hypotheses and discovering the truth of a matter in a scientific way. Relationships hadn't ever been his strong suit. He had a small group of friends and occasionally danced at a ball when it was necessary, but connection with other people wasn't a skill he had spent a good deal of time cultivating.

Today, though, he recognized a shocking fact in one explosive moment and it set everything in his world on its head. Evangeline was flirting with him. *Evangeline.*

Was she? It seemed outrageous that it could be so. He drew a breath and decided to address the matter as he would in a scientific endeavor.

The hypothesis: that Evangeline was flirting.

Now to analyze the evidence. First, she was looking at him in a different way. Staring into his eyes, leaning forward, smiling more. One could dismiss that as friendly, but her pupils were dilated like an animal's would be in a state of sexual arousal. He had a sneaking feeling his were the same. But then, he had always liked Evangeline in a more than friendly way.

Point one for the hypothesis.

The second bit of evidence was how she was talking. She had behaved as though he stood out in the crowd of thousands who traipsed through her father's door each year. Which meant she was either lying, which would be an attempt to make him feel special, or she was telling the truth and that meant he somehow *was* special to her.

Point two for the hypothesis.

"Henry, what are you doing?"

"Thinking," he muttered.

She tilted her head back and laughed. It was a rich, throaty sound that filled the small parlor with music and made it feel lighter. He found himself smiling along with her.

"Your mind is so remarkable," she said, inching a little closer on the settee. Her fingers wiggled across the cushion between them, closing the gap. Together they watched as she glided them over his own hand.

She was touching him. Oh, she'd touched him before, certainly. Shaken his hand, rested a palm on his arm as she laughed when he said something foolish to garner her attention, they'd danced a handful of times in the many years their fathers had been acquainted.

But this...this felt so different. Neither of them wore gloves. Her fingers felt heavy on the top of his hand. Warm. And when he looked at her, her lips were parted, almost in surprise.

Point three for the hypothesis. Evangeline *was* flirting with him. He felt he could make a strong argument for that if pressed. Like her hand pressed into his and sent shockwaves of awareness through his body. Settling in his blood. Heating the length of him that was suddenly and uncomfortably reacting to her proximity and the soft glaze to her stare.

He jumped to his feet and paced away to the window where he

stared out at the garden behind the house. He was having a natural, physical reaction to a woman. That was science. If he thought of something else, anything else, that would cut off the reaction.

Why couldn't he think of anything else besides the slight honeysuckle smell to her skin and the way it felt against his own?

"I was worried about you after the park," she said.

He sighed in relief. Her words put him to mind of his father and that certainly solved the problem in his breeches. He faced her with a shrug. "You needn't, though it is kind of you."

"Do you want to talk about your problem?" she asked, rising and moving toward him with slow, almost deliberate steps.

There was a lump in his throat and he struggled to speak past it. "Er, well...I'm not...it's just—"

He did not have the chance to finish the thought. At that moment, Evangeline's maid returned to the room, a book in hand. Her hawkish gaze flitted from Evangeline to him and back again. "I found the book, my lady," she announced, a little breathlessly, holding out the volume.

Evangeline's expression when she looked at her servant was one of pure irritation. "Wonderful, Tibby. That's wonderful. I wonder that it didn't take you longer."

"Because it was hidden behind your pillow, you mean?" the maid asked.

Evangeline lifted her brows and shot a look at Henry with a laugh. "What an accusation! If the book was behind the pillows, it must have fallen there by mistake. But...yes, thank you, Tibby."

Henry smoothed his hands over his waistcoat and moved forward. Right now his mind felt entirely addled and all he could think about was the way Evangeline's hands gripped that book. Why in God's name had she flirted with him when she'd never done so...or at least not like this...before?

It was very confusing.

"I think I must excuse myself," he said. "I suddenly am not feeling well."

Evangeline's lips parted and there was true concern on her face. "Oh, Henry, I'm so sorry. Yes, of course, go and take care of yourself. I'll see you out."

He nodded and followed her. She fell into step beside him in the hall and he felt her watching him from the corner of her eye. "Are you coming to my father's soiree on Sunday?"

Henry caught his breath. He had received the invitation for the gathering the day before, but hadn't opened it. "I-I hadn't intended it, actually, Evangeline."

"No?" she said. "Oh, that is disappointing. You know it will be all my father's ridiculous friends. I would very much like it if you were there."

Henry pursed his lips. His father would be there. His father was always at the Duke of Allingham's parties. He practically begged to carry the far more important man's train. If Henry saw his father it might give the viscount the opportunity to demand Henry's answer about his future. All very good reasons to avoid the party at all costs.

And yet, as they reached the front door, Evangeline leaned in, resting her hand on his forearm gently. Her blue eyes held his as she looked up at him. Her position must have been by design, for it put her in the very best light possible. She was as luminous as any star in the heavens.

"Please, won't you come?" she asked.

He found himself nodding, for there was no denying her. "Yes."

Her smile lit up the world and she squeezed his arm gently. "Wonderful. I cannot wait. Please feel better."

He continued to nod like a fool and stepped out toward his carriage. But as he climbed in, he couldn't help but wonder what the hell he was getting himself into.

And what exactly it was that Evangeline thought she was designing by her sudden change in behavior toward him.

CHAPTER 5

Evangeline stared as Henry's carriage ferried him away from her and felt a twinge of regret she couldn't quite understand. She was building a plan right now—there was no reason not to feel perfectly neutral about it.

"How did it go?" Tibby asked.

Evangeline turned to face her. "Well," she said softly. "Except that my maid insisted on interrupting my progress."

That wasn't exactly true, of course. Nothing had gone exactly as she'd expected that afternoon. She'd thought she'd have him eating out of her hand within half an hour. Instead, Henry had just...stared at her. Was the look one of desire? One of interest? It certainly wasn't one of acquiescence.

"Why are you doing this?" Tibby asked as they stepped back into the warm foyer and shut the door behind themselves. "Because it seems to bring you little joy."

Evangeline clenched her hands at her sides. Her existence was always one of careful control, but this afternoon that felt frayed. She shook her head. "Three times during this past Season my father casually mentioned my marrying soon. Three. I have no idea if he will follow through on that musing, but I wouldn't put it past him. He could use my dowry for connection of some kind to many a family or endeavor. You know how that kind of managing ended for my mother, my sister, my brother's wife, nearly every woman we've ever known! You yourself know what being arranged and controlled can do. If I don't design my future, it will be designed for me, and probably to my detriment."

Tibby's expression softened. "You're afraid."

Lips parting, Evangeline tried to think of a dismissive retort to that troubling observation but could find none. Her maid was right. She *was* afraid. Talking to Miss Lesley less than a week before had only sharpened the tip of that fear so it dug in deeper than ever. This was not an emotion she generally felt. She'd cultivated a life that didn't allow for it.

And now she wanted...*needed* to grasp back some of the power that kept those fears, and their causes, at bay.

"Well, if I could manage to woo Henry into marrying, at least I would be linked to a friend." She sighed as she thought of the moments of warmth between them in the parlor. When she'd touched his hand she'd felt an unexpected jolt of...something. Like she was more aware of her body than she had been before.

"Well, he seems in no hurry to get there," Tibby said with a shake of her head.

Evangeline clenched her teeth in frustration. Much as she hated to admit it, her maid was right. She felt Henry's attraction to her often, but he never made a move toward it. He would need a push.

"I think first I must know exactly what it is that is troubling him," she said, smiling as she glanced out the window and saw a fine carriage entering the drive. "And I know exactly who might have the answers. My father."

The carriage stopped and footmen burst from all sides, hurrying to help her father down. Their butler, Hughes, entered the foyer, but Evangeline lifted a hand to stay him from his course.

"Don't trouble yourself, Hughes. I need to speak to my father, I'll tend to him."

The butler nodded his head slightly and left her and Tibby in the waiting area. She tossed her maid a look filled with meaning she hoped Tibby would understand and then opened the door.

Her father bustled in. "It's blasted cold out there," he huffed as he pulled his coat away. He blinked as he found himself holding it out not to the butler but his daughter.

Evangeline smiled. "Isn't it, though." She took the coat and handed it to Tibby. "Welcome home, Father."

His brow wrinkled and his gaze darted over her. "Taken up the servants' duties, eh?"

She laughed as she held out a hand for his hat and gloves, which she also passed on to Tibby. The maid scurried away, leaving them alone. For all her sass with Evangeline, Tibby did not trifle with the Duke of Allingham. No one did.

"Not exactly," Evangeline said as she linked arms with her father. "I only wished to speak to you, and what a happy coincidence that you were coming in as my company had just departed. Would you like tea in the parlor or should we go to your study?"

He narrowed his gaze at her. "The parlor is fine if a set is already prepared there. What is it you want, Evangeline?"

"Want? Only to speak to you." They entered the room she had just inhabited with Henry, and she released her father's arm as she went to the sideboard and poured him a cup of tea. She sweetened it and then shot him a naughty look before she splashed a hint of whisky in the brew.

His expression softened a bit. "Just as I like it, eh?"

"It's the holiday season—why not celebrate with a little indulgence?" she replied, sitting on the chaise as he settled into a chair across from her. "Were you at the club?"

"Yes, and of course the whole discourse devolved into politics." He shook his head. "I went to play billiards, not listen to ramblings. Next time I'll just invite someone here."

Evangeline nodded to placate him, but this was the perfect opening. "Perhaps Lord Killam. He is always good company."

Her father shrugged one shoulder. "Good enough. He certainly wishes to impress me."

"It's funny you mention him." He lifted his brows and she ignored the unspoken fact that *she* had mentioned the viscount first. "For his younger son Henry was here calling today."

"Ah, yes. The scientist." Allingham chuckled. "How it sticks in Killam's craw that his boy is in what he considers a trade. He was going on and on about it after the ball Saturday last. Couldn't trip over himself fast enough to tell me he didn't approve."

"He considers Henry's research a trade?" Evangeline said, wrinkling her brow. "Many of rank have interest in the stars. It's all the rage, isn't it?"

"Perhaps, but that paper he published embarrassed Killam."

Evangeline nodded. Now the pieces of the puzzle were coming together. Why Henry had been so upset that day in the park. Why Henry had mentioned his paper.

"What does the viscount intend to do about it?" Evangeline asked.

Her father shrugged. "I know the boy has always been a particular favorite of yours, but why all the sudden interest, Evangeline?"

She leaned back. "A particular favorite?" she repeated. "Whatever do you mean by that?"

"You two put your heads together any time he's here," Allingham said as he got up and crossed back to the sideboard, where he splashed more whisky in his half-drunk tea. "And you said he was here, calling on you. You could have a duke, you know. Or an earl or a marquess…"

She waved her hand to interrupt him. "Oh, Father, you tell me this constantly. Don't change the subject."

"What was the subject?" He stared into his tea. "Oh yes, Killam's youngest. Well, he muttered about cutting him off to end the foolishness. I suppose he will do so if he thinks it will keep his own status from being devalued by, God forbid, *science*."

Evangeline caught her breath as her father droned on. Henry's position was being threatened and her heart hurt for him instantly. He loved his work—anyone who read that paper he'd written in his society's journal could not doubt his true passion for it. And his father threatened him, his very existence, over it. No wonder he was so distracted and upset.

"—Henry would have to marry an heiress, I suppose," her father said, drawing her attention back. "Perhaps one of your friends could save him. After all, you are constantly working hard to repair all those little birds with broken wings."

Evangeline rose to her feet. Henry marrying an heiress would certainly solve his problems. There were hardly any heiresses as well off as herself. Her dowry would keep him safe and them both in comfort for the rest of their lives. And of course, that had been her plan. To trade on his liking her in order to obtain her independence. It seemed she might have a different card to play now. Her fortune.

And yet that felt less...comforting.

Why? Why did it matter if she tempted Henry to wed her through her wiles or her fortune? What was the difference?

She didn't know. But there certainly was one.

"Why do you look so dour, Evangeline?" her father asked. "Do you need a nip of whisky in your own tea?"

She forced a smile. "I think not, though I do appreciate the offer. I was just thinking of some arrangements for your gathering in two nights. You know there is much to plan."

"Well, save me from those details," he said with a shudder. "When I marry you off, I think I shall hire a secretary to do these duties you so admirably perform. Certainly I cannot bear them. Good afternoon, my dear. I'm off to deal with the books."

He patted her hand as he wandered out of the room, teacup in hand. Evangeline flopped back onto the settee with a grunt and stared up at the ceiling.

Married her off. That was the *fourth* time he'd made a mention of such a thing. It put her situation in stark relief. She had to push aside any odd discomfort she had with the idea that Henry might wish to use her for her position as much as she intended to use him for his. That would only make it easier.

And she *did* still know he liked her. So there was nothing wrong with manipulating that fact first, before she turned to her ability to save him with her fortune.

CHAPTER 6

Henry stood at the edge of the ballroom, watching the people spin by to the time of the music. It would have felt like another normal, forced appearance in the heart of Society but for two things. First, that his father was here, glowering any time he caught a glimpse of him. Though they had not done more than say a cursory good evening, but the viscount's message was clear: Henry was still to give up his work. One way or another.

His stomach flipped, and he turned away from his father and found himself looking at the second circumstance that made tonight unlike any other ball or gathering.

Evangeline stood at the opposite side of the ballroom floor, peering through the bobbing couples and watching…*him*. He'd tried to convince himself that wasn't true, that he was seeing things that didn't exist and reading the wrong thing into the situation because he was under such pressure from his father.

And yet, he kept finding evidence that he was, indeed, in her sights, despite the fact they had hardly said more to each other than a quick welcome at the receiving line. Evangeline had hostess duties to perform, after all. Ones she was so very good at.

He loved watching her mingle, laugh, smile with her guests. Make them each feel warm and welcomed in her father's home.

He certainly always had, thanks to her.

She spoke for a moment with her companions, an earl and his wife, then began to move around the perimeter of the dancefloor. Step by step, she came closer, her gaze never leaving his. Her movements graceful and lithe and careful. Evangeline was always careful, like every single motion was planned. Perhaps it was. The woman had always been the epitome of control. Could a man take that control? Make her tremble? Make her come undone?

He blinked at the unbidden, heated thought and forced a smile as she reached him. "My lady."

"Good sir," she said, laughing.

"Your gathering seems a success," he said as they both took in the ballroom scene.

She shrugged. "I suppose it is, yes. Not that it is hard to make it so."

"A dozen hostesses in London who wish for half your style and flair would argue that point." He turned toward her. "Your father is lucky to have you as his representative."

A tinge of a blush warmed the apples of her cheeks to a fetching pink, and she dipped her head. Henry had rarely seen Evangeline blush, perhaps never now that he tried to find a previous memory of it. It was lovely to see her thus. To see her just a tiny bit vulnerable when she normally wore her confidence like knight's armor.

"I am glad you came," she said. "You were the only person I truly wished to see tonight."

He swallowed. "Me? Are you certain you are thinking of the right Henry Killam?"

She didn't laugh at the joke. "I am certainly only thinking of you." She broke the heaviness of the moment by looking around with a deep sigh. "You do not know how tired of this room I am.

Will you save me from my duties for a while and take me on a turn about the house? I need a moment with a friend."

Henry drew back. Evangeline had never asked to be alone with him, and here in the span of a few days she had manipulated conditions so they could be alone not once but twice. She wanted something, that much was clear. And since he could not determine it through pure deduction after reviewing the facts, he had only one choice as a scientist: to investigate the situation, to seek evidence directly. To go with her wherever she led and see what would happen next.

Something he most certainly looked forward to doing, perhaps more than he should. But he didn't argue with himself any further. He merely offered his elbow, thrilling when her warm fingers curled into the crook of it, and led her from the room as she had required.

Henry was very quiet as they strolled through the winding halls of her father's home. It wasn't that Evangeline had expected him to chatter on. It had never been his way to fill the silences with empty platitudes. But there was something different about this silence. It had a heaviness that had never existed between them. An anticipation of something she hoped he felt as strongly as she did.

She guided them to the music room and, with a gentle tug, led him inside. The room was dimly lit by a dying fire, as the servants probably hadn't expected anyone to come in here during the party. Which was why she had selected this room for her...well, it wasn't exactly a plan. She wanted it to be a plan, but she hadn't much idea of how to do what she wanted to do when it came down to it. If Henry had been a rake, well, that would have been easy. A little batting of the eyes and he would have had her against a wall.

But Henry wasn't that kind of man. He wouldn't sweep her away, so she had to do the prodding and poking to get them there.

"This is a lovely room," he said, pulling away from her hand and pacing the large space. "All the holly garland and gold makes it feel very much like Christmastide in here. And I haven't heard you play in an age."

"I don't do it to exhibit quite as much as I once did," she admitted, moving to place her fingers gently on the keys of her pianoforte. There was a soft ding of the note in the air.

"I've always like to hear you play," he said, watching her. She felt him watching even when she turned away. "You always capture the mathematics of any piece perfectly."

She laughed even though she suddenly felt unsteady. "You think of music as mathematics?"

"It's all it is. A series of equations." He cleared his throat and stepped closer.

"So is dancing, but you do not do that very often," she whispered, tracking him as he stopped at the edge of her piano and placed hand along the edge. His fingers were close to hers now. Almost close enough to feel their warmth as she had in the parlor the other day.

"The mathematics of dancing are complicated by the gangly nature of one's legs," he said. He smiled, but there was a hesitance there. "And the ability, or lack thereof, to move one's hips."

"I have danced with you before, Henry Killam," she said, her voice cracking in the most shocking manner. "And your hips move fine."

It was a scandalous thing to say, filled with a double entendre someone like her was never supposed to use. And yet Henry didn't step away. Henry didn't move at all, except to extend his fingers along the piano top and gently, carefully, brush them over hers.

Electric awareness jolted from that tiny point of contact and rushed through each and every nerve in her body. Pulses settled in the most sensitive places. Places she had touched before—she knew they could bring pleasure. Now she felt echoes of that pleasure with just his hand grazing hers.

"Evangeline," he whispered, the timber of his voice rougher, lower, more dangerous, even though she *wanted* him to lose control. Didn't she? Wasn't that what this entire performance was all about?

She couldn't quite remember now that they were standing half a foot from each other, now that he was touching her, now that she was staring up into green eyes behind glinting spectacles.

She inched farther into his space and lifted a shaking hand to rest on his chest. She felt the thud of his heartbeat against her palm, the cadence wild. She pulled the other hand free from his on the piano and lifted it to touch his cheek, then wound it around the back of his neck.

"Henry," she murmured back as she lowered his head to hers and let their lips meet.

She'd never kissed a man before. It wasn't that the opportunity hadn't arisen in the past. But there had never been anyone she *wanted* to kiss. This was not what she expected when she pictured the act, with a fair amount of disdain.

Henry's lips were soft against hers, but firm and warm. The pressure was uncommonly pleasant, and she leaned closer so she could feel more of it.

Henry made a soft sound against her mouth, and suddenly his arms closed around her. He tugged her flush to his body, molding all her curves to the surprisingly hard and unyielding planes of him, and the kiss's intensity increased tenfold. He angled his head and his mouth...opened.

She gasped at the unexpected warm heat and his tongue breeched her lips. He tasted good, so good, a hint of sherry, a taste of mint, something warm and needy and mesmerizing. She should have pulled away then, teasing him, but she didn't. Couldn't.

Instead, she let her tongue meet his and the room shrank into them, growing hot and close as she found herself lifting to be closer to him. As his hands dug into her back to bring her nearer still. As she felt the hardness of his body between them and realized, with a shock of awareness, that this was that thing she'd read about in naughty books she was not to read, but did anyway so that she would understand what exactly would be expected of her in a foggy future where she would be someone's bride.

Never had those descriptions seemed enjoyable until now when their bodies were grinding against each other and the world was fading away until nothing mattered but Henry and what he would do next.

And in that moment where it felt like she would burst from anticipation, he suddenly dragged his mouth from hers. He released her, steadying her by the elbow gently before he paced away, running a hand through his already unkempt locks.

When he turned back, he had removed his spectacles and was rubbing them on a handkerchief to wipe away the steam that had somehow gathered on the glass in those close moments.

She stared at him, this man she had told herself she would steer and seduce and manipulate. This man who had turned all that on its head by stealing her control and her plans with just a sweep of his tongue.

"Evangeline," he whispered again, his voice just as rough as it had been when he said it before they kissed. Then he shook his head. "I apologize, my lady. I have behaved in an ungentlemanly manner. Allow me to remove myself so I do not go further than I already have."

She stared, mouth agape, as he walked past her to the music room door. There he stopped, turned back and his face was lined with true regret. "I am...I am sorry."

Then he was gone without another glance in her direction and Evangeline was left to sag against the piano, her hands shaking and her mouth tingling with the memory of his lips and hers. With so much more than that.

She fought to catch her breath, for it was short and ragged and almost painful. Her heart throbbed, almost like she had been running, and she was just a little dizzy as she sat down at the piano to regather herself.

Regather. That was not something she had to do very often in her life. She had planned it that way, arranged it, created every circumstance that she never felt exactly as she did now: out of control.

What had gone wrong with her plan? She had chosen Henry as her target because she knew…*thought* she knew…that he could be navigated in the direction she wished for him to take. That she would be able to stay cool and collected and careful with him and put herself in a position where she no longer had to fear what could be taken from her.

A marriage of convenience, but not one based on money, only on a desire to keep her independence.

And yet, in the span of a few seconds, Henry had proven she could be put into the very position she had watched her mother take over and over and over again. The position she saw her sister in regularly, and her sister-in-law. That position was them wanting something *more* from a man. A man who didn't care enough to provide it.

When Henry had pulled away from her, she had felt the humiliating desire to beg him back. To follow him like a pathetic puppy, craving a connection he didn't feel.

She leaned forward against the piano, resting her head in her hands. She'd thought she would avoid all that with Henry. And now she had no idea what to do next.

And for Evangeline, not knowing was the worst thing in the world.

Henry staggered back into the ballroom, his legs barely keeping him upright and his spinning head making it hard to concentrate. The taste of Evangeline was still on his tongue, sweet and heady as spiced wine. The warmth of her was one his skin, hotter than any festive Yule log crackling in the fireplace.

And all of it led to a deep and powerful longing he had never allowed himself to fully feel, that he had always quashed when it dared to rear its head over the years, but now could not be denied. It was a longing for *her*. For a woman who had always been out of reach.

But now he'd had a taste of her, of what he could no longer deny he had craved for years, and he realized in that moment that he would never be able to pretend away that longing again. It would live with him always, a cold reminder every time he saw Evangeline. Nothing could ever be the same now.

She had made certain of that through her actions. Oh, he had elevated the kiss, certainly, wild and animal abandon taking him over in a way he'd never allowed before. But she had started it. She had steered them to the quiet music room where they would never be interrupted. She had flirted and leaned and ultimately, she had kissed him.

His body jolted at the memory of that kiss, sweet at first and then something far wilder and more wanton as they both let loose of control.

Why had she done it? After years of what he'd perceived as only a friendly connection, why was she suddenly and rapidly pressing for something more?

"Henry."

He froze, all heated thoughts of Evangeline's taste fading from his mind at the hard sound of his father's voice behind him. He turned slowly and found the viscount standing there with folded arms and a judgmental expression.

"We did not get a chance to speak much earlier. I did not expect you here tonight," Lord Killam said.

Henry was still so dizzy, he had a hard time measuring his response. "I was invited. I did not realize I was to remain locked in my tower until I did what you asked of me."

His father's eyes narrowed. "Watch yourself, boy."

Henry bent his head. There was nothing else to be done. His father held all the cards at present and would destroy Henry's future despite anything he did. At this point, it was a matter of degrees.

"I apologize," Henry ground out. "I hope my presence here doesn't make you uncomfortable."

His father shrugged. "Have you put any thought into what we discussed a few days ago?"

"Your ultimatum."

"Yes, that." His father lifted his brows. "Time is running out, boy. Don't make me use the worst option. Don't make me destroy you to save you from yourself."

His father tipped his head and walked off without an answer. Henry watched him, hands clenched at his sides. "You mean save yourself from me," he muttered, and reached out to catch a drink from a tray carried by a passing footman.

As he sipped it, his gaze moved to the door. Evangeline was stepping through the double doors, her gaze darting around the chamber. From her expression, no one would guess she had very nearly been ravished in a music room. She looked as bored and unbothered as she ever did.

As he watched her fall back into her hostessing duties, his mind turned to his conversation with Donovan a few days before. His friend had teased him about marrying an heiress to solve all his problems.

She looked at him, and when their eyes met, the color left her cheeks. So she was not so unaffected as she pretended. He was almost proud of that fact, but it also made Donovan's words even louder in his head.

If Evangeline was sniffing around him, she had to have a purpose. What if he could use that purpose to further his own future? What if it could actually work?

He bent his head. These kinds of thoughts and plans were not to be made lightly. He had to think on them, hypothesize, research, make lists of all the potential outcomes. He needed to think. And he certainly wasn't going to do that here.

So he made his way through the crowd carefully. At the door, he turned back one last time. Evangeline was watching him. Her expression had gone flat again. Control had returned.

But she held his gaze as he stood there. And it was he who broke it when he walked away.

CHAPTER 7

Evangeline very rarely allowed herself to get lost in life, but the one true exception was in a bookshop. Normally she could walk through the shelves, touching the spines, inhaling the heavenly scent and picking out the perfect story...or two...or ten...to take her away later.

Today that plan simply wasn't working. She stood in Mattigan's Bookshop, surrounded by its calming beauty, and her mind was most decidedly elsewhere. In a music room, to be precise, with Henry Killam's arms around her and his lips on hers—

She staggered as her slipper caught on the edge of one of the carpets and she nearly deposited herself face first on the floor. She smoothed her skirts and looked around, hoping no one had seen that inelegant display. The shop was mostly empty, so at least she hadn't made herself entirely into a cake. That was what one got when they strayed from a perfectly good plan and let emotion take over.

Perhaps she deserved to look a fool. She felt one.

She moved down one of the aisles and was about to try, once again, to surrender herself to the titles when another lady entered from the other end. Evangeline gasped as she found herself face to face with Miss Thomasina Lesley, the young woman who had wished to be lightly ruined...the one whose predicament had inspired Evangeline to look at Henry in this new light.

"Lady Evangeline!" Miss Lesley gasped as she rushed to the middle of the aisle to meet her. "What a pleasure it is to see you here."

"Indeed," Evangeline said, grasping Miss Lesley's hands in hers with a light squeeze. "I have found myself looking for you since our last meeting and wondering about you and your..." She looked around to make sure they were not being spied upon. "...your plan."

Miss Lesley's cheeks colored pink and she nodded. "Yes, my plan."

"Come, sit with me by the fire," Evangeline said, drawing her to the back of the shop where Mr. Mattigan always kept a fire blazing to warm the room and make the area cozy for in-shop reading.

They settled into the chairs together and Evangeline smiled at her companion. "How is it *really* going between you and Simon?"

"Fine," Miss Lesley said, and her tone sounded firm. "Perfectly fine, thank you."

Evangeline nodded. It seemed she was the only one in a state of weakness when it came to the pursuit of a man. How comforting.

"That's wonderful, I'm happy to hear it. And I suppose I must thank you for that night at the ball. Talking to you helped me put a great many things into perspective. I am also pursuing a gentleman at this time, though it is with an eye toward marriage."

Miss Lesley's eyes widened and she leaned forward slightly. "Marriage! Let me be the first to wish you happy. Who is the lucky gentleman?"

"Henry Killam," Evangeline admitted after the smallest of pauses.

Miss Lesley stared at her a moment, then a tiny smile turned up her lips. "You are to be congratulated in your choice. I understand now why you discouraged me from choosing Mr. Killam for my own plans."

Evangeline swallowed. She *had* done that. She couldn't deny it. And when thoughts of why she might so strenuously push her friend away from Henry arose, she had to set them aside with all her might. They were foolish musings brought about by the unexpected elements in her pursuit, that was all.

"Considering how well your plans with Simon appear to be progressing, I hope you are glad for that?"

Miss Lesley hesitated a moment and her cheeks turned red as she stared off toward the fire. "Indeed. Yes, it is indeed all for the best."

There was a silence between them for a moment, long enough that Evangeline felt a twinge of disappointment at her own uncertainty next to what felt like Miss Lesley's absolute assurance. When they had begun so oppositely aligned, it felt dreadfully unfair.

"Lady Evangeline? I don't want to intrude, but since you were kind enough to assist and advise me…" Miss Lesley cleared her throat. "I hope your plans with Mr. Killam are progressing according to your wishes?"

Evangeline hesitated as a world of imagery flooded her mind. Holding Henry's hand in the parlor, the way her breath had caught in the music room, him watching her, kissing him…him taking over the kiss. Him running.

She blinked the thoughts away. "Fine," she said, repeating what Miss Lesley had said to the same question. "It's all very fine."

"Lovely," her friend said.

The subject felt closed and Miss Lesley began to talk of something else, but Evangeline couldn't stop thinking about Henry. About how things had gotten so out of control. Here was Thomasina Lesley, who was lovely and friendly, and Evangeline truly liked her, but the young woman wasn't nearly as confident or certain of herself as Evangeline had always felt. Yet she was seducing a man...seducing him to her own ruination...without a care in the world while Evangeline fretted over kisses.

She jolted at the thought, straightening a little on the settee. Maybe that was the trick. She was dancing around Henry too much, spending too much thought and time in a gentle, soft temptation that would lead to a normal kind of marriage proposal. With Henry's calm, studious nature, that might not work.

Besides, it gave her too much time to analyze the situation. While Henry loved that, researching and testing had always been his forte. God, she remembered one summer party a year ago when he had spent an hour testing out different combinations of flavors for a fruited wine. Evangeline had watched him, astonished at his focus. She would have just poured the damn wine and been done with it. Knowing was far better, wasn't it?

Of course, the drink had been wonderful, but that was beside the point.

She *didn't* test. She decided what she wanted and went after it. She wanted to marry Henry, to have control of her fortune and to stop having these unwanted thoughts of the pressure of his mouth on hers. Perhaps Miss Lesley's idea of a ruination was a better one than her own. She would regain control by getting right to the point of the matter and harness the unwanted passion his kiss had inspired to something that had a purpose. If she could force herself to discipline her own reactions, which she had always been able to do in the past, then she'd be on track again.

Plus, it would force Henry's hand. Especially if they went beyond mere light ruination. He would marry her if they went too far. And that would be that.

"Lady Evangeline, are you well?" Miss Lesley asked, reaching out to cover her hand gently and drawing her back to the present.

"Yes," Evangeline said, shocked that her tone was a little breathless. She must have inhaled a bit of smoke from the fire.

She blinked and tried to focus. Her poor friend had been

speaking so earnestly and Evangeline had been rude. What had she been saying? Oh, something about her mother and using Evangeline's name to thwart Mrs. Lesley's overprotective drive.

"And please, you must call me Evangeline, for we are friends, are we not?"

Miss Lesley's expression softened. "Indeed, I would be honored. As I would be if you would call me Tamsin."

"Tamsin," Evangeline repeated, and smiled. She did like this young woman. Normally she only helped people and didn't get close, but there was something about Tamsin... "And of course you may use my name to further your plans with Simon. It's well known that I favor Mattigan's with my custom and am regularly to be found here." She stood, still distracted by thoughts of Henry and the seduction that had sprung to her mind. "But I realize I have another appointment that slipped my mind."

"Of course." Tamsin was staring at her as if she'd sprouted a second head.

The two women rose together and Evangeline smiled at Tamsin to reassure her. "I really do love seeing you, my friend. Perhaps before the new year, you and I could meet. I'll send you an invitation to tea."

"I would be honored," Tamsin said. "It was lovely seeing you again."

"Good day!" Evangeline called out as she hustled to the front of the store where Tibby was sitting, reading a gothic novel. Evangeline stopped and stared.

Damn. Tibby. She wanted to act on her plan immediately, but Tibby would never let her do something rash. Something like go to Henry Killam's house alone, for instance.

Evangeline smiled. She was standing right in front of Tibby, who hadn't even noticed her, she was so engrossed. "Tibby, I'm ready to go."

Her maid jerked her face up with a gasp and lunged to her feet. "Oh, my lady, I didn't even see you there!"

"Yes, you seemed quite riveted."

"I am," Tibby said with a smile. "But if you are ready to depart…"

She moved to set the book aside, but Evangeline stepped up and took it instead. "*The Mysteries of Udolpho* by Radcliffe. It is all the rage, isn't it?"

Tibby nodded. "And for good reason, for I am already captivated."

"Then we shall buy a copy," Evangeline said, "so that we may both read it and discuss it later."

Tibby smiled, but there was no shock on her face at the offer. Evangeline often bought books that she shared with her maid, since she knew Tibby adored a good story as much as she did. That today she offered this kindness for her own purposes… well…what was the harm?

"Mr. Mattigan?" she called out, lifting the book toward him. "Ann Radcliffe's *The Mysteries of Udolpho.*"

Mattigan grinned as he opened a book before him and made a notation. "I shall add it to your account, my lady. Very nice to see you again. And a happiest of Christmastide to you!"

"And to you, good sir," Evangeline said as they exited the shop into the sharp cold of the winter afternoon. She handed over the book to Tibby as they entered the carriage for the short drive back to her father's home.

"You don't wish to read it first?" Tibby asked, her gaze flitting greedily to the embossed cover.

"You have already begun and I find myself a little tired," Evangeline said, laying the frame of her lies with a false yawn. "I think I shall lie down for a bit when I get home. And you can take a few hours to lose yourself in a Gothic castle with a wicked villain and strife galore."

Tibby laughed. "It is as if you already read it."

"Just because I can guess the path does not mean I won't enjoy every moment when you've finished and are dying to talk to me about it." Evangeline's smile was not pretended, for she did love this part of her relationship with her maid. Many would have judged it, but she cared for Tibby. Which was why lying made her stomach hurt just a bit. She ignored it as they stopped on the drive.

"Come," Tibby said as Evangeline was helped from the carriage and her maid followed. "I will get your settled for your nap."

Evangeline followed obediently and fought the urge to let a wide smile cause Tibby any concern. When one controlled everything around oneself, it was easier to unwind the binds that kept her in place. And in a very short time, that meant she could pursue the next part of her plan.

Seduction.

Half an hour later, Evangeline had snuck down the back stairs and was back in the carriage, her driver at the door with a concerned expression. "You want to go to Mr. Killam's unattended, my lady?"

She pursed her lips. "Certainly not, Wilkes. My father is meeting me there, so I will not be alone. You needn't worry yourself."

Relief swept over his face, and that twinge of guilt that had been troubling her since she set this plan in motion ratcheted all the higher. What was a little deceit for the greater good? Were this plan to play out as she wished it to do, no one would be hurt. In fact, many would be *helped*. And if for some reason she was discovered, she would certainly take all the blame for her own actions.

It was a victimless crime she committed.

Wilkes closed her in and they rode along for the short turn around the park to where Henry's house stood alongside a dozen others with the same façade. As she stepped out, her stomach clenched. What if he was not at home? She had heard from several gossips that Henry had not been going to the Society of London Astronomical Studies hall for a few days, probably to keep his father's rage at bay.

But if he wasn't there, it would prove her words to Wilkes a lie, and that could cause trouble. She could always walk home across the park if Henry wasn't in residence. No one would be the wiser.

"Thank you, Wilkes," she said as the footman helped her down. "You may go home. I'll send for you if my father cannot escort me."

He still looked uncertain, but the driver tipped his hat and off the carriage went, leaving Evangeline alone on the stair to Henry's house. Her hands shook a little at her sides and she squeezed them into tight fists. What was wrong with her? There was nothing to be so worked up about. What she was about to do was a tactic, nothing more.

She pushed her shoulders back and made her way to the door. With a few deep breaths, she calmed herself, then raised her hand to the knocker and tapped three times. For a moment, she considered fleeing. Just racing into the park behind her and back to her house, where she could pretend she had not been so foolish. But before she could, she heard movement in the foyer. Whatever the prudence of her actions, they were done now. There was no escape.

She was going to do this, one way or another.

CHAPTER 8

Henry lifted his head from the line of figures before him and met Donovan McGilvery's bright eyes. "Was that my door?"

"I believe so," McGilvery said. "Were you expecting someone?"

Henry got to his feet and let out a long breath. "No. I certainly hope it is not my father. I've been avoiding the society in order to thwart his spies, but he will cause a scene if he discovers I'm here working on equations with you."

"Ah." McGilvery nodded slowly. "It's beastly, I'm sorry. Why don't you answer the door? I'll put away our mess and be ready to bolt out the back just in case."

Henry shook his head as the rapping of the door came again. His servants were out for the day. "Yes, yes," he called as he exited the room. "I'm sorry!"

McGilvery muttered something comforting, but Henry didn't fully comprehend it as he smoothed his waistcoat and made for the front door. He had no time to roll his shirt sleeves down or put on a coat to make himself presentable, so he prayed it was not his father as he threw open the door to the intruder.

He blinked at the shock of the visitor's identity. "E-Evangeline?" he said, then fought for propriety. "*Lady* Evangeline."

"Right on both accounts," she said with a small smile. "I-I did not realize you buttled as well as searched the skies for new planets. A man of many talents, indeed."

Her tone was laced with friendly teasing, but her gaze had flitted from his face and now settled on his bare forearms. She stared for a moment, then jerked her gaze back up to his. It was now slightly foggy and she blinked like she was trying to clear her mind.

"My—my servants have every third Tuesday off. Have I been indefensibly rude and forgotten an engagement between us?" he asked.

She swallowed hard. "Er, no. We had no previous arrangement to meet today. I simply...I want to talk to you, Henry."

He glanced behind him. Donovan was in his study waiting for him. Certainly when he'd heard a feminine voice at the door, he would have abandoned his plans to flee Henry's father. He glanced behind Evangeline and wrinkled his brow. "Where is your maid? And how did you get here?"

Her shoulders flexed back. "I...did not come with a maid." She was suddenly breathless. "And I sent my carriage away."

A sudden shot of heated awareness jolted through Henry and he felt an uncommonly powerful desire to tug this woman into his foyer, slam the door behind her and pick up where they'd left off in the music room the previous night. But he was no rake. He didn't ravish ladies.

But this one certainly tempted him.

"Come in," he said. "I do have company."

Her mouth dropped open slightly. "Oh, oh, I'm sorry. I didn't think. I can—"

He caught her hand to draw her inside and shut the door behind her. He had to lean past her to do it, and God, but she smelled good. Damned honeysuckles. She must have put some essence of it in her soap, because it clung to her. Made him wonder where else it lingered.

He backed away. "Don't be silly. Come."

He motioned her to follow him down to his study. As he stepped in, Donovan spun from where he was organizing Henry's desk back into some shape. "It didn't sound like your father so I did not flee—"

He broke off as Evangeline stepped into the room behind Henry. Her gaze darted down and heat filled her cheeks.

"No," Henry said with false lightness. "Er, Lady Evangeline, may I present my good friend, Mr. Donovan McGilvery."

Donovan's eyebrows lifted as he stepped forward, hand outstretched to Evangeline. "Lady Evangeline," he said as he bent over her knuckles for a brief kiss. Henry felt an odd urge to pull her hand away before she did that herself. "I have heard a great deal about you."

Henry's eyes went wide and he shot McGilvery a look as Evangeline glanced his way. "Have you now? I hope only good things."

McGilvery chuckled. "Only the very best of things, I assure you."

"And how do you two know each other?" Evangeline asked.

"The scientific society I am a member of," Henry said softly.

"Then you are a scientist," Evangeline said with a more relaxed expression. "Are you an astronomer like Henry?"

"Not quite as good as he is, but yes. The stars are my interest," McGilvery replied with a nod. "But I think it is time for me to depart. It was a productive day, Killam, but I can see you have duties to attend to and I admit I am tired of staring at figures. I shall certainly dream of numbers tonight. It was a pleasure meeting you, my lady. I'll see myself out."

"Good—good day, Mr. McGilvery," she called out, shooting Henry a look as the other man left them alone. All alone. In his house with no servants. Without a chaperone of any kind.

And in that moment, recalling he was not the rake was proving more difficult than ever.

"I'm very sorry, I don't know why he departed so swiftly," Henry said as he motioned toward the settee by the fire. "May I make you tea?"

"Tea would take a while if your servants are not in residence," she said.

"You doubt me?" he said with a smile. "I actually make very good tea, my lady."

"I'm certain you do, scientist that you are. It is only that my time is limited. Perhaps some of that sherry instead?" She motioned toward the sideboard.

Henry nodded and brought out two pretty crystal sherry glasses. When he handed hers over, she immediately took a sip like she was girding herself for whatever was about to happen. He had so rarely seen Evangeline nervous, he almost feared the reason. Feared it had to do with that amazing kiss they'd shared the night before. He'd been trying so hard not to lose himself in thoughts of it.

"Your friend said something about your father," she said, setting her glass aside and watching him as he took a place on the settee beside her.

He could have chosen any other seat in the room. But he hadn't.

He cleared his throat and wished he could clear his mind so easily. "Er, yes. I wasn't expecting the viscount, but feared it might be him when we heard the knock. I do not think he'd appreciate me hanging about with McGilvery and doing mathematics in my study."

"Mr. McGilvery seems a nice enough fellow," she said softly. "Your father would disapprove of him?"

"He isn't titled, and you know better than most what a toady my father is. He doesn't approve of anything 'beneath me.' He sees my work and anyone who joins me in it as that."

She leaned a little closer, and his heart felt like it might explode from pounding so hard. "Henry—"

He took her hand. The motion silenced her, and she stared at their intertwined fingers for a beat that seemed to last a lifetime.

"Why are you here, Evangeline? I know it isn't to make small talk with me about my friend or my father or tea or the weather or the price of ale."

"You're so certain I wouldn't care about any of those things?"

He arched a brow. "You came here unannounced with no chaperone. It can't have been for such mundane discussion."

"You are so direct," she mused, almost to herself. "I suppose that is in my favor. Henry, I did come here with a purpose. I wanted to talk about last night, about…the kiss."

He pulled his hand from hers and got to his feet. As he paced away, he ran a hand through his hair and shoved at his spectacles, trying to find purchase. Here was the moment. The moment when she told him he ought never have let that kiss happen. The moment when all his little fantasies would be dashed.

"I recognize what I did was very wrong," he began as he faced her with as much bravery as he could muster.

Her brow wrinkled. "What you did?"

"Kissing you." He swallowed. "Thoroughly."

She stared at him a moment and then she pushed to her feet. She took her time crossing to him, he thought that might be by design. But despite seeing the manipulation of her movements, he was still mesmerized by them. Step by step, she glided toward him, her dark blue gaze fixed on his. She held him in place with just a twitch of her hips, just a tilt of her smile. At last she reached him, nudging in far too close. Almost touching him.

And then she did touch him. She reached up, her bare fingertips skimming his cheek, his jawline and across his lower lip. It felt like fire when she did it, tingling, burning, wonderful fire that would consume him and he would love every moment of it. Even if it destroyed him in the end.

"*I* kissed you, Henry," she reminded him. "And I have been able to think of little else since."

His mouth dropped open. He was dreaming. That had to be it. He had fallen asleep over his figures and this was all a dream. A very vivid dream where he could smell Evangeline and feel her warmth seep through him despite her just coming in from the cold.

A dream where she was leaning up, lifting on her tiptoes, sliding that soft hand around the back of his neck. Their lips were less than a breath away and then their mouths met for the second time in as many days.

Both her arms came around his neck and he couldn't help himself. He caught her waist, drawing her even closer.

No, this wasn't a dream. Somehow it was fantasy come true. And just like the night before, he forgot reason and prudence and gentlemanly behavior. Everything but the pulsing need to taste Evangeline, to get drunk on her, to lose himself in her...everything else was gone.

He sank into the moment with abandon, driving his tongue past her parted lips, crushing her against his chest so he could feel the slopes and valleys of her curves mold to his own. She made a soft sound in the back of her throat, not of distress, not of refusal...it was a sound of pleasure. Of surrender.

Her hands clutched him closer, her fingers denting the muscles of his shoulders as he backed her toward the settee they had both abandoned. They fell onto it together, his body half covering her as he angled her head for better access and drove even deeper.

They were spiraling out of control now, her hips lifting beneath him perhaps without her knowing it. Her breath short, his too. And his body rapidly hardening to steel beneath his trousers. His mind screamed at him to recall himself, recall that he was a gentleman. All the while his blood burned at him, demanding he take, claim, pleasure, in a voice he didn't even recognize because he had denied its existence for so long.

Still, the gentleman was strong in him, even if it was weakening by the moment. At last he pulled away, jolting to his feet and pivoting from her so the hard evidence of his arousal wouldn't offend any more than his punishing mouth or hands already had.

"I'm sorry," he panted. "I'm sorry."

She was silent for a moment. For two. It felt like a lifetime. Then she said, "Henry, look at me."

It was an order, given in the tone of voice of a woman who was not accustomed to being denied. And he didn't deny her. He couldn't. Slowly, he faced her and stared down.

Evangeline had sat up from the reclined position, but her hair was mussed, her lips red from kisses, her dress slightly crooked in the bodice and wrinkled from where they'd ground against each other in reckless abandon. She looked ravished even if she hadn't been.

She made him want to finish the job.

"Evangeline—"

"Henry, if you apologize once more I will have my feelings hurt," she teased, but he saw the truth of that statement in her eyes, flashing there with rare vulnerability before she controlled it as she seemed to control all else.

"I wouldn't want to do that," he murmured.

She tapped the settee beside herself. "Please come back."

"That's a dangerous proposition," he said, staring at the small cushion so close to her own. "I'm not sure you know how dangerous."

She held his gaze once more and then slowly let it lower to where his cock was still outlined, hard against the fabric of his trousers. "I think I know exactly how dangerous. Sit."

He shook his head, but did it, drawn to her despite his own rational mind that knew the path this experiment could take.

They were working with uncontrollable substances now. Explosions were imminent.

"I came here, as I said, because I can't stop thinking about that kiss last night," she said, her voice calm even if she kept worrying her hands in her lap. "And what I want, Henry...what I want...I want exactly what you want. I want *more*. I want to be pinned to this settee and have your hands on me. I want all the things those...those naughty books I'm not supposed to read describe. I want...I want you."

Once again, he questioned whether this was a dream, despite all the evidence that it wasn't. Or perhaps he'd struck his head and this was something worse. He had a dozen questions. A hundred. He started with one.

"Wh-why?" he whispered.

Her eyes went wide, as if she hadn't considered that he might question her. And why would she? Most men would simply jump at the opportunity to touch this woman. How many times had he heard the whispers about her beauty and allure? Whispers that always made him bristle, for reasons he hadn't allowed himself to explore until...well, just *until*.

"I might not have the same level of experience as you do, but I certainly have the same longings," she said, her tone becoming slightly more peppery. "Why should a lady not want desire or something wicked? You men get to do so at your pleasure."

He drew back, for she seemed to view him in a light that wasn't exactly accurate. And perhaps if she understood this, the world would go back to turning in the direction it was meant to turn, rather than this madness that now surrounded him.

"Evangeline, I have not..." He shifted. "I am not a rake, my lady. I have no experience in the delights I believe you are describing."

Her lips parted. "Am I to understand that you are...you are a *virgin*?" she asked.

He nodded, though he felt blood heat his cheeks at the shock in her tone. Also at the directness with which they were addressing this sensitive subject.

"How is that possible?" She looked him up and down then repeated the question. "*How* is that possible?"

He shook his head at the way she asked that question. As if he had a dozen women falling at his feet. *That* was certainly not true. "I suppose men do have more freedom in these things and there is an expectation that men of a certain rank should cat around. God knows my brothers both do. But I...it never appealed to me."

"At all?" she burst out, and there was a lilt of desperation to her tone.

He chuckled. "Well, I think we've already established that it isn't *at all*. Certainly I have thoughts, desires, *longings*, as you described them. But I have enough control not to go chasing after every single thing that makes me...er...hard."

She twisted her mouth. "I see. That puts a wrench in things."

"A wrench in what?" he asked, watching as she stood and all but flounced to the fireplace. She turned there.

"Well, I came to seduce you," she said, tossing up her hands.

"You did?"

She tilted her head. "Of course I did. Gracious, Henry, you're very intelligent, do try to keep up." She folded her arms. "Of course, I have little experience in this arena and apparently you know nothing either. So how would I even do that if you can't guide us once we start?"

He lifted both brows. "I never said I didn't know anything."

She stared, confusion lining her expression. "What do you mean? How could you know anything if you haven't done it?"

"I'm a scientist, Evangeline." He got up, moving toward her because he couldn't stop himself even if he should. She watched him, her breath catching with every step. "I haven't experienced a great many things that I know to be true. I'm looking for a planet that has been nothing more than a rumor for hundreds of years. I can't see it, but I believe it to be there. I'm an *expert* in its potential existence." He stopped before her and reached out to trace her jaw, as she had done to him a few moments before. "I study my interests, my lady. And I have done a great deal of study on the topic we were just discussing."

Her gaze narrowed and a half-smile tilted her lips. "Have you now? Oh, of course you have." She rested a hand on his chest. "Well then, let me take this from another angle. Mr. Killam, you cannot be satisfied with only studying a subject in books, can you? As a scientist, would you not like to do some...some hands-on research of the topic?"

"What is the topic?" he asked, his breath coming short.

"You know the topic," she whispered, those blue eyes burning up at him. "And I am offering to be your test subject. You see, I have also studied this particular subject extensively over the years."

He dipped his head back with a groan. Damn it, but she tested him. She was asking for what amounted to ruination after years of mere friendship. He didn't understand why. He didn't understand it at all. And yet, he was a man, not a machine. He couldn't just pretend that this suggestion, scandalously made, wasn't so very tempting.

Couldn't he take what she offered? Couldn't he have this taste of utter heaven before he descended into the hell his father demanded? Didn't he deserve that? And he didn't have to ruin her, even though that was her request. He could do other things. Things he'd dreamed about doing to her. He had to be honest and admit they had always been dreams about her.

This was his only chance to pursue them.

He was still staring up at the ceiling, trying to figure out his answer when he felt the brush of her mouth on his exposed throat.

"Henry," she whispered, the words making swishes against his skin. "Stop thinking and hypothesizing and collecting evidence and just...touch me."

CHAPTER 9

Evangeline could hear the strength of her own voice, the certainty, and for that she was glad. Because she felt none of it. Not when Henry's arms were around her and her body was responding in ways she hadn't thought she'd ever feel. Ways that set her off kilter and made this plan feel much more dangerous and reckless. She was never reckless.

But she didn't have much time to think about that. He cupped her chin, tilting it up toward him again, and his lips came down to hers. He made a low groan in his chest, a very masculine sound of possession and pleasure. Between her legs there was a pulse of sensation and she gasped as she fisted her hand against his chest.

Back to the settee he pushed her, but this time when they reached it, he didn't collapse with her on the cushions. Instead, he stepped back. "May I undress you?" he asked.

Her lips parted in surprise. Once he'd capitulated to her demands, she had not expected him to need any more consent from her. This was a man's domain of taking and claiming and all those silly things. And yet here he was, asking permission. Allowing her to keep some control. It made her want him, want this, all the more.

"Yes. Please," she whispered, shocked at how shaky her voice was now.

"Turn around," he murmured.

She did so and he leaned in, pressing his lips to the bit of exposed skin between where her hair was bound and the top of the back of her dress. She jolted at the contact, her breath rasping out in a gasp.

He began to unbutton her dress. God, there were too many buttons. So many damned buttons, why had she worn the dress with all the buttons? Still, he made away with them, his fingers stroking the fine, silky chemise beneath. She struggled with the dress, pushing at it. This was about the claiming, and she wanted it now more than ever. For more than just her plan. She wanted to feel it.

To her surprise, he caught her arms and gently held them at her sides. "Don't rush, Evangeline," he said. "This is a first time for both of us—we should savor it."

His words reverberated at the side of her neck, against the sensitive skin there, and she closed her eyes, leaning back against him as a part of her surrendered. But the rest of her fought. Fought to keep this experience in the realm of her plan. Fought to keep her from losing herself. She didn't want to lose herself.

"We have little time," she said, forcing herself to open her eyes again and stare straight ahead. "So little time."

"We have enough time not to rush through this. What is the point of living if we don't *live*?"

He turned her toward him and hooked his fingers around the shoulders of her gown. As he held her gaze, he tugged and the fabric folded down over her chest, her stomach, her waist. Another tug and it pooled at her feet, leaving her in only her underclothes.

Everything in her told her to yank the dress back up. To run. Not because she didn't want this, but because she hadn't fully considered the intense vulnerability of it. And she wasn't even naked. According to those naughty books, she was going to have to be naked and so would he.

Of course, the part where he stripped down seemed more...interesting.

He reached for her a second time, but she stepped out of the way. His brow furrowed with concern. "You've changed your mind? It's fine, you know. We can—"

"I haven't changed my mind," she interrupted, shocked again by the fact that he was not trying to rend control from her grasp. "I only think it isn't fair that I'm standing before you in my chemise and you are fully clothed."

"Ah, a quid pro quo then," he said, nodding his head seriously even as his eyes twinkled. "Let me even the score, my lady."

He was already somewhat in disarray, his shirtsleeves rolled up to reveal those surprisingly muscular forearms she had been so distracted by earlier. It didn't take long for him to unwrap the cravat around his neck, dropping it aside. She caught her breath as he moved his hands to the four linen buttons that held his crisp shirt at the chest.

She could scarcely breathe as he loosened them, then tugged the long cotton fabric from his waistband and over his head in one fluid, graceful motion.

Her world stopped. She had always thought Henry handsome. He had an angular face, with beautiful lines and sharp eyes behind those spectacles. But she had not pictured...*this* beneath this clothing. He was all lean muscle and smooth lines. Not a fighter's body or a warrior's body. In past times Henry would not have wielded the heavy broad sword on the battlefield. He would have been the one in command.

Once again her body clenched at emptiness as she drank him in. What was she getting herself in to?

"You are suddenly pale," he said, catching her hand. "May I get you your drink?"

She shook her head, speechless, and that was a rare enough

occurrence. Finally she managed to squeak out, "I simply have not ever seen a man so…so undone before."

He smiled and glanced down at himself with what she thought was a slightly nervous gaze. "I hope I am an interesting subject for your first study."

"You are, indeed," she murmured, pulling her fingers from his and moving forward to trace the fascinating lines of his bare chest. She felt drawn to him, like a moth to a flame, and that image shocked her system out of its fog.

Moths died in flames. That was exactly what she was meant to avoid by choosing Henry, by enacting this wild plan. She had to stop losing herself in the anticipation and thrill of this moment, and remember her goals.

She yanked her hand back and lifted it to her chemise. She pulled and it fell at her feet. And now she was naked. Exposed. She forced herself to lift her chin, observing how his pupils dilated and his hands clenched at his sides like he wanted to touch her but was holding himself back.

That was right. This was what she wanted. To use what he desired against him in the game he didn't even know he was playing. And if there were other benefits to that game, well, she would take them, but that would be her *choice*. Not something she lost herself in.

Reestablished in her power, she sank down on the settee and took a deep breath before she lay against the cushions and opened her legs a fraction.

He muttered a curse, his cheeks growing red and the outline of his…the books called it a cock…pushing insistently against his trouser front fall. It looked dreadfully uncomfortable and she hoped that would convince him to move this along.

"Evangeline—"

She smiled up at him, cool and collected, or at least that was the incantation that flowed through her head. "This is what the books show, is it not? I open to you and you take me."

"That sounds rather clinical," he said, but he dropped to his knees on the floor before the settee like he was preparing to worship.

Her lips parted despite that cool and collected chant in her head. Seeing him on his knees and preparing for service to her was...it was wildly erotic.

"This is how it's done, trust me," she said, her tone too husky, but she had no way to stop it from being so.

"You are reading the wrong books," he said before he reached out, his hands smoothing across her bare stomach, up her sides, and then his thumbs traced the line beneath her breasts.

She arched beneath the touch. It wasn't something she chose to do, her body *had* to when he touched her and sensation went wild in her nerves.

"I believe you are to remove your trousers and..." She blushed. "Er...put your...your...your..."

"Yes, I realize what the end result is, I promise you," Henry said with a broad smile that lit his handsome face. He really was very beautiful. Why had she never fully comprehended that before?

"Then why aren't you—"

"Evangeline, I could remove my clothes and pump three times into you and be done with it," he said, and his voice grew low and dangerous. "And I would very much enjoy that, I'm sure. But I think that would violate the tenants of science."

"The tenants of science?" she whispered, her voice catching as he slid this thumbs up and over the crest of her breasts, teasing what were now very hard nipples. She turned her head against the settee pillows with a low moan.

"Any new venture," he said, leaning forward to press his mouth not against her lips but her stomach, "requires a bit of exploration. And I intend to do just that. So please stop trying to rush me."

Evangeline would have argued. She *had* to argue. This seduction, this pleasure that crested through her entire body, that wasn't what she'd come here for. But she was not given the opportunity to do so. Before she could exhale even a syllable, he leaned up on his knees and laved his tongue over one nipple.

The sensation of his thumb had been nothing at all compared to this. A jolt of electric pleasure crested through her entire body, bordering on pain, it was so intense and powerful. She heard herself moan, loud enough that she was glad no servants were in residence at present. Releasing that sound, letting go just a little, it made the sensation all the greater, and she squeezed her internal muscles, flexing her sex as he sucked her nipple.

She looked down at him and was shocked that he was watching her as he worked at her body. His pupils were fully dilated so that his gaze behind his spectacles was dark rather than the usual green. His breath came short, but he continued to focus on her.

And she realized he was watching her reactions. When she responded, he continued doing whatever he was doing. When she didn't, he tried something new. He was...experimenting. A test of her control and her pleasure.

But that wasn't what was meant to happen. This was supposed to be her way of getting what she wanted, not anything else. She struggled to sit up and leaned into him, tilted his chin up and kissed him.

He fell into her, lifting himself by those surprisingly strong arms and crushing his weight onto her body. The warmth of his skin merged with her own, and within seconds the kiss softened, deepened. She wrapped her arms around him and clung as he settled between her legs. She felt the hard pulse of him at her center and lifted out of instinct to rub herself against him.

Once again, pleasure ricocheted from that contact, and she gasped as the kiss broke. He stared down at her as he rubbed against her gently, letting the fabric of his trousers stroke along the slick heat between her legs.

Evangeline had touched herself before. It was a regular occurrence in the night, in her bed. Finding that release of quick, sharp pleasure was something that relieved tensions and helped her remain in focused control. She felt the echoes of the pleasure she gave herself as he arched against her yet again.

And then he was gone, dragging his mouth down her throat, her breasts, her stomach and across her hip. She squirmed beneath him as her skin came alive, as her blood burned, as her body lifted and none of it was in her control.

"That...that isn't what we're meant to do," she gasped as he placed a warm hand on each of her thighs and spread them wider so there was a bigger place for him. He was even with her sex now, watching her. He licked his lips and her body trembled.

"Evangeline, Evangeline," he murmured, almost crooning. "In such a rush. Study is the joy of life. I'm not going to deny myself that. And I admit, I have always dreamed of doing—" He leaned in and she felt the heat of his breath against the tender, wet flesh of her slit. "—this."

His tongue darted out and he traced her lower lips in one long, smooth sweep. She jolted at the sensation and her shoulders jerked up off the cushions as she stared down at him.

"Henry?" she said, guiding her hand to his hair. She meant to push him away, but as he licked her a second time, her fingers somehow pushed him closer.

He chuckled against her body and the vibration of that wicked sound made her flop back with a groan. This was no echo of that pleasure she secretly gave herself at night. This was a magnification. Something bigger and broader and oh, so much better.

He peeled her open with his thumbs, massaging gently as he licked her again. She felt him watching her, gauging her. A jolt of her heart told her to deny him her reaction. To control this. But that faded away as pleasure mounted and she felt herself let go at last. Maybe for the first time ever. Let go and surrender herself to him.

He smiled against her, she felt it rather than saw it, and the licking began again, this time in earnest. He laved her folds, he burrowed within them, and at last she felt him tap the tip of his tongue against the hood of that center of her pleasure. No book she'd read had ever named it, but she knew it. And he seemed to be acquainted, as well, despite his inexperience.

He swirled around her as he gently smoothed the hood aside, and suddenly the sensations magnified. She arched up, waves of pleasure hitting her. Too much, not enough. More. She wanted more.

He gave it without hesitation, swirling and licking and finally, when it seemed like this torture had gone on for a lifetime, he sucked her.

She fell over the edge with a scream that could have broken windows. She clenched the pillows of the settee, tearing at them as wave after glorious wave of release roared through her. She ground against him as she reached for more, as she begged for more with the jolt of her hips and the roughness of her cries.

She had no idea how long it went on. How long he continued to stroke her until she went weak, her legs shaking so hard she knew she couldn't have supported her weight with them. Luckily, she didn't have to. When at last she went limp, only then did he draw his tongue from her.

He traced his mouth up her body again, gently tasting her flesh as he rose up over her, covered her. She readied herself for the next part. The part she'd heard described as laced with more pain than pleasure. After that explosive power of what he'd just done to her, she was ready for the rest.

And yet as he leaned over her, his gaze flitting over her face, he didn't rush to claim. He leaned in and kissed her. She tasted salty sweetness on his lips. Her body clenched at the pleasure of that flavor. Her flavor.

"I'm ready," she whispered, and it wasn't a manipulation. She *was* ready. Ready for him.

He wrinkled his brow. "Ready?"

She nodded. "Yes. I assume you will take me now."

He stared down into her face, and she saw him struggle with wanting exactly what she asked for. Saw him struggle and conquer with the control she, herself, didn't feel.

He kissed her once more, this time gently, and said, "I have no intention of doing so, Evangeline."

CHAPTER 10

As Henry rolled away from her, Evangeline sat up, clutching her hands to her naked body as the exposure she felt multiplied. "You have no intention of doing so? What do you mean?"

The lilt to her tone echoed in the room around her and she froze. She'd heard that before. From her mother when she was begging Evangeline's father not to go. Not to fail her. Not to be who he was.

Her stomach turned and she got to her feet and snatched her discarded chemise. She tugged it over her head, smoothing it down her body so she was no longer naked while he was half-clothed. When she faced him, he was staring at her. Reading her, damn him. Like she was a project.

"You are angry," he said.

"Of course not." Except he was right. She *was* angry. And embarrassed. Those strong emotions she normally did not allow were terrifying. "I am merely confused. Please explain yourself, sir."

He tensed at the formality, but then he bent for her dress and handed it over. She snatched it, stepping into the fabric and reaching around to try to fasten herself. After a moment of helplessness, she glared at him. "Well?"

He moved behind her, gentle as he closed the gown. She walked away as soon as she was dressed again and folded her arms as she faced him.

He arched a brow. "How about *you* start, Evangeline? After all, you are the one who has something to hide, it seems."

She sucked in a breath as if she was offended, but in truth she was taken aback and needed that time to compose herself. Could he see past her façade? How?

"I hide nothing, Mr. Killam. I came here in honesty and laid myself bare for you. Actually bare." She didn't like that the words she said were true, not just a manipulation. "And you…I don't know what you're doing or what kind of game you are playing. Did you do this to hold something over my head?"

That was a very painful thought. And not very different from her own intentions, so her mind turned with guilt and worry in equal measure.

"No," he said immediately, and with force. "I'm just not as foolish as you seem to think I am, Evangeline. I can see your mind turning on some kind of plan. Some kind of reason why you would come here and so brazenly demand not only to be pleasured, but to be ruined. And by me! *Me*, who you have never noticed beyond a funny little friendship between goddess and bug. I merely want to know the reason. Especially after what just happened. I think I'm owed that before anything more takes place that can't be undone."

Evangeline drew a breath and wished it were not tellingly shaky. He was demanding answers, which was not what she'd expected when she chose him for this foolhardy plan of hers. He was challenging her, and that challenge felt like one she could lose. Perhaps she had already lost it when she gave over her pleasure in long, powerful waves against his tongue. When she wanted more, not for a plan but for herself. When she felt a longing for

85

this man that had nothing to do with anything beyond the way she felt when he gathered her in his arms.

Panic rose in her chest, pushing at everything else. His expression softened, as if he could see that panic. As if he understood. He moved on her a long step and caught her hands before she could evade him. He squeezed them gently and the fear subsided a fraction. A calm came over her that was unlike anything she'd ever felt.

"Evangeline," he whispered. "Tell me what you *want*."

That demand caused a hitch in her she'd never expected. A bending she had avoided all her life. A yearning more powerful than physical need. She pulled her hands away and put her back to him, carefully reassembling the walls she'd always kept between herself and everyone else in her orbit. When she felt she'd done that, only then did she speak.

"I am going to be honest with you," she said. "Perhaps I should have been from the beginning, it might have kept this entire situation more in line."

"What situation?" he asked.

She drew a long breath and then looked at him. It was harder to say this when she did that, but she *needed* to look at him. Needed to see his reaction as well as hear it. She needed to show him how controlled she was.

"I'm looking for a husband, Henry. And I'd like him to be you."

Henry took a step backward and nearly deposited himself on his arse. His ears rang and his hands tingled as those strange, unbelievable words filled the small room around them. He opened his mouth to speak, but found he could hardly draw a breath, let alone formulate a word in response. Still, he struggled to manage it and finally croaked out, "Husband."

She stared at him, those dark blue eyes unreadable now that

she'd returned herself to a cooler, more collected version of herself. Not the woman who had arched beneath him in pleasure, that was certain. "What do you think?"

He shook his head. "Think? I *think* I need an explanation."

Throwing up her hands, she paced away. "I just gave you an explanation."

His frustration mounted and he folded his arms as he glared at her back. "Evangeline, saying you need a husband and you've decided it should be me is a preamble, not a damned explanation, and I know you're clever enough to recognize that. Stop playing games, stop trying to control whatever you're trying to control, and tell me the truth. The only way I can make my next move is by having all the damned information."

She pivoted to face him, her cheeks pale as paper. "You've never spoken to me in such a way before."

He blinked. "It's ungentlemanly perhaps, and I will apologize for that later. Right now I think it is best for us to just be *honest* with each other."

She worried her lip a moment. He couldn't help but track the action. Want to claim her mouth again as he had a moment before. And yet everything had changed since she entered this room. Nothing could ever be the same again.

"Very well," she said, and he heard the tremor beneath her tone. The…fear. Evangeline was afraid and that set him back a step. Afraid of him? He didn't know. He couldn't tell. But afraid of something.

"Why don't we sit?" He motioned to the settee where he had ravished her. She blushed, but followed his direction and they sat together.

She pushed her shoulders back. "I am a woman living in a time of men," she said. "I may have power, I *know* I have power. I use it carefully and I hope never cruelly."

"I've never seen you be cruel," he said softly. "Often the opposite. I know you play savior to many a young woman who needs the benefit of your influence."

She turned her face. "I—no, I just—I—"

He drew back at her stammering and uncomfortable expression. "There is no reason to be shy about it."

"I don't do it so anyone sees," she said with a shrug and a half-glance his way. "In fact, exactly the opposite."

"I know. And I doubt anyone watches you more closely than I do," he said, wondering how that confession would be received.

Her lips parted a fraction and she tilted her head. "And why do you watch so very closely?"

Clearing his throat, he ignored the question. The answer was not one that would help him at present. "So you have power. How does that relate to you looking for a husband and deciding it would be me of all people?"

She shook her head like she was trying to clear it. "Yes, of course. I have power, but in this world, it will always be limited by my sex. My father wields my destiny, for better or for worse. He has mostly kept out of it. His heir was his main concern and my brother is situated nicely. When I didn't make a match, he allowed my younger sister to wed a year ago, which seemed to satisfy him. I play hostess since there is no duchess, and I think that has kept his mind from turning on whatever he would gain from matching me. Or it...it did."

His brow wrinkled. "You think he would match you against your will?"

"He would not think of my will or wishes and still believe he was helping me," she whispered. "A few times recently he has mentioned my future in terms of marrying me off, and I know the kind of man he would pick."

"One of his stature, I would assume," Henry mused, and there was a kick of something dark and dangerous low in his belly. Jealousy, he supposed. Hate for a faceless man who would have Evangeline in his life permanently.

Except she claimed she wanted him.

"Yes, one of my father's stature," she said with a disgusted expression. "A duke or marquess, even a higher-ranking earl. A man who would trip over himself for my inheritance and then expect me to dance to his tune. A man who would control my every move and expect me to smile while he did it."

"You think very ill of the men of Society," he said softly.

"Do you believe I judge them too harshly?"

He didn't answer, for he couldn't really. He had seen the world just as she had. He'd felt the particular cruelty of some of those who held the power.

She smiled sadly. "I thought not. At any rate, I realized that my best option might be to choose my own husband before my father devises a plan and cannot be turned from it."

"You believe he would allow you to choose for yourself?" Henry asked.

She nodded. "I believe he will until he won't. And I have no idea the day or time his mind will turn."

Henry held her gaze. "And why choose me for your scheme against him?"

For a moment, she seemed to struggle with the answer. Her mouth opened and shut, her gaze darted from his. And then she whispered, "You are a friend, Henry."

He arched a brow as response, and her eyes widened. "You do not believe me?"

"I don't know what to believe, but I know I see through you," he said. "How your gaze will not find mine, how your hands shake in your lap even as you grip them into fists to make it stop."

She sucked in a breath and clenched those hands even tighter in response.

"How there is a tremor to your voice, a lilt that tells me you are terrified, Evangeline. And also that you aren't being truthful. I see all of that evidence, and so no, I don't fully believe that your only reason for drawing my name out of your hat was because you like me as a person."

She pushed from the settee and flounced across the room in what he could see was a show of outrage. "Well, I never!" she huffed.

He chuckled despite the situation and followed her across the room. "I know you never," he said. "You *never* a great many things I think. It's actually one of the most charming aspects of your personality. But today, I need you to trust me. All the way. Please."

He had pushed back against her defenses and could see them wavering. Still, she was a woman unaccustomed to such things, and there was a moment when he thought she might just storm out his door.

But at last her shoulders rolled forward and she gave way. She sighed, and the sound was painful in the quiet room. "I know about your father's ultimatum, Henry. I know you need me as much as I need you, and that was *part* of why I chose you."

His brows lifted and his throat felt thick. "You know, do you? And what do you think you know?"

She glared at him. "Must you always make things so difficult?"

"I'm scientist," he said. "So yes."

"Fine," she ground out. "I *know* your father is going to cut you off because of that paper you published last month. I *know* if he does that, you'll be in dire straits because you depend upon your allowance to live. And I also *know* you don't want to give up your work because it's important, both to you and to the world at large. Marrying me could solve both our problems. Me, because I could retain some autonomy. You, because my dowry is seventy thousand and I would not give a flying fig if you went and found a dozen planets and published an entire tome about it."

He blinked. "Seventy thousand?" God, that was enough money to live comfortably for all their days. More than comfortably. And if Evangeline was being honest that she would not care if he pursued his interests…

Well, she was correct that it was a good match for them each on paper. And yet he felt less than satisfied at the answer.

"Yes," she said. "And the benefit of it can be yours if you agree to marry me."

"Under your terms, I assume," he said. "And that is why you chose me, because you think I will surrender to those terms because of my own situation."

His voice sounded hollow and her expression softened. She reached out and caught his hand briefly, squeezing his fingers and sending a jolt of awareness through his body. "Not entirely. Henry, I wasn't lying when I said you were a friend. I like you. I would not think of offering such a shocking arrangement to someone I didn't like."

"That is heartwarming," he said, and stared down at their intertwined fingers. Slowly, he lifted her hand to his chest and rested it there, forcing her closer. Her breath caught in a most delightful way. "And what about this?"

She swallowed hard. "This?" she squeaked.

He smiled at the fact that he had made the great Lady Evangeline squeak. "What I did to you on that settee."

"Oh." She pulled her hand away and her cheeks flamed higher than he had ever seen before. She was trembling now. "I liked that, too. But it is my understanding that this kind of connection doesn't...it doesn't last. That men grow tired of the same woman eventually and desire other company, whether they seek it out or not."

His brow wrinkled. There was such a lilt of resignation to her tone. Of pain. She believed women were disposable to men. And perhaps they had been, in her experience.

And yet as he stared at her, so lovely with her dress wrinkled and her hair mussed from the wicked things he'd done to her, with her bright gaze focused on him, with her sharp wit sparkling in his sometimes rather dull life...he had a hard time believing he could ever truly bore of that. Of her. Of touching her or being with her.

But if he said that, she wouldn't accept it. He could see that. That would be something he proved over months, even years. He'd have to draw trust from her slowly, carefully. If he earned it, then it would be an even more powerful gift.

"I don't know what the future will bring," he said carefully. "But I would not deny some men have a roving eye and cannot focus their attention on one lady. I, on the other hand, have a very focused mind. After all, this celestial body I'm trying to find has been searched for over centuries, not months. I can be singular, if that is what you fear."

Her expression didn't soften, but she nodded. "Then let us discuss the parameters of our agreement."

He tilted his head at her professional tone. Like she was a solicitor. But of course she would behave thus. She was all about control in the end. That's why stealing that control with his mouth was so satisfying.

"Go ahead. Lay out your terms," he said, sitting back down and folding his arms as he looked up at her in anticipation.

"I have three requests," she said. "First, if we are to marry, I do not wish to be subject to your control. I want to manage my own purse and set its limit."

"That doesn't seem unfair. With such a large settlement, there should be no reason to have to watch the finances all too closely. I assume I shall also have a personal account for pin money?"

Her eyes widened. "Pin money for the husband. Yes, that sounds fair. We each have our own personal account that the other does not have any rights to, as well as a household account for expenses."

"Second?" he pressed, loving the delight that lit Evangeline up when she got what she wanted. It made him never want to deny her anything at all.

"Secondly, I want to retain my independence in my friendships and in my actions." She met his stare. "I don't mean that I would do anything to embarrass you or bring shame to your name or my own. I only mean I do not want to have to explain my every movement to you. If you do not wish to attend an event, it should not preclude me from doing so and from dancing or enjoying myself while I'm there. I don't want my friendships interfered with."

Henry wrinkled his brow. What had she witnessed done to the women in her life? Not much more, he supposed, than any other woman, when he thought of it.

"Essentially you want to run your life like a dowager might, except that in this case I would still be alive," he said.

She nodded. "Something like that. The dowager part—of course you would be alive."

"That is heartening," he teased, and she flashed him a quick smile as a reward. "And having one's own interests doesn't seem too hard a thing to ask. What is third?"

"I do not wish to have emotional entanglements expected of me. We will be friends, I hope. I would not want to lose our friendship. But if you expect me to grovel at your feet for your love, that will never happen. I will not expect the same of you. We will have a marriage of convenience, and I don't want or demand more than that."

He frowned. She was truly against the very concept of romantic love, it seemed. So much so that she would pilot her ship right into a loveless union.

But perhaps time would change that. Or would make him more immune to the kinds of feelings stirring in him now.

"And what of this?" he asked. "What of ravishing you on settees or coming to your bed at night?"

Her lips parted and he watched her pupils dilate with renewed desire. It all gave him hope. Faint, perhaps, but hope nonetheless. Then she straightened her back and pushed her shoulders back.

"As long as you do not have an emotional expectation tied to such things," she said, "then the pleasure we just shared is certainly something I'd like more of. And procreation requires such acts, so I might as well enjoy them."

"Very pragmatic," he said, using humor to hide the sting caused by her casual disregard for emotional connection. "And I can agree to all those terms to a marriage."

Her shoulders rolled forward and she let out her breath in an unmistakable sound of relief. In that moment, he saw how much a lack of control over her future had weighed on her. How much solace he gave her with his surrender to her requests.

"Good," she said. "Now I must return home. My maid will soon discover I snuck out if she already hasn't. Will you call on me tomorrow? I'll be sure my father is there for you to make the show of asking for my hand."

He pushed to his feet and stepped in front of her as she scuttled toward the door. She stopped, staring up at him.

"Evangeline," he said. "You have forgotten to seal the deal."

She blinked. "Oh...yes, I suppose we should, if you want to be gentlemanly about it." She stuck out her hand between them, as if to shake his.

He chuckled. "Gentlemanly isn't exactly what I had in mind."

He caught her waist, curling his fingers around the softness of her as he molded her to his body. He was gratified when she let out a great shudder and lifted her chin toward him as her eyes fluttered shut.

She knew what he wanted. She was willing to give it. And so he took, dropping his mouth to hers and drinking of her deeply. Her tongue met his with abandon and he tasted her surrender as she sagged against his chest and gripped his forearms hard enough to dig her nails into his flesh.

Oh, how he was going to enjoy learning her body. Studying her pleasure. Teaching her his own. He was going to enjoy that very much.

She pulled away at last, unsteady on her feet as she stared up at him. Then she nodded and said, "Yes, well…good…yes. Good—good day Henry."

She staggered to the door and exited, leaving him half-dressed and alone as he stared after her. He heard the front door close and rushed to the window to watch her making her away across the street and to the park. As she disappeared from view, he knelt on the window seat and let his forehead press against the cold glass.

Evangeline didn't want emotion and he was in deep, deep trouble by agreeing to her terms. After all, emotion was already something he felt. And it wasn't going to get any better, no matter how many limits she put onto their future.

CHAPTER 11

Evangeline snuck in through the servant entrance to her father's estate exactly seven minutes after she'd left Henry's house and crept up the backstairs. There was no one in the hall and she smiled as she slipped into her chamber. She tossed her wrap aside and was about to lie down on her bed when she heard a throat being cleared behind her.

She pivoted and found herself face to face with Tibby. Her maid was seated in the corner of the room, arms folded and face lined with concern.

"You frightened me half to death!" Evangeline exclaimed as she raised a hand to her chest. "What are you doing in the corner there?"

"Waiting for my wayward charge to return from God knows where," Tibby explained. "As I have been for the last half an hour."

Evangeline frowned. Well, there was no use in lying and saying she had only just stepped out. "And how...how do you know I wasn't in the library or the study?"

Tibby pursed her lips. "Because I searched there when I came up and found your bed empty. And also because your cheeks are bright from the cold. I *know* you left the house."

Evangeline sighed. "Well, I had to take care of some business."

"I can only imagine what kind of business you needed to attend to unchaperoned." Tibby got up. "You put yourself in danger, my lady!"

Evangeline flashed to an image of Henry perched between her legs, her body shaking as he did such scandalous things to her. Dangerous, indeed, for in that moment she would have given him anything. Everything. It had taken every ounce of control in her to gather herself afterward and present her plan to him calmly and with detachment.

"I was not in danger," Evangeline muttered. "I'm quite capable of taking care of myself. It's rather ridiculous that I must be followed around like a child at any rate."

Tibby let out her breath in a long, put-upon sigh. Then she took a step closer. "You met with Mr. Killam?"

Evangeline worried her lip. Tibby didn't approve, but she did so need to speak about what had happened. Not all of it, of course, gracious no, but just say out loud her plan so that she would feel better.

"I did," she admitted, and ignored the strangled sound of frustration that escaped Tibby's throat. "You know you are my maid, don't you? You aren't supposed to judge."

Tibby shook her head slowly. "It's not judgment, my lady, I assure you. You have been so kind to me since you demanded I be hired all those years ago. I only worry about you."

Evangeline turned away from the strangely emotional reaction those words inspired. She gathered herself and focused on the problem at hand. "I know you don't approve of my sneaking out, but it worked out for the best, so I don't regret it. Henry and I… we…we were…well, it doesn't matter. He has agreed my terms of the marriage. Tomorrow he'll come and speak to my father about taking my hand."

Tibby was silent for so long that Evangeline turned to look at her. The maid's mouth was slightly agape in surprise, but her eyes were bright with what almost looked like...pity.

"So you have gotten your way at last," she murmured.

Evangeline tried to force a smile, but found it impossible. "I have."

"Then why do you seem disappointed, my lady?"

Evangeline gasped at the observation. Worse was how true it was. She *was* disappointed, even though she had found incredible pleasure with Henry, even though she had been able to convince him to give her what she wanted, needed. Somehow it all felt...*flat*. Not like her usual triumphs.

"I'm not," she lied. "In fact, I got more than I hoped for in our bargain. There will be unexpected benefits that do not require me to give any more than what I originally planned." She shivered as she thought of the pleasure again and all the promises of more to come that he had made to her.

Tibby wrinkled her brow. "And that will be enough?"

Evangeline turned away and walked to her window. Her view was of the park across the street and she looked through it, toward Henry's home. She couldn't see it, of course, but she knew it was there. *He* was there.

"Of course it will be enough," she said softly. "What he's agreed to is all I want. I can't want more."

"Can't want it or are afraid to want it?" her maid asked.

She pivoted back to Tibby and was pleased she could harden her countenance at last. "You are being ridiculous. Now, let's fix my hair and help me change for supper. Father has the Wilkinson brothers joining us tonight because he is determined to purchase some racehorse of theirs." She rolled her eyes. "I shall not miss playing hostess to these kinds of events."

If Tibby had more to say about the matter of Henry and her impending engagement, she did not do it. She only inclined her head slightly and moved to Evangeline's dressing room to bring out a few dresses for her to choose from. The moment she was alone, Evangeline took a long breath.

Everything was working out just as she wanted it to do. She had to shake off this odd sensation that she should wish for more before it caused her grief. Before it made her do something foolish that she would regret in the end.

Henry followed the duke's butler, Hughes, down the twisting halls of the manor the next day, and it was like he was seeing this place for the first time. Oh, he'd been here many a time, following his father as the viscount toadied about for the duke's favor. But today wasn't about the viscount or the duke. It was about Evangeline, and Henry took in every detail around him that would make him understand the woman who would be his… well, she'd be his bride soon enough if their plans went well.

An odd thought, considering where they had begun a week ago, a month ago. Just friends, nothing more. He wanted her and never dared hope he could do anything more than watch her from a distance as she brightened the world. But now she would be his and that had kept him up all night, dreaming of her sweet scent and the way her flavor had burst on his tongue as she erupted in pure pleasure.

He pushed those heated thoughts away and continued his observations. The house reflected her taste as much as the duke's. Henry knew her mother had died five years before, when Evangeline was seventeen. As the eldest daughter, she had taken over the hostessing duties that had once been the duchess's. It had truly been her first entrée into Society, even more than her coming out. He recalled the first party he had attended after the family ended their official mourning period. There had been Evangeline, mingling through the crowd, being herself and making everyone at ease.

She had turned toward him that night and he had caught just a flash of sadness in her stare before she smiled and it was all erased. Now that moment rushed back to him, reminding him that she was very good at hiding her heart.

"Mr. Killam, my lady," Hughes said as he stepped into the parlor ahead of Henry and announced him to Evangeline.

She turned from the sideboard where she was fussing over the tea and smiled at Henry. His heart stuttered. She was beautiful. Her thick black hair had been elaborately done in a twisted and curled mass of coiled silk atop her head. She wore a dark blue gown with a pattern of swirls stitched through it in gold thread. The blue matched her eyes perfectly and brightened them. Although it was meant to be a casual dress, something a lady would wear to tea, she could have strolled into a ballroom and caught the eye of everyone in attendance.

And she would be his. His to laugh with and touch and watch as she charmed the world for the rest of his life. A strange thought, but oh-so-very pleasant.

Of course, she wanted nothing more, but in that moment he could forget that troubling thought.

"Evangeline," he breathed.

She nodded to the butler, who stepped away and left them alone. "Will you close the door a moment?" she said softly.

Henry's entire body clenched and he reached back and gently did as she asked. She folded her hands before herself and said, "I wanted to talk to you alone before—"

He didn't allow her to finish. In three long strides, he closed the distance between them, cupped the back of her neck and dropped his lips to hers.

She was still for a moment, he thought perhaps in surprise, but then her hands lifted to his forearms and she clung there, opening her mouth to his, sighing against him as he tasted every inch of that delectable mouth of hers.

At last, he found the strength to break the kiss and she stared up at him with a foggy, unfocused gaze. "Well, that was unexpected. And very welcome, I assure you."

He grinned at her bewilderment. It was actually fun setting her control to the side and making her blink like she'd never seen the sun before.

"I have been thinking about doing that since the moment you left my home yesterday," he admitted. "But I interrupted you, my lady, very ungentlemanly of me. What was it you were saying?"

She shook her head like she was trying to clear it and then shot him a playful glare. "As if one could retain any kind of focus after *that*. We will have to make some kind of arrangement once we're married so you'll know when I have something important to say and won't interrupt me."

"I think I will not tire of interrupting you." He shrugged. "But certainly I am happy to devise systems to make you happy, Evangeline."

She laughed and the sound was like music on the air. "Oh yes, I recall now what I wanted to say. I wanted a moment alone with you to discuss the best way to approach my father today."

Lightness escaped Henry's body and he focused as she wished him to do. The Duke of Allingham was a serious and rather terrifying person, truth be told. Henry had been trying to avoid thinking about how he would explain to the man that he wished to take his eldest daughter's hand.

"I am all ears, as you know the situation best. I defer to your judgment."

She blinked. "You respect my opinions, you mean?"

"Of course," he said. "On this and many topics."

There was a shadow of a smile that crossed her face. "I spent all of last night priming him for you. I mentioned my spending time with you more than once and got him to speak highly of your family and your father. He ought to be in a receptive mood when you go to him. I would suggest you be polite but direct.

Look him in the eye, he likes that. Try not to push your spectacles up."

He drew back. "Push my spectacles up?"

"Yes, you do that when you're nervous and he'll mark that," she explained.

Henry stared at her. "I don't do that."

"Of course you do!" Evangeline laughed. "You're doing it right now!"

He jolted as he realized he was, indeed, fiddling with his glasses, shoving them up his nose. He jerked his hand away and shook his head. "Trust in me to marry the most observant woman in London. We will be quite a pair."

"Unstoppable if we play our cards right. He is in his study. I'll have Hughes take you. In a few moments I'll come in and help the situation along if you need it." She moved to ring the bell, and as they waited for Hughes, she held out her hand for him.

Henry moved to her, taking it, and for a moment there was a deep peace that came over him. It was so strange, for Evangeline was a force of nature. And yet, when he touched her, there was a calm to her storm. A protected place where everything could be quiet.

She leaned up and pecked his cheek. "You'll be fine."

She released his hand and smiled at the butler as he entered the room. "Mr. Killam needs to speak to my father, Hughes. Will you take him?"

The butler's expression fluttered with surprise at the statement, but the reaction was gone in an instant. "Certainly. Come with me, sir."

As he followed Hughes away, Henry cast one last look at Evangeline over his shoulder. She smiled, gave a little wave and mouthed, *I'll come in soon.*

And so, buoyed by the fact that she would save him if need be, he made the rest of the walk with Hughes to the Duke of Allingham's study. He was announced and entered the room as the duke rose from his desk in greeting.

"Mr. Killam," he said, nodding to Hughes to send him away. "I did not realize you were calling today. Did we have an appointment?"

Henry felt his hand stir toward his spectacles but forced himself to stop and instead meet Allingham's gaze. It was very much like Evangeline's: dark blue, sharp, impossible to read. All of which did not help his nerves.

"Mr. Killam?" Allingham repeated with a tilt of his head.

"I beg your pardon, Your Grace," Henry said, stepping into the room further. "We did not have an appointment. I was here to meet with Lady Evangeline, actually."

Allingham's eyebrows lifted. "You two have been seeing each other a great deal lately, it seems."

"We have, Your Grace," Henry said slowly. Now was the time. Though how did he do this? How did he say this?

In the end, he had to be truthful. It was the easiest way to proceed, after all.

He straightened his shoulders. "You should know how much I admire your daughter. How I have always admired her, though from afar." He paced another step closer. "Recently I have had the honor of being allowed a bit nearer. I understand what a rare thing that is, for Evangeline could have any man she desired, I think."

Allingham chuckled. "She would take whatever she wanted regardless. Too much like her father, I suppose. But what you are saying, I think, is that you care for my daughter beyond a mere friendship?"

Henry cleared his throat. "Indeed, I do, Your Grace. I care for her very deeply and I came here today with the wish to ask for her hand in marriage."

CHAPTER 12

Allingham's smile fell and he stared at Henry in what looked like pure disbelief. Immediately, Henry's tension increased and he had to force himself not to push up his glasses. Damn Evangeline, making him aware of his nervous habit.

After what seemed like a silent eternity, Allingham came around his desk slowly. "You do realize you aren't the first man to ask this. *All* have been adeptly swatted away by her. She can have a cruel tongue and seems to have no wish for love in her life. Do you have any hope that my daughter would agree to a union?"

Henry wrinkled a brow. Allingham was speaking of Evangeline in such cold terms, as if she were more machine than woman. But that had *never* been his experience of her, even when she was not pursuing him. Evangeline was kind, he'd seen it a dozen times with those who needed her influence. She was never cruel to anyone who didn't deserve a set down.

If she was standoffish or cool, he was beginning to understand why. It was a shell she wore, a protective layer that kept the world and all who would hurt her away. Getting past that layer was a worthwhile endeavor, indeed.

He set his jaw, and this time meeting Allingham's gaze was far less difficult. "I have every hope that she will want a future with me," he said, his voice stronger than it had been since he entered the room.

There was a light knock on the door behind him, and he turned to find Evangeline standing there, her gaze locked on his in support. He smiled at her and she returned the expression.

"I see," Allingham said with another chuckle as he looked between them. "It seems this was all a manipulation on my daughter's part. Come in, Evangeline, since this is your doing."

Again, Henry found himself feeling defensive of Evangeline in the face of her father's characterization of her. But she seemed unbothered and entered the chamber to stand beside him.

"Mr. Killam has asked for your hand, my dear," Allingham said with an arched brow. "It is not the lofty match I might have made for you myself…" He shrugged at Henry apologetically. "…but I wouldn't stand in your way if this is what you truly desire. Is it?"

Evangeline licked her lips and Henry saw a slight crack in her façade. She was as nervous as he was. Somehow that was comforting rather than frightening. He longed to reach for her, to hold her hand and bring them both into that calm center of the storm, away from where the rain and wind lashed.

He couldn't, of course. Not yet. But if they resolved this, he could do that any time he wished.

"It is," she said softly. "Henry and I have a friendship and a connection that I think would make for a happy union, Father. Please grant us your approval."

Allingham tilted his head. "I see. I have no objection save one, but it must be dealt with before I give any consent to the match."

Henry glanced at Evangeline, but she looked as confused by this statement as he felt. "What is it?" she asked, her voice calm, very calm, *too* calm.

"Recently you published a paper about your mathematics work, Mr. Killam," Allingham said. "Which is all fine and good—a man should have a hobby, though I do wonder at your choice.

Still, the problem is that you have published this under your own name. I know your father shared my concerns, as he railed about it endlessly during the most tedious game of billiards I have ever had the displeasure to be a part of."

Everything in Henry felt like it had sunk a few inches. Publishing his paper had seemed such a small thing when he did it, and yet these men, these men who cared nothing for study or science and everything for appearances...they judged him harshly for it.

"If you are to marry my daughter, I would have to insist, as I know your father has, that you cease such activities immediately. It is one thing to drag your father's little name through the mud of trade, but to do so to the House of Allingham is another. I would not wish my son-in-law to be associated with trade of *any* kind."

Henry barely kept himself from glaring at the man. People of his ilk were so judgmental of those who actually did something. It was disgusting, really, for these men of rank made their entire lives off the backs of those they looked down upon.

"Your Grace," he began.

"Is that your only objection?" Evangeline asked, interrupting Henry with a hard look in his direction.

Allingham thought a moment and then nodded. "Yes."

"Then there is nothing to worry about, Father," she said with a light laugh that was nothing like the real, musical one she sometimes gifted Henry with. He felt the falseness of it. "Henry and I have talked about this at length. I am of your same mind that it would not do for my husband to be seen as a man of work. So he has agreed to give it all up and focus on pursuits more suited to a gentleman."

"With seventy thousand he'll be able to do so, eh?" Allingham said with a laugh.

There was a flutter across Evangeline's expression even as she said, "Quite. Isn't that so, Henry?"

She shot him a hard look that cut through the ringing in his ears. "Y-Yes."

"Well, then I have no further objection," her father said with a shrug. "You have my permission to wed. When would you wish to do so?"

Henry gaped, but Evangeline stepped in effortlessly, managing the entire situation as she always did. "Just after the new year, I think. Before February, certainly. We could begin to read the banns just after Christmas is over."

"Very good," her father said. "In these cases, I think it makes no sense to wait. If that's all..."

Evangeline caught Henry's arm and guided him toward the door. "Yes."

"Yes," Henry repeated. "Thank you, Your Grace, and good day."

"Good day." He was already back at his desk, working at his figures as if he had not just agreed to this union. As if it meant little to him.

Evangeline didn't seem troubled by that fact. She grinned as she all but dragged Henry back to the parlor where they'd originally met. She shut the door behind them and proceeded to flounce a little jig across the floor. He might have been charmed by the rare lack of decorum in his future bride, but for the sentence that rang in his ears.

"You did not mean what you said to him, did you?" he asked, sitting down hard on the settee. "About my giving up my pursuits. This wasn't all some deception to get your way, was it?"

Evangeline stopped dancing around in glee and spun on Henry. He did not look like a man well pleased to make an advantageous match at all. Rather, he looked sick. And like he didn't trust her, which stung a great deal more than it should have.

"You and I discussed this at length," she said, moving to take the seat beside him. "*Of course* I do not expect you to stop researching your astronomy and math and whatever else strikes your fancy. But one cannot be truthful with a person who is being unreasonable. My father wanted to hear a certain answer. I gave it to him. Once the money for my dowry is safely under our control, what can he truly do to us?"

"He could insist that we no longer be invited to events," Henry mused.

For a moment she froze. *Would* her father do that? More to the point, *could* he damage her socially? She ran through the scenario in her head, and it was terrifying. And yet...

She waved her hand. "I could manage that. Can you imagine how sorry everyone will feel when I talk about my great love and how my father is punishing you for your superior mind?"

His brow wrinkled. "Great love?"

She halted and her heartbeat increased. "A—a stretch, of course. But everyone loves a love story, don't they? It won't hurt us for them to believe our friendship developed into something more."

"If it serves your purpose," he said.

She worried her lip at his tone, but nodded nonetheless. "*Our* purpose. Perhaps the old guard will limit us a fraction, but that story would make the younger set invite us all the more, I'd wager."

He stared at her a beat and she was surprised that didn't make him happier. "Another collection of lies."

She shrugged though her defenses raised in the face of what felt like his disapproval. "You want to benefit from this match, don't you? Then let *me* handle the details. You must pretend a disinterest in your work for, what? A month, perhaps six weeks? It is not so much of a surrender as all that, is it? To have a lifetime of freedom?"

She could see him processing that question. When his mind

turned, he got a wrinkle of concentration in his brow that she longed to lean up and smooth, though of course she didn't. That would be a foolish action.

He moved a little closer at last and traced a finger along her jawline. She felt her smile waver, then melt away as her body reacted to that simple touch.

"You are correct, but of course you always are," he drawled. When had he started drawling? Like a rake! And why did her stomach clench at that sound when she'd always found it mightily annoying in other men? "But for the next month to six weeks, that means I'll be quite *bored*. Will you provide my entertainment, my lady?"

Her throat worked as she swallowed. Who would have thought Henry Killam could be so seductive? If she'd guessed, she might not have risked this plan with him, for it felt like she couldn't resist what he implied. What she already knew he could do to her.

She wanted that. Wanted more. And they had agreed more was exactly what they'd have together, at least until the shine wore off and they both moved on from the physical attraction.

For now, though…

She placed a hand on his chest and loved how his heart pounded against her palm, even through all the layers of clothing he wore. His breath hitched and his pupils dilated. There was power in that. Control. Which meant this was a situation she could manage and win, despite how he had made her shatter the day before.

"I'm certain I can think of something that will fill your time," she whispered before she lifted on her tiptoes, her mouth lifted toward his.

He met her halfway and his lips just brushed across hers. She opened slightly, trying increase the pressure and the pleasure. To her surprise, he drew back, continuing a gentle exploration of lips. She gripped her hand into a fist against his chest and he chuckled, then guided his hand against the back of her head. He angled her slightly, and at last his tongue met hers.

She let out a sigh of relief, hating herself for how much she needed what he had withheld. Control, she was supposed to have control. This was not control, not by a great margin. And yet she surrendered even though it wasn't her nature to do so, letting him be her guiding light as he brought her anticipation up notch by notch, caress by caress.

She was overheated with it by the time he broke away, smiling as he shifted around. She saw the proof of his desire, outlined against his buff-colored trousers. And yet he had not yet allowed himself pleasure, at least not with her.

Didn't he want that?

"I ought to go tell my father our news," he said. "Before I do something we might both suffer from."

She worried her lip with a nod. "Very well. Although I must point out that our engagement will make it all the easier for us to be alone. At least in theory."

"Theories are something I like to test," he said with a laugh. "And I very much look forward to that one."

He leaned in and kissed her again, this time with more distraction and less purpose. Then he moved to the parlor door, where he paused and turned back.

"I know this future we are so carefully designing means as much to you as it does to me," he said, meeting her gaze evenly. "And I swear to you, I will do everything in my power to make sure you aren't sorry you chose me for your madcap plan."

The warm feelings she'd been experiencing froze to ice with those words. Here he was making promises. She'd heard enough of those to wonder if they'd be broken. She nodded slowly. "I appreciate that, Henry. Goodbye."

He wrinkled his brow in confusion at her cooler tone. Then he tipped his head and was gone, leaving her alone to ponder all her unexpected reactions to him. And torture herself with all the ways they could make the future go so wrong.

Henry entered his father's study a quarter of an hour later, his mind cleared by the crisp winter air. Or at least somewhat cleared. It seemed he was never far from thoughts of Evangeline and the powerful ways she affected him, despite her constant refrain that their marriage was going to be nothing more than one of friendship and mutual benefit.

"Henry." His father rose from his desk and eyed him carefully. Of course he would. The viscount had to believe Henry had come to speak to him about his ultimatum. The one he was supposed to answer by tomorrow afternoon.

Funny how that had fled his mind so easily once he touched Evangeline.

"Good afternoon, Father," he said, reaching out a hand to the viscount.

He shook it warily and motioned his head toward the seat across from his desk. As Henry settled in, his father narrowed his gaze at him. "Did you come to finish our discussion?"

"In a way, I suppose yes. I actually have news for you," Henry said, watching his father's every move. He'd never been able to make the man happy for longer than a five-minute span. It would be interesting to see what that would look like.

"Great God, tell me it is good news," the viscount said with a frown.

"I think it is good for me and for you." Henry leaned forward. "I am to marry Lady Evangeline after the new year."

His father stared, unblinking and unspeaking for almost a full minute. Long enough that Henry began to worry he might have been struck by an apoplexy. Then he shook his head slowly. "The

Duke of Allingham's daughter?" he asked, incredulity all but dripping from his words.

Henry shifted at the lack of faith in his tone. He lifted his chin slightly. "The very one, my lord."

His father rose from his seat and looked down at him through a narrowed gaze. "Just how did you manage that?"

Henry shrugged. "The lady and I have always been friends. In recent weeks that has…blossomed. I asked for her hand today and the duke agreed."

For a moment his father remained silent, but then he let out a great whoop and began to pace the room. "Great God, what news, what news! You have linked us to the very family I have spent decades infiltrating. It will solidify our friendship and make my entry into every level of Society all the easier."

Henry fought the urge to roll his eyes. "Good that you see the benefit to yourself, Father."

The viscount cast him a side look. "She is a comely girl, of course. And her dowry is a thing of legend. Good things for you. Yes, I'm very pleased."

Henry got up and walked to the window. He'd been trying to please this man for years, and it was just this manipulation that did it. Wonderful. "I'm glad you are happy. I am happy, as well. I'm sure the duke will want to do an engagement ball, perhaps after Boxing Day since the Christmas holiday is just days away."

"Excellent, excellent. I will co-sponsor it, of course. A very good way to make our alliance public." He clapped his hands together and then he froze, staring at Henry. "I spoke to him about my concerns regarding your…activities."

"He mentioned it," Henry said with an arch of his brow. "You seem to be regretting that mention of my work now."

"God's teeth, boy, don't call it your *work*, it makes it all the more vulgar." His father ran a hand through his graying hair. "So he mentioned it, did he? You know it is more imperative than ever that you give up your nonsense. He will force it and I would assume that young woman will also turn up her nose at linking herself to someone who makes their pursuits so public and ostentatious."

Henry let out his breath slowly. Here was the lie. Evangeline might be good at it, but for him it was harder. He'd never had much of a face for cards…which ironically his father would have been more accepting of as a vice.

"The duke made his thoughts on the matter very clear," he said, sticking to facts. "It was a term of his agreement that I agree to give up my work in astronomy." His stomach turned. "I said yes."

His father's face lit further. "Very good, you have sense in you yet. You and Lady Evangeline. What a lucky man."

There was something slightly lewd to his father's tone and Henry straightened up a little as his hackles rose. "Indeed, for who could ask for a more intelligent and witty bride?"

His father looked confused by that statement, but then shrugged. "To each his own. Well, I shall send word to Allingham right away. This shall be the engagement party to end all others, I will make sure of it." He sat back down at his desk and waved his hand. "You are dismissed."

Henry walked from the room slowly and went to the foyer where he could make his way back to his home across the park. Although he had done exactly as was asked and expected of him, he felt less than victorious in his actions.

After all, it seemed he was trading one control for another. And for the first time in his life he wanted something more than to just study his books and be left alone. He wanted something more than to be managed by his father or his brothers or even Evangeline.

He wanted the life he suddenly saw as a potential future. A life where he and Evangeline were equals, were partners, were truly bound together in spirit and soul and yes, in heart. Where control or manipulation didn't come into the equation.

And he wondered if there was any chance for that life at all.

CHAPTER 13

The party to announce the surprise engagement between the Duke of Allingham's eldest daughter and the Viscount Killam's youngest son was the party of the decade, just as their fathers had desired. The ballroom was full to the point of bursting, and around Evangeline people were drinking and making merry and toasting not just her happiness, but the spiraling end of the old year and the near arrival of the new.

It all should have made her happy. After all, her plan was in full swing and everything was falling into place. And yet there was a nagging sensation in her chest, one she didn't like. That sensation told her she was missing something. And if she was missing it, that meant she could not prepare for the contingencies it might bring.

She let out her breath in a long sigh and looked around the room. Her brother and his wife and Evangeline's younger sister and her husband were all standing together. The women looked dutifully quiet and utterly bored as the men laughed with each other. She shivered.

Her gaze shifted and she found Tamsin Lesley in the crowd. There were *many* people watching her friend, actually, since her plan to be ruined had very much succeeded. Which was exactly why Evangeline had been certain to invite her, for she certainly wasn't about to let her friend be destroyed by her plans.

Not that Tamsin was making it any easier by standing with Simon. Not just standing, but moving onto the dancefloor to take a turn with him. Evangeline wrinkled her brow as she wondered if ruination and a life with cats was still what Tamsin required. The way the two looked at each other certainly felt like…connection.

She'd have to talk to Tamsin about it later, for at that moment she caught a glimpse of Henry. Henry, who she would wed in just a few weeks, once the banns began being read that coming Sunday.

He was standing alone by the punch table, an untouched drink in his hand and a faraway gaze in his eyes. He had not been himself all night. In fact, she hadn't felt he was himself in the entire time since their engagement.

Something was off. Something she longed to uncover and fix. She was becoming emotionally attached and the fear that realization created was painful. Still, she couldn't ignore her desire to help him…or even to be near him, and she found herself going across the room to him with a false smile on her face.

"You look very serious for a man celebrating his engagement," she said, nudging him gently as she stepped up to take a place beside him.

"Marriage is a serious business," he said with a flash of a smile in her direction. She had no idea if it was any less false than her own.

"Still, you will have people saying I'm forcing you to the altar with that dour expression."

He chuckled, and now there was a relaxation of his mouth and shoulders that made her own do the same. "Based on our positions in life, I would guess some people are arguing I'm forcing *you* somehow."

"Then dance with me—let's show them we are both very pleased with the match," she said, holding out a hand to him as the first bars of the waltz began.

He inclined his head and took the hand, guiding her onto the dancefloor, where they began to turn in time to the music. His arms were warm around her, his hand heavy on her hip and his gaze locked with hers as they sashayed around the floor again and again.

"What is troubling you, Henry?" she asked at last, uncertain she wanted to know the answer. It felt very personal.

He held her gaze. "A—a few things," he admitted. He seemed to struggle with the words a moment and then he let out a huff of breath. "I suppose one thing is that it is difficult for me not to work."

She frowned. She had thought he might struggle when his active mind was asked to be idle. And with the holiday, they'd had little time to see each other in the past few days.

"Would you have worked so very much during the merriments of the past few days?" she asked gently.

"I would have to escape those celebrations." He shook his head. "Instead I was forced into a room with my father, my brothers and their families. Everyone was crowing over our match, of course, but also so very tedious about everything else. The things I care about are so different from what they find important. I think they feel they've won something by my giving up my endeavors toward science."

She frowned. Henry defined himself so strongly with his search of the stars, his figures and experiments. She wasn't certain she had fully understood that until now.

"I can imagine that is difficult," she said, squeezing his hand gently as they turned around the ballroom floor yet another time. "But it is only short time. The sacrifice of a few weeks will result in a lifetime of freedom for us both."

"I know you are right," he said. "And I suppose it must sound foolish to you, my avoidance of societal norms. After all, you love the company of those of our rank. You must have enjoyed the past few days immensely."

Evangeline worried her lip a little at the statement. She knew she should just agree and toddle off to the next benign subject, but before she could, he stared into her face.

"Didn't you?" he asked.

She swallowed, and when she opened her mouth, words came out she hadn't expected or planned for. "To be honest, not all that much."

"Why?" he asked.

She sighed. "I spent the last few days with my family, too. My brother and sister brought their spouses. It should have been a very happy group, and often if was. But…"

She trailed off, trying to cut off the vulnerable revelations that seemed to be forced from her lips by a power beyond herself.

"But?" he pressed gently.

"But whenever I spend time with the women in my family, it only makes me…sad. My brothers, both in blood and in law, are men of rank and privilege. They do not expect or desire for their wives to have opinions. And they married women who comply, even when they are not in the company of their spouses. And like you, I was regaled with advice whenever I was alone with the women."

"Advice about marriage?"

"Yes." She shook her head. "How I shall have to give up my opinions, be ready to come at your beck and call, make my interests only your own."

"That sounds utterly depressing," he said with a twist to his expression. "And boring. The fact that you have your own opinions and pursuits is very attractive to me. I look forward to hearing them over our supper table. Two people should not become one when they are united. The best marriages I have seen, the true love matches that seem to last, are those where each partner *does* have their own separate life. They choose to unite with each other, not become...a—a symbiotic unit like a fungus on a tree."

Evangeline couldn't control the laughter that bubbled out of her lips at that image. She broke her hand from his and covered her mouth as the giggles kept coming. Luckily the waltz was coming to an end at the same time.

Henry laughed with her as he bowed, and she took his hand to let him lead her from the floor. "I'm glad to have amused you, though I'm not sure how."

Tears were streaming down her face as she continued to laugh. "I'm just trying to imagine which of my siblings is the fungus and if any of them could be the tree in their marriages. I rather think my entire family is fungus. My father might be the tree."

"Well, neither of *us* will be fungus," he said, and held up a hand. "I solemnly vow as much. We shall be very separate trees, both of us."

Her laughter subsided at the "very separate" part, even though that was exactly what she'd told the man that she wanted. He continued to stare at her, his expression changing and then he glided a thumb along the hand he still held.

"Will you escape with me?" he asked. "To one of the parlors for a quiet moment...alone?"

Her lips parted, for there was no denying the seductive tone to his voice. And no denying the way her body called back to that seduction, willing and able to surrender to whatever he planned.

She nodded. "I'd like that."

"Good. What about the music room where we first kissed what feels like a lifetime ago, even though it wasn't? I'll step out first, you make your rounds and then follow?"

"An excellent plan, Mr. Killam," she said. "I'll see you there."

He lifted her hand to his lips and brushed his mouth across her knuckles, letting her feel the steamy heat of his breath on her skin before he winked at her and walked away. She watched him go, her heart pounding, and one thing became patently clear as she did so: she was in trouble. And she didn't want to escape it, even though it was in her best interest to do just that.

Henry moved around the music room, lighting a few candles and stirring the fire. He wanted the room to be beautiful when his fiancée arrived. His *fiancée*. That was still taking some getting used to. And the moment he became accustomed, she would then be his wife, and he wasn't certain *that* fact would ever set in.

When Evangeline had asked him what was troubling him, he'd turned to the subject of his work and his family, and that had been true. But it was also proof of his cowardice. There were other reasons he was distracted, and all of them had to do with her and the riot of emotions that had been building in him over the past few days since their engagement.

Emotions he was going to have to resolve. Discuss. Express. But not in a ballroom. Not in a public place where they could be interrupted or she could escape him too easily.

So he had a plan. A very good plan, or so he kept telling himself and hoping it would be true.

The door behind him opened, and he straightened and turned to watch Evangeline enter the room. In the soft glow of the candlelight, she was even more beautiful than ever. Her shiny black hair reflected the light when she turned her head, almost with blue tones. Her dark eyes scanned the room, settling on him at last with both interest and anxiousness. She wanted him.

Which was the first step in his plan. Evangeline clung to control and he was beginning to understand why. But when she'd shattered with pleasure a few days before, she'd let all that go and given him her trust. He would claim it again before he asked for even more.

"You asked earlier what was distracting me," he said, stepping toward her. "And I told you a portion of the truth. Another part of it is you..." He caught her hand and drew her closer. She didn't resist and molded to his chest with a shuddering sigh. "...this. Have you also thought about that day in my parlor?"

For a moment he thought she might deny that charge. Deny him because giving even this inch was so difficult for her. But then her expression softened and she squeaked out, "Every day, Henry. Every night. Every moment."

He bent his head and swallowed the last words, cupping her cheeks as he plundered her mouth and drowned in the sweetest taste of her. He felt her give over to him as her muscles loosened and her mouth opened, and he could have crowed in triumph. Earning what she did not easily give was all the more pleasure. He wanted to never give her pause in doing so.

His arms tightened around her back, and she lifted into him as the heat in the room ratcheted up. Slowly he moved her toward the settee. Someday he would really like to do this in a bed, but that wasn't going to happen right now. He laid her back, settling her against the cushions and going down on his knees before her, just as he had the first time.

"Are you going to do...to do that again?" she whispered, her voice breaking in the quiet.

"Oh yes," he murmured as he pushed her skirts up slowly, reveling in the reveal of silky stockings, long legs, slightly parted thighs. "Assuming you'd like me to do so."

"Yes. I have thought of little else since you did it last time. But I wonder how you know how to please me like that without experience."

"I told you I study," he said, dipping his head to stroke his cheek up the inside of one thigh. "I read books, I saw images, and once I was with you, once I could watch your reaction, I adjusted to you. This is for you, after all."

His hands settled on her knees and he pushed, opening her

wider, making the gap in her drawers part so he could see her at last. Just as perfect as the last time, dewy wet for him already, scented with earthy sweetness. He reached out a finger and traced the length of her sex, loving how she arched against his hand and nearly pushed him inside.

She gripped at the edge of the settee and stared at him, her brow furrowed like she was trying to cling to whatever control she had left. "And why didn't…why don't you…" She gasped again as he stroked again. "Why don't you take me? I'm yours, we're engaged."

He smiled at her, at the eagerness she was trying to hide by couching the question in terms of him. "Because you are *not* mine. We aren't married. Life is not predictable, and I would not leave you in a worse position if something happened that would prevent our union. Society's obsession with a maidenhead may make no sense to me, but it does to those in power. I wouldn't disadvantage you."

Her lips parted and then she reached out, cupping his chin and tilting his face toward his. Her jaw was set, her face pink as she jolted against his fingers. But she managed to whisper, "I want to touch you, Henry. Even if we cannot do the other, I don't want to be a mere receiver. Isn't there something I can do to make your experience better?"

He caught her hips and dragged her forward on the settee, opening her wider to him as he licked his lips in anticipation. "Trust me, Evangeline, there is nothing lacking in my experience when I do…this…"

CHAPTER 14

Evangeline's hips lifted as Henry's mouth settled firmly on that spot between her legs. Pleasure flowed through her, starting with the tip of his tongue and making its way through her body until she felt limp and warm and tingling from head to toe. He did that with a few mere swipes of his tongue, and this time he knew more about what she wanted. He used that knowledge against her...or for her? It was hard to tell the difference as he swirled his tongue around and around her clitoris until one hand bunched in the settee cushions while she pressed the other hard against her lips so she wouldn't call the house down with her sounds of pleasure.

He watched her while he licked, his gaze bright beneath his spectacles as he tasted and teased, drove inside of her clenching channel and always returned his attention to the tingling bud of nerves where she wanted him most.

It didn't take long for the desire to crescendo and her hips jerked as pleasure-pain rocked her, too swift, too intense, too powerful. He rested a hand on the fabric gathered around her belly and forced her to ride through his ministrations until she whispered his name in a plea for respite.

When he did stop licking her, he looked up at her with a wicked smile that twisted her stomach in knots. Still, she beckoned him up to her, forgetting her worries as she drew him in for a long, deep kiss. She tasted herself on his mouth and loved it, craved it, ached for it in ways she never could have imagined she would do.

He broke from her, helping her push her skirts down as she sat up and made a place for him beside her. She cuddled into his shoulder and she sat there for a moment. She could once again see the outline of his cock against his trousers. He denied her, but right now she needed a little control back.

Slowly she reached out and placed her palm on the hard ridge of him. He jerked beneath her with a sharp exhalation of breath, and she glanced up to see his face. It was taut with need, his pupils dilated wide as he watched her hand pet over him a second time.

Their gazes met and then he reached down and unbuttoned the placard of his trousers. His cock bobbed free from the confinement and bumped her hand. She gasped as she caught it. It was silk on steel and it filled her palm as she stroked him from base to tip.

"Evangeline," he grunted, his head lolling back against the cushions.

She liked that sound. The sound of him pleading out her name. It almost erased the fact that she had done the same with a moment before. There was power in that. And power in the fact that when she stroked him, his neck muscles tightened and his fists clenched open and shut in the rhythm of her strokes.

She wasn't exactly certain what to do next, but then again, he had learned how to touch her by doing it. She could do the same. She increased her strokes over him, gliding her hand until he tensed and then slowing down again. A sound came deep in his throat as he lifted his hips to force a cadence.

She obeyed because she liked the sounds he made when she stole his strength and control. She liked the hardness of his lips as they pursed together in concentration. And she liked how he cried out softly and then pushed her hand away as thick ropes of liquid escaped his cock.

He stroked himself a few times and then flopped back with a curse that echoed in the room.

Smug, she settled her shoulder back against his. "Now we're even," she said.

He lifted his head a little as he tucked himself back in place. "Were we counting something here, Evangeline? I'm not certain that is how it works. I could make you come a dozen times and not feel you owed me something in return. Though if you are going to unman me, I will never argue against it. That was...that was far more enjoyable with your hand working me than with only my own."

She turned herself slightly and met his gaze. "You keep acting like life is not a quid pro quo, Henry, but you must know you're wrong. Everyone counts their costs, everyone expects payment for whatever they receive. They may not say it, but they do. And you must always be ready to pay the piper when he arrives."

"You are so jaded," he murmured, lifting a finger to trace her kiss-swollen lips gently. "I hate that your life has taught you that."

She jerked to her feet and walked away, not wanting his comfort. Hating that she *did* want it even though she knew it was dangerous.

"You are afraid," he said.

She pivoted with an unsteady laugh. "Me? Please do not sport with me, of course I'm not."

"You are," he said but stayed in his place, not chasing her or pushing her. "I understand why. A few weeks ago, we were friends. Now there is...there's *this* between us. There could be more. If there's more to gain, that means there's more to lose."

She stared at him, his words so powerful and yet said so calmly. They weren't a question—they were a statement of fact. And she found herself nodding. "Yes."

His eyes widened a little that she would admit as much, and now it was too late to take it back. Too late to pretend she hadn't said it or felt it. She could sense the promise of more, exactly as he said. But she had seen the damage such a promise, when unfulfilled, could create.

He stood up at last and moved toward her. "What if we could be something more than friends? What if I could offer you more than orgasm and independence, Evangeline?"

"I don't want more," she whispered, panicking but unable to turn away when he took her hand and lifted it slowly to his heart.

"You're *afraid* of more. That's not the same as not wanting more," he said, his gaze holding hers so steady and so certain. "What if I could give you that, those things you've feared to crave?"

"I don't know," she said, her breath short and tears stinging her eyes. "I have never seen that work out."

He tilted his head as if considering her opinion. "But what about all those recent love marriages, Evangeline?" When she caught her breath, he rushed to add, "We may not be there yet, I know."

She flinched, uncertain why that caveat felt like a little twist to her heart. "Even the love matches don't last, do they? Lord and Lady Fitzwallis were a love match. He was publicly unfaithful with her friend and she was humiliated and socially damaged."

He frowned. "Yes, I recall that."

"Miss Regina Black thought her marriage to the Honorable Richard Holland was a love match, enough that she defied her father's wishes that she marry a duke. She was cut off by her family and then Mr. Holland ran off to the continent with a maid."

"Also true." He was wrinkling his brow now, furrowed so deep that she had to believe she was convincing him.

"And then there's—" She stopped, cut herself off. If she gave her next example, that would be too revealing of her own heart.

He already saw her fear, she didn't want to tell him why. She didn't trust enough in what he offered to do so.

"Who?" he pressed, gently squeezing her fingers.

She pulled her hand away and walked to the fire. "I'm just saying I could list a dozen off in my head."

"You are presenting evidence to support your hypothesis that love matches don't work," he said. "And I understand why and appreciate the examples. But you cannot pick and choose the evidence you believe. What about Lord and Lady Ribbonworth? Two years ago their love match was all the talk of London. Still married and he scandalizes the world when he kisses her in full view of the public. He dotes on the woman."

Evangeline sighed. "I suppose I can think of other stories like theirs, yes."

"But the frightening ones mean more," he said. "I understand."

"You do?" She blinked at him.

"You've guarded your independence carefully over the years. I appreciate that about you. I always have."

"What?" she asked, confused about this turn in the conversation. In the look in his eyes, like he was certain and afraid at the same time.

"Evangeline, you must understand I have always admired you." He swallowed. "How deeply I care for you."

She jerked back a step, nearly depositing herself on her backside as if staggering away would help her escape what he'd just confessed and how that confession wound its way into her heart and her soul and made her ache to rush to him and take it. Take him. Take everything.

"Please," he said as he caught her hand and forced her to remain in place. "Let me finish. I need to tell you everything and then we can decide our next step."

There was no way any intelligent man could look at Evangeline's pale face and not see her abject terror. It was palpable as she stared at Henry and more genuine than any emotion she'd ever revealed to him before. But there had been one thing he realized as they connected so powerfully...as he tried to convince her to want more...and that was that he didn't just care for Evangeline. He didn't just want her.

He loved her.

It hadn't hit him like a thunderbolt, it hadn't rocked him to his core. The thought had flitted through his mind as she tried to convince him against love matches and it had just been...true.

Not only that, but the feeling didn't seem new. It was as if he'd always felt it and only just discovered there was a name for the reason why his heart leapt when she spoke to him or why he sought out her face in every crowd. *Of course* he loved her. He had always loved her.

And he wanted a future, a real future. But that would take risk on his part and enormous patience because he recognized she *couldn't* risk anything herself. At least not yet.

"Henry—" she began, her tone telling him she was desperately working to rebuild those walls she so expertly erected between herself and anyone who might let her down.

"All I am asking is that you let me prove myself," he interrupted.

She froze, staring at him. Then she shifted gently. "Prove what?"

It was a good sign, that curiosity. An indication she hadn't eliminated all chance before they even began. He drew a long breath.

"That this thing between us, this *thing* that so frightens you—" He cupped her cheek and she shuddered. "—it could be good. It could be happy. It could be more." He smiled. "It could be the shining example some other hapless gentleman holds up to convince an uncertain lady that love matches do exist."

Her eyes fluttered shut. "Oh, Henry, that is quite a leap of faith."

He touched her chin with the tip of his finger and she opened her eyes. "Or you could see it as an experiment. A way to test the hypothesis that this *could* work." He smiled again, and this time a flutter of her own smile was his reward.

She worried her lip a little, and it made him want to kiss it and nip it himself, but he held back. Push too far and she would run and perhaps never let him close enough to propose this again.

"You are so comfortable trying and testing and…and *failing*." She held up her hands almost helplessly. "Henry, my nature is to need to *know*."

Every word she spoke was further evidence of a pain she didn't reveal to anyone in her world. He took them carefully, reverently, in the hopes that he might one day use those pieces to fill the holes of fear that kept her distant.

"You risk nothing," he offered. "Keep yourself under control as you have, as you do and have done your whole life. Give only what you feel you want to share. Let me prove my theory to you. Let *me* give you evidence, like I've given you pleasure." She shivered just a little and he drew her a fraction closer. "You didn't believe that kind of pleasure could exist, but I did give it, didn't I?"

"You know you did," she huffed out, sounding more herself.

"Then please trust me this little bit. If you don't end up believing me or it turns out you don't care for me at all, then your marriage of convenience will play out just the same as we originally discussed. We will be nothing more than friends, with separation and independence. I won't expect or demand emotion. I'll only give you pleasure if you desire it."

She looked confused by the offer, as if it hadn't occurred to her that failure in this case was only a return to their original bargain. Which he would surrender to if he lost this war, though knowing his heart and being rejected would not be easy. But he couldn't think of that now.

He had to think about what would happen if he could convince her to let him in. To let him love her and hope she could love him in return.

She nodded slowly and his heart leapt. "All—all right."

"Yes?" he asked, uncertain if he was dreaming after all that battle to get to this moment.

"Yes," she repeated.

He tugged her closer and pressed his mouth to hers. She wound her arms around his neck and clung to him, letting him in physically as she swore she couldn't emotionally. But that was a start and he wouldn't let go of the hope it gave him.

He drew back at last and steadied her on her feet. "I look forward to this experiment, my lady," he said with a grin.

She shook her head. "God help me for admitting it, but so do I." She glanced toward the door. "But now we should go back to the ball. Someone will be looking for us, and I would hate for a scandal to disrupt all your careful plans."

He offered an arm without argument, because he could see that she needed the escape. That letting him in as far as she had was uncomfortable. But if science had taught him anything, it was how to be patient.

And if patience led to a real marriage with Evangeline, he was willing to do whatever that took. However long it took it.

CHAPTER 15

It had been almost three weeks since the engagement ball and Henry still felt like he was walking through a dream. He had feared his days would be boring since he couldn't work, but Evangeline had filled his time effortlessly. Thinking of her, planning things for her and spending time with her as he slowly, gently tried to show her that their future was worth trying for.

He thought he was succeeding too. Just one night prior she had stood on a terrace with him during a party and reached out to take his hand. She'd told him she was happy, and it was like someone had lit the world ablaze with marvelous color.

Such a simple thing, but it brought so much pleasure to his life.

"Pardon me, Mr. Killam?"

He glanced up from the letter he hadn't been paying attention to as he daydreamed of Evangeline and smiled at his butler. "Yes, Deacon, what is it?"

"You have a visitor, sir."

"Evangeline?" Henry asked as he jumped to his feet. She often made the little walk across the park to meet with him. They'd taken many a stroll around the frozen lake and even tried ice-skating with friends. He had never enjoyed the pleasures of the winter more.

Deacon shook his head. "No, sir. Not this time. It is Mr. McGilvery."

"Oh." Henry shook away the disappointment that shouldn't have accompanied the announcement of his friend. "Please show him in."

He moved to the sideboard and poured them each a sherry, and smiled as Donovan entered the room a moment later. His smile fell when he saw Donovan's expression. Dark, concerned, frustrated.

"What is it?" he asked, setting the drinks aside as McGilvery closed the door behind him.

Donovan shook his head. "The better question is, where have you been?"

Henry held up his hands. "The moratorium on my participation at the society stands until my wedding to Evangeline is complete, you know that. I wrote it to you in that letter."

"I never thought you'd go through with that nonsense!" McGilvery said, flopping into the closest chair. "Don't you care about the research? You know we were close to obtaining a new patronage before you went off to seduce your bride."

Henry nodded. Donovan had said something about that what felt like a lifetime ago. Patrons for the cause of science were always good to find. They were about more than money—they were about respectability for the field, about expanding the knowledge.

"Who was it again?" Henry asked. "Some merchant, yes?"

"Grayson Danford, but he's not a merchant. He's...I suppose an investor. Interested in the *application* of science. He wants some more data, though, and I'm stuck on an equation. I cannot for the life of me figure it out. I need your help, Henry."

Henry drew back and stared at Donovan. "I-I can't. It isn't that I don't want to, but I made a promise to my future bride."

"The woman who doesn't care if you do this in a few weeks after your wedding?" McGilvery burst out, jumping to his feet.

"Yes, and if you ask me in a few weeks, I'll bloody well do it then." Henry folded his arms.

"In a few weeks, Grayson will have moved on to something else," Donovan said. "A man like him is unaccustomed to waiting. If I don't submit the research to him right away, it won't happen at all. Please, all I'm asking you to do is look at a few figures. Help me see where I'm going wrong. No one has to know."

Henry shut his eyes. He had promised Evangeline, and *he* would know he hadn't kept that promise even if she never did. But McGilvery was right that there was a brief window of opportunity for the society in this matter. He couldn't be responsible for it closing.

"Fine," he grumbled as he motioned to the desk.

Relief flowed over McGilvery's features as he drew a rolled up piece of vellum from his inner pocket. He unfurled it onto Henry's desktop, and for a moment Henry's heart rate increased wildly. God, but he had missed figures like these. This was a particularly complex equation, filling the entire large sheet from corner to corner.

He leaned over it, beginning a slow examination of every number and letter before him so he could find the segment that was incorrect.

"Mr. Killam?" Deacon said again from the door.

"Yes?" Henry didn't stop looking at the numbers.

"You've received a message from Lady Evangeline," the butler said.

"Leave it there," Henry said, motioning vaguely toward the sideboard. "I'll look at it shortly."

As the butler left, Henry lost himself in the figures again. And he forgot everything else, as he always did, including the discomfort in his chest that told him he was doing something wrong.

Evangeline sat at the table in her dressing room, staring at the beautiful hothouse flowers sitting on the surface before her. She propped her chin into her palm as the soft scent of honeysuckle and roses tickled her nose.

"Honeysuckle in winter," Tibby said as she passed by the table, tidying up from that morning's toilette. "He does know how to woo a lady."

"Indeed," Evangeline sighed. "Every day for the three weeks since our engagement ball, it is something new. Flowers, books he thinks I'll like, and the man is *always* right. He took me to that exhibit of Mary Linwood's worsted work because he knew I'd like the intricacy of the stitching."

"And Covent Garden," Tibby added. "How you both laughed at the pantomimes."

Evangeline shook her head. She could not deny so many parts of the past few weeks had bound her closer to Henry, but it was two things altogether different that were melting her icy heart toward him.

First were his letters. Each day she received one at half past three. His handwriting was neat and careful, that of a scientist, she supposed, who had to take good notes to be understood. But when he got excited about a subject the hand became a bit wobblier. And there was so much he thrilled at. Discovery was an act of pure love to him. And he shared new discoveries with her with passion.

He also wrote about his family, his friends, his reasons for pursuing astronomy. His story of seeing a comet the year his mother died...it had brought a tear to her eye and made her feel so much closer to him.

She wrote back, of course. To not do so was abominably rude. But she had not yet felt brave enough to confess any of her own deep secrets. Not that he pressed. He stayed true to his word that he would only convince her of his intentions. He made no demands.

Sometimes she almost wished he would.

And the other part that had bound them was something she would *never* discuss with Tibby. Henry had continued his dedication to her physical pleasure. If they had a moment to sneak away together and he could do so discreetly, he could have her moaning with a few flicks of his tongue or circles of his talented fingertips. She found herself waking in the night, hands between her clenching thighs, dreaming of him poised there to take her.

She wanted him to take her so damned much. She wanted to surrender herself to him fully, she supposed because she trusted him with her body.

And that was frightening because it wasn't just her body he was involving now. She already felt a strong pull of her heart. One she wasn't quite ready to submit to.

"Lady Evangeline?"

She blinked and forced herself back to the present, where Tibby was standing beside her door, staring at her. "I'm sorry, I was woolgathering. What were you saying?"

"I was wondering if I should prepare your riding habit for later today. It's a little warmer out and you wished to go riding with Mr. Killam at some point."

Evangeline nodded. "Yes. I'll write him and see if he would like to meet me at our spot in the park later. He answered my letter a few days ago so late and I haven't seen him since, so it would be good to reconnect."

She bit her lip as she said it. Damn, could she not go even a few days without him now? Was that how far she'd fallen?

"Very good," Tibby said with a bit of a smug smile. "I will—"

There was a sharp rap at the door that interrupted the maid's thought. She glanced at Evangeline with a shrug and then opened the door. It was Hughes on the other side, his expression tight.

"Excuse me, Lady Evangeline, but your father has demanded you join him in his study immediately."

Evangeline rose and moved toward the door. "I thought Father was at his club. When did he return?"

"Just now, my lady, and he is not in a good humor. He asked me to fetch you at once."

Evangeline fought the rising sense of dread in her chest and nodded. "Of course. Tibby, ready those riding clothes. I'll write to Henry when I return."

Tibby's mouth was a thin, worried line, but she inclined her head as Evangeline slipped past her and Hughes and made her way to her father's study. She had no idea why he might be upset today. Normally his club days were anything but upsetting, for he held court with all the other men who wanted his favor and influence.

But she would soon know why he wanted her, for she paused at the closed door to his study to gather herself. Then she forced a bright smile as she breezed into the room. "Good day, Father, you are home early. You wished to see me?"

He was sitting at his desk, staring at a paper, and he rose as she entered the room. His expression was twisted and angry, a darkness to him that she rarely saw.

"What is it?" she asked, dropping her façade and moving toward him.

"Have you had word from your fiancé today?" he said, tilting his head at her in what felt like accusation.

She blinked. "Henry sent me…he sent me flowers this morning. I have not yet received his daily letter today. Why?" Her heart sank. "Is—is something wrong with him. Is he well?"

"He seems very well," her father growled. "Get your wrap, daughter. We are going to see Mr. Killam."

"Father," Evangeline said, raising her hands. "I must demand that you tell me what is going on. Why are you angry with Henry? Why are you angry at all?"

"We will discuss it with the gentleman himself," her father said, getting to his feet and slamming his hands down on the desktop. "I'll call for the carriage."

Evangeline stared at him, helpless in her lack of understanding, and then turned and left the room. As she staggered back up the stairs, her hands shook. Her father was not a man quick to rage and yet here he was, clearly barely managing to control himself.

She pushed into her chamber and Tibby looked up from the clothing she was carefully arranging. "That was quick." She frowned. "What is it?"

"I don't know," Evangeline admitted. "He is very angry at Henry and insists we go to him right now, but he will not tell me what is going on."

The world swam a fraction and she caught the back of a chair to steady herself. Tibby rushed forward, supporting her elbow. "Lady Evangeline, you are pale as paper."

Evangeline shook her head. She was being weak, so weak, and she hated herself for it. It proved what she already knew, that growing too close to a person was dangerous. But she *was* close to the man she'd arranged to become her husband.

And she feared whatever could have caused her father to be so unhappy with him.

"Evangeline!"

Her father's voice echoed from all the way in the foyer and Evangeline flinched as she motioned for her heavy pelisse. "He is waiting, I must go."

Tibby patted her arm and followed her to the top of the stairs as Evangeline rushed for her father. He was already out at the carriage and he gripped her hand a little too tightly as he helped her into the vehicle.

They began to move around the perimeter of the park toward Henry's home and he glared at her. "If you are involved in this, Evangeline, I shall be *very* angry with you."

"Involved in what?" she asked. "I am in the dark, Father, and you are starting to frighten me."

He glowered and merely stared out the carriage window for the few moments it took to arrive at Henry's home. He didn't wait to help her out, but let the footman do it as he strode up the stairs. Henry's butler, Deacon, opened the door before they could knock.

"Your Grace," he said in surprise. "Lady Evangeline. I—"

Her father ignored him and started down the hall. Evangeline rushed to keep up, sending the servant an apologetic look as her father reached Henry's study door and pushed it open.

Henry got to his feet as they entered the room. He at first looked confused and then his gaze flitted to the papers on the desk before him. Star charts. Equations. Notes that were obviously about his project, the one he was not supposed to be pursuing for the short time they were engaged.

She lifted a hand to her mouth.

"Your Grace," he said, waving off Deacon as he came around his desk. "Evangeline. May I—may I get you a drink?" He was trying to pretend calm, but Evangeline heard the slight lift to his voice. The tension.

"You lied to me," her father growled.

"Your Grace—" Henry began.

Her father reached into his pocket and whipped out pile of folded paper. "*This* will be made public in a few hours time," he said softly. "Will it not?"

Evangeline stepped closer as Henry shook the bundle open. It was the newsletter for the Society of London Astronomical Studies, and she saw the first article on the front page was written by the man she had met here weeks ago, Donovan McGilvery…and the Honorable Henry Killam.

Henry stared at the paper that had been thrown in his face and his heart dropped. He shook his head slowly. "This was not to be published until…until…"

He drew off, for those words would help no one. Evangeline's father was angry, and certainly didn't need to hear that his daughter had conspired against him and that Henry had gone along with the deception so they could flout both their fathers' rules.

"Your father's name may not mean much," the duke said as he snatched the paper away and threw it on top of the research materials on Henry's desk. "But mine is worth a great deal. I told you that you were not to continue this foolishness, certainly not to publish again under your real name. And yet I go to my club today and my friends are asking what it feels like to marry my daughter off to a man who insists on doing *work* in the world."

Henry should have kept his gaze on the very angry man standing across from him, but he couldn't. Instead he let his eyes move to Evangeline. She was staring at him, her arms folded, her cheeks pale. She was stone, no emotion on her face or in her eyes. Not anger, not sadness, not fear.

Nothing.

"Your Grace," he began. "Please allow me to explain."

"Explain that you lied to me? That you embarrassed me? What is there to explain, Killam? The fact is that we have read the banns twice and yet I question now if I should allow you to marry Evangeline."

Henry gasped at the magnitude of that statement. The duke was far angrier than he'd thought to even consider such a move. To do so would be to harm Evangeline socially. Ending an engagement so close to the actual wedding?

"Father, you have every right to your feelings," Evangeline said softly, her tone still blank as she stepped up and took her father's arm gently. "Perhaps a walk back home would clear your head? I'll speak to you about this situation after I return in the carriage."

"And what will *you* do?" her father barked, though his tone had softened a little at her managing.

"I want to talk to Henry," she said, and she cast a quick, dismissive glance in his direction. "Alone. Please. I know it isn't a regular request, but I'm asking you to grant it."

"I will walk," her father growled. "But I will expect you before half an hour has passed."

She nodded and he stepped forward, looking over Henry's notes in disgust. Then he stormed from the room and left them alone.

CHAPTER 16

Evangeline could hardly control the shaking of her hands as she moved to Henry's study door and quietly closed it. She wanted to slam it and then scream, but that would give him too much. Right now she wanted to share nothing with him of how much this hurt her.

She turned to look at him. He was staring at her, helpless, and he motioned to the papers behind him. "Please let me tell you why."

She shrugged. "What would it matter? What would *why* matter, Henry? It still takes us right here."

"He's being unreasonable," he said.

She smiled, though there was no pleasure left in her. "Of course he is. Men like him always are because they are accustomed to getting their way. It may seem like a simple, silly thing to you, but you thwarted his rule. Worse, you made him feel foolish in front of people he keeps close because they are beneath him and worship him. *That* is an unforgiveable sin."

Henry shifted. "I wasn't thinking."

She almost laughed at that statement. Nothing had ever been so obvious. "It doesn't matter now, I suppose. As I said, it all leads to this. And when he says he may end the engagement, I'm sure he is being honest. He doesn't make idle threats."

"He would do that to you, despite the potential for social consequences being visited on your head?"

She folded her arms. "My happiness and future have rarely come into his mind. *Anyone's* mind, it seems."

"Evangeline." He breathed her name out softly.

And it broke her. The façade she'd been trying to maintain cracked and she stepped toward him. "Why was I so foolish as to believe you?"

He jerked his head up and she could see he wanted to speak, but she held up a hand to silence him.

"I watched my mother do this, you know. She believed that she could have faith even when every piece of evidence around her said that nothing was real. That my father was not true to her. And I said I would never do the same. That I would *never* put myself in a situation where anyone had control over my heart or my life. But that is exactly what I've done myself. I believed the occasional bouquet meant love and ignored all other evidence to the contrary."

His lips parted and she could see she'd struck a blow at the heart of him. Because of course he believed he was doing the right thing. He believed he cared. But he hadn't. Not enough to protect her, to protect their future.

And her anger peaked again at that thought. "Henry, you only had to wait to do all this..." She waved her hand around the room toward his notes. "...you only had to wait a few weeks. That's *all* I asked. Once we were married it would have taken away his leverage over you. But you cared more about this than me, no matter what pretty words you wrote to me in letters or whispered as you touched me."

"That isn't true," he said, reaching for her. She dodged him and his shoulders rolled forward. The pain that flitted across his face was so powerful she almost wanted to rush to him and comfort him.

And there was the trap again. If she opened up to him, she would spend the rest of her life chasing him. Longing for something he wouldn't give.

"I'm not blind, Henry. I see the truth perfectly clearly," she said.

"Donovan was stuck on an equation," he explained, even though she had denied she cared. "He came to me a few days ago with the paperwork and asked for my help. It was to garner an important patron for the society. I was foolish not to send him away, foolish not to stick to our agreement."

"And how did that lead to this?" she snapped pointing at the paper without touching it. She didn't want to touch it.

He ran a hand through his hair. "When we solved the problem, we could both see how important the equation was. It *had* to be published. Donovan told me then that the paper your father is in a rage about would be published under both our names. He wanted me to get the credit for the work I did. He insisted. I asked him to postpone it. I thought he had, but it seems I was wrong. Perhaps he didn't understand the vital nature of my request or perhaps there was confusion when he asked for a delay. Either way, the paper will be out by the end of the day and I did the wrong thing."

She nodded, working hard not to let that explanation sink into her skin. She would excuse him if she found any justification to latch on to. She could feel that down to her very bones. Once she did, she would be lost for the rest of her life.

"I see. I suppose that makes me feel better, that you weren't in complete disregard. But you didn't talk to me about it, did you?" she whispered. "You didn't warn me that this publication was a vague possibility, even though it could...*would*...affect us both."

"I'm sorry," he said, ducking his head. "I was wrong. I was caught up in the moment and I was very wrong."

"Yes, you were," she said, straightening her pelisse as if she could pull the bends and wrinkles out of her own soul. Ones she'd let herself create by being vulnerable to this man. "And now I must fix it." She clenched her hands at her sides. "Just as I must always fix *everything*."

She opened the door and moved into the hall. He followed her, catching her arm and turning her back. Just the touch made her body tremble, and she yanked her arm away to break off that unwanted reaction to him.

He stared down at her. "What will you do?"

"Go to my ridiculous father and convince him that we will still marry. To save myself, if nothing else." She shook her head. "And he'll agree in the end because I know he will. Ending the engagement will cause him more harm than even your silly paper would do, and he'll see that once his stupid pride is less sore. So I'll fix it, Henry. But as for us?"

He caught his breath and she could see him waiting for what she'd say next.

She backed away a long step. "This experiment of yours is over. My hypothesis was proven right and yours wrong, so that is the end of it. We will have our marriage of convenience. You will return to your precious research soon enough."

"No," he said, catching her arm again, this time to draw her closer. "No, Evangeline. I won't accept that. I can't. You must know I love you. I love you."

She stared up at him, hating that her eyes flooded with tears at those words. Hating that her heart soared at his confession. That her mind screamed at her to forgive him and tell him that she, too, loved him.

But she couldn't. She *would* not.

Gently she extracted her arm from his grip and backed away. "Good afternoon."

Then she stumbled down the hallway and back to her waiting carriage so she could go home to her father and fix what the man she loved had so foolishly mangled because his own needs so exceeded the promise of their future.

Evangeline stepped into the house, her head throbbing. As Hughes took her pelisse and gloves, for a moment she considered just running up to her room and hiding in her bed for the rest of her life. Well, perhaps just the afternoon. She didn't want to face her father when her nerves were so raw. She didn't want to face anything, including her own heart, which felt like someone had stabbed her. Henry had said he loved her.

She knew she loved him.

None of it made her happy. It scared her.

Her father stepped from the parlor and tilted his head at her. "Evangeline."

It seemed there would be no avoiding the mess now. She had to go clean it up. She set her shoulders back and forced a smile on her face as she entered the room and crossed to where her father had had tea delivered probably the moment he came home. From the looks of the open bottle of whisky on the table beside the pot, he had flavored his own cup with something extra.

She poured for herself and then shook her head as she added her own whisky to the tea and cream and sugar. When she turned, she found her father staring at her.

"You are very upset," he said.

She blinked. She'd spent a lifetime making sure no one ever saw her real emotions so that they could not be touched or used against her. And here, thanks to Henry, she seemed to have lost that ability.

She sat down and took a sip of her tea. She flinched at the bite of the whisky as it burned down her throat. Now she just had to remember how to be detached.

"Of course I'm not upset," she said at last. "That would imply I had far deeper feelings than I do."

He took a place beside her on the settee and reached out. When his hand covered hers, she jolted in surprise and jerked her face up to his. The duke was rarely attentive, but he looked truly concerned for her.

She pulled her hand away. "I swear to you, Father, I am simply frustrated. Like you, I had certain expectations of the agreement I'd made with Henry and I'm not happy he violated those. Especially since you are now saying you will break our engagement two weeks into the reading of the banns."

He let out his breath in a huff. "I thought his father was being rather ridiculous about the situation, truthfully. There are plenty of men who have this sort of hobby. The publishing was the troublesome part, but after you wed I was willing to discuss with Henry the idea that he could continue to do his work quietly, *anonymously*, if he needed to share his ideas for the purpose of... whatever the purpose is of his publishing these long strings of facts and figures."

"The purpose is to share scientific knowledge," she said. "I suppose in the hopes that others could use his brilliance to find the planet they all seek or some other celestial body they have not ever considered."

"That is very unselfish," her father grunted, almost as a curse. "If I were him, I'd want all the accolades in such an endeavor."

Evangeline bent her head, for she was certain that was true. But Henry wasn't like her father. He was giving, both professionally and personally. She had no doubt that if this planet was one day proven by some other person, he would be the first to celebrate that accomplishment.

And when it came to her...well, he had been very giving, indeed. Physically, certainly, but also in other ways. He'd shared his past with her and his hopes for the future. He'd treated her as his equal. He'd...he'd told her he loved her, and there was no doubt he meant it.

She drew in a sharp breath. She was finding reasons to convince herself that she could trust him even though he'd gone behind her back.

"I recognize you're angry and you have every right to be considering that Henry violated the terms of a very simple agreement." Of course, she was referring to her own with him, not her father's. "But to say that you will end the engagement, I must say I think you are cutting off your nose to be revenged of your face."

Her father sighed. "You think I'll be more damaged by the breaking of the engagement."

She flinched at his regard only for his own feelings, not her own, but plowed forward to obtain what she wanted. "Yes. We are a week away from completing the reading of the banns and the marriage will occur almost directly after. All of it is utterly public already and much talked about since I waited so long to choose a husband."

"That is true. It is not a day that goes by that I do not hear your name on the wind." He sounded positively proud of that fact, as if he had anything to do with her machinations to marry Henry.

"Well, you will hear more of it if you do something rash. This time not in a positive light." She leaned forward to punctuate the seriousness of it all. "If you cut him off, no one will believe it is only for some silly reason like a paper his name was attached to, especially since you knew he'd published another time before our engagement."

"They'll make up their own reasons, ones that would not benefit me," he mused.

She nodded. "Any leverage you had in arranging a situation for me would be over, for my social standing will be hurt."

He blinked as if he hadn't considered her in any of this. Not a shock to her, but still a sting. He frowned. "I suppose it would be."

"Please do reconsider, Your Grace," she said. "This is still a good match and the one of my choosing. It links us to the family of your friend, a man of standing and honor."

"And what do I tell people when that damned paper circulates at large by sundown?" he asked.

"Act as though it was your idea, Father," she encouraged. "Great God, you know that if you act like you're excited to have Henry do this, you can turn the tide. You could tell them you think he might consider naming any discovered planet after *you* because of your great patronage. Say that and everyone will decide it is an *honor* to have a man work on such important business."

He wrinkled his brow. "You think he might name the planet Allingham?"

She almost laughed at that thought. A sky full of gods and her father. But she fought the urge. "I could speak to him about it. But only after I'm his wife."

He nodded. "Very well, I'll consider all you've said."

She patted his arm, finished her tea and got up to excuse herself, but he caught her hand to keep her there, staring up at her pointedly. "I also think *you* should take some time for consideration, Evangeline."

"Consideration of what?" she asked.

"I have never seen your face so pale and pained as I did when you looked at Henry's work spread out across that desk. When you realized he'd lied about his intentions. And when you came into this room a moment ago, you looked like someone had died. It's obvious you care for the man."

She jerked her hand away and took a step back. "I don't know what you mean."

He held her gaze a beat. Two. "I might have done a disservice to you, allowing you to see the troubles between me and your mother before her death."

She flinched. "Don't be maudlin, Father."

He shrugged. "My point is that if you cared for this man, if you loved him, I would *never* consider breaking you apart. If that gives you some permission to feel as you fear to do."

She shut her eyes. Here was her father, giving her some push toward her heart, but he had to use it as a manipulation. And that her feelings had given him ammunition to do so only made her harden herself more.

"I do not care for Henry Killam beyond a friendship and a desire to marry him for both our benefit," she lied. "And *you* will not keep us apart because it serves your purposes more than reacting in a fit of pique would do. Now I shall go upstairs. It's been a long and difficult morning."

She didn't wait to be excused, but exited the room. It felt like the stairs were so steep as she took them slowly. She stumbled as she reached her door and rushed inside. Thankfully, the chamber was empty. Her hands shook as she staggered to the freshly made bed. She was trying so hard not to cry, trying so hard not to let disappointment make her weak.

But in the end, her hated emotions bubbled up, and she leaned against the side of the high bed and wept for what she'd somehow been foolish enough to let herself want.

And for what she felt she'd lost in just a few short moments.

CHAPTER 17

Henry strode across the empty park, oblivious to the sharp chill in the wind and the light flurry of snowflakes around him. Right now he cared not for weather. He really cared for nothing except for the place he was going and the person he was determined to see.

Evangeline.

It had been three days since his encounter with her and her father in his home. He had sent a letter each of those days and apologized, trying to explain further what had been in his heart when he helped Donovan.

But she had not replied and it forced him to sit in what he had done. It wasn't about the research, of course. Evangeline didn't care if he invested time in his pursuits, she had encouraged him to do so…the first person in his life to truly support his endeavors.

He realized that it was the *lie* that bothered her. The fact that he had promised one thing and done another. He hadn't considered the full effect it would have on her.

He hated himself for that. And now he all but sprinted through the park and out into the neighborhood on the opposite side where he hoped he could have an audience with his fiancée and try to tell her he understood her feelings.

Try to get another chance with her.

He rapped on the door and Hughes answered. "Good afternoon," Henry said as his coat was taken. "I am not expected, but I need to see Lady Evangeline. Please tell me she is in residence."

Hughes nodded. "I will inquire, Mr. Killam. Will you wait here, or shall I show you to the parlor?"

Henry knew that if he waited here, he would be less easily ignored. "I'll stay."

Hughes looked slightly annoyed but hurried off to find his mistress. He was gone a while, and when he reemerged, his face was drawn into a frown. "I am sorry, sir. Her ladyship is not here at present."

Henry's heart sank and he bowed his head. "She's here, isn't she?" he asked. Hughes didn't respond. "She doesn't want to see me."

The butler shifted. "She is not available."

"Of course she doesn't want to see you." Henry turned at the sound of the duke's voice coming from the parlor just outside of the foyer. He was leaning on the doorjamb, watching Henry carefully. He crooked his finger and motioned him into the room. "Come. We have some things to discuss."

Henry glanced toward the longer hall on the opposite side of the foyer. Hughes had come from there. Perhaps Evangeline was down that wing of the house. In her music room or the library.

He hated that he was so close and yet so far away. But what could he do? He had to respect her desire for distance. To violate it was to be no better than her father or any other man who had proven to her that the male sex was not trustworthy.

So he followed the duke into the parlor instead and flinched as the man closed the door behind him. "Tea?" Allingham asked, his tone short. "Or perhaps something stronger?"

"No, nothing," Henry muttered, moving to stare into the fire.

The duke was silent a long moment and then he cleared his throat. "Perhaps my daughter has informed you already, but if not, you should know I won't break your engagement, Mr. Killam. The final set of banns will be read as planned this Sunday and the wedding will happen as scheduled."

Henry faced him in surprise. "I see. Thank you, though I wonder if that is wise considering Evangeline will not even see me."

Allingham shrugged. "Perhaps, but I do this at her request."

"She asked for the marriage to move forward?" He shook his head. He wished that meant something, but she had made it very clear to him that their union would be only one of convenience. If she wished to wed, it was for her original reasons, not because she cared. He had lost that right.

"I have never seen my daughter so upset," Allingham continued.

Henry stared at him. "No?"

"Never. She does not really let herself care enough about anyone else to give them the power to hurt her like you have." The duke sighed. "I suppose that is a function of losing her mother at such a vital age. And perhaps of seeing me..." He drew off slowly. "Well, I was not the best of husbands, and my wife suffered for it more than perhaps some might."

Henry worried his lip, surprised that Allingham would reveal something so personal. "Evangeline has mentioned her mother before." Just the once, of course. In anger when she compared him to the man who had let her down all her life.

"Has she?" Allingham drew back a fraction. "Then she must care for you. She never speaks of her to me or to her siblings." He sighed. "Honestly, I'm not sure why she's so upset with you. After all, what you did affects me more than her."

Henry flinched. And there it was. Even if the duke had some awareness of his failings when it came to Evangeline, he still didn't have much empathy for her. He viewed the world in terms of how it touched him, not anyone else. Even Evangeline's pain could be co-opted.

It was no wonder she managed everyone in her life so carefully. There had never been anyone in her world who had offered to carry even a portion of the load. No one she could trust enough to set down some of the weight and rest while they took care of her. She was secondary to everyone.

And suddenly it was very clear what Henry needed to do.

He pushed to his feet from the settee. "I'm sorry, Your Grace, but I have something I must do." He dug in his pocket. "Will you see that Evangeline gets today's letter from me?"

"She won't answer," Allingham said, but he took the folded papers.

"She doesn't have to," Henry said softly. "Good day, Your Grace."

He raced from the room, barely hearing Allingham's farewell and ran for home. He needed a carriage and he needed it now.

~

Evangeline stared at a line of spools of ribbon laid out before her in the shop and did not give a damn about any of them. She supposed she should, as they were some of the finishing touches for the gown she would wear for her wedding. And yet she looked at them and none of it mattered.

"My lady, you must choose one. I rather like the blue," Tibby said. When Evangeline didn't respond, she sighed. "You must speak to the man, you know. It is the only way to end this terrible temper you find yourself in."

"I know you're right," Evangeline muttered. She had thought of talking to Henry many times since he'd arrived at her door a week before and she refused to see him. It was fear that kept her from seeing him now, not anger.

She would reveal too much if she saw him. She would say too much.

"I will take the blue," she said softly. "Will you let them know?"

Tibby let out a sigh and then slipped off to find the shopkeeper for the length of ribbon. Evangeline turned, and just as she did, the bell over the door rang and Donovan McGilvery entered the shop. He caught sight of Evangeline and though he looked startled, he made his way to her.

"Mr. McGilvery, what a surprise," Evangeline managed to choke out, though she thought of Henry as she looked at him. She resented this man, for it was helping him that had put them all in this position.

That wasn't really true, but it helped to think of it that way.

"Yes, yes," he said. "I have a sister, you see, and she sent me to pick up some fabric she wanted. A brother's work is never done."

She nodded, somehow managing to retain some normalcy when all she wanted to do was ask after Henry. "Very lucky for her."

He shifted a little and picked at the edge of some fabric on the table before them. "Lady Evangeline, I realize it is very forward of me, but I must ask you about Henry."

Her lips parted. "Ask *me* about him? Certainly you have seen him more than I have as of late."

He shook his head. "No, I haven't. About a week ago he came into the society meeting house with all his equipment. He donated everything to us and gave up his membership. He asked that his name be removed from any future publications he had a hand in. Then he walked out. I have not seen him since, despite many attempts to meet with him or reach out to him."

Evangeline stared, hardly able to speak for the total shock that settled over her in that moment. "I don't understand. He gave up his work?"

"Entirely." McGilvery's concern was real in the lines along his face. "He was grim about it, but determined. He said it was what he must do for his future. I assume that means this is something you required of him."

Evangeline stared. "No. I would *never* have asked him. In fact, I encouraged him to continue."

She thought of that day in his parlor when she'd accused him of caring more for his work than for her. Was that the catalyst of this change?

The very idea of it tore at her heart, partly because she hated to think he thought he had to surrender something so important for her. And partly because he would. And he did so without show, without performance. McGilvery said Henry had done this a week ago, but he'd made no mention of it in his letters. Her father had said nothing.

"Mr. McGilvery, I promise you I'll go to him straight away. I will talk to him about this and encourage him to speak to you." She turned and waved to Tibby.

"Thank you, my lady." He smiled at her. "I can see why he cares for you so deeply."

His words sank into her and she lifted a hand to her heart. "Good day, sir."

"Good day," he said as she and her maid rushed from the shop together and toward the carriage that would take her where she belonged.

To Henry Killam.

∼

Henry sat at his desk, drawers open all around him, papers stacked high. He sorted them into piles with a frown. Burn and keep. Burn and keep.

The burn pile was teetering with copies of notes he had already delivered to the society. His chest ached as he looked at them, the work of nearly a decade, and knew that part of his life was almost over.

And yet if it brought him to Evangeline, perhaps it was worth it.

"Mr. Killam," Deacon said, pushing the door open slightly. "You have a visitor. Lady Evangeline."

Henry froze, hand poised over another stack of papers, and looked up at the butler. He was dreaming or hallucinating. Those were the only two options. Evangeline could not truly be here.

"Shall I send her in?"

"Yes," Henry said, standing and smoothing his waistcoat. "Please do."

The servant stepped away a moment and he heard voices coming down the hall. Evangeline's voice, the one he adored more than any other.

When she stepped into his office, she stopped, looking around the mess in shock as Deacon announced her and stepped away. She swallowed and reached back to shut the door behind herself.

He tensed at the motion. It could mean something good or bad.

"You are here," he said, rather foolishly, he knew.

She smiled. "I am, indeed."

"I did not think you would come. I had given up hope," he said. He watched her look around the room again and rushed around the desk. "I am sorting, not working."

She flinched a little and ran her fingers along the top of a wobbling pile of pages. "Sorting what?"

"What will be destroyed and what will be kept. I'm afraid my papers for the house and other holdings were bound up in my work. So I must parse it all out before I get rid of what doesn't matter."

She let out a gasp. "So it is true, then? You really are divorcing yourself from your research?"

He tensed, his hands clenching at his sides. "I am. But…but you ask if it's true, does that mean you already knew?"

"I ran into Mr. McGilvery earlier today and he expressed his concern over your actions." She moved toward him and then stopped herself. "*Why* are you doing this?"

He sat on the edge of his desk slowly. "For you."

She lifted a hand to her mouth and her eyes went impossibly wide. "For me? Henry, I never asked this of you. On the contrary, I arranged this entire thing so that you would never have to give up your work. Why in the world would you do it for me?"

"Because of just what you said," he explained. "This is not what I intended. I wanted to speak to you about it after we were married, so you wouldn't see it as a manipulation. Damned Donovan."

She shook her head. "Forget Donovan for a moment. Just tell me what is going on."

He sighed and reached out. She took his hand, and relief flowed through him as he guided her away from the piles of papers to the settee by his fire. The settee where he had first touched her what felt like a lifetime ago.

He pushed those thoughts away and stared into her face, memorizing every line of it, every movement. He could only pray that what he was about to tell her would give him back the chance he had lost out of foolish distraction.

"You keep your stories close to your heart, Evangeline," he began. "But I understand some of them. I have seen firsthand how no one in your life has truly considered you. I know that's why you are so controlled both in action and emotion. If you aren't, there are consequences. You must manage everything because if you don't, no one will. Am I correct?"

Evangeline bent her head, and to his surprise, tears filled her eyes. "Y-Yes," she admitted softly. "Yes."

He nodded and gently stroked the hand he still held. "I imagine that has been very painful. Despite that you allowed me the chance to prove I was different. But I let you down, just like the others. No wonder you were hurt and angry. I earned that."

"You love what you do," she whispered. "Perhaps I was wrong to react so strongly."

"Don't do that," he said, touching her chin and tilting her gaze back up to his. "Don't excuse me. I made you a promise and I didn't keep it. Worse, I hid it from you. It might not have been the most terrible promise to break, but a promise nonetheless."

"I still don't understand why that means you must give up your work," she said.

"No one has put you first," he explained. "Including me. But I hoped that if I gave up what you know is important to me, it would send a message to you through my actions, since my words are empty, that you are the thing in this world that matters most to me."

He leaned forward, and now he caught both her hands. "Evangeline, when I said I loved you, that was true. I do love you. I have loved you for a very long time, though I thought I had no chance in the world with you and was too cowardly to do anything about it. When I had my opportunity, I should have moved heaven and earth to make certain I didn't lose you. I'm sorry I didn't. And I hope that this action I took will show you how serious I am. If not, that's fine. I accept your reticence. But please know that I intend to keep trying to prove myself to you from now until the day I take my last breath. And that's all. That's everything."

She pulled one hand away and rested it on her forehead. "You would give up everything just for a chance to have my faith?" she asked, he thought more to himself than to her. "You would surrender all you are."

"I would," he said, and when she was sitting with him, the sting of that surrender was far less harsh.

She was silent for a moment, then surprised him by leaning forward and cupping his cheeks. "Oh Henry, you great, wonderful *idiot*. I…"

She drew a very deep breath and her face flamed scarlet. "…I love you too."

CHAPTER 18

Evangeline smiled as she said those words, and it was the most beautiful thing he'd ever seen. As was the confidence in her tone when she said them. It almost made him think they could be true.

He stared at her, his eyes wide and his lips trembling. "This is a dream. I believed it before, I know it now."

"Because I said I loved you?" she asked with a laugh. "Well, if it is a dream, I say we work hard to not wake up."

"And you don't say it as some kind of…I don't know, way to manage me?" he asked.

"You do know me well, but no. I think I realize love is utterly unmanageable." She reached up to cup his cheek. "Dearest Henry, I *never* wanted you to do this grand gesture, as much as I appreciate the sentiment behind it. I have watched multiple generations of women surrender all they were for men who didn't appreciate it. Saw them wait around for those same men to grant favor. It was horrible. I didn't want that for myself, but nor do I want it for you. I want us to each have our independent interests and lives. I love the idea of coming to our table or…or our bed and talking about your latest venture at the Society or my current project secretly taking over London's most influential."

He laughed. "Is that what you're doing?"

"As often as I can."

"But if I cannot have this grand gesture, as you put it, how can I prove to you that you are most important in my life?" he asked.

"Just as you have," she said. "I admit, I was upset, and those feelings made my heart so clear to me. That was frightening, perhaps it still is. But you have restored my faith in you. In us and our future. But can you get back your equipment and your membership?"

"I'm certain I can. I've had desperate messages all week asking me not to walk away." He leaned closer. "Do you truly want me to do this?"

"Of course. At any rate, I wouldn't want your quitting to undo all my work on my father. I almost have him convinced it was his idea for you to carry on with your work and make it public what you do."

He blinked. "What? Would he really agree to that?"

"If you let me alone to trick him into it, certainly," Evangeline said. "And I will stand beside you proudly as you become the one to prove a planet into existence and whatever else strikes your fancy after that."

He leaned forward and wrapped his arms around, dragging her into his lap as he kissed her. God, but he loved her taste. He'd almost forgotten it after what seemed like a lifetime apart. He never wanted to lose that or her again.

She ground down against him gently and then pulled away. "Henry, I would like to…to be with you. But I want all of you. Not just a taste. All."

He sucked in a breath. God, but he wanted that too. "But what about—"

She held her hand up to his lips to silence him. "No more what ifs. I cannot control the future, try as I might. But what I want in this moment is perfectly clear. Please? Please won't you give that to me?"

He stared into her eyes, that dark blue capturing him as it always did. He couldn't deny her. He didn't want to. So he leaned in and just before he kissed her again, he whispered, "Yes."

∽

Evangeline's heart raced as Henry broke yet another searing kiss and moved to the door. He locked it and stood there staring at her. "Your maid is here, and my servants," he said. "So there will be very little time to make this as perfect as I want to."

"It will be perfect because it's us," she reassured him, and stood to unfasten the line of buttons along the front of her dress. She pushed the gown away, then the chemise, and stood before him naked.

He caught his breath, just as he had the first time he'd seen her like this. Unlike that time before, she was not embarrassed to have him see her. After all, she was his. He hers. This was meant to be.

She beckoned him closer, and he came in three long steps and gathered her to him with a passion that quickened her blood. Her heart raced as she tugged at his jacket and he cupped her backside with both hands and rubbed her against his cock. She arched with a soft sigh as pleasure ricocheted through her.

"Hurry," she murmured, not only because the time was short but because she needed him, needed this, needed to solidify in a physical way the promises they'd just made.

She wanted to be loved in a manner she would feel throughout her whole body and to love him that way in return.

He unfastened his trousers and she licked her lips as she gripped him, stroking him as he backed her toward the settee. They fell onto it and he half-covered her as his hands roamed up the length of her body, lingering in the places where he'd studied her pleasure over the past few weeks. She gasped at his fingers grazing her side, cresting over her breast, playing with a sensitive nipple as she sucked his tongue gently.

"Hurry," she repeated, opening her legs a fraction.

He drew his head back and stared down at her. "This is the first time either of us will ever do this," he said, his breath short. "And you will be the only woman I will ever share this with. So please look at me, Evangeline."

She held his gaze and smiled. "Never look away."

He didn't as he positioned himself at her wet entrance. He didn't look away as he eased a fraction inside of her and they both moaned in time. Her body stretched, a mixture of pleasure and pain, and she fought to keep her eyes on his.

He brushed his thumb against her jawline and whispered, "I'm sorry."

"I don't mind," she said, and it was true. He pushed farther and she dug her fingers into his shoulders as he fully seated himself.

They rested that way for a few seconds, their breathing slowly matching as their gazes remained locked. At last she gripped her sheath around him and he made a garbled sound that swelled her sense of power to new heights. She liked making him surrender this way. She liked doing the same with him.

He ground his hips, thrusting gently, and she gasped a second time. Those short, focused movements put pain in the background and rubbed their pelvises so her swollen, sensitive clitoris was massaged. And it felt good, so very good as pleasure built like a wall within her. She crested that wall with him, meeting his strokes, holding his gaze until finally the pleasure was too much and she fell into the oblivion of release.

Only then did he break their stare, catching her soft cry with his mouth and kissing her through the crisis as his thrusts increased. She felt him straining, reaching for his own release, and she clawed at his back as he arched his head back and groaned her name. He pumped hot into her body and she took it all as tears began to roll down her face.

His breath slowed and he leaned back. Immediately horror registered in his expression and he rolled away, parting their bodies as he crouched beside her.

"I hurt you, I'm so sorry," he murmured.

She shook her head. "No, it's not the pain," she said. "It's the knowing that you are mine now. Truly mine. And I'm yours. And once we say our vows, we never have to be apart again."

He smiled at those words, which had been so hard won and hard fought for. She was glad she had never gifted them to another man, nor tried to seek out someone else's affection. She loved that her heart belonged fully and completely to Henry Killam.

And always would.

EPILOGUE

The wedding of the year happened long before the beginning of the Season, and the lucky guests invited to the big day were treated to the party of the century afterward, as well. Evangeline smiled as she passed by one of the debutantes who would be coming out in the spring. The girl was pouting about how no one would even look at the new batch of diamonds when they could talk about Evangeline and Henry and their winter romance.

Of course, that wasn't true and Evangeline knew it. Life moved on and everyone would forget the love story of the scientist and the diamond long before the summer began. Then that story would only belong to her and to Henry, just as she liked it.

As she stepped around a giggling group of her acquaintances, she found herself face to face with Donovan McGilvery. He bowed. "Mrs. Killam."

"I'm so glad you could come," she said, and meant it. She liked her husband's partner in astronomy.

"As am I. And very glad that your new husband has come back to the fold." He did look truly happy.

She nodded. "I would have him nowhere else."

He shifted slightly. "I never apologized to you for the trouble I caused with the article in the society journal a few weeks ago. I realize it created pain and I...I should have been more strenuous in making sure it wasn't published until Henry was ready."

Evangeline reached out and briefly touched the other man's arm. "I don't know the circumstances of how that all happened, but in the end they pushed us to where we needed to be. Mr. McGilvery, I know you care for my husband. I never wanted him to be kept from his work or from the credit he deserves."

McGilvery was still for a moment and then he inclined his head. "I only hope I shall be so lucky as to find a lady as invested in my hopes and dreams. If such a woman exists, I can see she would be worth winning."

Evangeline blushed at the compliment and her smile widened. "I hope you'll come and dine with us, once the excitement calms down."

He looked surprised at the invitation, but inclined his head. "I would very much like that. And now I see a lady racing across the room and she can wish to speak to no one but you. I will leave you to it."

He stepped away, and just as he did there was a cry behind her. "Evangeline!"

She turned and found Tamsin coming toward her. She had a bright smile, making her happy face all the more beautiful. Evangeline moved toward her and folded her into her arms for a brief hug that seemed to surprise her friend.

"Thank you for coming!" Evangeline said as they parted. "*Mrs. Cathcart!*"

Tamsin's smile became dreamier. "I am still not accustomed to being called by my married name. It all happened in such a whirlwind."

"I imagine so!" Evangeline said. "Considering not so long ago, you wanted a peaceful man-free existence."

"I thought I did." Tamsin laughed. "Until I didn't."

"So you love him then?"

Tamsin nodded with enthusiasm. "I do. More than I thought was possible. Simon is my perfect match. Thank you for kicking him awake that fateful night. Otherwise I might never have known him."

Evangeline let out a happy sigh. "I could thank you for the same, for I love Henry with the depth that you describe. But I'd known him forever and never admitted my heart to myself. None of this would have happened had *you* not put the idea to pursue him for my own purposes into my mind."

"Then I suppose we needed each other to point ourselves in the right direction," Tamsin said.

"Indeed, we were each other's compass. And that means we must be the closest of friends just in case we need direction in the future." Evangeline squeezed her hands. "I insist on it. As soon as we recover from the celebration, I shall ask you and Simon for supper."

"We would love to join you." Tamsin sent a glance across the room and then blushed. "Though right now I must leave you, for I can see my husband sending me a look across the room. If you'll excuse me..."

Evangeline smiled as she looked in Simon's direction and saw he was, indeed, focused very intently on Tamsin. She shook her head, for she'd always written Simon off as a bit...silly. *Un*focused. But it seemed love had all the power in the world to make people...better.

It certainly had for her.

"Best go to him then," she said.

The two broke apart and Evangeline continued her way across the room to where her new husband stood by with both their fathers. For the first time ever, the viscount actually looked like he was proud of his son. She pursed her lips. At least she'd given Henry that.

She couldn't wait to give him more. But first she had to save him.

"Husband," she said, smiling at the fathers before she winked at her groom. "I would dearly love to dance with you."

Henry bowed toward her and then tipped his hand to their fathers. "I cannot deny my lady what she desires. Excuse me, gentlemen."

He took her hand and to the dancefloor they went, falling into the spinning crowd together with a few graceful steps. "Thank you for saving me," he said with a bright smile.

"I will always save you," she reassured him as she gripped his hand all the tighter, "and know that you will do the same for me."

"Aye, I will," he agreed. "That is part of our future."

"Part? And what is the rest?" she said, smiling at his teasing.

"Well, every day we'll come to know each other more," he said.

"Trust each other more," she added.

"So you do know the future," he said. "I do not need to tell you at all."

"Not true." She leaned a little closer. "I want to hear my future from your lips every day for the rest of my life. I demand it."

"If you demand it, I must obey," he said, his fingers brushing along her hip quite scandalously. "For as you know, I am hopelessly devoted to you."

And as he spun her around the floor once more, she realized that fact was the only thing she really knew for certain. And it was more than enough.

Author's Note

The planet Henry is so earnestly seeking in *A Lady's Gift for Seduction* is Neptune. There are some who theorize that Galileo first predicted the existence of Neptune in the 17th century. By the regency, astronomy (especially comets, like the one Henry viewed with his beloved mother) was all the rage and amateur astronomers were seeking celestial bodies all over the sky. Telescopes of the time obviously couldn't find planets so far from our own, so mathematical equations were developed to predict orbits and provide proof of existance. At the time what we know now as Neptune wasn't known to be a planet or a meteor or some other body, but our Henry is convinced and of course he was right.

But poor Henry would be skunked by a Frenchman, Urbain-Jean-Joseph Le Verrier almost thirty years after our story, who proved the existence of the planet mathematically in 1846. I would like to think in our Jess Michaels story world that he used some of Henry's equations to do so, and that Henry would simply be over the moon pleased with the proof of what he always believed to be true.

I hope you enjoyed Henry and Evangeline's love story. Happy reading!

A LADY'S GIFT FOR SCANDAL

ELIZABETH ESSEX

*All thanks for this wonderfully fun project go to
my brilliant co-author and co-conspirator, Jess Michaels.*

Your friendship and encouragement made this project an utter delight!

CHAPTER 1

London December 1814

M iss Thomasina Lesley was desperately disappointed in London.
Well, not London itself—the city at Christmastide was a delight of bright, festive sights and sounds. But the people in Society, and in this dimly lit room in particular, where a score of supposed gentleman were gathered around a flaming punch bowl, included a great deal too many, "Japes and jackasses, if you ask me."

"I do not ask you." From her place beside the holly-bedecked mantelpiece, her mama was quite emphatic. "Smile, for heaven's sake. You'll frighten all the gentlemen away with that scowl."

"Good." Tamsin was rather emphatic herself. "I shouldn't like to let such simpletons near me." Just because she was pretty did not mean she was sweet or unintelligent. Or without expectations.

Tamsin had expected the gentleman of London to be more… Urbane. Cultured. Sophisticated.

But the snow-cold fact of the matter was that the gentlemen

arrayed before her seemed to be nothing but idiots—witness the fact that they were engaged in lighting themselves on fire by attempting to drink from their flaming punch bowl. And laughing like braying jackasses while they did it.

As if it were the greatest joke in the world to set one's eyebrows on fire.

"The fellow in the green coat is smoldering." If that wasn't the very definition of an idiot, Tamsin did not know what was.

Her mother nearly throttled her fan in exasperation. "Had you rather pack your bags back for home," Mama asked in a furious whisper, "and be married to your cousin Edward, who is the only man in Somerset to overlook your errant tongue and ask for you?"

Heaven forefend. "No." A duller, more pompous man than her cursed cousin had yet to be born—he was thirty going on sixty, if he was a day. But at least he had never set his own eyebrows on fire. That she knew of—this idiotic game of Snapdragon seemed just the sort of male jollity Cousin Edward would extol as manly.

"Then smile, for heaven's sake, girl. You're a diamond of the first water, prettier than any of your sisters," her mama reminded her. "Pray smile and look like it."

It was all humbug, this diamond business—Tamsin had never felt more like paste, being given the chance to go to London instead of her older sister, Anne, just because of her looks. She was a counterfeit diamond at best, a determined bluestocking being made to masquerade as a marriageable ninny in search of an equally marriageable ninny of a man. She looked the part, certainly, rigged out like a dressmaker's doll in the latest styles from the London modistes, but she felt nothing but an absolute imposter.

A frustrated, bored imposter, sore from biting her own tongue.

Exactly how she had felt at home, deep in the Somerset countryside, where nothing exciting or intellectual ever happened. As much as she loved her sisters and their intelligent, well-read company, she longed for a wider acquaintance than their benighted neighborhood provided. She yearned for newer ideas. The country was a vast, tedious, snow-covered prison, if you asked her.

But no one asked her.

Especially not Mama. Under her escort, London had become more tedious—the city jackanapes who set their tailcoats on fire excepted, of course—than the country. Here, Tamsin could not even for one minute be herself. Here, she was an ornament to be displayed and disposed of—preferably to a man who was both titled and rich. Anything above a lord, and Mama would be in alt. Anything below, and Tamsin would be accounted a failure.

Frankly, Tamsin preferred to fail on her own, without reference to anyone else—father, mother or future smoldering husband.

Her frustration made her tone far sharper than her mama would like. "I suppose a game of Snapdragon can't be counted a success until at least one idiot has lost an eyebrow."

"Sometimes two," a stunning young woman murmured at her elbow. Lady Evangeline, eldest daughter of the Duke of Allingham, was a true diamond of the first water—the sort of raven-haired, creamy-skinned English rose Mama was forever extolling as the epitome of beauty. The young woman was like an elegant swan gliding across the gilded surface of Society, regal and serene, as if she didn't need to paddle madly beneath the water like Tamsin.

"I do beg your pardon." Tamsin felt she had best apologize, for Lady Evangeline was a noblewoman—a duke's daughter—and her opinion was listened to. "I fear I should not be so critical of the fun, especially at this time of year."

"Do not go back now," Lady Evangeline's laugh was tempered by a wry smile. "I need an ally. You are utterly correct that they are all idiots. They're not the sort of fellows one wants for a husband, are they?"

"Heavens, no," Tamsin was too straightforward not to admit the truth, though she was both surprised and relieved to find anything like an ally in Lady Evangeline.

"Lord, grant me the confidence of a man of supposed education who knows absolutely nothing in truth," the lady intoned.

"Indeed." Tamsin was thrilled to find the lady possessed such an arch wit—it gave her permission to add her own rather acerbic thoughts. "If this is what's on offer, I don't think I want any sort of a husband at all. It seems a devil's bargain at best."

"True," Lady Evangeline agreed. "But what sort of life can one have without one?"

"An independent life," Tamsin vowed. The sort of quiet life where she might be left alone to read. And write. And think for herself.

She knew it was impossible—she and her sisters had been told so, over and over until she was blue in the face from hearing it. But somewhere in the last stubborn corner of her character, she had refused to accept it. "I had rather entertain myself, not with silly parties with flaming punch bowls, but with intelligent salons where ideas and ideals might be exchanged. Where books might be discussed or poetry recited." Where she might get advice and encouragement about the study of Bess of Hardwick that she had undertaken.

"You're a secret bluestocking."

"It's no great secret," Tamsin admitted. "I would be a true bluestocking if I were allowed, like my aunt Dahlia—she has her own establishment here in London and has the most elegant salons, full of the most interesting people." But Tamsin was not allowed go to any event that smacked of intellectualism. She had visited her aunt but once, before Mama had decreed such salons—as well as trips to museums or lectures—a waste of their precious time when they might be at balls instead, securing Tamsin's future. "But the sad truth is that if I don't marry one of *them*"—she gestured to the rowdy young men on offer—"I'll only be married off to my odious cousin who is to be a baronet someday but cares nothing for books or ideas, unless they're to do with beef cattle or crop rotation."

"Great God," her new friend said with feeling. "Might you be able to manage him into thinking better? A good woman can often make a mediocre man into something more."

"I doubt it." A more vain, self-convinced man than her cousin Edward, Tamsin had yet to meet. Every sentence out of his mouth began with *Actually, Thomasina...* He was positively enraging—even Mama said so, and she was normally enthusiastic about anything with a title and a pulse.

How different it would be if clear-sighted people like Lady Evangeline and Tamsin had charge of their lives. "I wish *we* were truly allowed to choose instead of only being chosen. Don't you, Lady Evangeline?" she mused. But the lady made no response. "Lady Evangeline?"

"Yes?"

"I was only saying I wish we were truly allowed to choose, don't you?"

"I'm sorry, Miss Lesley, I was just woolgathering—thinking of your situation. So you do not wish to marry this dreadful cousin?"

Tamsin could only shake her head.

"What is it you *do* want, then?"

No one, not in all the days she had been in London, nor in any of the days that had passed before, had *ever* asked Tamsin what she wanted for her life. Not Mama, nor Papa. And certainly not odious Cousin Edward.

But Tamsin knew her answer. "I'd rather be a spinster, like my aunt Dahlia. My mama does say she ruined herself, coming to London on her own, but she's left to live in peace with books and cats, and no men. It's heavenly." Especially when compared to the smoldering idiots. "That is what I want. But my mama will never approve. I must choose, and by the end of this little Christmas season."

Tamsin had never felt so helpless, or so angry. Heat scratched her throat. "The very thought of Cousin Edward makes me want to ruin myself like Aunt Dahlia, so he'll have nothing to do with me." Cousin Edward would get her father's small estate regardless, so why should she let him torture her with his odious opinions for the rest of her life?

Lady Evangeline's eyes lit with mischievous excitement. "Why not do it then?"

"Do what?"

"Ruin yourself."

The suggestion had Tamsin instinctively shaking her head—it was one thing to give vent to her secret fears and frustrations, but it was another thing entirely to act upon those wishes. Yet everything within her shrank from the suggestion at the same time that she yearned toward it.

Lady Evangeline was all confident decision. "It would have to be light ruination," she mused, smiling as if she already had a perfect plan percolating behind her equally perfect face. "To maintain your standing on some level. It all has to be done very carefully, in a controlled fashion—a bespoke sort of ruination, if you like."

Hope—crazy, unrealistic, exhausting, exhilarating hope—slid into Tamsin's veins like too much French champagne, lifting her up on the possibility. "Do you really think so?"

"Absolutely," Evangeline said.

Tamsin urged her brilliant new friend away from Mama so there was no possibility she might overhear. "Pray, tell me more."

Lady Evangeline tossed up a shoulder. "If you truly do not want to fall victim to the machinations of your parents, you must do a little *machinating* of your own."

The idea took root in Tamsin's head and began to grow stronger. "How?" Tamsin could barely hear her own voice over the strident, hopeful beating of her heart.

"We must simply think like the men, mustn't we, when they

want to find a biddable bride." Evangeline clapped her hands together like a magician conjuring a trick. "And who is a biddable bride, at least in their minds?" She opened her hands wide as if the answer were self-evident. "A wallflower!"

Of course. So simple. So practical. So perfect.

"A wallflower," Tamsin repeated, trying the idea out for size—tailoring it to suit her needs. "A *masculine* wallflower."

"Exactly!" A mischievous smile of angelic radiance and devilish determination gave something more than beauty to her new friend's already-beautiful face. Lady Evangeline took her arm with purpose. "And I know just where they are."

CHAPTER 2

Tamsin cast a wary backward glance at Mama. While she might have secretly thought of rebelling against her mother and her draconian strictures, she had never actually put so much as a toe out of line.

But where had that got her? Watching idiots set their eyebrows on fire.

So despite the fear beating a hectic tattoo on her heart, Tamsin followed in her new friend's wake like an ugly duckling swimming after a swan. Lady Evangeline led the way to a tall door that stood slightly ajar, spilling warm, mellow light into the darker corridor and threw open the portal to reveal row upon row, and shelf upon shelf of rich, jewel-toned volumes.

"The library." Of course. Why had she not thought of seeking like-minded intellectuals here, in this temple to learning, instead of wasting her time standing by the side of the dance floor?

Lady Evangeline smiled like a cat in cream. "And just as I promised, here are the wallflowers."

There they were—two gentleman sitting in perfect peace, reading beside the fire. And not a one of them smoldering.

"Who is that?" Tamsin gestured to a third fellow, a bespectacled gentleman quietly focusing a telescopic glass out the window at the night sky. He looked to be just the sort of kindred spirit who would welcome intellectual discussion. Perhaps she might even become acquainted with him without any sort of ruination required.

"Do you not know Henry Killam?" Lady Evangeline's tone indicated that everyone did. Everyone but Tamsin.

But she was happy to correct that mistake. "Might he do? He seems quite a bluestocking sort himself." And she rather liked his sort of gentle handsomeness.

Lady Evangeline took a long time before she answered. "Well...he is a thorough, scientific sort of fellow, who never does anything by halves, so that would be an advantage in your predicament, specifically..." Lady Evangeline trailed off, staring at this Henry for a long moment, as if she could divine his flaws. She shook her head. "Do you know, I don't think Henry will do at all for your purposes, not at all."

"No?" Tamsin could not keep the disappointment from her voice.

"No." Lady Evangeline's tone firmed. "Because he's... Because he's not... Simon!" She headed for the other side of the room to an alcove where a tall fellow Tamsin had not noticed reposed upon an upholstered sofa. "Oh, yes. Simon Cathcart ought to do quite nicely."

"Really?" This time, Tamsin couldn't keep her skepticism from her voice. The fellow in question lay full length upon the sofa, with his buff-clad legs crossed comfortably at the ankle. Apparently asleep. In the middle of a ball. "He looks rather too indolent. And too..." The man was so tall, his booted feet stuck well out over the arm of the sofa. "...too everything."

"Hmmm, yes," Evangeline considered, "but he's only indolent at these types of things. He used to be a soldier—a very good one, by all accounts, commended by Wellington himself, and part of the delegation to the Congress of Vienna last summer. Superior with languages or some such. But he came back from the war... different, they say."

"Different?" This did not sound like a good thing. "Is he violent?"

"Quite the opposite—a sworn pacifist!"

Tamsin fetched her spectacles out of her reticule and put them on, the better to see this interesting, pacifistic specimen. The man had a sort of beauty in repose—as if his conscience were as clean and unruffled as his cravat. "Perhaps he was too long at war?"

Lady Evangeline shrugged. "Either way, no one has any expectations of him. So no one could expect him to make an offer for you. He's the second son—hence his place in the army—but he's sold out or some such. Insufficient ambition, some say."

Such facts might be accounted in the fellow's favor, if she were seriously considering Lady Evangeline's idea. Which she wasn't. Not seriously.

Not yet.

"He accompanies his aunt, the Countess Cathcart, in Society, as the earl doesn't care for these things," Evangeline went on. "Rumor has it the earl doesn't care for the countess, but I suppose that's nobody's business but theirs. He always retires like this, Simon does. Never socializes, never dances, but also never gambles. Nor, more importantly, lights himself on fire."

Definitely a point in his favor.

"What's more, he doesn't have opinions. And he's as handsome as the day is long. Just look at him."

Tamsin was looking. At the tumble of sandy hair. And the sweep of too-beautiful lashes. And the smooth cut of his jaw. "I *suppose* if I were going to all the ugly trouble of being ruined, I might want something beautiful to look at."

"Exactly. He's eminently suitable for the purpose," Lady Evangeline concluded. "Uncomplicated, simple Simon. Aren't you, Simon?" She prodded the sleeping man awake with her slippered foot.

But instead of leaping up in an embarrassed haste to be caught sleeping at a ball by two young ladies, or rage at being so rudely interrupted mid-masculine slumber, this Simon just opened his eyes and gave them a warm, sleepy smile. "Of course I am. Is that you, then, Evie, old girl?"

"It is. Good evening, Simon. Do get up, dear man. Miss Lesley has a proposition for you."

Simple Simon did not get up, but merely turned his sleepy eye upon Tamsin as if he were perfectly used to being awakened from slumber by females with propositions. "Does she?"

"Do I?" Tamsin echoed, and then firmed her voice. "Yes. Yes, indeed, I believe I do."

He looked at her with the same sort of simple, happy expectation that her father's dogs exhibited whenever Papa so much as rose to his feet. But this Simon Cathcart did not, in fact, rise to his feet. He just lay there smiling, happy to be propositioned. Or not. "Don't dance, I'm afraid," he offered. "Three left feet, don't you know?"

Tamsin did not know, especially as he had but two such long appendages stretched out before him. But if she doubted his mathematical abilities, she had to admit his smile was personable and his demeanor pleasant. "Not dancing, I thank you. I'm seeking...more of a personal, private favor," she hedged, unsure of how best to phrase a ruinous proposition to a gentleman wallflower. Unsure if she *should* make the proposition. "A temporary alliance, if you will."

His happy countenance clouded. "Don't know about an *alliance*—had a bit too much of that sort of thing in the army. Treaties, pacts, alliances—not worth the paper they're written on."

Lady Evangeline let out an elegant sigh and then bluntly declared, "Miss Lesley desires to be ruined."

"Lightly ruined." Tamsin lowered her voice in the hope that not everyone in the house might have overheard them. "*Very* lightly. For appearance's sake, and not in actuality."

"Not in actuality?" Mr. Simon Cathcart frowned and smiled and turned down his mouth all at the same time in the perfect picture of sleepy confusion. "Where's the fun in that?"

Tamsin strove for logic, even in the midst of an illogical situation. Which meant that she really was considering ruining herself with *someone*, if not this illogical, smiling, *different* man. "Our agreement would be more of a business arrangement, sir, not for...amusement."

"Right ho." He took the correction amiably. "So I'm to be in the business of ruining young ladies?"

"Only me, sir," Tamsin clarified in as quiet a voice as possible. "No other young ladies."

"Not at the moment, perhaps." He grinned up at her. "But if I'm successful, who knows who else might come knocking on my door? Don't know if I can chance it, Miss..."

"Lesley. How do you do?" Tamsin fell back upon civility to allay her confusion at his nonsensical style of talk.

"Like a fellow, Lesley," he observed apropos of nothing. "But you're not a fellow at all, what?"

"No, I'm not." She wouldn't be in this predicament if she were. "I wonder if we might speak privately?" Where she might more logically evaluate if this Simple Simon really was the suitable masculine wallflower Lady Evangeline had thought him.

"Oh, I shouldn't think so," he refused baldly. "Load of trouble, that—being alone with a young lady."

"But I should like our arrangement to remain private, known to no one but the three of us assembled here. And I give you my word that no other young lady will hear it from my lips."

"Nor mine," Lady Evangeline swore. "And to make sure I know nothing of the affair, I shall leave you to arrange it as you will." And she swanned herself off, leaving Tamsin alone with the recumbent, reluctant man.

"Don't know if such a thing can be arranged," Mr. Cathcart observed. "Least not by me."

His willingness to admit to this fault was actually a decided mark in his favor. Tamsin began to see more and more the advantages of an amiably biddable man.

"I shall do all the arranging, Mr. Cathcart—you needn't fear. I will instruct you," she informed him in the same kind of quiet but firm tones her governess—who was the very picture of a dedicated bluestocking—had used on Mama whenever she got sniffy about Tamsin's studies. "I shall teach you how to go on."

Simon Cathcart's face cleared in obvious relief. He was the very picture of a man who was a proverbial open book. "Very thoughtful of you, Miss...?"

"Lesley. Miss Thomasina Lesley. My father is Colonel Oliver Lesley of the Royal Marines and His Majesty's Ship *Audacious*." Even as she said it, she hated that her *bona fides* were not her own, but borrowed from her father. But as she seemed to be arranging her own ruination, perhaps it were best if she kept her old-fashioned papa out of it. "Tamsin," she offered, "to my friends."

"Colonel Lesley? Know a deuced load of colonels—was one myself—but don't think I know any marines, if that's what you want, Miss..."

"Lesley." Tamsin began to understand the depth of his *differences*. "I do not seek a marine. I seek to be lightly ruined."

He nodded and smiled as if she made every sense. But then he frowned. "Why?"

This was actually a very good question. One she had best have the answer to—for her own sake, if not for his. "Because frankly, I had rather not marry, Colonel Cathcart. I would rather pursue more serious intellectual studies and write books than be a wife. I am what some people call a bluestocking."

"Books? You don't say?" Cathcart's amazed gaze dropped to her skirts. "Don't know that I've ever seen a lady's blue stockings," he observed with some wonder.

Tamsin found herself both embarrassed and amused by his still-sunny befuddlement. "They are not, in actuality, blue, sir. The appellation is just a name—an expression to connote a person of intellectual interests."

"You don't say." He was smiling at her as if she had just explained all the secrets of the universe.

"I do say." She gave him her own smile, for it seemed pointless, and rather rude, not to join in such happy affability, even if it was confusing. "Are we agreed?"

"To what?"

"To lightly ruining me. For appearances," she clarified. "Under my instruction."

"Under instruction—like being under orders. I reckon I can do that." But then he closed his eyes and scratched his sandy head as if he were searching his brain. "Aha—the very thing." His face grew rather blankly serious. "If I ruin you, then I'll have to marry you."

"No, no," she hastened to assure him. "I have no want to marry. In fact, the reason I should like to be ruined is so I'm beyond the pale, and *un*marriageable."

"Right ho." His brows rose and his face cleared. "Put some fellow off, is that the brief?"

"Yes, exactly." Tamsin began to have some hopes for his intellect despite other appearances.

"Right ho!" The sunshine dawned in his face again. "Rather not get married myself, either. But parents and relations and the like—they have a deadly bad habit of insisting upon such things, don't they?"

"Yes, I suppose they do. I take your point, Colonel. But I give you my word that I will not be forced into marrying you—my papa is away at sea and shall not bother us, so we shall only have my mama to contend with. And my plan for her is to arrange to leave your name out of it entirely."

"Right ho. Well, that's a relief." His smile widened, if possible, until it reached all the way up to the corners of his eyes. Which were a rather lovely sort of green. Not that that mattered. "No need to saddle you with me, then, is there?"

"No." Tamsin felt her own lips curving in response—it seemed impossible not to join in such easy joy. "Not that you're not a perfectly agreeable sort of man, I'm sure." And most perfectly, most agreeably handsome. "But as I said, I've no want to be trapped either, so I give you my word that should someone, somehow, someway, force you to propose, I shall refuse. Here is my hand on it." She offered him her pledge.

He finally stood and took her hand, his big palm covering hers entirely.

The feeling—of relief, she supposed—was nearly overwhelming. Or perhaps that was him, bending over her, sheltering her like some tall tropical palm tree.

Lord help her, but he was a tall, well-favored man. "So you'll do it?"

He smiled at her as if *she* had given *him* a gift. "I don't see why not."

Tamsin felt as giddy with hope as if she'd drunk an entire bottle full of French champagne.

Ask and you shall receive, the Bible always said, but Tamsin had never really believed it. Perhaps because she'd been asking the wrong people all that time.

CHAPTER 3

Simon Cathcart couldn't remember the last time he'd been so completely surprised. Probably at Vitoria on the Peninsula when that retreating French officer's cavalry saber had arced toward his head.

But ruination was a far pleasanter prospect than either the scar across his shoulder, or the bloody war that had begotten it. And he was bored out of his allegedly damaged skull.

So Simon raised himself up from his pose of idle relaxation on the plushly upholstered sofa, extended his hand in pledge and prepared to break all his hard held rules. Because ruining the delightfully serious Miss Tamsin Lesley was going to be fun. And Simon hadn't had the kind of fun that involved young ladies in a long, long time.

Years of soldiering, of disciplining his body and mind, of simultaneously honing his instincts while curbing his impulses, had left him tangled in such knots that he no longer trusted himself. No longer trusted his ability to make the sort of decisions they prized in the Army. No longer wanted to.

And so he had become someone new—someone so simple and dull that Society could not conceive that he had ever served under

Wellington or assisted his uncle, the Earl Cathcart, in the delicate diplomacy of negotiating peace at the Congress of Vienna. So simple, diamonds like Lady Evangeline and her friend thought him *different*.

He had heard it all before—their whispered assessment of him, people saying he'd lost his mind. And he had been horrified at first, angry and diminished. Until he realized how useful it was to be thought *less*—it gave him peace and quiet to think. It gave him a reason to prefer quiet to company, and library sofas to balls. A reason to listen instead of talk.

But the sofa had, of late, become tedious. He tired of playing the part of everyone's favorite idiot. And it wasn't every day a lass asked him ruin her.

Especially a lass who looked like a strange spun sugar confection of a governess. The bright glint of her spectacles against the clever spark in her eye added to her air of mischievous, myopic, fairy godmother. "I'm happy to oblige you, Miss—"

"Lesley," she supplied politely, despite it being the fourth time he had very purposefully asked. "Tamsin, please." She clasped his hand in the sort of nervously overconfident shake generals had given him when they had wanted difficult orders followed and impossible gains made—hopeful that he would be their man. "But only lightly ruined, you understand?" she queried again.

"I understand you perfectly, Miss T." He stepped back and gave her a smart salute. "I'm just the fellow for the job."

Relief transformed her face. If she had been a tolerably pretty lass before—all fey, elfin features that gave her that fairytale air— she was rather ravishing now, with a lovely warm, satisfied determination beaming from her face through the glinting lens of her spectacles. "Thank you, Colonel."

"Simon, please. Don't know who he is, Miss T, but serve him right," he assured her. "We'll rout him, and put him off, what? See if we don't."

Miss Lesley smiled slowly—the sort of genuine, honestly

pleased smile that seemed so rare in Society, where most people hid their true emotions and intentions behind a false mask of pleasantness.

God knew he did.

"Oh, thank you. That's lovely. Now, we'll have to plan it out quite carefully." She stepped closer to speak more confidentially. "Nothing left to chance."

Up close, Miss Tamsin Lesley was even more delicious—all that doe-eyed, fey innocence masked a sharp determination.

For some reason he could not name, he liked her. He liked the bossy bundle of deliciousness who couldn't see past her own nose, but assumed all the world beyond her gaze should be as she saw it. There was something hopeful about that assumption. Something reassuring. And reassuringly human.

She wanted to be the heroine of her own story.

In short, just his type. "I await your command."

"Really?" She peered at him through those glossy spectacles with slightly narrowed eyes, as if she wanted to trust him, but feared he really was as thick as the wet bale of wool he pretended to be. "I've never met a man inclined to give rank to a mere woman before."

"Had entirely too much of being in charge, I assure you," he said, because it was the truth. And because he was not nearly as thick as he so purposefully tried to appear. Nor too addled by his years of army service—and that French saber—to look a gift horse in the mouth. "Happy to be led to water, as the saying goes." And to drink.

Especially from such rosy, charmingly bitten lips.

"You are the most remarkably accommodating man." She said it with such wary wonder that he wanted to thank all the unaccommodating men who had disappointed her. They were idiots.

But their loss was his gain.

"When do you think you might become available to start?" she asked.

Simon felt his grin widen. "No time like the present, what?" He gestured to the sofa.

Miss Tamsin Lesley lost some of her governess-like assurance. "I hadn't thought to begin straightaway." She took an awkward step backward, and promptly smacked into a side table, sending the brandy he had settled there sloshing. "Perhaps we might discuss the particulars first? Some place less..."—she glanced across the room where Henry Killam sat in his usual sentinel at the window, as well as at the two fellows reading by the fire —"...crowded."

"Oh, I should think we're safe enough here. Especially if a light ruination is all you want—should actually think Henry is the right person for the job of observant witness. Very scientific and observant, is Henry."

"Oh, no, I shouldn't ask that of a stranger." Miss Lesley pushed her spectacles more firmly up her pert nose. "It will be my mother, and my mother only, whom I want to discover us in... some compromise."

Some compromise. Simon was charmed. "In *flagrante*, as the French would have it, do you mean?"

"Yes, although the phrase is, I think, not French but from the Latin, *in flagrante delicto*—in the act of a blazing offense," she corrected.

Simon could only smile—damned if he didn't adore the clever ones. His childhood governess, the beautiful Miss B—Beatrice Bancroft—had a lot to answer for. "Let us blaze away. It's all Greek to me, Miss T."

"And that's Shakespeare." Her smile was only a temporary reward, because her now-keen gaze focused on his face in a way that made him suddenly less sure about having agreed to her proposition—she looked too clever not to find her way through his defensive charade.

Perhaps it was time he gave it up?

But not just yet. Simon gave her the happy lunatic smile he had perfected when he wanted people to leave him alone—even though the purpose was to be left alone *with* Miss Lesley. "How should you prefer to be compromised, Miss T? Kissed or cuddled or something more? Say the word and I shall do my best not to disappoint."

"That's very good in you, Colonel." She pleated up her forehead in an adorably fierce look of deep thought. "I should think a sort of straightforward caress will do."

"Ought to call me Simon, what? Under the circumstances." The circumstance being that there was no such thing as a straightforward caress. Which also meant Miss Tamsin Lesley clearly did not have as much actual experience in ruination as she wanted him to believe. How interesting and amusing.

And how delightfully dangerous.

Well, perhaps not dangerous—how dangerous could a bespectacled confection of a governess-y lass be, really? It wasn't as if she were French cavalry.

"A straightforward caress?" he echoed as if considering the maneuver as carefully as she. "Like if I touched your hair"—he reached out to demonstrate, catching the backs of his fingers across the sweep of soft, light hair looped behind her ear—"or your face."

Her mouth opened into a gratifying expression of silent astonishment before she recalled her both her wits and that decisive, instructive voice. "I had thought something more definitive, sir." She pushed her spectacles more firmly up her nose.

But she was not so self-possessed as she might like him to believe—her face had pinked up quite nicely. "More definitive? Do demonstrate for me, Miss T. I shouldn't like to get it wrong."

She moved fractionally closer. "I should think your arms might simply go 'round me"—she moved her arms into an awkward, patently inexperienced version of a caress—"as if you were pulling me into an embrace."

"Right ho, an embrace," he echoed with all the appearance of studious attention. "Like this?" Instead of following her careful instruction, he gathered her almost roughly to his side, so they were mashed up, shoulder to shoulder.

"Well." Despite being squashed against him like a trooper in a cart, she gave every appearance of considering the pose seriously. "That seems rather more like comrades than lovers. Perhaps something a bit more purposefully amorous?"

Purposefully amorous. Oh, she was delightful, with her awkwardly specific vocabulary.

"I should rather recommend the sort of face toward face embrace that might be mistaken for kissing," she continued.

"Right ho!" he said as if he could never of thought of such a thing on his own. "Well, if it's kissing that you want—" He swept her 'round, across his lap in a rather stylish, ready-to-ravish embrace, if he did say so himself. "A good bout of kissing is bound to do the trick."

He was gratified to find her flustered and instantly holding him off with straightened arms pressed against his chest. "Yes, perhaps, but if you don't mind, Colonel Cathcart, I think we might postpone the actual embrace until the appointed time. Though I am pleased to find you sufficiently versed in the art to effect the requisite pose without any difficulty."

Requisite pose! "Glad you think so, Miss T. Happy to oblige."

"You are very kind," she said with obvious sincerity. "But there are one or two things that I must take care of—things I must plan and prepare, you see—before we can commence in earnest."

"Plan the thing out, what?" He gave her his sunniest, dimmest smile, all toothy pleasure. "Strategy—learned that in the army."

"Yes, exactly—strategy." She disengaged herself from his arms and stood to shake out her skirts. "I'm so glad you understand."

"Don't understand much." He regaled her with his best idiot's delight. "But happy to oblige."

"For which I thank you." She put out her hand to shake, even as she took a step back, as if she feared he might seize her up again. "Thank you for agreeing to help me."

"Always a pleasure to help a damsel in distress, what? Though you don't seem distressed at all."

"No. Because I've got you to assist me."

Something that had to be his conscience stirred within, like a dull sword being pulled out of a rusty scabbard. Damned if he didn't feel like he ought to act something of the hero she was making him out to be.

But she was entirely her own heroine. She repossessed herself of her hand, all self-possessed, self-determined governess. "Until next time."

"Right ho." And because he wanted to have the last, most idiotic word, he added, "Tell you what, Miss T. I'll use the time till then to practice up on the various embraces, shall I? See if I don't."

CHAPTER 4

In for a penny, in for an entire pound—after what she had arranged with Colonel Simon Cathcart, Tamsin felt she had put enough of her foot on the road to ruination that she might as well continue on down the path.

She readily gave way to a small falsehood—that she had an appointment to meet Lady Evangeline at Mattigan's Bookshop, no more than a few short blocks away on Piccadilly. Her mama generally depreciated Mattigan's as a place that catered to bluestockings, but she could not object to any appointment that put her daughter in the circle of the much-admired, deeply influential Lady Evangeline. And truly, Tamsin *would* make an appointment to meet Evangeline there, just not on that particular day.

Her object in the subterfuge was to visit her aunt Dahlia and make those *alternative arrangements* she had told Mr. Cathcart about—it would do no good to ruin herself if her punishment were to be trapped in the tedious country for the rest of her natural-born life. She was not such an idiot to think that being alone without comfort or companionship was anything to be desired.

When she arrived at her aunt's smartly elegant house on the curve of Manchester Square, there was a smattering of the intellectual set taking morning coffee and tea in the drawing room to ward off the winter's chill. Much as Tamsin might have liked to sit and listen and chat the whole morning through, she had business that needed attending to. She would have time to chat later, after she was ruined.

So as soon as a lull in the conversation opened, Tamsin inserted herself into it. "I was wondering if I might seize this opportunity to speak with you privately, Aunt Dahlia?"

If her aunt was surprised at her urgent tone, she made no public sign. "Of course, my dear." She led the way toward her private sitting room near the back of the house and took a seat on an elegant chaise in front of the warm fire. "Come, tell me what has occasioned your visit this chilly morn without your fiercely protective mama to breathe fire at us all?"

The mental image of Mama as a dragon who would alternately guard and scorch her for the rest of her life was enough to embolden Tamsin. She took her courage in hand and envisioned the life she desired—the life that would not be possible without her aunt's—as well as long, tall Colonel Cathcart's—assistance. "You must know how ardently I admire you and the life you have made for yourself here in London," she began.

"I am so glad you've enjoyed your visits."

"I've more than enjoyed them—I long to accept all of your invitations, and to be able to visit every day."

"So you might," her aunt said kindly, "when you are married and mistress of your own acquaintance."

"But that is just the thing, Aunt Dahlia—how can one be sure that one will be mistress of one's own acquaintance? That one's husband will not object as much as one's draconian mama?"

Aunt Dahlia smiled as if she knew all the secrets of the world. "By choosing carefully. And wisely."

Such advice, although well meant, could only frustrate. "Choice is one thing, Aunt Dahlia, but the law is quite another."

"Ah, yes." Another understanding smile wreathed her aunt's face. "I am pleased to find that your education has been so thorough."

"Indeed it has." Despite Mama's—and occasionally Papa's—objections, their governess had given Tamsin and her sisters a very liberal education. "I am glad I've been educated in what my rights will—and more importantly, will *not*—be under the law. It makes me more desirous than ever of being in charge of my own fate, even if that means becoming a spinster. What I desire above all else is to be like you."

"I am flattered." Aunt Dahlia looked at her with fresh concern. "But are you...averse?...to men in general, or simply to this Cousin Edward that I've heard my sister Violet speak of?"

"Not exactly averse." Tamsin weighed her words carefully, not wanting to misspeak. "I'm sure some men are perfectly acceptable." For some strange reason Colonel Cathcart's genial face leapt into her mind, smiling and giving up command. "But I much prefer books, and my own rights, to men."

Her aunt smiled. "Books don't keep you warm at night, my dear girl. Not in the same way someone who loves you will."

"But you've no husband," Tamsin pointed out, sure of her logic. "Your life is heavenly—you do as you like and pursue your own interests."

"True," her aunt acknowledged. "But that is not exactly by choice. And not exactly heavenly—despite the fact that I have many friends and acquaintances, I am still without a chosen helpmeet. Such an existence can become decidedly lonely."

Tamsin's face must have shown her shock, for she had always believed Mama's assertion that her sister Dahlia had freely and defiantly chosen a life of intellectualism in London despite her family's objection.

"Tamsin, I might have married had I been able—had the one I loved..." Dahlia shook her head and collected herself. "What I've created here"—she gestured to the house and all it symbolized—"was the life we had planned together, had we been able. So this life of intellectual and artistic pursuit you admire is not necessarily incompatible with a successful marriage."

Her aunt's surprising story of unfulfilled love made Tamsin ache with pity—and with more determination to fulfill her own destiny than ever. "I take your point, Aunt Dahlia. But I've no time to find the right fellow. With the peace, Papa plans to sell out of the Royal Marines, and wants our futures—and his estate—settled, and Mama says this season is my only chance to find someone other than Cousin Edward. It's most unreasonable to think I must decide about the entire rest of my life in so short a span—it simply can't be done."

"I take *your* point—you'd like me to appeal to your mama to let you stay in town longer, with me?"

"Why, yes! That would be lovely." But as much as her heart lifted at the thought that her object might be so easily and practically gain without recourse to ruination, Tamsin had little realistic hope that her mother would agree—Mama already thought Aunt Dahlia's set too "fast" for Tamsin to even attend salons, let alone stay permanently.

"Then I shall ask her, to please you," said Aunt Dahlia. "Though you must prepare yourself to be disappointed—your dear mama does not always like to listen to me. She thinks you're too beautiful for intellectualism."

"Beauty is not the same thing as character," Tamsin scoffed.

"Indeed." Aunt Dahlia smiled in her gentle way. "But do not be too hard upon your mama—she thinks you beautiful *because* of your character."

It was typically kind of her aunt to say so, even if Tamsin doubted it was true. "What Mama thinks is that beauty is currency, and that I must spend it whether I want to or not."

"It is the way—"

"—of the world," Tamsin finished. "So I've been told, though I should rather change the world than adapt myself to it."

"You are young and passionate, as you should be. I agree that you should have more time to choose your way, and I shall do my level best to persuade your mama to give it."

"Thank you, Aunt Dahlia. Thank you." It was both a pleasure and a relief to know she had such an ally within her own relations. "But what I should love more than anything would be to stay here with you always, and be your companion so you are never again lonely. Even if Mama does not approve."

"Sweet girl." Aunt Dahlia reached for her hand. "You are most welcome, my love, anytime, whether my sister Violet approves or not. But do not be in such a rush for spinsterhood, no matter how enticing it looks at present. My situation was only made tolerable because my mother and father had both died and I was able, through the disinterest of my guardian, to take control of my fortune. But I don't know if you shall be so lucky?"

"No," Tamsin had to admit. Though she and her sisters had respectable enough dowries, there was no guarantee that her parents would settle the money on her if she chose not to marry.

"Is there no one?" Aunt Dahlia asked. "No one that you might have singled out for your attention? Someone who might improve upon further acquaintance?"

Again, Colonel Simon Cathcart's sunny smile beamed out of her mind's eye. But she had singled Simple Simon out for attention for reasons that would hardly please her relations, even her liberal-minded aunt.

So she gave in to the lie that seemed to come too easily to her lips. "No one particularly special. No one at all, really."

But Aunt Dahlia was not born yesterday—she sat back and assessed her niece with narrower eyes. "Oh, my. I am almost afraid to ask what it is you're hatching in that too-clever head of yours."

"Nothing untoward, Aunt Dahlia."
At least nothing *too* untoward.
If she planned carefully.
And if she and Simon Cathcart got her ruination *just* right.

CHAPTER 5

"We have to get it just right," Miss Lesley instructed in her delightfully bossy way—Lord, how he loved a governess—when she sought him out in the library of the Viscountess Malmesbury's palatial house on Pall Mall.

"I am at your service, Miss T," Simon assured her, "if you will be so kind as to tell me what it is I'm to do."

"I've given it a great deal of thought," the young lady explained, donning the spectacles she dug out of her reticule, giving her that deliciously pert, governess-y air. "It is imperative that we be found privately rather than publicly. While I should like to be ruined—"

"Lightly ruined—do I still have that right?"

"Oh, yes." She was all serious scholarly consideration. "But I should like to be ruined with as little *éclat* as possible, so as to lose as little of my reputation—or yours—as can be managed."

Simon clearly didn't give a damn about his reputation—who else would pose as an idiot? And while he had no great confidence that ruination could be achieved without any *éclat*, he would give the attempt the old army try. "Don't worry about me, Miss T. I'm immune—no one wants a muzzy-brained dunderhead for a son-in-law."

201

Miss Lesley looked rather adorably put-out for him at such a characterization. "You're not such a dunderhead that you light yourself on fire," she said earnestly. "You're a very good, generous sort of person who will make some lovely woman a wonderful husband." She patted his arm in consolation. "Just not me."

Simon was surprised to find her words—though certainly kindly meant—gave him a pang. He had played his part too well, it seemed. And he needed to continue doing so. "If you say so, Miss T."

"I do." She gave his arm another consoling pat. "Now, I have arranged as best as possible to be found by my mama and not someone else, as that should serve our purposes best." She led the way upstairs, toward the back of the house. "The viscountess has a small, seldom-used morning room where she meets her housekeeper and writes her letters—"

Simon acted the dunce. "Never heard of a viscountess who writes letters to her housekeeper instead of just telling her what to do. But that's the nobility for you."

"No, she— That is—" Poor Miss Lesley's earnestness could not hold the line against such stupidity.

Simon pressed his idiot's advantage with another nonsensical speech. "But I suppose that's how generals order a battle—sending out dispatches and missives instead of merely shouting them at the top of their lungs—which they do an awful lot, I can tell you—so nothing gets garbled or mistaken in the furor. Superior strategy, I suppose. I salute Lady Malmesbury."

"I'm sure she'd be gratified at such praise," Miss Lesley offered kindly. "But what I meant to say was that the room should be suitable to our particular purpose—remote and private."

"Leaving nothing to chance, Miss T? Already reconnoitered? I salute you, too. You're a credit to your father, the marine colonel, what? You'd have made an excellent quartermaster."

She cast him a funny little sideways glance over the top of her spectacles. "Only a quartermaster and not a colonel? I thank you, but I should rather be the one giving the orders, rather than the one receiving them. Wouldn't you?"

"Damn me, no," he said, entirely honest. "God keep me from such a fate—I quit the army so they couldn't promote me."

"Really?" She turned to face him—man to man, as it were. "I've never heard of a career officer—or any man, for that matter—who didn't want promotion, or at least recognition."

"No, no." He had glanced too close to the truth—or at least a small portion of the truth. There was nothing for it but to renew his bid for incompetence. "Had more than my share of that sort of responsibility. Makes my brain ache something fierce, it does."

She sent a very long, considering glance his way, and seemed on the verge of saying something to the point, when they thankfully arrived at their destination. "Oh. Here we are."

The room was as small and discrete as she had described—it would do perfectly for a little light ruination.

"I think we should start in a basic position of compromise." His Colonel Lesley began to order the field of battle. "Here, where we can be readily seen, across from the door."

He was certainly a man who knew how to take an order. "Right ho. Which one?"

She stilled. And frowned. "Which door?" There was only one.

"Which position of compromise do you prefer, Miss T? There are, after all, so many."

Her face turned an enchanting shade of pink, and he didn't know when he'd last been so pleased with himself. Or so charmed. "Ah, yes, of course there are." She nodded, as if she had spent quite some time thinking of any number of intimately compromising positions to choose from. "I think a deep embrace."

"Deep embrace," he repeated, as if this required concentrated study. "But face to face, as I recall. Like this?" He came close enough to take a firm grasp of her upper arms, but no closer, as if they were about to dance.

"Yes, well," she hedged. "A bit closer, I should think. More like a waltz where one might not be interested in keeping one's proper distance."

"Right ho. Closer then." He gathered her into a more satisfactorily intimate embrace, sliding his arms across her upper arms and around her back, settling her snugly against his chest.

She stiffened and held her breath, clearly trying not to shy away, but as clearly not comfortable with the contact, and that rusty conscience of his inched its way out of its scabbard, forcing him to reconsider.

He loosened his embrace. "We'll just stay like this then, until we hear the door?"

"Yes, thank you." She nodded, trying to give every appearance of confidence, but her voice was thin and unsure, all breath and bravado. "Then perhaps I'll engage you more closely when she does come, if I may?"

"Right ho." Yes, poor Miss Tamsin Lesley had no idea what she was doing—behind her calm veneer, she was shaking like the veriest greenhorn at the sound of the charge.

Simon damned his rusty, creaking conscience, and abandoned his plans to amuse himself, setting himself instead to amuse *her*. "Your first time, then, being ruined?"

He was rewarded for his efforts by her lovely little huff of laughter. "Yes. Indeed." She nodded and took a steadier breath, and looked to the side so her pert chin brushed against his chest, and he found it suddenly strangely hard to breathe. "You?"

"Well, let me think on that." He winced up his eyes like a proper dunce so he might ponder that question. And so he wouldn't look down at her mouth, so close to his chest. "I don't suppose it is, really. Though this is my first *formal* ruining—never tried to get caught before."

"No." Another small, secretly sweet smile curved her lips, just down there, so deliriously close. "I don't imagine you would have done."

"No. And never before as a civilian, what?" He prattled on to keep from thinking about lips and closeness and the febrile heat from her small, perfectly lush body. "So that's new."

Another small infinity passed, during which he grew more and more aware of the shallow pattern of their breathing, chest against chest. Breast against—

Simon was racking his brain for another nonsensical idiocy when she asked, "How long have you been out of the army?"

Her question surprised him into honesty. "A while now, it's been," he reckoned. "Since the autumn. Glad to be back, what? When so many other, better fellows didn't make it."

Her level gaze met his for a long, serious moment. "I am very sorry for your losses, Colonel Cathcart. You must have lost a good many friends."

"Simon, please." He found himself clearing his throat and affecting an easy tone to cover the unexpected knot of emotion her kindness tangled up in his chest. "Lost a lot of men that weren't friends, too—not that that makes it any easier. See their faces at night sometimes." He couldn't seem to stop himself from rambling on. "It used to frighten me at first, but now I've come to rather like seeing old friends."

Damn him for a sentimental fool. Simon would have given himself a good shake if his hands hadn't been otherwise engaged.

"How difficult." There was something in her voice—something kind and not pitying—that had him blustering on, as if he might reassure her.

"Don't think it is, really," he rattled on. "Loads of chaps in my boots, so to speak, tell me the same. Not the coming to like it, of course." He truly was an idiot. "Not every one can come to grips." A talkative idiot. "Some of them tell me I'm mad."

This was why he hid out in libraries and pretended to sleep—so he wouldn't make a mad ass of himself.

But in the face of his madness, Miss Tamsin Lesley tucked her chin and considered her answer for only a moment. "I don't think you're mad. I think you're rather nice."

If he could have stopped up his ears against the kindness in her voice, he would have. "That's big of you, Miss T." Because his resistance to her bespectacled, governess-y charms was falling alarmingly low—any moment now he was going to have to bury his face against that soft slide of skin down the side of her neck and inhale the delicate warmth of her fragrance, and then where would they be?

Ruined, deliriously happy, and unhappily married. In that order.

Simon forced air into his lungs, and affected patience. "How much longer, do you think, your mama might be? Don't want to keep you overlong, if there's deserving fellows you ought to be dancing with."

She let out another lovely little self-deprecating huff of laughter before she shook her head. "Not a one. And not long—any moment now, I should think. It's been ten minutes since I told her I'd be gone for five." She glanced at the mantelpiece clock. "I can't think what might keeping her."

It really didn't matter what was keeping her, only that whatever it was went on keeping her. Because the moment the woman came and they were found out was the end of this lovely little charade. And, Simon realized with a sharp pang, he didn't want his interlude with the lovely Miss Lesley to end.

So he took the last shreds of his courage in hand, and spoke the truth. "I must say, Miss T, this has been rather delightful. Don't know when I've been so diverted. Rather hate to see the fun end, what?"

"Thank you, Colonel Cathcart."

"Simon, please."

"Simon, then. Under the circumstances," she murmured as she tipped her face up toward his, and he was already leaning down, nearing those soft, bitten lips, knowing that he shouldn't and doing it anyway.

"Sweet T," he heard himself murmur. "Are you sure—"

"Yes?" she breathed, before he could finish.

But before he could act upon the impulse and kiss her properly and assuage the strange ache within him, her face turned abruptly toward the door.

"Oh, bloody drat! She's here!"

CHAPTER 6

"Tamsin Lesley," Mama hissed the moment she was through the door and had it securely locked behind her. "What in heaven's name do you think you're doing?"

Tamsin kept herself from stating the obvious. "Oh, Mama! It's not what you think—" She clung to Colonel Cathcart for a moment longer than was strictly necessary before pushing apart, as if she were trying not to be caught. Though his arms had at first tightened around her, much to her disappointment, Cathcart let her go.

Granted, Mama was advancing upon them like a force of nature—all frost and frowns as hard as hailstones. "Come away from that man! And take those hideous spectacles off." She interposed herself between them and glared at Colonel Cathcart. "Who," Mama asked in her most thunderous tones, "are you?"

Tamsin answered before Colonel Cathcart might say something nonsensical about her engaging him for the business. "Pray do not blame him, Mama. I—"

"Oh, never fear, I've blame enough to go around, my girl. What on earth were you thinking?"

Tamsin cast what she hoped was a longing look at Colonel Cathcart. "I can't help it, Mama. He quite took my breath away."

"Well, fetch it back this instant." Her mama kept her forceful sense of logic even in a crisis. "Now, tell me, who *is* he?"

"I fear you will not approve." Tamsin attempted to look suitably apoplectic. "He is a handsome face who has won my heart and turned my fancy—"

"You just turn that fancy back around, my girl." Her mother was not buying a Drury Lane farthing's worth of her show. "Get out of his arms this minute, before anyone sees." Mama turned her ire on Colonel Cathcart. "Speak up, sir. Who *are* you?"

Colonel Cathcart smiled and bowed to Mama, as if they were at the side of the dance floor and not caught in an illicit embrace. "Simon Cathcart, at your service, Mrs. Lesley."

So much for keeping the man's name out of it.

Mama was nonplussed. "I rather think you were already at my daughter's service, sir. But Cathcart, was it?" Tamsin could all but see her mother leafing through the pages of the peerage stored in the attic library of her mind. "The Scottish Cathcarts?"

Simon was all enthusiasm. "Why, yes, ma'am! My family are from Renfrewshire."

Mama's ambitions lit her face like a chandelier—it took only a short leap for her imagination to travel from Castle Cathcart in Renfrewshire to St. George's Church in Hanover Square. "The Honorable Simon Cathcart?"

"That is my father!" Colonel Cathcart crowed. "Do you know him?"

Mama's hopes instantly dimmed into disappointment. "I have not that pleasure. I but know the name."

The colonel was entirely undaunted by her waning enthusiasm. "Makes sense, what, as Pater rarely leaves Renfrewshire. Prefers the country, you see."

"So you're the—"

"Second son of a second son, Mama." Tamsin decided to speed things along. "I know it's a scandal, but I love him anyway."

"We'll see about that." Mama too, wanted to get the heart of the business. "Mr. Cathcart, have you any money?"

"Afraid not." He patted his pockets as if they might miraculously have filled with gold while he was sleeping, and was astonished to find a sovereign, which he offered to her mama. "Need it for the cards, do you? Happy to contribute."

"I most emphatically do not need money for cards!" Mama had seen and heard more than enough—she shackled Tamsin's wrist in an implacable grip. "Come along!"

"But what about the scandal?"

"There will be no scandal," Mama vowed. "Not if I have anything to say about it." She turned a cool eye on Colonel Cathcart. "You, sir, would do well to keep this unfortunate interview entirely to yourself. Do you understand me?"

"Ma'am, yes, ma'am." Colonel Cathcart gave her mother a smart salute. "Happy to oblige."

"I imagine you are," her mama concluded.

Tamsin was not yet ready to give up. She broke from her mother's grasp and pushed toward Colonel Cathcart, who had enough presence of mind to put his arm around her, gathering her comfortably in the shelter of his broad chest. "But Mama, I cannot lie, though it shames me. I know I am ruined and—"

"Hush." Mama held up her hand in absolute command. "Do not say such a thing. Not another word!"

"But you saw us—I fear we were in the most embarrassingly compromising position," Tamsin insisted. "The scandal—"

"Don't be silly!" Mama was once again emphatic. "You're not ruined because of one little kiss or cuddle." She busied herself slapping the creases out of Tamsin's skirts. "You're very lucky it was me who found you and not some tattletale." She reached again for her daughter's hand. "Come along, Thomasina. And for the last time, take off those wretched spectacles."

Tamsin turned to poor Simple Simon who, true to his name, stood as placidly and unbowed as a tall tree in a storm. He gave her that amiable, hail-fellow-well-met smile, as if the whole affair had gone swimmingly and was not an utter disaster.

"I'm so sorry, Colonel Cathcart." Tamsin didn't know what else to say.

But Colonel Cathcart did. "Simon, please. And not at all," the big fellow rejoined. "Can't remember the last time I had such jolly good fun." He tossed her a remarkably happy but at the same time nearly naughty wink. "Let's do it again sometime, shall we?"

Though the evening had turned out to be a complete disaster, the next morning brought a flower shop's worth of posies and stems. Enough blooms to put roses in her mama's cheeks, as well as on every flat surface of the reception rooms in their cavernous, rented Mayfair townhouse.

Most were the usual hothouse posies—roses, scented carnations and forget-me-nots sent by men whose names she had already forgotten. But someone had set a dozen stems of ravishingly beautiful lavender tulips. And though the accompanying card was unsigned, it contained two lines written in a bold but carelessly slanted hand.

Great fun, what? Hope I served honorably.

Just the sort of happy, kind and somehow appropriate thing she was pleased to find characteristic of Colonel Simon Cathcart.

"What an unusual bouquet," Mama noted.

"Mmm, yes." Tamsin palmed the card and attempted to sound uninterested.

Her mama was not fooled. "Who sent them?"

In for a penny, in for several hundred pounds. Tamsin schooled back her smile and attempted to look pensive, while letting the card slide into a convenient splash of water that had beaded on the tabletop. "That handsome chap, what's his name, that you introduced me to...?"

"Lord James Beauclerc? The Duke of Albany's heir? Tall fellow, sandy blond hair?"

Tamsin pictured a different tall, handsome, sandy-haired man. But she conjured Lord James Beauclerc's image into her mind's eye, and described someone else. "Blue Bath superfine coat? Buff trousers?

"Good Lord, no. No, Lord James was in an impeccable black merino coat with a cream satin waistcoat, breeches and evening slippers, just as he ought." Her mama liked the old fashioned ways of dress best. Nothing of the modern era had any appeal for her.

"Oh, yes. Now I recall." Tamsin glanced down to make sure the ink on the card had sufficiently run. "At least I think it is from him, but it's so badly writ, I'm not sure. I can't make it out—at least, not without my spectacles. See if you can make anything out of this, Mama."

Her mama gladly took the proffered card. "Why, it's hopelessly damp—the ink's all run out."

"Must have been jostled and wetted by the Beauclerc footman on his way here, though I didn't see who brought it. Perhaps we could find who brought them to the door, to confirm they came from the Duke of Albany's house?"

"No, no," Mama objected. "No need to involve the servants in your business—that would be hopelessly gauche." Her mother's mind was made up. "And there are posies enough to ensure your reputation as a diamond of the first water."

Reputation was all—currency and capital—in her mama's way of looking at the world.

Tamsin would definitely ensure her reputation—if not exactly in the way her mama intended. But she would have to reapply to Colonel Simon Cathcart for his ready assistance.

Let's do it again sometime.

Sometime was now.

If she could conjure up enough nerve for another try. If she could make it more convincing next time.

And what did she have to lose, aside from obnoxious Cousin Edward?

"Mama, I'll be in my room, writing letters."

Arranging her next faux tryst.

CHAPTER 7

His utterly transparent ploy worked—an elegantly brief missive from Miss Lesley was delivered to him in the Cathcart House library by the afternoon post via Mahoney, his resourceful batman.

> *I will not allow my mother's interference to be anything other than an* <u>obstacle</u> *to my ends. I would make another attempt if you are game. If so, I will look for you in the library of Worcester House—for we go there this evening.*
>
> *—T*

Simon found that he was indeed game, though he had no idea if he was to be at Worcester House that evening—normally, he simply presented himself, appropriately dressed at the appropriate hour, and went where his aunt's carriage took him. He accompanied her to dinners where he found food for his weary body, wine for his addled brain, and gossip as fodder for his fertile imagination without taxing himself. After the dinners, when the gentlemen retreated to cigars and cognac and self-serving lies about sacrifice and patriotism, Simon took his leave and headed for the peace and tranquility of the libraries, where he could rest his head and dream amusing dreams.

But for Miss Lesley, he would inquire. He would *arrange*.

Even if it meant exposing his flank.

"Mahoney, where am I to be found this evening amongst the *Beau Monde*?"

If Mahoney was at all surprised to find his former superior officer inquiring after something in which Simon had never before expressed any interest, like any good solider, he kept it to himself. "The countess requires escort for dinner with the Wallingford's on Mount Street, and then will attend either the Basingstoke or the Worcester Ball."

"Need it to be the Worcester ball, Mahoney. Can that be arranged?"

The clever Irishman tipped his head, and revealed some of the resourcefulness that had seen them through years of arduous campaigns. "A hint, sir, can be placed with her ladyship's dresser. I understand the arrangements at the Worcester affair will be vastly superior to the Basingstoke decorations."

"Excellent. I am all appreciation for a superior arrangement. Good man."

"Thank you, Colonel. Any other particulars I might arrange for you, sir?"

"No, nothing else, I thank you."

And if Simon took extra care with his appearance that evening, his batman was canny enough to say nothing. Neither did his aunt, the Countess Cathcart, when Simon arrived with her at the Worcester Ball and did not immediately seek the sanctuary of the library, as was his wont.

Instead, he took the opportunity to escort his aunt to a seat of honor in the ballroom, from whence she might regard the whole of the room. And he might reconnoiter his Miss T across the lines, as it were. Purely for observations purposes—know your allies as well as you know your enemies was as good a practice in love as it was in war.

Not that this was love. Or war. It was simple fun.

An interesting way to pass a tedious evening.

His interest had nothing to do with the thrill of anticipation, the intoxicating rush of blood through his veins at the thought of having the delightful Miss Tamsin Lesley in his arms again. Nothing to do with her personally, really. Nothing to do with her irresistibly governess-y air.

Nothing at all.

But finding her in the crowded ballroom was difficult. Firstly, she was attired in the same sort of flowing skirts of white as all the other young ladies, like so many identical columns in a Grecian temple. Secondly, she was so small in stature that it took only two taller gentlemen—and damn their heads—to block his view. But mostly because she was not wearing her lovely spectacles.

That they were needed was evidenced by her narrowed-eyed squint when she turned to check the time on the clock mounted over the mantelpiece, as if she were perhaps as anxious as he for their appointment.

Not that he was anxious. Not at all. He was simply drawn to her.

That he was bored and she was diverting—so very diverting with her wide, questioning eyes magnified by those strangely seductive spectacles—was adequate to explain his strange sense of...*hope*.

Which was ridiculous, of course. To Miss T, he was simply the means to an end—a happily spinsterish end. And end he would help her reach most enjoyably.

"Well, Simon, to what do we owe your presence and attention in the ballroom?" his aunt Cathcart finally asked in a low, amused voice. "Do tell me her name so I might be the first to wish you happy."

Simon deflected her interest with his usual nonsensical banter. "Thought I might give it a try, what? But no, my darling aunt—still makes my head spin, what? Afraid I must be off to my usual haunt."

"Haunting, or rather hiding, in the library?"

"Keeping peacefully in the library, never you fear." He bestowed a quick kiss upon her cheek, and a fond pat upon her hand. "Take your time and send for me when you are ready to leave, but not before."

And away he went down the stairs to the library wing to arrange things to tell the story his Miss T wanted told.

The first job was to clear out extraneous characters. "Make yourself scarce, Hastings, old man." He tipped up the fellow's chair to all but spill him out of it. "Go find somewhere else to hide this evening."

"What? Where am I to go?"

"Some. Where. Else." Simon didn't have time to sketch out the particulars for young Hastings. "If you make yourself scarce, I promise to return the favor someday very soon."

Hastings balked. "I don't have anywhere else to go."

Simon dug deep into his pocket and extracted a golden guinea. "Here, go find the card room and have a flutter."

The young man stood stubbornly flat-footed. "But I don't gamble."

"Then now's the time to try," Simon rejoined with decreasing patience. "Do what you will with it. Just leave me in peace, if you please."

"What about my peace?" Hastings grumbled. "What's gotten into you?"

"Haven't the slightest idea, old man. I'm eccentric like that, what?"

Simon had the library to himself and had made himself negligently comfortable in an armchair before the glowing hearth by the time Miss Lesley poked her myopic nose around the door.

"Miss T!" Simon covered his strange jangling excitement by hailing her amiably. "Over here."

She retrieved her spectacles from her reticule and returned them to their proper place on the end of her divinely pert nose, resuming her delightfully curious, deliciously governess-y air. "Colonel Cathcart. Good evening."

"Simon, please, Miss T." He found himself standing, rubbing his hands together in happy anticipation, too nervy to sit. "What's it to be this evening, then?"

But Miss Lesley shared none of his enthusiasm for a rush to ruination. "Before we do get started, I should like to thank you for the tulips, but urge you to greater caution should you ever be required send flowers again. Though I can't think of why you would be—this evening should see the end of our association."

Her warning doused the spark of his enthusiasm like a bucket of sand. "Caution?"

"My mama remarked upon their beauty and extravagance straightaway."

Discretion was clearly the better part of valor, and he needed to re-learn what it meant to be discreet. He took her meaning, even as he pretended not to. "Thought they were pretty, what? Reminded me of you."

The lovely warm blush that pinked her cheeks was his thanks. "You are very kind, I'm sure, sir." She gave up trying to urge him to any greater sense, and turned to the business at hand. "As to our agreement, I should like to make a slight change from my original plan."

His disappointed hope made him puckish. "Indeed?" His object, he decided, would be to see how many euphemisms he might elicit from her—how many inventive ways she would politely circumvent the delicate topic of trying of only appear to have *sex*. "Is it kissing that you want?"

Her blush went from pink to a deep, rosy coral, but she held her ground like a trooper. "I think our object can be achieved with only an *escalation*, if you will, from our first…*embrace*."

Two points straight off the line. "I'm afraid I don't have the pleasure of understanding you, Miss T. Are you sure it's not kissing that you want? Best to give me clear orders, what?"

She did so, as politely and euphemistically as possible. "No. That is… I think it best, if this evening, when we are found, if your hands were rather particularly upon my person."

Particularly upon my person. Four more points to Army.

He schooled his mirth into a show of dim curiosity. "Right ho! Which part of your person? In particular?"

"Well," she hedged. "I don't think it really matters which, just that when Mama comes through the door this time, things appear a great deal more…advanced."

"What a capital idea." He beamed at her. "But if I might make a suggestion?"

Simon was ashamed to find she looked a little astonished that he might have cobbled two thoughts together at all. "Please!"

"To achieve the effect you're after—"

"Lightly ruined," she reminded him.

"Indeed, lightly ruined, Miss T." He arranged his face into a serious, considering frown. "In order to be lightly ruined, I suggest that my hand be found *lightly* upon your breast."

That she was shocked was apparent by the widening of her already wide eyes. That she was also seriously considering his proposition was made manifest by their slow narrowing. "I see your point, Mr. Cathcart." She cleared her throat slightly. "Which breast, do you suppose?"

He gave every appearance of studious thought. "While they are both equally lovely, I assure you, Miss T, I should think whichever of them is closest to the door, in order to provide the view you are intent to achieve?"

She took a shaky breath of equitable consideration. "Yes, very sensible."

"Thank you." And because he had clearly spoken too sensibly, he added, "I thought it was a jolly good idea, if I do say so myself."

And because he was a considerate, thoughtful sort of idiotic cad, he rubbed his palms together to warm them. And then he smiled and asked, "If I may?"

CHAPTER 8

Tamsin *ought* to have known what to do. And say. Because she was the one arranging this ruination, wasn't she? But she hardly knew how to act. Or where to look. Or how to breathe.

But she heard herself say, "Yes, do," and hoped she sounded more worldly than she felt while her heart stuttered in her chest.

She leaned back in an awkward attempt to grant him some sort of greater access.

And still, she was entirely unprepared for the indescribable feeling of his palm closing 'round the whole of her breast. All at once.

Her lungs seized up in some strange attempt to make herself as small and still as possible. But then, of course, she held her breath too long, and practically had to gasp for air. Which, of course, made her chest expand into the warm pressure of his hand in a sort of involuntary, but entirely too-pleasurable caress, when his thumb, most particularly, brushed against her bare skin above the neckline of her gown.

Heat scorched across her face and down her neck, no doubt pinking her from forehead down to where his hand sent a thrill blazing across her brea—

Best not to think of the thrill. Best to keep her eyes closed and concentrate on breathing evenly. In and out. In a normal sort of cadence. Nothing untoward.

"That's it, what?" he murmured as if he knew all about what was normal. "Just keep breathing."

Tamsin attempted to do so, though his other arm had made its way to the small of her back, where it urged her closer to his chest. Closer into his embrace. So close, she could smell the bright scent of starch on his cravat. And feel the warmth of his body seeping through the intervening layers of clothing. And sense the extraordinarily intimate press of his hand subtly changing position upon her breast.

Oh, holy heavens. A mixture of heat and mortification and want washed across her skin so strongly that for the first time in her life, Tamsin feared that she might actually faint.

Because she liked it. Very much.

But this was meant to be an *arrangement* with Colonel Cathcart, not a tryst.

Tamsin attempted to assert logic to keep the topsy-turvy feelings at bay. "What can be keeping her?" she asked at the same time that she hoped whatever it was took a good deal longer. Hours or even days longer.

Because she had never felt so...*everything*. Everything so utterly delightful.

"Patience," he whispered closer to her ear. "Would it help if I..." And as if he meant to soothe her with his hand as well as his low voice, he began to absently brush his thumb back and forth along her skin.

"Oh, yes." Though she did not feel the least bit soothed—beneath her stays and chemise, her nipples went tight and achy. It was the most disconcerting, uncomfortable, pleasurable thing that had ever happened to her. And she prayed he would stop.

She was happy he did not.

Because the feeling was extraordinary. And rather wonderful.

"Such interesting things, breasts," he murmured, as if he were talking about the weather or the stock market, or some other phenomena wholly out of his ken. "Lovely, soft, firm things. Yours has gone a bit firm, hasn't it, Miss T?"

"Yes." She swallowed over the sudden drought in her throat. "I suppose it has."

He must have heard unease in her voice. "Too much, Miss T?"

"Yes." She was relieved and embarrassed and bereft, all at the same time. "A bit."

"Right ho." But he said it quietly, as if he were thinking. And then he slowly slid his hand away toward her back, where his clever fingers began a careful exploration of her spine, from the bare skin at the top of her nape down, over the layers of silk and linen and whalebone, to mesh snugly with its partner in the small of her back. "Better?"

Now the firm pressure of his hands urging her deeper into the embrace was comforting instead of titillating. And when she gave in to the temptation to find out what it would feel like to lean all the way against the solid breadth of his chest, his hands swept up to lightly play with her hair.

"Yes." She grasped for something to say that wouldn't make her the veriest, most breathless ninny. "I thank you."

His fingers traced little spirals at her nape. "This is rather lovely, what?" But his tone held none of his former hail-fellow enthusiasm, but instead a sort of quiet wonder. "I think we're getting a better feel for this ruination, now."

"Yes, quite." She felt it, too, the lovely wonder. It really was quite nice to be held so securely within his arms. It felt as if she wasn't…alone.

Even though that was exactly why she was doing this—to be left alone.

How…odd.

"If I might make another suggestion, Miss T?"

"Certainly," she agreed, because it seemed necessary that one of them think, and she didn't seem capable of rational thought at the moment.

"Perhaps we might sit? In this chair? Bit tiring, all this ruination, standing up."

"Oh, I did not realize—"

But Colonel Cathcart didn't wait for her apology—he had already somehow picked her up, and settled her upon his lap as effortlessly as if they were making a turn at the waltz. "That's better." He made himself comfortable against the back of the chair and urged her to relax against his chest. "I can put my hand on your lovely breast again now, if you'd like, Miss T?"

That was the stratagem for the evening, wasn't it? Her mama couldn't ignore something so personal. So deeply intimate. "Yes, that would be...suitable."

Oh, holy heavens. There it was again, that thoughtfully gentle, but somehow firm, press of his palm against her breast, and the indescribably lovely, full feeling that followed.

So personal. So deeply intimate. Tamsin was mortified and gratified and aroused, all at the same time.

"That's nice," he murmured. "Almost as if it fits there, what—my hand on your breast," he clarified helpfully, in case she was somehow unaware of what he was talking about, or where his hand was.

But it *was* almost as if his hand was the exact right size to comfortably cup her breast, or perhaps her breast was the right size to fill his hand—she had no idea of how one measured such things. Or if one should. Or anything else, except the strangely thrilling feeling of delicious, curious, comfortable anticipation that was enveloping her.

"Do you mind if I...?" His other hand seemed to have found its way to her hip.

"Oh, yes," she answered. "I think it will look correct if your other hand is covering my haunch."

He cocked his head, as if he were not sure if he had heard her aright. "Your…?

"Haunch," she repeated, feeling her face flame higher. "My backside."

"Ah. Right ho." But this time, his nonsensical banter felt more like a benediction. "Your sweet bottom, do you mean, Miss T? For it is lovely, as bottoms go."

"Thank you." *As bottoms go.*

"Quite welcome, Miss T. Happy to oblige. Quite happy."

And so they were still quite alone, for her mama still did not come.

Tamsin redirected her mind to marshal her arguments for when Mama did come. She took a deep, clarifying breath and edged herself bit to the right, away from the chair arm poking into her bottom so that Mama would get such an eyeful, she could not possibly gainsay the scandal.

"Right *ho*." Colonel Cathcart's voice took on a different pitch—he sounded almost…pained.

"Are you all to rights, Colonel?" She tried to shift again, to make him more comfortable as well. "I beg your pardon, but something was pressing into my…my…"

"Lady bits?" His voice was curtailed, and abrupt. "Yes, mine too."

"Oh. Oh, I see." But she didn't really. Because how could Colonel Cathcart have *lady bits*? But then as she shifted again, the bit pressing into her seemed to…move. Or…grow. "Oh!"

He met her shocked gaze. "Indeed."

"Is that your…"

He drew a short breath. "Cock, Miss T," he specified. "Indeed, that's my cock. Apologies."

There was a pause the length and breadth of Tavistock Square before she could even begin to formulate any answer. "I do beg your pardon, Colonel. How…uncomfortable that must be."

"Simon, please, under the circumstances. Don't trouble yourself, Miss T. I assure you, I'm well used to the phenomenon."

"Phenomenon?"

"Aye. It's not always in this state, my cock. It's just the circumstance of having you so near." He smiled down at her in his sunny, uncomplicated way, but it was as if the longer he held her eye, the harder it was to keep the expression upon his face. As if the sunshine was overshadowed by something deeper, something darker and more honest and intimate. "Pray don't concern yourself."

His voice was low and quiet and very, very near. So near, she could see the flecks of gold and black in his green eyes. Could count his individual eyelashes. So near, she was already imagining what the firm fruit of his lower lip might taste like against hers.

So near. Just...there. If she straightened up just a little more, she might find out. Might discover for herself what all the fuss was about.

"My dear Miss T," he whispered. "Perhaps, since we've touched on breasts, and haunches, and cocks, we really ought to spare a moment for lips?"

"Yes." She finally found her breath. And her voice. And her nerve. "Yes, that would seem eminently suit—"

"Good Lord Almighty, Thomasina Lesley! I told you to stay away from this man."

They sprang apart this time, flustered and awkward, fumbling to stand.

But Simon seemed to have some presence of mind. "Dear Mrs. Lesley." He stood and stepped behind the chair. "How nice—"

"Don't you *dear* me." Mama snatched Tamsin out of his reach as if she feared her daughter might catch something. "What on Earth are you playing at with this man? You know they call him Simple Simon."

"Mama!" Anger, and something that had to be shame scorched her skin. The poor man was right there. He might not be the smartest whip in the race, but he was a very nice man, and he had ears enough to comprehend the slight against him. "Please."

"If *you* please," her mother returned. "Simple Simon," she repeated. "Not to put too fine a point on it, but they say he's not right in the head and would be in Bedlam but for his well-connected relations."

Tamsin found herself stepping in front of him, as if she might shield him from her mother's casual cruelty. "Mama, I know what we've done is wrong, but there is no reason for you to attack poor Colonel Cathcart like this."

"Listen to yourself—*poor Colonel Cathcart*. A colonel," her mother huffed. "I won't let you make the same mistake I did and be brought to grief over a shining uniform. And if that isn't reason enough, I don't know what is. You've lost your head, girl, and I aim to make sure that this"—she gestured from her daughter to Simon—"unfortunate liaison goes no further. Come along."

She took possession of Tamsin's arm, and rather than turn her into a ragdoll being pulled between them, Simon let her go.

"Nice to see you, too, Mrs. Lesley," he said in his sweet, sunny way.

His easy self-possession took Mama aback. She turned to Tamsin. "He really isn't all to rights in his brain, is he?"

"The Peninsular War—" Tamsin began

"Took a saber at Vitoria, what?" Simon explained helpfully. "Hell of a thing."

"Indeed it must have been," Mama said, not unfeelingly. "And indeed it were best for you to rest quiet and recover yourself after such an injury. So best to end things with my daughter here, yes?"

"If you say so, ma'am." He was the picture of helpful concession.

"I do." Mama was nothing if not emphatic. "Though it is a shame—you do have a lovely sort of face."

"I like yours, too, ma'am. And your daughter's. She's a lovely sort of young woman. A credit to you, ma'am."

"Thank you. You've manners, I'll grant you that, Cathcart," Mama admitted. "But keep your distance from my girl. For your own sake, as well as hers. Do I make my self clear?"

"I think so, ma'am."

"Then back to your spot here in the library." She shooed him toward the fireplace. "Or the conservatory with the rest of the potted plants," she muttered more unkindly under her breath as she towed Tamsin out the door.

As soon as they were alone, Tamsin pulled from her grasp. "Stop it, Mama. I won't have it."

"I'll tell you what you won't have, my girl—any more of that fellow." She reeled Tamsin into a sheltered nook beneath the stair. "You're too intelligent for this to be an accident, Tamsin. And I'm too intelligent not to see your ploy for what it is."

If Tamsin had thought she felt breathless and foolish before with Simon, it was nothing to the way her mother's stare made her feel—small and stupid. "And what is that?"

"You think you can eat your cake and have it still—you think you will manage this witless Simon Cathcart into agreeing to marry you. That he won't object to your salons and studies and books and biographies of Bess the Bitch, and who knows what else. But who is to keep you—who is to pay for you to take tea and talk? Not your father, I can tell you. He's barely got a penny set aside that's not to go with the entailed estate, you mark my word. You'll have nothing to live on nothing. Nothing."

Mama's face was white with the stark truth of her words. "Mark my words, Tamsin, and think hard."

CHAPTER 9

The new day dawned so clear and so cold, the wind off the Thames drove all the way up to Simon's snug retreat on Hampstead Heath—whence he decamped from Cathcart House after his rout at the Worcester ball—and rattled its way under the sash of his bedchamber window. He would have closed his eyes and burrowed back under the covers to dream about the divine Miss T and her even more divine haunches, if Mahoney had not come bearing a tale of mischief.

"Note for you, Colonel, delivered by an urchin who didn't even wait to be paid."

"What kind of self-respecting urchin doesn't wait for a vail," Simon groused.

It was rhetorical question, but one that his self-respecting batman felt bound to answer. "One sent from Cathcart House, sir?"

That fact got his attention. "Really? My aunt hardly seems the sort to employ urchins." Simon resigned himself to his fate and threw back the covers. "But the ways of the female mind are mysterious and deep and likely forever unknown to us mere men."

Mahoney handed him a heavy robe. "If you say so, sir. The note doesn't appear to be from her ladyship, the countess, but merely forwarded by her."

Simon breathed a sigh of relief and reached for the steaming cup of coffee in Mahoney's other hand. His aunt was one of the few people he had trusted to tell about the house in Hampstead, his secret bolt-hole to retreat to and be himself away from the prying, judgmental eyes of Society. "So who is it from?"

"My guess would be a determined, enterprising lass."

Ah. There was only one determined, enterprising lass he wanted it to be—the sprightly, determined lass who had literally stood up for him last evening.

No one—not his uncle or aunt, the Earl and Countess Cathcart, nor even the Duke of Wellington, for whom he had fought and bled for many long years—had ever objected to the characterization of him as "Simple" Simon. Tamsin Lesley stood alone in his regard. And his attraction.

Simon took the missive and cracked the seal. "Right in two, Mahoney. Brilliantly determined, and sublimely enterprising." The note of course, was from the determined Miss Lesley.

"What's the reccy, sir? So I know what kind of clothes I'm to put out."

The few short lines from his characteristically to-the-point young lady asked him to yet another rendezvous. "It seems I am going ice-skating, Mahoney—on the Serpentine River in Hyde Park. So make of my wardrobe what you will."

The terse Munsterman let out a low whistle. "Oh, there's a lass behind that outing, and no doubt."

"No doubt at all, my good man." Simon was nothing if not scrupulously honest with his servant—because there was no lying to a man who had stood by him at his worst, and prompted him to be his best through three arduous, bloody campaigns.

"I should advise two pairs of wool socks, sir."

Simon took a long sip of the blessedly scalding morning brew. "Just like the old days in the Peninsula?"

"Aye, sir. They do say courting is just like going soldiering."

"Do they?" Simon wasn't courting. He was just having fun, helping a lovely young woman he had come to admire. And like. And find delightfully attractive.

But clearly he was doing something very like courting, if he was rigging himself out to skate. Something…risky.

"It might be so, Mahoney—I reckon it's nearly as dangerous." Because there were two glaring problems with such a plan—he would have to ice skate. And he would have to ice skate *with her*. And keep his hands—and other, more tender parts of his body, like his reckless heart—to himself. "I'm not even sure I remember how."

"I shouldn't let that bother you, sir. They say it's like riding a horse—or a wife. Once you begin, you'll remember how soon enough to get on."

There was nothing for it, of course. "While you're dispensing socks and dubious advice, Mahoney, I also stand in immediate need of a pair of ice skates."

Miss Lesley, the efficient, practical minx, had arrived at the frozen Serpentine ahead of him, and already wore her skates. And her delightful spectacles, which glinted in the winter sun. But as she was seated on a bench next to a bevy of other cloaked and swansdown-wrapped young ladies, Simon waited until she had glided away from her escort before making his approach.

Mercifully, Mahoney's prognostications proved correct, and within a few strides, Simon was gliding along like a Dutchman, tipping his hat as he came up beside Miss Lesley. "What ho, Miss T. Grand day for it, what?"

"Colonel Cathcart!" She came to a neat, controlled stop, as if she had spent countless winters skating on Somerset's ponds.

Oh, how he liked the competent ones.

"Thank you so very much for coming, Colonel. I thought such an outing—without my mama—might provide a better chance to talk and arrange things."

"Simon, please. At your service, Miss T."

"Why don't we—" She gestured for them to skate along, in the opposite direction from her friends, keeping a goodly distance apart from him until they were well out of range. "Thank you for meeting me yet again."

"Apologies I can't seem to get you sufficiently ruined, Miss T," he offered in bluff, idiot mode. "Sorry my efforts at a convincing embrace were not up to snuff."

"It was not your embrace that was not up to snuff," she consoled as she glided along. "As determined as I am to be ruined, I fear my mother is equally determined to keep me from being declared so."

Simon said the first simply natural, and simply stupid, thing that came into his clearly damaged head. "I fear your mother could find us naked in a snow bank, with you riding my cock and whipping me like a racehorse, and still say nothing."

Miss Lesley stumbled and Simon just barely kept her from going down and cracking her knees against the ice. "Your pardon, Miss T. Shouldn't have said that, what?"

But he had said it. It was likely the crassest thing he had *ever* said—and he had lived amongst soldiers for years on end. Perhaps all this playacting had actually gone to his head, and he was becoming as mad an idiot as they said.

Because lovely Tamsin Lesley had gone as pale as a candle in one breath, and then burst into flame on another—spots of high color radiated from her cheeks.

"Well, yes, exactly," she stammered before she regained some of that marvelous, governess-y aplomb. "But should that happen, even my mama would be forced to give way."

Oh, how he *liked* her.

Liked her self-possession. Loved her dry sense of humor.

"I should bloody well hope so." Because if he was mad, he was mad for her. And growing madder by the minute.

"While I hope such extremes won't be necessary"—she resumed their conversation where she had left off—"I have come to the conclusion that you were in fact right, Colonel—it is kissing that we want."

"Right ho!" Perhaps he wasn't so mad after all.

"It will be most disagreeable, of course, but I fear it must be attempted."

Simon's ears rang as if he'd taken another French saber. "Most disagreeable?" He could not have heard her aright. "How so, Miss T?"

She shrugged and wrinkled her nose. "Well, you know, all slop and press. But I am convinced a kiss, however disagreeable, will be something that not even my mother can ignore."

All slop and press. Truly, Simon did not know whether he wanted to kick or thank all those stupendously unaccommodating men who had given her disagreeable kisses her in the past.

"Reckon you're right about your mater." He addressed one subject before he was confident enough to address the other. "Not to act the blaggard Miss T, but I've never had a kiss that I would describe as all *slop and press*."

"Oh, well, that must be because women are kissing you, and not the other way 'round."

Simon could not let that piece of illogic pass. Yet still he tried. "Tell you what—why don't we give it a go? Bit of a reccy run, so we go into the live fight with dry powder, what?"

She turned that spectacled focus upon him. "Are you saying that we ought to practice?"

"Just so," he enthused. "Shouldn't like you to have to endure

233

anything like slop and press." The very words offended him. He would hand her a pistol and ask her to put him out of his misery if she ever described his kiss thusly. "You can give me directions, just like last time, to make sure I get it right."

"That's very thoughtful of you, Colonel Cathcart."

"Simon, please." One of these days she was going to call him by his Christian name. Like an intimate. "Just shouldn't like to be thought of as sloppy, Miss T."

"Indeed," she agreed. "When might we meet to do so?"

No time like the present was still good advice. But the frozen Serpentine was no place for a tryst. There was, however, a small, wild island, covered with snow-dusted trees that would provide more than adequate coverage. "Why don't we go there? Now?"

Her brows rose, but she took in one of her strengthening breaths and firmed her chin. "I suppose that would do."

It did do—there was even a conveniently fallen tree trunk jutting out onto the ice that acted as a bench for them to remove their skates. But they never got to unstrapping the metal blades.

Because once they were seated side by side, it seemed quite natural to take her mittened hand in his, and give it an encouraging squeeze. And raise it to his lips for a wooly kiss. And since he was already there, and she was so close, he leaned in.

Slowly.

So slowly, she could adjust and turn away from him if she chose. So slowly, she could not mistake his intentions. So slowly he could not mistake hers.

He slowed time even more by turning his hand so the backs of his gloveless fingers caressed the soft curve of her cheek. And in those extra seconds, gained a world of sensation—her skin, soft against the rough of his hand. Her warmth against his chill. Her steadiness against his onslaught.

No. He wouldn't allow it to be an onslaught—this wasn't a charge, cavalry mounted and swords drawn. It was an invitation, slow and sensuous and as pleasurable as he knew how to make it

—so she was the woman kissing him, and not the other way 'round.

He tilted his head to better fit hers, and waited until she did the same. He let his gaze fall to her mouth, and watched patiently, until hers did as well. He parted his lips in readiness, ever so slightly, breathing in her essence, all but willing her to do the same.

Willing her to ease nearer. And nearer still.

He meant to watch—to watch and wait and understand—correctly interpreting her actions, gauging her interest and consent. Keeping himself from anything that could be in any way thought of as a *press*. Assessing her enthusiasm.

But he could not sustain the detachment, the distance required to hold himself back. His eyes slid shut, and all he could do was feel. And wait for the first cool, tentative fluttering of her lips against his. And the exquisite sensation of her lips settling more firmly upon his.

And then she was kissing him, and nothing else mattered, or even existed. No ice, no snow, no chill. Nothing but the sweetness of her lips. And the warmth of her breath. And the cold, clean scent of her.

He slanted his mouth, and without leaning any weight into her, gently took her plush lower lip between his teeth, and worried at it without biting, luring her with the promise of more. Hoping there was nothing *disagreeable* about the kiss.

And perhaps there wasn't, because in the next moment, she angled her own head, and kissed him more deeply, her mittened hands sliding up the lapels of his coat.

But then she drew back.

For a moment he thought she meant to stop—and he meant to stop with her. But she only paused long enough to strip off her mittens—letting them fall where they would on the ice—before her fingers were at his nape and pushing into his hair, knocking his beaver hat askew and then off, to fall with a soft *shush* into the snow.

But he didn't care, because she was kissing him with something more than mere tolerance—with growing heat and hunger. And he was falling or rising, soaring into the sweet span of her lips, flying away on the decadent tang of her tongue tangling with his.

Kissing him the way he was kissing her—with heady abandon.

It was everything he could do not to pull her into his arms. Not to press, but to let her set the pace, and the pressure, and the contact. To follow her lead, and take his orders from her like a good soldier.

Damned if he wouldn't.

CHAPTER 10

Who would have thought that kissing could be so heavenly? Tamsin never wanted to stop. She wanted to kiss and kiss and taste and feel and experience.

Experience *everything*.

Every sensation skittering across her skin. Every thought that caromed about her head. Every ounce of joy at this new discovery.

If she had known that kissing could be this marvelous, she would have done a vast deal more of it. But then she had not been kissing handsome, cheerful, kind, clever Colonel Simon Cathcart.

Who could not possibly be as simple and *different* as she had thought. How could a man be an idiot and kiss like an angel?

Tamsin opened her eyes to look at him—to marvel at his sandy-haired, sunny handsomeness. But all she could do was laugh.

He drew back. "Miss T?"

"I can't see." Their kissing had raised such heat that her spectacles were completely fogged.

"I am sorry," he said. But he didn't look sorry—he looked quite pleased with himself. And with her.

"I'm not sorry at all, either." She tucked the spectacles into the pocket of her velvet-trimmed Spencer. She could see up close well enough without them. And he was very close. "Please don't let that be a reason to stop."

"No reason at all."

There were, of course, many reasons, but she couldn't seem to remember them now. And she didn't want to.

But the colonel did nothing to resume their intimacy—nothing to *press*. He just smiled at her and waited as if he had all the time in the world. As if he would wait all afternoon long for her to kiss him again.

So Tamsin took pleasure in drawing out the moment of anticipation. In extending her own patience to the limit. In taking the opportunity to touch his face, and run her thumb across the barest beginning of scruff, as if he had come out to her before he had even had a chance to shave his morning beard. In letting the tip of her finger delve into the deep dimples that creased his cheeks beside his mouth.

But she could not resist that mouth—wide and pliant and clever. So clever, that once she had kissed him, he smiled and quipped, "Something better than slop and press, what?"

"Much, much better." She was so happy, so full of joyous sensations. It was a remarkable feeling.

"Happy to oblige, what?"

There it was again—that feeling that something was amiss. He kissed with such awareness, such focused intention, that she could not reconcile his actions with his careless words.

Or was it only her imagination that wanted him to be more? To be *different* in an entirely different way?

The thought made her felt strangely uncomfortable in her own skin. She must have shivered, because he asked, "Are you cold?" and immediately hugged her close and began to rub her back.

"No, truly." One look at his sunny, smiling face restored her equanimity. And the truth was she hardly felt the cold—she felt warm from the top of her head to the tips of her toes. She felt as breathless and muzzy-headed as if she'd had a teacup full of gin. "That was certainly very agreeable."

"Most agreeable," he agreed.

"The best."

Their lips seemed to meet of their own accord, as if they were meant to be together always. Always meant to be making this taut pleasure. Always searching for ways to be closer.

And so she searched too, her kiss a slow exploration of his mouth and tongue. He let her set the pace, let her kiss when she would and where she willed, sliding her lips along the firm line of his jaw, finding the salt-kissed corner of his eye. Marveling at the wonder and contradiction that was Simon Cathcart.

He was *different* to her now—a different man than the simple, helpful fellow no one could have any expectation of. A real man, and not a pasteboard cutout of a masculine wallflower whose help she needed. A person who might have needs and wants of his own.

What were they?

"Privacy and peace," she murmured, because that was what she wanted more than anything.

"Oh, aye," he agreed. "Just the thing for kissing—and other things—privacy and peace."

Other things. Heat pooled deep in her body at the thought.

Tamsin closed her eyes to savor the sensation, the keen tension that coursed through her veins at his words. If he did *other things* with the same grace and ease that he kissed—

"Are you all to rights, Miss T?"

"I'm not sure." She straightened her skirts as if it would straighten out her spine, and tucked her loosened hair back behind her ear as if she could tuck away her loosening morals. "I feel all at sixes and sevens. Maybe even eights."

She was happy to make him smile. "You'll do, Miss T, you'll do nicely."

"Thank you." But she was anxious for her own performance—

she had complained of *slop and press* but heaven forefend she had done either. "Was it all right then, the kissing, do you think?"

"Superb," he said. "Eminently gratifying."

The heat in her veins spread across her skin to other, less sensible parts of her body. "Ah. Good then. That's good." She cleared her own throat. "Thank you for being so accommodating. And understanding."

"Happy to be of some use. Best to know the strength of your powder before you light your charge."

For some reason she could not presently fathom, his cheerful military metaphors could not help but make her smile. "And we'll light the charge tonight."

"Your wish is my command, Miss T. Give your mama quite the show, what?"

The reference to her mama reminded Tamsin it was past time she got back—even if Mama wasn't there, the others in her party might be looking for her. "Yes. At the Grenville musicale." Mama had heard that the Duke of Albany's heir, Lord James Beauclerc, was musical.

"The library?"

"No." Tamsin knew from previous visits to the Grenville mansion that the library was dangerously close to the music room. "The orangery is more private. Although Mama..."

Mama was so stubbornly set against Tamsin's plans that some alternative arrangement needed to be made. "I fear we may have to ask Lady Evangeline to be our witness after all, though she is so well known that I fear word of our..." She forced herself not to use the word *tryst*. "...encounter would be spread too widely. Especially after she did urge us to discretion."

"Did she? Tell you what—I'll enlist someone to find us, or report us to your mother. She can hardly ignore the offense if someone else has witnessed it, what?"

Tamsin was no longer sanguine about anything her mama might do. Her own determination was clearly inherited from that lady, who did not give up easily. "If you think they could be discreet?"

"Oh, aye—as discreet and silent as a tomb. I've a mind to rig up my pal Sergeant Mahoney in an officer's uniform and trot him out, what? No one will know who he is, but your mama is bound to listen to a man in scarlet regimentals. You leave it to me."

She did. Mostly because it seemed a serviceable enough plan, but also because she was too happy, too enchanted with his kisses to think straight. She felt marvelous—giddy and exhausted and exhilarated all at the same time. So exhilarated she couldn't stop herself from rising up on the tips of her skates and pressing a kiss to his lovely dimpled cheek. From wishing she might kiss him more.

"Thank you, Colonel."

"Simon, please."

"Simon, then."

He raised her hands to his lips and kissed her fingers. "Until tonight then, Tamsin."

She was such a bonfire of hope, it was a wonder she didn't go up in flames right there in the snow. "Until tonight.

CHAPTER 11

By ten o'clock that night, Tamsin was alive with something more than mere anticipation—she was tingling with an exquisite sort of happiness. Beneath the layers of linen and silk and velvet, her heart was dancing a lively reel within her chest. Her toes tapped against the floor. She hummed along with the orchestra's tune.

It was almost as if she were…happy.

But of course she was happy. Tonight she would accomplish what she wanted—she was sure of it. Her emotions were not truly engaged with Simon himself, but with the situation. It was only her more excitable sensibilities that made her so giddy.

"Tamsin! What is wrong with you?" her mama complained. "Sit still. You haven't attended to a word I've said."

"I'm sorry, Mama, but—"

"No buts." Her mother closed her eyes to signal that there would be no further discussion. "And no running off to dark corners with the likes of that misbegotten Colonel Cathcart, who is exactly the sort of ne'er-do-well you once complained about."

"Not exactly," Tamsin protested.

"Exactly," her mama pronounced with far more force than Tamsin liked.

Mama's insistence was going to play havoc with Tamsin's plans if she wasn't careful. But at least it meant Mama was already on her guard, and their discovery would be quick and she would not have to endure the exquisite torture of standing in Simon's arms for overlong.

"You'll need to make yourself more agreeable to the gentlemen, my dear, if you want to have any chance. No one likes a judgmental, standoffish girl."

Especially not the judgmental men. But that was—

"—the way of the world," her mother continued as if she had read her daughter's mind. "You must present yourself as amiable and desirable to the gentlemen—"

"Oh, I'm desirable," Tamsin murmured. She had felt the evidence of Simon's desire in the throes of their intimate embrace. And when he had kissed her in the Serpentine. And kissed and kissed her until her lips had felt strange and—

"Tamsin!" Her mama's brow grew thunderous. "I declare, it's almost as if you want to marry that idiot cousin of yours."

For a moment Tamsin's heart had suggested another name—another supposed idiot, a different sort of man from Cousin Edward entirely. But she did not mean to marry Simon Cathcart any more than she would Cousin Edward. And Simon didn't want to marry her. He didn't want to marry at all. So there was an end to that.

"I do not want to marry Cousin Edward, Mama."

"Then apply yourself to finding someone else—someone else *suitable*!"

"Suitable being rich and titled."

"Certainly rich, if you'd like to have any comfort, for your father is like to settle nothing on you if you do not marry well, or marry Cousin Edward." She shuddered, as if even saying the dreaded man's name was distasteful. "Odious man—you know he's made it plain that he will do nothing for me once your father is dead."

"What?" This was news to Tamsin, who, if she had not hoped for better for herself, had at least assumed better for her mother.

"Edward even took the time," her mother went on, "to inform me that he's made a thorough inventory of the furnishings of Five Bells so he'll know if I've attempted to abscond—*abscond*, he said!—with anything when I'm asked to make my removal. Abscond from my own house, with my own things that I've had about me all my life. Why, the very nerve of him. Ungrateful, hateful odious man."

Tamsin could only agree with her about Cousin Edward. But what was she to do? Could she really set herself to marry one of the men arrayed before her in the music room? The prospect was not encouraging. "I'll do my best, Mama. For us both."

Mama reached out to take her hand. "Please see that you do. You must understand. You are our only hope."

Mama's words drowned out all else, muting the rest of the chatter, and nearly all of the music. Even as it played, Tamsin could hear nothing else.

It was not only her future that she played with, but her mother's, and very likely her sisters' as well. What would happen to her quiet, shy older sister Anne, as well as Mary, Edwina and sweet young Lolly, if Cousin Edward put them out? It might happen—even in the Peace, Papa was still a military man, away on his ships in harm's way for most of the year.

She had grown too accustomed to dismissing the chance of his death from her mind. She had put the danger, the risk to them all, out of her mind. She had thought only of herself, and what she wanted, not understanding how their fates might be so tied together.

And so when the time came at last to keep her appointment with Colonel Cathcart in the orangery, every instinct told her to stay put. To turn away from the selfish course she had set.

But she could not just sit. It would be intolerably rude were she not to give him some explanation. Some accounting of why she had changed her mind. "If you'll excuse me, Mama—"

"Where are you going?"

"The withdrawing room." Tamsin was ashamed of how easily the little lies came from her tongue. She would need to change that. She would have to apply herself to reforming her character.

Just as soon as she spoke to Colonel Cathcart, and told him she had had a change of heart. And a change of several other organs, too.

But there he was, awaiting her in the corridor. "Miss T! Well met. Off we go, what?"

A small pain, as if her heart were tearing, just a little, gripped her chest. He was so handsome. So smiling and accommodating. She really was going to miss him and his cheerful, kind ways.

"Left here, Miss T." He put a light hand to her elbow to guide her around a corner and into the tall stone room lined with fruit and palm trees kept warm in the winter by glowing hot braziers. "Reconnoitered already, what? Always know the ground, Miss T. Always know the field of battle."

It was so like him—so instinctively military at the same time as being so offhand—that Tamsin felt herself smile. She was going to miss him. So very much.

Because she truly did like him.

Apart from the other things she liked. Things that had to end.

And so she took a deep breath and looked him in the eye. "I'm so sorry, Colonel Cathcart, but I've had a change of mind."

She put back her shoulders like a martyr entering the arena to face the lions, head held high, as straight as a promise
Absolutely adorable.

And absolutely unnecessary—he would rather do anything than cause her pain.

And she looked pained, with a furrow pleated between her light brows and her sweet lips pressed together.

"Right ho, Miss T." Simon played the befuddled idiot, even as his heart—or was that a different part of his anatomy?—was sinking. "Change of mind about what, exactly?"

"Our arrangement," she said solemnly.

"Right ho." But he couldn't keep the very real disappointment from his voice. "Do you mean you'd rather not be lightly ruined?"

"I'm afraid not. Not that I haven't enjoyed it—the attempts at ruination—along with your company, very much. But I must...I must do other things."

"What sorts of other things?" Perhaps she wanted something stronger than light ruination. Perhaps she thought he wasn't up to the job.

"I must think of my family. And do what's right."

Simon had had a lifetime of doing what was right—what he was ordered, what needed to be done. He didn't want to do it any longer. And he didn't want her to do it either.

But her eyes, so luminous and bright with tears, held his, and he could not hold on to his resolution. Or his resentment. "I see, Miss T. All for the good of the troops, what?"

"Yes, indeed. For the good of my family. I'm so glad you understand."

"Don't understand much." He fell back upon his doltish persona to mask his disappointment. "But if you say so, Miss T."

"I do. This must be our last meeting. Though I do appreciate everything you've done for me. I am most grateful." She put out her hand to shake.

Simon stared at it. He knew he was meant to play the idiot and give her a naffy salute, or some such. But he didn't want to. He wanted to kiss her.

And so he asked, "Might I perhaps kiss you goodbye?"

She went as pink as a sunset at the waning of the day, and tilted her head ever so slightly to the side. "Surely that would do no harm," she murmured. Almost as if she were trying to convince herself.

He would help her. "One last kiss, Miss T. Something to remember me by."

Her answer was so quiet he would not have heard it if he was not already leaning down. Already set to kiss her. "Yes."

He wanted to swoop down upon her lips and kiss her with every ounce of disappointment and need and hope in his body. But he had learned his lesson well. So he took a steadying breath. And focused his gaze upon her lovely lush lower lip. And asked in his idiot's sort of way, "Not quite sure how one goes about a farewell kiss, Miss T? Do you know?"

"Not really," she said with a bittersweet, rueful smile that told him she was perhaps as reluctant to part as he.

"Well, I suppose to give a proper farewell kiss, like in those books you're so fond of, I'd need to get a vast deal closer." He stepped so close the toes of his boots nudged against her slippers. "And if I were the one writing the book, the hero would take the heroine's hand, so he could hold it one last time." Simon followed this direction with the action, leaning closer still. "And then he'd clasp it to his chest, so she might feel the pounding of his heart. And then, I should think, he would lower his lips to hers."

All of this he did, until his lips were but a hairsbreadth from hers. And then she was leaning toward him, closing the last, desperate, unspannable inch. "And then what?"

"And then I would kiss her."

Their mouths met as if of their own accord and meshed as if they had been made for each other, crafted by a benevolent creator to fit as perfectly as two halves of one whole. Her lips were still as soft, still as pliant. They moved ever so slightly against his, as if she, too, were holding back. As if she too feared the end as much as he.

So he did nothing more to touch her, keeping only his lips pressed lightly to hers, tasting slowly, sipping slightly, waiting for want and need to build. Waiting for her to deepen the kiss and take something more. Take all she wanted.

All he had to give.

She did so, finally, settling her hands upon him, gripping his lapels, pulling him down to her, so he could not move away and leave her before she thought better of kissing in the brazier-lit dark.

But she did not think better of it. She kissed him with her own want, her own need, sighing into his mouth, pressing her lush body nearer to his. Filling his mind and his senses with her.

His hands went around her back, pulling her close, encouraging her to follow her own unspoken desires. Willing her not to be done with him.

Kiss by kiss, he gave himself away, using every ounce of remembered skill, battering open the siege doors of his passion. Tasting her sweetness, and breathing in her delicate clean scent. Giving way to his own possibilities.

What would it be like to keep such a lass forever? To have this sweetness and levelheaded charm in his life to ease his way? To drop his mask of idiocy and finally be completely himself?

Whoever that was.

"Simon," she whispered.

"Yes." It was his only answer to anything she asked.

"I think we ought to stop now."

Anything she asked but that.

But stop he did, because he was a gentleman. And because he *liked* her. For herself alone and not only for her kisses.

But nothing could ever be stopped completely, for the world turned, and even if plans changed, arrangements progressed on their own schedule.

"I say." A deep voice cleared its throat. "Is that you, Colonel Cathcart?"

Mahoney, damn his eyes, right on cue. "Colonel, forgive my interruption."

And because fate was not in the least bit kind, a second voice joined Mahoney's—Tamsin's mama, looking at him like a French grenadier, ready to run him through with her saber.

"Thomasina Elizabeth Lesley. For the last time, get yourself away from that man."

CHAPTER 12

Two hours of applying herself to being agreeable to the assembled japes and jackanapes were almost more than Tamsin could stand. But stand she did, as well as dance, though her toes were frequently and painfully trod upon. Her mother had rung such a peal over her head that she dared not make so much as a peep.

So she smiled with as much good humor as she could muster at every pronouncement that fell from the assembled jackanapes' lips, just as her mama had adjured her. And was bored out of her skull.

"And then I said, 'Well, how's a ruddy fellow supposed to know that, what?'" one of the titled jackasses—some lord or another—brayed.

It annoyed her to hear Simon's familiar way of ending a sentence from anyone but him—these fellows had none of Simon's sunny, self-deprecating wit.

She was annoyed enough to finally answer them. "By reading a book."

"What was that?" The fellow gaped at her as if he had no idea what she was talking about. Or no idea that she could speak. Or perhaps no experience in anyone having the temerity to speak to him in such a tone at all.

Tamsin sighed and smiled just as her mother had instructed, to mitigate the sting of her words. "A book, Lord James. You might find such information in a book. The city is full of them, if you know where to look. If you'll be so kind as to excuse me…"

She didn't wait for his say so, but returned to her mother's side, where she was for the moment safe, until her mother deployed her to some other skirmish—that was what Simon would have called the encounters, with his funny military metaphors, wouldn't he?

Tamsin strove not to give further vent to her feelings.

"Don't sigh," Mama warned. "And don't squint so."

"If I had my spectacles, I wouldn't need to squint to see who's next to me."

"Don't be ridiculous," her mama muttered. "Who ever heard of a girl wearing spectacles to a ball? Now there's Viscount Wainwright."

Tamsin let herself be towed in the direction of the bluff, young puppy of a man who seemed to repeat "I say!" either before or after every word he spoke.

"I say, how do you do, Miss Lesley?" But then the puppy fell silent.

"Miss Lesley," came a smooth voice at her side. "I wonder if you might do me the honor of a dance, if you have this one free?"

Simon beamed down at her with his never-fading smile.

Tamsin was so startled to see him in the ballroom and so conscious of her mama at her side, that she hardly knew what to say. "Colonel Cathcart. I thought you didn't dance. Three left feet, you said."

"Did I?" He looked mildly amused by this admission. "I promise to use only two this evening if you would do me the honor."

Tamsin stole a glance at her mama, who, for perhaps the first time in Tamsin's life, had nothing to say. And so she had to answer for herself. "That would be…acceptable." She settled on a word intended to keep the peace, if peace needed to be made.

"The next set it is." He bowed rather more beautifully—graceful and masculine at the same time—than she had expected. "I look forward to it." And then he went away, back to stand silently behind his aunt, the Countess Cathcart.

Her mama, who had held her tongue throughout the awkward exchange, now spoke. "What goes on here?"

"I have no idea," Tamsin answered honestly.

"It were better if you had nothing at all to do with him, Tamsin. I've told you before and I'll tell you again—he's not the sort of man you marry."

"I know." He wasn't the sort of man to marry anyone. "But I hardly knew how to refuse him in public."

"Just so long as you intend to refuse him in private," her mother said for her ears only. "Then we'll have no trouble."

"No," Tamsin agreed as the musicians scratched up their bows and Simon began to make his amiable, unhurried way to her side. "No trouble at all."

"Miss Lesley." He took her gloved hand within his own, and led her to the floor where the set was forming.

"Colonel Cathcart." She felt the heat of his fingers through her gloves—she felt the heat of his entire *presence* all the way from the tips of her fingers to the ends of her toes. "This was not what we had arranged."

"Indeed. But I got to thinking." He moved away to take his place, and she was left in uncomfortable anticipation of just what that might be, because the measure started up and she was obliged to put her mind to the complicated steps of the "Marquess of Wellington" dance.

When they finally chanced to come together for longer than a moment, she asked, "And? What did you think?"

"That I used to like dancing, before I came to dislike it—

thought it was all humbug and social pretense, but there is a great deal more to it that that, what? All this getting to hold your hand and..." He trailed off before he added, "And you smell rather like a night garden, Miss T."

His strangely offhand compliment made her unaccountably pleased. "It's jasmine."

"Whatever it is, it's lovely—heady and oh, makes me think all kinds of things. Which is dangerous for a man with my brain, what?"

"Your brain is just fine, Colonel Cathcart." They passed away from each again, but his words had insinuated themselves into her mind, until they came together again and she had to ask, "What kinds of things does the jasmine make you think?"

He smiled as they stepped together, face to face. "Of warm summer nights. Not all this ice and cold and mistletoe."

With her mama's warning fresh in her ears, Tamsin answered, "Pray let us steer clear of any mistletoe, Colonel."

"Right ho, Miss T."

The steps of the dance took her away, rotating around another couple before she could catch a glimpse of his face again —his expression, though he smiled, was too acute for his usual mirth.

"But I was wondering about that fellow," he began when they came together. "The one who was driving you to make *arrangements*." He stepped away to revolve around another lady in turn before he came back to take Tamsin's hand. "Must be someone god-awful to keep you at it so determinedly."

His question surprised her entirely—she was both embarrassed and touched by his perceptiveness. But by the time they had danced down the set and could catch their breath, she had her answer. "My cousin Edward, you must mean."

Simon nodded. "Tell me about him."

Tamsin could not see the harm in laying out her complaint against Edward—it would serve to remind her of her duty. And the fact that she had scant days left to accomplish the impossible —finding herself a rich, titled husband.

"My cousin is set to inherit my father's small estate, so my papa naturally wanted him to marry one of his daughters. The miserable man wouldn't deign to ask for my older sister, Anne, because he didn't think she was pretty enough. So he asked for me instead. But I won't accept, for despite his offer, I know he doesn't even like me," she finally admitted. "I think he likes *disliking* me. He's odious and contrary in that way. He only wants a pretty wife, as if that would reflect better upon him. As if my supposed beauty were his accomplishment."

"What an idiot," Simon said succinctly.

His instant condemnation could not but cheer her. "Yes, thank you. He is."

"Now I understand why you went such a long way out of your way to avoid marriage. Must be the same fellow who gave you such a fright of kissing—'all that slop and press,' you said."

Since the memory of what she said coincided with the passionate kissing that had ensued, Tamsin felt her face flame. "Indeed."

"Well, damn his eyes. Damn him for making you so afraid."

There was such heat in his voice, she almost put her hand on his arm to reassure him. But she was too conscious of her mama's all-seeing gaze to forget herself. But some explanation was called for. "I wasn't *afraid* of the kissing, really."

Now that they appeared to be getting to the heart of the matter, why not expose herself? No one but Simon had ever asked. No one as innately kind as Simon might ever understand. "I was more afraid of losing my personal sovereignty to someone else—to any man. All women are afraid of that, I should think."

"Well, damn *my* eyes," he swore with that lovely, kind heat.

"I had so hoped things would be different in London. More progressive. More modern than the benighted country."

"Somerset, you said?"

"Yes, in Somerset. In the village of Winchett." She had hoped never to set eyes on the place again. "Where I had an acquaintance—a particular friend of my older sister, Anne, and in the way of small villages, a friend of mine by extension. Arabella was a perfectly lovely girl, the loveliest, kindest creature, just like my sister, who never put a foot wrong. Quiet and kind as the day is long. But she caught the eye of the local squire's spawn, Arabella did. And they married. But the whole village knows that he treats her worse than he treats his dogs—and he kicks the dogs in public. We all know he knocks her about something awful."

She closed her eyes, and lowered her voice to impart the dreadful truth on a whisper. "She says that he can only engage in marital relations if he is enraged. That otherwise his…" She squeezed her eyes shut and shook her head, because it was awful, and because there was nothing she could do about it. "It's terrible, the way he treats her. But what's more terrible is that the whole of the village, and I daresay the entirely of the shire, knows of his violent tendencies, and still do nothing. And they will do nothing until he kills her, and then they will do nothing more than shake their heads at her funeral, and say behind their hands that they always knew she'd come to a bad end. As if it were all her fault."

Tamsin gave vent to all the fear and all the worry and all the awful, choking hate. "It is awful. It's odious. She has no rights to anything—no rights to even complain. The only right she seems to have is to a decent funeral once she's dead. It's a wonder she hasn't taken her own life."

She drew a deeper breath to keep herself from an unmannerly display of all the emotions she was desperately trying to keep in check. The last notes of the music faded to a close, and they were left standing upon the dance floor as the other couples moved apart and away. But Simon stayed beside her.

"That is awful," he agreed quietly. "It's enough, I daresay, to put one right off marriage. Indeed, it might put one right off men forever."

"Not forever. Not all men." She tried to lighten the awful seriousness of the moment. "Just the ones who want to marry me."

"And what do you want, Tamsin?"

It was the second time in about as many days—she had lost count of how long it had been since she had set her plan in motion—that someone had been kind enough and perceptive enough to ask her that question.

And her answer was just the same. "To be a bluestocking, like my aunt Dahlia and other ladies like the famous playwright Joanne Baillie, and read books and write histories and be my own woman."

"Why should you not be?" He smiled at her in that sunny way of his, as if he could not fathom why it was not the easiest thing to accomplish.

"Because it is not the way of the world."

"Is it not? It can be," he insisted. "Come, meet me tomorrow and I will show you how."

She hesitated—behind Simon's back, Tamsin could see her mother advancing across the floor, parting the waves of dancers like a ship making for port. "I need to get back to Mama."

He bowed over her hand and Tamsin felt that simple kiss on her wrist like a benediction. "Please?"

Her resolution began to give way under his determined kindness. "Where?"

"The east side of Berkeley Square, ten o'clock," he said in a low rush. "I'll have a carriage. I'll be looking for you."

Mama was almost upon them.

"Will you come?"

"Yes," she said, determined to trust him, even if she did not trust herself. "I will."

"Excellent. And Miss T? Prepare yourself to be surprised."

CHAPTER 13

At half-past nine the following morning, Tamsin stepped into the corridor and made her voice as sure and calm as a governess. "I'm headed for Mattigan's Bookshop, Mama," she called at the door to her mother's private sitting room. "Shall I get you the latest copy of the *Lady's Magazine?*"

Her mother raised her head from where she lay upon her chaise. "Yes, please. How thoughtful. It is good to see you taking some greater interest in fashion."

"I'm trying, Mama." Tamsin hated the small lies more than the larger ones, if only because she disliked so easily giving up her principles to the expediency of convenience.

Mama rose and reached out her hand, bidding Tamsin enter. "You'll see, my darling," she assured her. "We'll come right out of this thing, and then you'll see. The next few balls, before Christmas—"

"Yes, Mama."

"I tell you what," Mama began, and Tamsin could see that her mother was talking herself into some Christmas spirit. "I'll come with you to Mattigan's myself. Won't that be lovely? We'll have a lovely morning of it together."

Tamsin hardly knew what to say. "Oh. That would be a treat," she lied. "I'm almost ready. Just give me a moment to go up and fetch my heavy cloak."

"Not that old country cloak," Mama scolded. "Your new purple Spencer coat looks so well—so stylish."

"Thank you. I'm glad you think so." Tamsin attempted to look flattered. "But it is fearful cold out this morning—I popped out into the garden just this minute to gauge the temperature. I shouldn't want to catch cold at this point in the Season. Better safe than sorry, I think, and find myself in bed with a putrid fever, missing those balls."

Her mother, who had grown sensitive, as she called it, to extremes of temperature, began to think so, too. "Cold enough for a coat *and* a cloak?"

"Oh, yes. And my eiderdown muff as well. I know it's nothing as fashionable as your swansdown, which I did think of borrowing, but after getting so cold at the skating, I'd rather be comfortable and warm than stylish."

"I tell you what," Mama began, and Tamsin began to relax. "I have remembered that I must speak to the housekeeper about... the supper for this evening. I particularly want Cook to get us a good haunch of pork. I hope you will forgive me for not accompanying you on this errand, but needs must—"

"Of course, Mama." Tamsin managed a reluctant smile. "Perhaps another time."

Tamsin barely saw the carpet under her feet as she hurried down the stairs and out the front door—she could see nothing but her own duplicity. She definitely saw nothing between Hill Street and Berkeley Square. But once she reached the fashionable square, she saw everything—the seemingly enormous number of carriages tooling up the Davies Street side of the square, the curving arabesque of the frost-withered leaf litter crunching under her feet, and the faces of every passerby who must surely see by her own face that she was headed for an illicit rendezvous with a man who would never be her husband.

She heard everything, too—the clattering of the birds in the bare branches of the trees over head, and the chattering of passersby, and the *clop, clop, clop* of hooves and carriages rumbling by, keeping time with her racing heart.

And then his voice from a carriage pulled alongside. "Miss Lesley," Simon called her from the darkened interior. The carriage barely slowed as the door opened and the step fell down, and she seized the hand that reached for her and leapt aboard.

Simon efficiently closed the door to plunge them into the strange twilight of the closed interior. After the bright winter sunshine outside, it took several moments for her eyes to adjust to the lack of light. When she did so, he was smiling down at her.

"Miss T," he greeted her.

"Simon." She shook the hand he had extended as if they were out in the square, in public, instead of in a closed carriage, off on an illicit adventure. "This is all very mysterious.

"Excellent. It's a present, what? For putting up with me. And my failure to help you."

"That was not a failure on your part," she assured him. "But what sort of a present?" Gracious, she hoped it wasn't a Christmas sort of present—she had nothing to offer him in return. She hadn't even finished making presents for her own family, who would be exchanging small presents at home on Epiphany. "Where are we going?"

"Hampstead."

He might as well have said John o' Groats at the far tip of Scotland—the idea of leaving London was so surprising. "But I can't be gone that long. Mama—"

"A short morning visit to the heath. Or rather a house near the heath—at the home of someone you said you admired and wanted to meet—Joanna Baillie."

Tamsin's heart clutched up hard in her chest. "The playwright?" Had she said that? Last night while they were dancing and sharing her secret most fears and desires? "You know her?"

"Neighbor of a sort. Have a little bolt-hole up in Hampstead myself, and one of my neighbors moves in Miss Baillie's circle—poets and playwrights and the like. Your sort of people."

He had told her to prepared to be surprised, but she was more than surprised—she was overcome with gratitude. That he would arrange such a thing for her—

"You really are the most remarkable man."

He smiled in that sunny, sometimes silly way of his, as if her words were of no particular account. But Tamsin could see the warm spots of pleasure color his cheeks.

Her own face must have been bright with pleasure as well. She could barely contain her enthusiasm—she didn't want to. "I've never been north of the city. I've never been anywhere but Winchett village and Mayfair and the road in between."

He peered behind the shade, and then raised it. "We should be far enough away from the fashionable areas to pass unseen."

Tamsin couldn't decide between looking at him, and watching the scenery roll by as they made their slow way up the Hampstead road past Camden Town and Haverstock Hill. Her chest felt too tight, her palms too damp. Was she wearing suitable attire? She hadn't cared overmuch about her clothing because she knew she had been dressed to blend into Society, and appear much the same as other girls her age. And her one prior outing with bluestockings had been at her aunt's house, where everything was made easy.

She smoothed the creases out of her countrywoman's red wool cloak.

"You look charming," Simon told her. "Just as you ought."

"Thank you. I know it's silly to be nervous, but I am. I have always wanted to meet Joanna Baillie and her circle, but now I worry that I am not accomplished enough."

"You don't need to be accomplished," he assured her. "You only need to be yourself."

But was she enough?

The question was taken out of her hands when the coach rolled to a stop at the top of the hill, in front of a tall, neat red brick residence labeled Bolton House.

"You see," he said. "Nothing too grand. Let me hand you out." And he did so, opening the door, and taking her hand to help her alight. "Off you go."

A fresh wave of anxiety took hold of her chest. "Are you not coming, too?"

"Me? What would they want with a fellow like me? Say the wrong things, what? No, no." He shook his head. "No place for a fellow. Off you go," he repeated. "They're expecting you."

She was torn between her anxiety and her desire. But Simon had gone to a lot of trouble for her to meet her idol, and it would be foolish, not to mention ungrateful for her to refuse now. And really, when was she going to have another chance? "If you're sure?"

"Are you not?" He turned the question on her. "Is this not what you want for your life?"

It was exactly what she wanted for her life. And he was a rare man to see that. And to help her get it. "Thank you."

"Most welcome. " He tipped his hat and tossed her that delightfully naughty conspirator's wink. "Now off you go."

She stood there on the side of the lane watching his carriage drive off, until there was nothing for her to do but gather her courage and ring the bell. But she need not have worried—the door was almost immediately opened by a very respectable-looking housekeeper, who queried kindly, "Miss Lesley? Do come in, miss. They're expecting you."

They? Tamsin had expected Miss Baillie alone, but the playwright's cozy parlor held more than just one of her idols.

"Miss Lesley, you are most welcome." A kind-faced older lady in lace and shawls stood to greet Tamsin. "I am Joanna Baillie. I am pleased to meet you and welcome a kindred spirit into our circle. Let me make you known to my friends."

Three other women rose to greet her, each more accomplished than the next. Anna Barbauld, the essayist, critic and author of the new type of children's literature, reached out her hand. "We are happy to have you amongst us, Miss Lesley."

"Tamsin, please."

"Tamsin, then. Let me make you know to my niece—"

"Miss Lucy Aiken," Tamsin breathed. "I am honored. I have read your histories, and have used them as a guide for my own fledgling efforts at a—"

"— history of the esteemed Countess of Shrewsbury, Bess of Hardwick?"

Tamsin was all astonishment. "Why, yes. How did you know?"

"Your aunt, Miss Dahlia Green, is another of our acquaintance."

So perhaps she had her aunt to thank for her attendance, too. But that would mean that Simon Cathcart and Aunt Dahlia were acquainted, and had joined forces against Mama, which seemed unlikely. How curious it all was.

But not as curious and interesting and enlightening as the women around her. The last to be introduced was the most famous, the novelist Miss Maria Edgeworth.

Tamsin was in alt. "I don't know when I've ever been in such illustrious company."

"Oh, we will seem far less illustrious once you get to know us," was the kind woman's response.

The morning flew by with conversation ranging from one more interesting topic to another, along with a very great deal of good sensible encouragement for her history.

"You must of course pursue that line of inquiry. Lucy will, I'm sure, be happy to write you a letter of reference to Dr. Dain at the Royal Philosophical Society, who will no doubt be able to get you access to the Hardwick and Chatsworth muniment rooms for your research."

"Thank you, ma'am. I would like that very much."

It felt as if no time at all had passed before the housekeeper was back, and speaking to her mistress. "Your pardon, ma'am, but Miss Lesley's carriage awaits."

Simon's carriage.

Tamsin was filled with another sort of joy—one that came from more than gratitude.

"Dear Miss Lesley, I hope you will visit us again. And do bring your manuscript with you, as well as your aunt, dear Miss Green, next time."

"I hope I might—I should like nothing more. Thank you so very much for a lovely morning."

"It has been a pleasure. Come again! " Miss Baillie stood and shook her hand. "And do thank our friend for bringing you to us today."

"Colonel Cathcart?" Tamsin was relieved to finally be able to say his name, but she hoped that only her admiration, and not her growing attraction and attachment to the man, showed in her face, for she would hate to appear to be nothing more than a calf-eyed girl in front of such accomplished women.

"Ah, yes, Simon," and "Such a dear man," and, "So very like him," they chorused, but said no more.

So all Tamsin could say was, "Thank you. Until next time."

And hope that there would be a next time. Hope that she had the courage and daring to make it so.

CHAPTER 14

Just as Simon had hoped, Tamsin was glowing with happiness as she clambered into the carriage. "Oh, Simon, how can I ever thank you?"

Her unprompted use of his Christian name sent pleasure sliding down his veins. Heady stuff.

"Tamsin." He gave her mittened fingers a quick squeeze, but did nothing more until the door had been shut and the carriage began to roll down Windmill Hill. "Did you have a pleasant morning visit?"

Her smile lit the interior of the carriage as brightly as a campfire. "I did not have a pleasant morning visit—I had an absolutely *brilliant* visit. Oh, I don't know how I am ever going to thank you for arranging it all. It was the most thoughtful thing anyone has ever done for me."

Despite the fact that he had adjured himself to play his cards close to his chest, Simon showed his hand. "A kiss will suffice."

"To thank you?" She was too happy to object to his outrageous suggestion. "Just one?"

Oh, how he liked the clever ones. "We'll start off with one and see how you go on."

She laughed. "Oh, Simon."

It was heaven hearing her say his name with such a smile on her lips—it was like a prayer already working its benefit, easing his heart, bolstering his intent. Especially when she kissed him completely, with hungry lips and playful tongue. She showered her kisses upon him, over and over, with no reserve, no thought of the dreaded press or slop.

"Tamsin," he found himself saying again and again, like an incantation, as her kisses filled the strange yawning emptiness he couldn't quite fill on his own.

She cupped his face between her small hands and he had to close his eyes against the steady, steely joy in her gaze. Against the potent, sweet shine in her eyes behind her governess-y spectacles.

"You have no idea what your eyeglasses do to me."

"Tell me, then." Her demand was half question, and half disbelief.

"They make me mad for you, you intelligent, clever, beautiful woman." He kissed his way to the bridge of her nose, and placed a buss upon the gold wire of the spectacles. "They make me want to fog your lenses, so the only thing you can see is me."

"Oh, Simon. That is without a doubt the nicest thing anyone has ever said to me about my eyeglasses." She laughed. "Tell me more!"

"I'll tell you more, if you're very clever, and very nice, and say my name, and kiss me again."

Her smile was all the answer he needed. But still she obliged him. "Simon."

He met her lips with equal enthusiasm, sliding his mouth up the sensitive side of her neck, and she arced her head away, granting him access, sighing her permission. He kissed her with everything he was, every hope and dream, every fear and failure, willing her to want him. Willing her to want more.

To want to be with him.

He slanted his mouth across hers, kissing her more deeply,

satisfying his lust, or at least trying to. Assuaging his need with her sweetness, blunting his passion with her goodness. He let his thumbs fan along her cheeks, then set one hand at her nape, drawing her closer—as close as possible and still be two people—kissing her with heat and purpose. Everything else faded, until there was nothing but the longing for the feel of her mouth, and the pleasure so bright it all but blinded him.

Perhaps it was too much for her—she pulled back. But she was still smiling.

"Now, I'm sorry I didn't ask for more than a kiss."

She pinked and let out one of those lovely little huffs of laughter. But then she looked up at him with that level, inquisitive gaze of hers and asked, "How much more? How much more is there?"

It was his turn to laugh. "My dear Tamsin—a vast deal."

"A vast deal of what?" she challenged him. "Today I am a bluestocking, and I find that bluestockings are independent and intellectually curious. And quite, quite determined."

"You were already quite determined enough," he said. He never would have met her otherwise. But he gave himself a long, considering moment before he decided to answer the rest of her question. "More involves more kissing and touching—kissing and touching with more intimacy. And in more intimate, more personal places."

Two spots of colors bloomed high on her cheeks. "The kissing or the touching?" Her voice had gone very quiet.

"Both." His answers up to that point had been a bit teasing, a bit tongue in cheek. Perhaps because he did not want to admit—even to himself—how much he wanted to tell her. How much her wanted to show her. And for that he needed the truth. "To assuage all the tight, aching needs that arise within."

Her color rose higher and her voice got even quieter. "And without?" Her gaze dropped to the obvious bulge in his breeches. "That arise like your cock?" She whispered the word delicately, but still it sounded so wicked that it hit him with all the force of a fist.

A force he would marshal—he was not alone in his need. "And your nipples."

She gasped—not in shock, but in pleasure.

And on that particularly intimate note, the coach drew to a quiet stop on Berkeley Square.

They sat for a long moment in the still silence, before he cleared his throat and dared to ask the question that was burning on the tip of his tongue. "Do you want to know? Do you want to find out? Do you want me to show you more?"

She swallowed. "Will it hurt?"

He felt the breath leave his body. What a question—what an unfair world they lived in that she thought she had to ask such a question. "No. I promise you that," he pledged. "I give you my solemn oath as an officer and a gentleman, and your friend. I will never hurt you."

She took another perilously long moment before she took him at his word. "Then yes, I'd like you to show me. Please."

The air slammed back into his lungs with all the force of a French cannon.

But he kept his composure and kept his eyes on hers, honoring her trust while he reached up to the trap, and called his instruction to his batman. "Drive on, Mahoney. Drive on until I tell you to stop."

"Sir?"

"An hour, no more. Spare the horses—just keep them moving and warm in this weather. Steady as she does."

"Aye, sir."

Simon closed the trap with a snap, and reached for the windows. He put up the shades one after another, plunging them into a half-light twilight that dappled the plush interior. "Prepare yourself, Tamsin—"

"To be surprised?" she finished, echoing his invitation of last night. "I already am—at myself."

CHAPTER 15

There was that smile—lazy and sunny but full of a sort of slow, focused intent. "You'll do, my lass. You'll do."

The low words sent her already hectic pulse pounding in her veins. "And what is it we are about to do?"

"Patience," he counseled. His voice was the same warm baritone, but his tone was…more commanding. She began to envision him as the military officer he must have been, not the muzzy-headed layabout she had thought him.

"We are about to do many things. And if you don't like any of them," he offered, "or want to stop at any time, you have but to tell me."

Everything within her stopped and started and tensed and eased all at the same time. She didn't know when she had ever felt so breathless and terrified and excited. Because she believed him. "I will, Simon."

His smile softened the corners of his eyes. "I am glad. A man can't seduce a lass properly without her consent. And I do mean to seduce you, Tamsin Lesley, my sweet Miss T. Just so you're prepared."

How she was to prepare herself, she had no idea—she had

never been seduced before. Not like this, where his words alone seemed to light her into flame—her skin already felt hot and sensitive.

But he seemed to be done talking, because he turned to her, and slowly—so slowly that she felt herself taking a long full inhalation as if she might draw him in like a breath—he leaned down to brush his lips against hers.

The effect of that first touch was instantaneous—she had to be kissing him. She had to be pressing her lips to his and opening her mouth to him. She had to be taking his lapels and pulling him closer. Close enough to loop her arms around his neck and hold him tight, and run her fingers up his nape to comb through his beautiful, unruly, sandy hair.

"Simon," she said, because she loved saying the name that echoed around and around her head, day after each more interesting day. Deviously un-simple Simon, who hid so much behind his sunny, baffling facade.

"Tamsin," he murmured against her lips, and everything within her, every ounce of her blood and every inch of her skin went hot and tingly with longing. As if her body knew what her mind did not—that she had been longing to hear her name whispered so intimately, as well.

"Yes," was her answer. "Yes, please. Yes, yes, yes."

He took her words for the permission they were and kissed her in earnest, delving his tongue into her mouth to twine with hers, kissing and kissing until there was nothing else in the whole of the world but his kisses.

She leaned into him, nestling into the broad warmth of his chest, inhaling the brink, intoxicating scent of his starched linen and polished leather. Drinking in the whisky-warm taste of his lips.

She closed her eyes to thought, and tipped her head away, giving him access, hoping the exquisitely slippery feelings were leading her someplace...more. "How far, do you think, will we go?"

"My sweet Tamsin." He punctuated each word with a kissing nip of the sensitive skin down the side of her neck. "We're going all the way to heaven."

There was such kind confidence in his voice that she could not help but smile. "That would be lovely. I've never been."

His lips curved against hers. "Then we shall make up for that deficiency by taking the long way 'round."

And around she did go—he kissed her again and then picked her up, so her back was to his chest and her legs fell slightly to each side of his thighs, as if she was on an armchair made of man.

Wondrous, clever, warm man.

But a man she could no longer kiss. "I want—"

"Patience," he counseled one last time before his hands went to the clasp of her cloak. And then stilled. "Perhaps not just yet. Shouldn't like to overwhelm."

She shivered at his words, though she felt breathless and light, buoyed up by his good humor and obvious delight. "I'm not overwhelmed."

"You will be—if I get this right." He let the delicious weight of the words settle upon her, urging her to lean back against his chest. "How do you feel now?"

"Giddy," she admitted, feeling the excitement and anticipation rise up against her uneasiness. "And a little achy."

"Tell me what aches." His mouth brushed against the shell of her ear. "Tell me what I need to soothe."

Beneath the layers of her clothing her skin seemed to be alive with sensation. Her breasts felt heavy and tight. Her thighs clenched together in unconscious spasm. "Everything."

"Right ho." She felt his smile rumble through him as he nuzzled the skin behind her ear. "I do think I'll fold this back." He drew the edges of her cloak over her shoulders, like a curtain parting upon a stage. "For now. Because I want to see you. I don't want anything in the way while I take down your bodice. I want to see your lovely breasts."

Her hands immediately fluttered up as if she might cover herself. But she didn't. She wanted this—she had asked him specifically for this. Pretending otherwise was disingenuous.

But he understood her even if she didn't—he covered her hands with his own, the broad span of his palm warming her cold fingers before he interlaced them with his, and brought her hand up to his lips for a kiss.

She half-turned her head toward him, and he caught her in a kiss that relaxed some of the stiffness in her spine. "Simon." His name was answer and entreaty all at the same time.

"Yes." His answer was encouragement. "So lovely," he murmured. "So sweet."

He released her hand to caress her face and kiss her while his other hand swept up from her waist. For one exquisite moment, he cupped her needy breast before rounding to brush the backs of his fingers along the skin above the line of her bodice. "Such beautiful, interesting things, your sweet breasts."

She felt herself arching into the warmth and weight of his hand. Her head went back, resting on his shoulder, opening herself to him. Hoping he would do exactly as he did, loosening her neckline and scooping his fingers beneath her stays and linen to touch and tease her tight, aching nipples.

Tamsin gasped her astonishment and appreciation at the extraordinary contradictory sensations his attentions evoked.

"Steady on, my lass. Steady." His murmur echoed in her ear. "Because there's more. A vast deal more."

"I want more," she insisted.

"So determined. So curious," he teased, but his voice held admiration. Or at least no admonition as he pushed her bodice lower so it gaped across her chest, sliding her sleeves off her shoulders so her upper arms were held snug by her sides.

"Do we leave the stays?" he queried quietly against her ear. "An awful lot of work to lace them back up after, when we only have so much time," he mused, answering his own question. "When we might just make free of the straps"—he untied the bows securing the straps—"and perhaps tug a bit down on this lovely lawn shift instead."

His hand went to the hem of her skirts, pushing aside the wool of her Spencer coat, gathering up the layers of skirt and petticoat to find the hem of the shorter shift beneath. He pulled the fine lawn taut beneath her long stays, tugging the neckline of her shift down just far enough to expose the tips of her breasts. "Perfect. So much lovelier without all that interfering cloth."

She felt imperfectly perfect—a diamond of the last water, perhaps, but not the least bit counterfeit.

Especially not when Simon cupped her breasts within the confines of her stays, his clever, clever fingers rolling and tweaking her nipples into tight furls of needy pleasure. A low hum of something more, something deeper began to thrum within as his clever fingers plucked and played her body. And he knew just what chord to play.

He rucked her skirts up to her thighs but raised them no higher. "Spread your legs for me, sweet," he urged. His big hands covered her knees, pressing them lightly, showing her the way. Leading her to expose herself to his touch. "Yes," he encouraged before he traced his beautifully articulate fingers along the length of her thighs until she thought she would burst from the anticipation.

And then he cupped her mound, and it was…*everything.* "Just so," his low voice crooned in her ear. "Exactly so."

He set his fingers in a gentle rhythm upon her until it was almost too much, the pleasure and need and achy, incandescent joy. Until it wasn't enough, and she began to move her hips, chasing her rising passion, riding his hand as it played against her.

"That's the way of it." He slowly slid one long finger within, and Tamsin felt her body clench and release and clench again in an agony of pleasure and anticipation.

She turned her head toward him in mute appeal and he kissed her deeply, his tongue tangling with hers in rhythm with his hands. In the next moment, he eased another long finger alongside the first—a rush of heat and desire blossomed from her belly and spread to the edges of her being.

Tamsin closed her eyes to stop thinking and only feel, as he touched and played and murmured. Her body wound itself higher and higher. Closer and closer to some unseen place—some not-so-distant meeting of mind and body and soul and pleasure so beautiful she wanted to laugh and cry all at the same time.

She wanted this. She wanted more. She wanted nothing less than absolute bliss.

Tamsin could not stop the sound of want and desire that flew from her lips when he touched her *there*, at the center of her pleasure and need, grazing ever so lightly against the sensitive nub his fingers exposed. She arched wildly one last time and he swallowed her cry as her climax shuddered through her, hot and delirious and imperfectly perfect.

Simon wrapped his arms around her and held her, safe and secure, as she collapsed against his chest, sated and numb and more alive than she had ever felt before.

She turned in his arms to hold him, to put her lips against the hollow of his throat and feel the strong pulsing of his blood and hear the hard pounding of his heart. "Heavens."

"One of the bright stars in the sky," he said as he slowly and systematically began putting her clothes to rights as neatly as if he were a dresser.

"You'd make some lucky woman a marvelous lady's maid."

"Thank you." He placed a sweet kiss upon her mouth. "As luck would have it, you are that woman."

"Lucky indeed." Lucky to have found such a man, this strange, masculine wallflower.

The coach began to slow, and Simon leaned over to check out the window. "We're almost to Berkeley Square."

"I wish we would never arrive." She wanted to stay with him, stay with the warm feeling of sated satisfaction as long as possible. But it was not possible. "Thank you," Tamsin said as she checked her clothing and hair more attentively. She knew she must look a fright, but she was too happy and sated to care or blush. She was too happy to do anything but smile. "For everything."

"You are most welcome. Happy to help, what?"

There it was—the return of his idiot's persona, come back as if he'd never had a thought in the world of so competently and completely bringing her to a shattering climax not so many minutes before.

"You don't have to do that with me, Simon—talk like that."

For the briefest moment she thought she saw a spark of acuity —of consciousness—in his eyes. But then it was gone before she could name it. "No, with you I can be my muzzy-headed self. And you don't care. That's why I like you."

Like you.

He liked her. Just as she was—by turns inexperienced and afraid, confident and curious to find out more about the world. More about life. He never questioned her choices or told her what to think. He never once corrected her.

Simon Cathcart was that rarest of rare creatures—a man who could become her friend. Perhaps he already was.

The only question remained—what was she going to do about it?

CHAPTER 16

Tamsin was happy to find her legs still worked when she alit from the carriage, and that she had enough presence of mind to remember her errand in Piccadilly before she could return home.

But not even thoughts of Mama could turn her thoughts away from Simon, and the strange conundrum of his behavior. There had been nothing simple or sleepy or stupid about Simon today. He had spoken so directly, without any of his usual verbal tricks—the *whats* and *right hos*. He had acted for all the world like a man in full possession of his faculties until she had spoken to him about it.

It was baffling.

And intriguing.

Tamsin found herself at Mattigan's Bookshop, and went straight toward the high counter where Mr. Mattigan kept the coveted copies of the *Lady's Magazine* and *La Belle Assemblée*, ensuring that customers would purchase the magazines before they pored through them. "One of each please, Mr. Mattigan."

"Nothing else for you, Miss Lesley?" Mattigan's twinkling eyes peered over the top of his spectacles. "I still have a few copies of that new book by Maria Edgeworth you had your bright eye on —*Patronage.*"

"Oh!" She had indeed looked at the novel on her previous visit—thinking she perhaps could purchase the book as a Christmas present for her sister Anne, who was deeply fond of Mrs. Edgeworth's novels. But now she might use the gift as an excuse to return to Hampstead so the authoress herself might inscribe it. "Yes, please."

"Just along there." Mr. Mattigan gestured to the shelves. "You know the way."

Tamsin did indeed know the way. But she had to hurry—she had already been gone many hours more than her mama would like.

She darted into the row of novels, only to come face to face with— "Lady Evangeline!" What a happy coincidence—she could use their meeting as an acceptable excuse for her lateness. "What a pleasure it is to see you here."

Though she should not have been surprised—Lady Evangeline might not have identified herself as a bluestocking, but clearly she was a lady of progressive thinking.

"Indeed." Lady Evangeline pressed Tamsin's hand warmly. "I have found myself looking for you since our last meeting, and wondering about you and your…your plan."

"Yes, my plan." It had seemed simple enough—to lightly ruin oneself. But in actuality, there was nothing simple about what had just happened in the carriage. Nothing simple about the way she was beginning to feel for Simon. But she could hardly tell Lady Evangeline that. And certainly not in such a public place.

But her blushing face must have betrayed her.

"Come, sit with me by the fire," Lady Evangeline offered, taking Tamsin's hand, and leading her to the private reading space near the back of the shop. "How is it *really* going between you and Simon?"

"Fine." Tamsin firmed her voice in an attempt to sound brisk and easy, anxious not to betray herself with any more blushes. "Perfectly fine, thank you."

And he was—the most perfectly fine, most perfectly gentlemanly man in all of creation.

As Lady Evangeline expressed her approval, Tamsin took a deep breath and bit down on the inside of her lip to keep from smiling. And to keep herself from confessing all.

"...I am also pursuing a gentleman at this time, though it is with an eye toward marriage."

"Marriage!" Tamsin could not keep her surprise from her voice, though she worked to hide her dismay. What would it be like to be pursuing marriage to Simon, instead of chasing ruination? "Let me be the first to wish you happy. Who is the lucky gentleman?" Some duke or marquess, no doubt. The news would send Mama into another paroxysm of hope and renew her push for Tamsin to seek out a nobleman. Poor Lord James Beauclerc would be in for an unfortunate amount of toadying manipulation from Mama—if he wasn't Lady Evangeline's choice.

"Henry Killam," Lady Evangeline said.

Tamsin didn't know when she had last been so surprised.

No, she knew exactly when she had been *more* surprised—less than an hour ago when Simon Cathcart had put his lips and his hands upon her—

Tamsin cleared her throat, and strove for something to the point about the Honorable Mr. Killam, who didn't seem at all the sort of gentleman a peeress like Lady Evangeline would seek for a husband—while the lady had advised Tamsin to seek a masculine wallflower, she had never indicated that she would do so herself. "You are to be congratulated in your choice. I understand now why you discouraged me from choosing Mr. Killam for my own plans."

"Considering how well your plans with Simon appear to be progressing, I hope you are glad for that?"

"Indeed." Tamsin felt her face warm with telltale heat. Her

plans had progressed far beyond her expectations, hadn't they? "Yes, it is indeed all for the best."

Ruination *was* what was best for her, wasn't it? She wasn't going to find a suitable masculine wallflower for a husband in the time Mama had allotted—Simon had on numerous occasions stated that marriage was not for him. "Rather not get married myself," he had said, and "no want to be trapped…"

Or was that her?

But it was Lady Evangeline who wanted to get married, though she looked…uncharacteristically wistful. "Lady Evangeline? I don't want to intrude, but since you were kind enough to assist and advise me…" Tamsin trailed off, unsure how one asked such a woman as Lady Evangeline if anything was wrong. She was sure to tell her everything was fine, even if it were a lie. Or else she would simply tell Tamsin off for being too presumptuous. "I hope your plans with Mr. Killam are progressing according to your wishes?"

"Fine," Lady Evangeline assured her with a bright, serene smile. "It's all very fine."

"Lovely." Tamsin was glad to hear it. At least one of them should get their heart's desire. It wasn't Lady Evangeline's fault that Tamsin's heart seemed to have changed its mind without consulting her.

Tamsin strove to be grateful. "I am very glad to have met with you here. Indeed, I had hoped I might. I must confess to having used your good name to further my plans"—she lowered her voice to the barest whisper—"with Colonel Cathcart. I hope you will forgive me for being so bold as to use your name—telling my mama I was meeting you here, when in reality I was engaged in meeting the colonel."

But Lady Evangeline wasn't attending her—she was staring off into space with that beautiful but somehow bittersweet look of wistfulness across her face.

"Lady Evangeline?" Tamsin called softly, not wanting to

impose herself. "Lady Evangeline, are you well?" She reached out a gentle hand.

"Yes." The lady recalled herself with a brisk breath. "And please, you must call me Evangeline, for we are friends, are we not?"

"Indeed, I would be honored. As I would be if you would call me Tamsin."

"Tamsin." That beautiful, luminous smile warmed her new friend's face. "And of course you may use my name to further your plans with Simon. It's well known that I favor Mattigan's with my custom and am regularly to be found here." She stood. "But I realize I have another appointment that slipped my mind."

"Of course." Tamsin rose to take her leave.

"I really do love seeing you, my friend. Perhaps before the new year, you and I could meet. I'll send you an invitation to tea."

"I would be honored," Tamsin said again, sensible of all the advantage Lady Evangeline conferred upon her, though she knew that Tamsin's feet were set on the road to ruination. "It was lovely seeing you again."

Lady Evangeline smiled and took her leave. "Good day!"

"Good day," Tamsin repeated, though her friend had already passed out of earshot.

And just as well—the clock at the front of the shop chimed out the hour, sending Tamsin scurrying for the front desk to purchase her wares, so she could run for home.

She had been six hours away.

She'd be lucky if there were only hell to pay.

CHAPTER 17

"Well, you seem to have made a rather long exercise of your errand." Mama's cool voice carried into the corridor and warned Tamsin to think better of rushing by.

"Yes, thank you." Tamsin bustled purposefully into the drawing room where her mama was taking her tea. "I took a long walk before I went to the bookstore—I needed to think." It was the best and only excuse she could think of—Mama had been used to Tamsin and her sister Anne taking long walks at home in the country. "And I met with Lady Evangeline at Mattigan's. We talked for some time."

"Very nice." But her mother was not yet convinced. "Your color is high," she observed. "I hope you didn't take a chill?"

"I assure you, I was well bundled—I hardly felt the cold at all." This at least was true. She had felt many other things over the course of the past few hours, but not the kind of chill her mama worried about. Tamsin plastered an unconcerned smile upon her face. "Here are your magazines."

"Thank you." But Mama did not look pleased. She was looking at Tamsin with something more than mere concern—something that was perilously close to censure. "I hope, while you were taking your very long walk in the cold and talking with Lady Evangeline, that you were thinking about your situation. We've had nigh unto a month here, Tamsin. A month full of parties and balls full of handsome, eligible men—handsome, eligible, *marriageable* men. And still here we are, with you disappearing from the dance floor with ne'er-do-well, living-with-his-rich-relations, dim-witted, sold-out officers, and taking *very long walks* the whole day through."

Tamsin kept herself from leaping to that particular officer's defense by telling her mama that he wasn't nearly so dim-witted as people liked to think. Or perhaps, as he wanted them to think—she wasn't sure which. But discretion was definitely the better part of conduct, so she kept mum.

Yet some portion of the truth was overdue—Mama was too intelligent to entirely bamboozle. "I also met with some friends of Aunt Dahlia's. Some bluestockings." She put up her chin, for she wasn't ashamed in the least. "I went to Hampstead to meet Joanna Baillie, the playwright, and Anna Barbauld and her niece, Lucy Aiken, *and* the novelist Maria Edgeworth."

"Hampstead?" From her tone, one might think Tamsin had gone to the devil and not the heath. Mama's mouth pinched in a tight show of indignation. "I should have suspected as much, though my sister promised me she would not interfere."

"Don't blame, Aunt Dahlia, Mama. This was something I arranged of my own accord."

"Oh, you and your *arrangements*," Mama scoffed. "Always thinking you can arrange things the way you like. What good have those arrangements done you? How will they settle your future if it is to be anything other than strife and woe."

As little as Tamsin wanted to enter into argument with her mother, she could not let the point pass. "The life of a bluestocking is not strife and woe."

"Perhaps not," her mother countered. "But if you don't reconcile yourself to finding a more suitable husband, your life with your cousin Edward will be nothing but strife and woe, for you're too determined to have your own way, and too combative to have anything but a dreadful time with him. You're sharp chalk to his moldy cheese, but he'll take the upper hand—and if he's anything like his father, the baronet, he'll take that hand to you. Is that what you want?"

"No!" Tamsin cried. "You know I revile him."

"Then you *must find an alternative.*" Mama punctuated each word for emphasis. "Or there will be *no money.* Do you not understand that? A few thousand pounds of prize money your father sends home will not see us through our days when Cousin Edward takes over the manor and farm. He will put me and your sisters out. And you too, if you disoblige him by still being about after not marrying him. Is that what you want?"

Tamsin had heard such arguments before—they were the reason why she was in London, why she had consented to this farce, in the first place. "Why must it be my job to sacrifice myself to secure everyone else?"

"Why must it be such a *sacrifice* to marry a rich, handsome man of your choosing? That is why I have brought you here—you and not one of your sisters, who are not so beautiful as you—so you may escape both Edward and poverty."

"Why must I do it now? What is the unholy rush?"

"London is expensive, and money does not grow like mistletoe on trees. You had until Christmas to get yourself betrothed. Have you forgotten? Have you forgotten that we must go home? That you have other sisters I must see to besides yourself?"

Tamsin was at the end of her patience with this line of thought. "Then go to them, I beg you. Go home for Christmas and leave me with Aunt Dahlia. Give me time to find someone who will truly suit."

"Leave you with Dahlia!" Mama's face crumpled into her handkerchief. "You have no idea how that wounds me—or how it pained me when she first suggested it, and pains me still. That you prefer to go to her after all I've done for you—all the trouble and expense, for where do you think the money for this rented house, for this season came from? From my portion. From what little money I will have to live on when I am a widow and your father's odious nephew puts us out. *I* spent that on you."

Tamsin could not but be moved. She went to her mother's side. "But you are not a widow," she consoled. "Papa is very much alive and well and coming home for Christmas."

"I don't know that," Mama countered. "I never know. I only know he is alive for sure and has not met with some terrible accident when he finally crosses my threshold. I live in constant —*constant*—fear of him being already dead and cold in his grave at the bottom of the sea by the time someone sends me notice."

As much as Tamsin could empathize with her mother's fears, she could not join them. "Please be sensible, Mama. Papa is alive and well. He is safe and we are comfortable."

"But for how long?" Mama railed. "Even if he comes home, he will retire and sell out of the Royal Marines and there will be no more prize money or pay."

"Then let us spend no more of it, and no more of your portion. Let me stay with Aunt Dahlia—she has said I might. That will give me the time I need to find the right person. Someone more to my liking." More masculine wallflowers, who might not be so averse to marriage as Simon. Surely there was someone she could at least learn to like, if not love as much as him.

Someone who liked her *and* was free and able to love her back.

"Stay with Dahlia—" Mama scoffed again. "How are you meet men in the sole company of women?"

"Mama." It was Tamsin's turn to chide. "There are many gentlemen who visit her salons—intellectuals, writers and poets and—"

"Ne'er do wells with not tuppence to their names." Mama dismissed such men with a wave. "You'd be better off with that idiot, sold-out officer."

Tamsin did not know what shocked her more—her mother's disdain for intellectual gentlemen, or the suggestion that she would be better off with Simon.

"The type of men Dahlia keeps company with aren't interested in marriage," her mother insisted. "You know that, don't you?"

"No, I—"

"You know that's what she likes, why she lives here in London without a man for a husband? Because she prefers the *company* of women."

It took Tamsin no more than a moment to understand what her mother was implying—it was Dahlia who was *averse*. Averse to men.

That was why Dahlia had asked—because she understood that not everyone was suited to marriage. Not everyone wanted such a life.

That *everyone* had hopes and dreams and wants that were entirely their own.

Whatever shock Tamsin might have felt was quickly turned to righteous indignation. "I don't care who or what she likes, or who she loves. I only care that she likes and loves me. And listens to me and understands me. She is open and kind and generous and has a wide circle of acquaintance I would be happy and proud to call my own."

"You are impossible to reason with," her mother accused.

"And you are impossible to live with!"

Her mother's face went white, and Tamsin knew she had gone too far. She had given vent to feelings that were far better left unspoken. "Mama, I am sorry—"

Mama held up a hand to stop her. "You're not. Not sorry in the least. And you've wasted my time and money."

"It's not wasted," Tamsin insisted. "I know better now what I like, what sort of man would suit me." A masculine wallflower who did not frequent balls, but who was not averse to marriage. Or perhaps Simon might, with time, begin to think differently.

"All I'm asking for is time."

Mama took a deep breath. "You ask the impossible."

Tamsin wanted to stamp her feet in frustration, if only to keep herself from giving way to the hot press of tears. But she was not a child to have a tantrum because she did not get her way. So she asked, "Why?'

Her mother turned her head and gave no answer.

And the stubborn, determined, and yes, disobliging part of Tamsin's soul turned away as well, and set its course. It was *not* impossible. All it would take was courage and will.

Tamsin rose, determined.

"Where are you going?" her mother called.

Tamsin was determined enough to give her the truth. "To pack my bags."

"I won't let you go to her," Mama vowed. "I won't."

No matter. Tamsin would find a way. "You said we had to leave in two days time, Mama—to go home for Christmas. To do so, I'll have to pack my bags."

"Go ahead." Her mother waved her away. "You'll only do as you please anyway."

Perhaps she would. Perhaps she could choose what she wanted instead of worrying about what might happen. Perhaps she could make them all happy.

If she asked the right person for what she wanted.

The time for making arrangements had passed. The time for simply taking action had come.

CHAPTER 18

Tamsin packed her trunks, but when twilight fell, she stood at the door to the garden wearing her country cloak and carrying only one small valise filled with her most necessary possessions. All else she left behind—all the gowns and velvet pelisses and swansdown muffs. All the comforts of her life as she had known it.

Because, hard as it was, she had to leave it all behind.

Heat scalded her throat and salt tears stung her eyes, but she would not cry. She would not falter. She would not give in to Mama's worst fears. Tamsin had fears enough of her own, and they were real—Cousin Edward and his dislike were real. Having no money was real.

But she did have friends. And one friend she was sure she could depend upon.

Tamsin pushed open the door, and was through the back garden and out the gate before she could change her mind and think better of her rash decision, or let her tears blind her way.

"Why my dear Miss T," a quiet voice greeted her. "Dare I ask where you are going, and with a valise, at this time of evening?"

Tamsin's heart cracked and flooded her chest with bittersweet relief. It was as if she had conjured him out of her thoughts and brought him to stand on the pavement behind her. "Simon. What are you doing here? I was just coming to find you."

"The same." He took the valise from her cold hands. "Where to?"

"I hardly know." She chanced a glance back at the house. "Come away before my mother sees you."

"Right ho," he agreed quietly, and fell in beside her hasting down Farm Street. "I might ask you the same thing, although I reckon I can guess. Tamsin," he asked, "are you...leaving your home?"

"I am."

His arm came around her, as if he would protect her from whatever fate had in store for a girl who abandoned her home and family. Or perhaps just prop her up when she wavered. "You've a plan, no doubt?"

Tamsin had every doubt, especially now that she had to articulate the loose handful of hopes and ideas that constituted her plans. "Yes, I— That is—" She seemed to be having some trouble throwing herself at the poor man, despite her recent practice. "I wanted to propose—"

He stood still on the pavement. "Yes?"

No. She wasn't going to act in the same way that had got her in all this trouble. She wasn't going to simply inform him of another new arrangement—she was going to *ask* for his opinion. And his help.

"Simon, what do you think of ..." Her voice cracked and her palms went damp and cold inside her mittens. She didn't have the nerve. "A sham elopement?"

He looked astonished and pleased all at the same time. "I think it's a jolly good idea," he said immediately. "I've still got the carriage, and with a change of fresh horses, we could be away and off to Scotland at once. We could have Christmas at Castle Cathcart with my family. I daresay we might even catch up with my uncle and aunt, the earl and countess—they left for the holiday in Scotland this morning, and travel is better in style and comfort. Not that the hired carriage wasn't comfortable, what?"

The ease and enthusiasm with which he acquiesced took her by surprise. And he was smiling at her in his open, sunny way, full of that strange, almost happy befuddlement that she could swear was some sort of act. Some way of keeping people at arm's length.

She could not tell which was the real Simon. Not that it mattered at this moment. "But Simon, I don't think you'd want to get your family involved—this is a sham elopement, not a sham engagement."

"Are you quite sure, Miss T?" Despite his use of the familiar moniker, his voice was low and even sincere. "I find I've rather warmed to the idea, myself."

Her heart, which had already withstood so much that evening, stuttered to a near halt, beating painfully in her chest. "Really? You've warmed to…?" Elopement or engagement? She couldn't bring herself to say the word that was on the tip of her tongue—marriage. Not when both she and he had so vocally opposed it.

But hope was like opium in her blood, heady and stupefying. She longed for him to say the word—love. That was what she wanted from him. Nothing more. Nothing less. Nothing else would do.

But what he said was, "Christmas in Scotland. With you. I really do like you, Tamsin. We'd have a jolly good time of it."

He liked her. Disappointment and reality leeched the hope from her. As if two friends could pretend to elope up the Great Northern Road and spend Christmas together with his family with no mention of marriage, or even a sham engagement.

It was impossible.

"Simon, I like you, too. You've been a very great friend to me—a better one than I deserve. But the whole point of the elopement would be to be caught, so my mama would have absolutely no choice but to wash her hands of me and let me go."

"Or force us to marry," he countered. "And we would need to go on up to Scotland if that happens."

She was tempted, so awfully, wickedly tempted to let the scenario play out—to let fate make the decision for her. But she didn't want to be a coward. She wanted to decide for herself, even if she decided wrongly. "Simon, I gave you my word. I would never let anyone force you to marry me."

"Aye, you did." His hand slid into the small of her back, where he began to rub warm circles of encouragement through the layers of her clothing and cloak. "But I tell you what, now that I think on it, I've a better idea."

Her hope was too worn out for surprise, and heaven knew her prior plans had come to nothing but a load of mischief. "I'm all ears."

"What you want is a *sham* elopement." He smiled and spread his hands as if such a thing were self-evident.

"Yes. That's what I said." Had she not proposed just that? How was it that she was confused and not he?

"No." He gripped her hand as if he would make her understand. "We don't actually elope. But your mama thinks you have, what? She chases me in my coach on the way to Scotland while you're tucked up safe and quiet at my house in Hampstead."

"Hampstead?" But she should not be surprised that he, who had clearly known both the neighborhood and the neighbors so well, should have a house there—he was so full of unexpected, unexplained surprises.

"Aye, that snug little bolt-hole on the heath I told you about. It will serve to hide you away quite satisfactorily in safely and comfort until your mother's been brought to book. You could meet your bluestocking friends while you're up there, and get a start on that book you were talking about."

Relief leavened her disappointment. His proposal wasn't exactly what she had hoped for, but it would certainly make do.

She gestured to the tattered valise. "I've already made a start."

"You see! What could be more perfect?" His enthusiasm was like a balm, easing her way. "Give you time to sort things out—time to think while you're chaperoned by my housekeeper, a very respectable widow who will no doubt be very glad to swap you out for me. I know she's got a goose set in, just in case the weather should turn and I had to stay in town."

"You would do that for me?" Her relief warmed into gratitude. "That would be extraordinary."

"Think nothing of it." He waved away her praise. "If you really are determined to strike out on your own, then Squire's Mount is the place for you."

"Strike out on my own." She tried the idea on for size. "I like the way that sounds."

His smile softened the corners of his extraordinary eyes. "Then it's decided—you'll come."

"I will."

She would strike out on her own—with the help of her extraordinary, loyal, kind friend. She was decided.

She had looked so weary and undecided—she who had before been so calm and determined—it was nearly more than Simon could bear. He wanted to take her up in his arms and tell her it would all work out. He wanted to carry her home and keep her there where she would always be safe and loved and at peace.

But to be at peace, she needed to be on her own. So he would take her home and leave her in peace, and trust the kind fate that had seen him safely through the war would keep her safe as well.

The relocation took only the slightest of efforts to arrange, and in what seemed like no time at all, the hired hack brought them back to the top of Hampstead Hill. "We're here. Squire's Mount. My house."

His bolt-hole, he called it. The house he bought with his army pay and the price of his commission when he had sold out. The quiet house at the end of the lane, across from the wild expanse of the heath. It was the place he could laze about without reference to a calendar after so many years of rigorous schedules, agendas and precise timings of assaults. The place that had buoyed him back up after the near crushing weight of responsibility for the lives and fates of men and nations.

Some of his friends had celebrated the lucky stroke of being alive at the end of the war by diving into affaires or marriage with the first available lass, suitable or not. Simon hadn't wanted sex—he had wanted serenity. And he had found it here, where he had learned at long last how to have not a care in the world—how to have not so much as a dance card planned out in front of him.

Where he had found a purpose and a calling in making other people feel as light and happy as he, even if that avocation had required him to occasionally interact with Society at all those gossipy dinner parties that served as such great fodder for his imagination. But he had found his bolt-holes in Society, too, finding quiet sofas to dream upon. Until Miss Tamsin Lesley had found him in that library.

Simon showed her into the house and stood in his foyer in his caped greatcoat, not allowing himself to take more than a step or two into the cozy interior lest he be tempted not to leave. So he stood and twirled his hat in his hand in a ridiculously telling gesture—uneasy at leaving her, but anxious to be gone so as not to prolong the misery of having to go.

Tamsin turned about the hallway, looking about the place with a wide, fascinated gaze, which he followed across the amusing prints and myriad books stacked everywhere, trying to see the place through her curious eyes, wondering what she would see. He felt strangely exposed, as if all his secrets were tacked up upon the shelves and walls for her to see.

Because they were.

"It's very lovely," she assured him. "So wonderfully homey, I already feel at home. Thank you, again, for arranging it all."

"Easy enough to arrange, once you'd thought the whole thing out."

Her look—that governess-y pleating at the corner of her lovely mouth—told him she was not buying the act he was still so desperately selling. "No. Simon, please. You must let me thank you—"

"Right ho. I expect you to be well on your way to writing that history you spoke of. Just the place for it, what? Library's as crammed with books as a bluestocking like you might like." And before he could do anything else to give himself entirely away, he donned his cap and tapped it down on his head in a bizarrely awkward gesture of finality, as if he could prove in a single gesture to her that he was an idiot. "I'll be off then. Best to get on the road before any snow, what?"

Her shoulders sagged a little—hopefully in disappointment—but she rallied and put out her hand to shake, just like a man. Like a friend. "Godspeed. And thank you again."

A friend who wanted to be more.

He allowed himself the painful pleasure of grasping her hand one last time. "Happy to oblige. Really."

And then, before he either said or revealed too much, he took himself through the door, and into the coach, and set to rattling down the road. Just to prove to one and all that he really was an idiot.

CHAPTER 19

Simon's two-story Georgian manor house sat at the corner of Squire's Mount, across the lane from the darkened heath, which, when she looked through the rows and rows of windows, was slowly being illuminated by a dusting of new falling snow.

She hoped Simon had gotten away and on the road to Scotland ahead of the wintery weather. His house was so very much like him—handsome and well-proportioned, full of light and interesting, unexpected things. The blue-painted plaster made the soaring rooms cozy. The furniture was comfortable rather than fine. The walls were hung with charming, amusing prints of ordinary people doing ordinary things—not an aristocratic seal or staid portrait of an illustrious Cathcart ancestor to be found.

The house was perfectly looked after by a sensible, brisk woman named Mrs. Walters, who conducted Tamsin on a tour of the rooms and cooked and cleaned and "made do as needed for the colonel."

"Now the colonel says as you're to have the run of the place, library and all, to write your book. So you just make yourself to home there"—she hustled Tamsin into the cozy room—"and I'll see to everything—elevenses, nuncheon, tea, even supper if you're mad for the work and want it brought in to you." The woman bustled over to the lovely scroll-legged desk, perfectly situated before the library windows. "There's paper and fresh pens, and a pen knife, thought I daresay he's left you plenty of well-cut quills. Cuts a good pen, the colonel does. Nice and tidy. A place for everything and everything in its place. Keeps the colonel bright and cheerful, doesn't let him get blue and broody."

"Is he"—Tamsin felt her way along carefully with a woman who was clearly loyal to her employer—"often blue and…" *Broody* seemed the wrong word for sunny Simon. "Out of sorts?"

"A touch, though not so much as before. Low and hard on himself he was, when he came back. Not sleeping the night through, roaming about at all hours. Cagey-like, poor lad."

Of all the things Tamsin had thought about Simon, that he could be characterized as either a lad, or cagey, was not one of them. "But he's better now?"

"When he writes—though I'm not supposed to say about that. Colonel will have my hide, so we'll just keep that between you and me, miss. But it is so. And he'll be better still if he gets himself a missus—a mistress for this fine house." A steam kettle began to whistle in the distance. "That's me kettle. But as I was going to say, you just set to writing yourself and leave it all to me."

"Thank you, I will."

And Tamsin did because there didn't seem to be anything else to do that was not exceptionally nosy. She shut herself into the library where she was not tempted to poke her nose into his bedchamber and open his closets and chests and inhale the divinely singular scent of starch on his shirt.

But each book on the library shelves—and there were hundreds there, and more scattered throughout the rest of the rooms—held some new question. Had Simon read it? Did Simon sit here, in the wing-backed chair before the fire, when he read? Did he like this book, or that?

There were books of every kind. Some she might have

expected of a military man—atlases of the continent with maps of different countries. But others seemed an odd choice for a man who professed to be muzzy-headed—plays and poetry, and a vast many novels, many by a Scottish authoress, whose books Tamsin had seen at Mattigan's but never yet read, Essie Greenock. There was even a copy of the novel she had only just purchased —*Patronage* by Maria Edgeworth—which carried a personal inscription from the authoress to Simon.

Simon. Not Colonel Cathcart. But *My dear friend Simon.*

Tamsin racked her brain to remember what he had said—a friend of his knew the bluestockings. No—a neighbor moved in Joanna Baillie's circles. But Simon was a neighbor—Miss Baillie's house was only a few streets away.

And once her curiosity was aroused, Tamsin could not resist poking her nose into every shelf and drawer—for hadn't she been especially granted the run of the place?—and examining every painting for more clues about their owner.

Everything around her told her that he was a well-read, organized, private man, who liked his simple comforts. The house gave her new and not entirely surprising insights into his character which were in complete contradiction to the man she had met in the library that first night—the addled, indolent, masculine wallflower.

Tamsin turned her attention to the desk positioned directly in front of the windows overlooking the snowy heath. It was a beautiful desk, made of carved cherry wood, warm and well-polished with gracefully curving legs—as beautiful and polished as the man himself.

And what had Mrs. Walters said?—there were plenty of fresh-cut quill pens. Tamsin opened the writing case set in the middle of the desktop. And indeed there were plenty of pens, as well as ink and paper. Plenty—far more than Mama, who had a large correspondence, or than Lady Malmesbury had kept in her desk in her private sitting room where Tamsin and Simon had embraced.

So what was Simon Cathcart, a man who slept in libraries from one end of the Ton to the other, doing with so much pen and paper?

She dove into the drawers, pulling out each and rifling through the contents. And what she found astonished her—page after page of what must be notes filled with a bold, carelessly slanted hand she recognized at once as Simon's. But that wasn't all —in the bottom drawer she found a box filled nearly halfway with more sheets, covered in a neater, more careful version of that same, unmistakable, boldly slanted hand.

A manuscript. In Simon's hand.

Tamsin ignored the hectic beating of her pulse in her ears and took the box to a chair next to the window. And began to read.

Simon decided not to make a mad dash for Scotland after all. The weather—always something one had to take into account on a campaign—helped him decide, as did the sense that both he and Tamsin would be exonerated far more quickly and at far less inconvenience to both himself and Mahoney were he to simply stay in London and let himself be found.

And so he stuck like burr on the hide of Cathcart House, letting himself be seen coming and going, and going and coming in the snowy dusk. Making a spectacle of himself.

Waiting to play his part.

Mrs. Lesley did not disappoint, though she did take a good deal longer to arrive than Simon had anticipated—it was early the next morning by the time she darkened Cathcart House's door and insisted upon seeing him.

The butler conducted the lady to him—stretched out on the library sofa in his evening clothes, as if he lay where he had fallen the night before.

He did so like a scripted stage piece.

"Colonel?" The butler gently shook his shoulder, although he was already well awake. "There's someone to would like to speak to you—a Mrs. Lesley."

"Mrs. Lesley." He opened one eye. "What ho?" He sat up slowly —it wouldn't do to give up the game all at once. Especially since Tamsin didn't seem to want him to—what *he* wanted would have to keep for another time.

"Pray forgive my appearance, madam." Simon attempted to look chagrinned. "I seem to have fallen asleep inappropriately attired, what?"

"Colonel Cathcart." The lady had the good graces to look uncomfortable. "I had thought to come to you on a matter of some...delicacy. For some intelligence about my daughter."

"Miss T? Lovely girl. Very intelligent. Didn't see her here." He pretended to reconnoiter behind the lady's lines. "Is she not here?"

"No. That is—I wondered if you might have some news of her?"

"Haven't heard a thing, but I just woke up, what? Anything from you, Steller?" he asked the butler.

"I'm sorry, no, sir."

Simon turned back to Mrs. Lesley, who nodded and pursed her lips and nodded again. "I see."

"Is there anything—" he began.

"No, no, I thank you," Mrs. Lesley answered quickly. "No, I'm sure it's all just a misunderstanding."

"Indeed," he said as kindly as he might. "I hope that is exactly so."

"Yes. Thank you. I—" Mrs. Lesley fought for her composure, and Simon began to see from whence her daughter's characteristic determination came.

And clearly, no matter their differences, the woman cared deeply for her daughter, and was genuinely upset and worried for her girl—the snow on her shoes was evidence that she had hastened there on foot from Hill Street.

Simon couldn't help but be moved. "Lovely lass, Miss Lesley. Clever and sensible. Been a very good friend to me, what?" He was running out of kind but misleading things to say. "Clever, lovely lass. Lass to be proud of. She'll come right, don't you worry. She'll come right as rain."

"I do hope so," Mrs. Lesley sniffed into her handkerchief. "I do so hope."

CHAPTER 20

The day dawned bitingly cold and glaringly gray, with the promise of even more snowfall on the wind. "Do you think it will keep snowing like this?" she asked Mrs. Walters at breakfast.

The housekeeper waved away any involvement in such a wish. "Oh, it'll do what it's going to do, no matter what we want."

Yes, life was like that, wasn't it—life went on no matter what one did, or didn't do. Tamsin had meant to do something life-changing, but life was still very much the same as it had been at home in Somerset—she rose and ate breakfast, Last night she had dinner and read, and went to her bed. Alone.

Alone with Simon's story for company, for she knew to her soul that the manuscript was his. And it was strangely intimate, reading his words and sharing his thoughts. Aunt Dahlia had said that books didn't keep her warm at night in the same way a man might. But Simon's books had made her extraordinarily warm. They had changed the way she saw him. All of him, and not just the strange facet he presented to Society.

She knew now that façade was not the true measure of the man.

Outside a dog barked in the yard, and she turned to see a shadow loom at the door—a tall, snow-covered figure carrying—

"Simon!" It was exactly as if her thoughts had conjured him out of the snow this time. Tamsin threw open the bolt. "What are you doing here?" Excitement made her breathless and giddy and demanding.

"Well, look what the storm's blown in!" Mrs. Walters was in alt. "Thought as you'd be back to us in this weather. Come you in, colonel, come you in."

"I thought you were meant to be in Scotland," Tamsin stammered. Not that she wasn't ecstatic to see him. "You must be frozen in this weather."

Simon set his snowy burden—a now-wet wicker hamper—on the table, and said, "I admit I am."

"I'll put the kettle on." Mrs. Walters bustled to her hob. "Where's yer man?"

"Right behind me." Simon turned back for the door and opened it to admit his manservant, Mahoney, who carried in an armful of firewood.

Tamsin worked to keep from bouncing on her toes in happiness. "I didn't think you would be coming back—that's not what we had arranged."

"The weather had another arrangement in mind." He shrugged as if it were self evident that he needed to come and check on her. "I wanted to make sure you had everything you needed out here, in all this snow. It being Christmas and all. "

She had never been so grateful for a storm. Yes, let it snow. Let it snow even harder, so he would have to stay. Let it snow so much the roads became impassable and the whole of the world came to an ice-frosted stop.

Just this once. Just for a little while.

She did not care why he was there, only that he was. "Let me help you. Come in and get these wet things off. You are frozen—your hands are like ice."

"The colonel insisted on taking the reins himself," Mahoney told them, "when I got too cold to feel the ribbons."

He would do that, wouldn't he? No thought for himself, but always for others, even his servant. "Come in," Tamsin urged him, "to the fire."

She divested him of his cold, clammy coats until he was in his dry shirtsleeves and waistcoat and seated in a comfortable high-backed chair before a toasty fire in his snug library. He surrendered himself to the warmth, propped his numb feet upon the brass fireplace fender and closed his eyes.

"You must be exhausted," she said from nearby. "I'll leave you in peace." She would find something to do, some chore from Mrs. Walters to keep her busy and away from him.

"No." Without opening his eyes he reached out and found her hand. "I'd actually prefer company. I'll rouse myself to amuse you in a moment, see if I don't."

"You don't need to amuse me, Simon. In fact, I should be the one amusing you."

"Oh, you do, my friend. You surely do."

Tamsin was not sure if that was a good thing. Or if she was still content being called his friend. But he was holding her hand in a way that was surely more than merely friendly.

She would start there. "Let me thank you again for the use of the house."

He smiled again without opening his eyes. "Happy to oblige. It's a snug little bolt-hole, isn't it?"

"Indeed." Her eyes went to the desk where her manuscript sat. And where that other manuscript was tucked back up in its drawer. "Just perfect for writing. But you already knew that."

One wary green eye cracked open at that. But he said, "Glad you find it so."

"I do. Your library is filled with exactly the kind of books I needed—histories and diaries of all sorts of interesting people. Just the thing for a historian or a writer. Just the thing for me."

Tamsin hesitated before playing her last card. "And for you, Essie Greenock."

"I read your manuscript, Simon."
The siege was up—his carefully erected ramparts were crumbling. Just as he knew they must when he had invited her here. For surely he had known she was too clever, too determined not to find evidence of who he truly was.

"Why did you not tell me?" she asked, her voice laced with confusion and disappointment, but also kindness.

Simon closed his eyes again, and made himself find the truth he had hidden—perhaps even from himself—for too long. "Because I didn't want anyone to know. It would have interfered."

"With what?"

"With everything. With my privacy and peace."

"I don't understand—you've adopted this pose, let people think of you as Simple Simon on purpose? You would rather people think you stupid, and damaged by the war, than—"

"A sentimental novelist?" he finished for her. "Aye."

He closed his eyes again so he would not have to see her reaction, would not have to swallow his own disappointment.

But she didn't disappoint him. "You're a rather exceptional sentimental novelist," she averred. "I read it. You may chastise me roundly for taking such a liberty, for violating your privacy, but once I had started, I could not stop. I had to keep reading and find out what happens to Lillianne. But I couldn't find the rest of the story."

"That's because I haven't written it. My heroine has not yet decided what she is going to do."

"Then you don't know what happens to Lillianne?"

"I know what I *want* to happen," he said. "But I'll have to wait and see if it comes true."

She let out that delicious little huff of laughter that he so loved. "You know that makes no sense. You are the author, Simon—you decide."

"That's what you would think. But what has to happen is that she lives happily ever after. It's a rule of all good tales," he told her. "The good must be rewarded and the evil punished."

"Like a fairy tale," Tamsin sighed. "It isn't like that in real life, is it?"

"Sometimes," he conceded. "But we have to work very hard to make it so."

"And sometimes, even when we work hard, like you and I did to convince my mother, it doesn't work anyway."

His question was quiet. "Was it hard work then, kissing me?"

"No," she assured him. "That was no work at all."

He drew in an easier breath and let his mind drift where it would. "I missed you," he told her. "In the carriage. The journey wasn't the same without you."

"Did you set out for Scotland and turn back from the weather?"

"Oh, no. Never wanted to go to Scotland in the first place. Mostly because you're not there."

"Simon," she chided. But he could hear the warm smile in her voice.

"So I stayed in London and slept on a sofa. And I dreamt of you."

"Oh?" She sounded startled and unsure.

He would reassure her. "Hmm." He turned to look at her, so beautiful, and so curious with her spectacles glinting at him in the firelight. "I dreamt we waltzed."

"Did you?" She was smiling. "I've never waltzed."

"You should—it's marvelous. Learned it on the Continent during the war. Funny the things that stick with you. Funny the things you do to try and make yourself forget everything else."

"You mean the war?"

"Hmm." He made another sound of vague agreement. "The waltz is marvelously close. And intimate—your partner never leaves your arms. Spinning and spinning together. Makes you quite lose your head."

"And were you happy waltzing, in your dream?"

"Intensely. I was happy to lose my head." He gathered what little courage he had left, and let the tension in his gut tighten another notch. "I'd be even happier to make you lose yours."

Heat blossomed across her cheeks, but she kept her aplomb. "And how would you do that?" she finally asked.

He gave in to his need to tease. "Secrets of the guild, Miss T. An officer and a gentleman—even an ex-officer—never tells."

She smiled at that—from relief and something else.

Something he hoped was at least the beginnings of love.

"But I would demonstrate. If you liked. If you asked me, Tamsin, I think I would do anything." He held out his open palm for her to take. "I doubt I could resist."

She clasped the hand he offered. "I don't want you to."

CHAPTER 21

She came to him, leveraging herself against him, angling her mouth to his, offering him her body, her self, her very soul. She would not just passively wait for him to accept her offer. She would not let this opportunity slip from her grasp.

Softly at first, she moved her mouth across his, feeling her way toward passion, using his sleepy kisses as stepping stones on her way. She kissed him gently, pressing her lips against his lightly, shifting to place little busses along the rough line of his jaw, until her lips seemed to want to move of their own volition, until she was opening her mouth and delving in to taste him. And then her hands were fisting in his linen, and wrapping around his neck, sliding into his hair, holding him still and near so she could kiss him as she pleased, as she had always wanted to do.

"I don't want to be alone tonight, Simon," she whispered with all the painful longing she had bottled up inside. "I don't want to sleep in a bed while you sleep in this chair or anywhere else that isn't with me. Please. I know what I'm asking of you. I know the sacrifice I'm asking of your honor. But please, please don't turn me away. Please let me be with you. Please."

If she could have tonight, if she could have just one chance to be with him, then she felt she could bear whatever hardships, whatever loneliness might come her way.

She pressed what she hoped were persuasive kisses to the sensitive slide of skin beneath his ear. "Please, I beg you. I love you, Simon Cathcart, and I want to be with you. I need to be with you. Please, if you care for me, if you like me even a little, then you'll do this for me."

"Tamsin." He looked at her for a long time, it seemed, his eyes dark and unfathomable, in the low firelight. And then his hand came up to caress her face, carefully outlining each and every curve and plane, brushing his fingers lightly over her lashes, skimming along the outline of her lips. "You know I can't resist you. And I don't want to, either."

"Simon." She pressed her mouth into the hollow of his throat where his pulse beat strong and steady beneath her lips.

In answer, he cupped her face with his hands, drew her toward him and kissed her—a kind, gentle kiss that filled her with bittersweet hope.

She felt the moment when his will weakened—the moment when his resistance gave way. His arms tightened around her and drew her snug against his chest, and he began to kiss her back in earnest. His tongue delved into her mouth, and he let his hands roam over her back, until they came up to rake through her simple braid, holding her still for a blistering kiss.

"Yes," she gasped. Heat began to pulse through her veins, warming her enough to drive out the cold that had been knotted there for far too long.

She abandoned herself to the warm pleasure, losing herself in the blessedly forgetful force of each new sensation, until he finally broke away from the kiss, gasping for air just as she was.

He looked down at her for another long moment, while his chest rose and fell, heaving with the effort to draw a collected breath. And then he picked her up, and began to carry her toward the narrow stair as if she weighed nothing. As if he was no longer the spent, sleepy man of the library, but another man entirely. A man of passion and action.

She wrapped her arms about his neck and rested there, safe in his arms for a blissful moment, until he reached the top of the stair and turned for his bedchamber.

The door gave way to his boot, and in another few steps they were at the foot of his bed. His dear, kind face was solemn in the wash of silver light from the window. "Tamsin, are you absolutely sure? This is..." He closed his eyes and tipped his head up to the ceiling as if he were seeking some divine guidance. "This is not part of any *arrangement.*"

"No. This is different." As *different* as he was. "This is just for me. And for you."

He set her down upon her own two feet, but held her close, brushing the hair that had fallen over her eyes away, tucking the strands carefully behind her ear. And then he traced the line of her spectacles back across her temples to the bridge of her nose. He kissed her there, and murmured, "Leave them on. I want you to see everything."

And then he cupped her face with his hands, tenderly caressing her cheeks with his thumbs, touching feather-light kisses upon her nose and cheeks, pressed infinitely light busses upon her lips.

In answer she pressed her lips to his and deepened the kiss. He tasted of brandy and warmth and strength. She gave herself up to him, using her lips and tongue and the force of her love to convince him to become one with her, body and soul.

She stepped back to unbutton her dress and shrugged it over her shoulders, rending the seam in her haste. But she wanted to be naked, with nothing between them, bare of all traces of cloth and restraint.

Simon shucked off his own waistcoat and linen shirt over his head as he came to her. He reached out to deftly untie her stays, letting them drop into a heap at her feet, until she stood before him in nothing but her stockings and shift.

"You are so beautiful," he said quietly, all trace of the laughing, happy idiot long gone from his face. "Let me. Please."

He kissed her again, with heat and something more of insistence, before he scooped her up and laid her across the soft mattress. He came down next to her, and his hands immediately began roaming over her torso, lightly skimming over the sheer fabric of her shift, over the length of her body, up and down her arms, around her face and into her hair. Each touch, each whisper of his breath along her skin wound down through her belly until the sweet tension coiled throughout her body.

"Yes." There was no other answer. There never had been.

He speared his fingers through her hair, unraveling her careless braid and spreading the long strands out around her head. He buried his face in it, inhaling deeply.

"Tamsin," he whispered into her ear. "My God, Tamsin, how I have wanted you. How I have dreamed and hoped for this moment."

Her eyelids crashed closed as his fingers traced the contour of her lips, so sweet and tender under the veneer of all that sunny, careless charm. So easy to adore as the soft, slippery sensations washed under the surface of her skin, seeping into her bones. Simon's hands heated her skin and she let the glorious tension pulsed upward through her veins, leaping and tumbling along while he kissed and touched, touched and stroked over the curve of her hip and down around to grasp her bottom.

His lips were at her ear, even as his hands cupped her, the words a heady, evocative murmur. "My sweet Tamsin. So lush, so sweet."

She needed little else to inflame her. The heat of his hands on her body, the touch of his tongue at her ear, were all she needed. She opened her eyes to watch him, wanting to see more of him. She reached up to touch his handsome face, holding his rough cheeks in her hands, guiding her thumbs across the strong planes of his cheekbones as she set herself to memorizing each and every facet of his dear, dear face.

This was Simon, with the fair, sandy hair and deep green eyes. This was the man she had chosen—was choosing now.

Tamsin ran her fingers up the sides of his temples to trace the faint crows feet at the corner of his eyes. Her hands delved into his short locks, and she could feel the strong cords of muscles in his neck as she pulled herself back up to his mouth.

She slanted her mouth across his, deepening the kiss, heedless of restraint. She wanted and needed to feel the heat of his skin next to hers, to feel the comforting strength of his body wrap around her, and chase away the last vestiges of the cold inside.

Tamsin abandoned herself to the glorious feelings. She gasped aloud with pleasure and relief from the sheer joy of the sensations streaking across her skin like lightning. Even her hands felt hot and tingly as she ran them over his body, so different from her own. His skin was pale and golden and warm, and the strong, corded muscles in his neck and shoulders flexed as she ran her fingers across his taut flesh, tracing the sleek, sculpted curves of his chest, marveling at the sprinkling of sandy hair that lightly abraded the sensitive tips of her fingers and palms.

"That's it, lass," he encouraged on a whisper that was more of a groan. "Just like that."

She needed no more encouragement to reach down between them and tug up the hem of her shift, baring herself to the friction of his body. Baring her to his gaze.

Her breath began to come faster, in audible pants that should have embarrassed her, but she was beyond embarrassment, beyond even the recall of sanity. Simon was here, next to her, and she would have him now. Now, before he changed his mind. Before anything or anyone else could come between them, or stop them. She would have this one perfect night, so she could live off its memory for years to come.

Tamsin trailed her hands down his long torso, to the edge of his breeches, loosening the buttons on the close, grazing her fingers across the growing bulge at the apex of his thighs.

"Easy, sweet," he whispered on a low laugh, covering her hands with his own, guiding her hands to clasp his firmly. "Patience, love. We have all night."

She ignored his instruction and returned to slide her hand beneath his linen and close her hands around the rigid length of his cock. "I'm tired of being patient."

He kissed her hard, pressing her head into the mattress. "I'm tired of being clothed. I'm especially tired of you being clothed." He dragged the shift off over her head and pinioned her wrists there. "I've waited a very long time for us to be naked and I aim to look my fill."

He traced the sensitive underside of her breasts, before his hand brushed lightly across her nipples—first one breast and then the other, until she felt the pink flesh contract into an almost painful burst of bliss.

She gasped, a sound of need and desperation, and arched her back, pressing herself forward into his hands.

"Please," she said again.

Above her, Simon looked down and smiled. "Now that is an excellent arrangement."

CHAPTER 22

Simon had never seen anything so beautiful. Or so beautifully ardent. He had anticipated a slow seduction—Tamsin was, for all their arranging and embracing and kissing and carriage rides, a young woman who ought to need easing into the fuller intimacies of sex, not the young woman making insistent, highly erotic sounds, and calling his name in a voice laced with desperate, carnal need.

Damn him, but he had never met a lass who seemed so determined to be well and truly ruined.

"Tamsin, love," he murmured again, but she was entirely heedless. She drove her hands into his hair, directing his mouth to her breast, insistent with need. A need he hastened to fulfill. He ran the edge of his tongue lightly across the sweet peak of her nipple, wetting the lovely tight bud before he abruptly nipped, abrading the sensitive flesh against the sharp edge of his teeth.

She cried out, and threw her head back, her eyes clenched shut tight to absorb the intense sensation. As he watched her, some of her wild abandon began to creep under his skin, heating the fire of need deep in his belly. He rasped the other peak while his hand dove down across the sleek scoop of her belly and into the nest of soft curls between her sweet thighs.

"Simon." She was almost keening now, urgent little panting cries that rose with each shallow, rapid breath.

He rose over her, and ran his free hand all the way down her shapely legs, kneading the straining muscles rhythmically until she caught the cadence and began to move her hips in time, riding his hand as it covered her mound.

"That's the way of it. " He slowly slid one long finger inside and felt her inner muscles close around him, hot and slick and delicious, and his need to join her, to put his arching cock within her, gripped him like a fist.

But he would control his need until he met hers.

Simon kissed her deeply, his tongue tangling with hers in rhythm with his hands. When he felt her body ease a fraction, he slid another long finger alongside the first. A rush of heat and desire ripped into his gut as Tamsin let out a high moan and lifted her hips off the bed. She was so bloody close, he resisted the urge to tear off his breeches and instead concentrated on grazing his thumb ever so lightly against the sensitive nub shielded by her petal-soft flesh. She arched wildly one last time and he swallowed her cry as her climax shuddered through her.

Simon kissed her again and slowly withdrew his hands from her body as she drifted on the ebbing tide of her ecstasy. Her skin was beautifully flushed a silvered pink from the sheen of her heat even in the chill of the dark room.

When her ragged breathing began to slow and ease, he ran his hand down the long, sinuous line of her side, stirring her to anew, relishing the way her body rose again to passion. Her arms, which only moments ago had been still and relaxed against the sheet, reached to bring him back within her embrace.

He dipped his head and kissed her again, closing his eyes and indulging his other senses, letting his hands flow lightly over her sinuous, responsive body. Her skin felt so soft and inviting. His cock twitched insistently, as if to remind him of his own need.

He wanted her so badly he ached. For her, this strangely determined, tiny lass in his arms, and he wanted to make the most of the precious time he had with her. God knew what might happen on the morrow—she was here, now, and they were together, and she was naked.

And she was his and no other's.

He kissed her again, and again his hands delved into the silky glory of her hair, sliding it across his palms. He meant to kiss her lightly, to give her time to recover, but she stirred and nuzzled delightfully at his throat, and his lust and his cock rose with each supple stir of her body, every subtle rustle of the soft sheets. Moonlight glanced over the dewy slide of her skin, illuminating the beautiful contours of her small, lush body.

He nosed her damp hair aside to kiss the sensitive hollow of her neck, and her eyes fluttered open on a beguiling, inviting sigh.

And then she laughed and removed her fogged glasses. "I don't need these anymore—you're close enough that I can see."

Simon rose on his arms so she could see all she wanted. Could watch as he joined her body. Watch and feel as they became truly one.

Merciful God, but he couldn't wait another moment to have her.

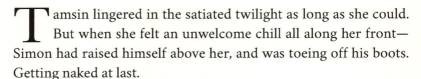

Tamsin lingered in the satiated twilight as long as she could. But when she felt an unwelcome chill all along her front—Simon had raised himself above her, and was toeing off his boots. Getting naked at last.

She eased back onto her elbows and watched with fascination by the cool silver light of the moon as he stood at edge of the bed and peeled his tight doeskin inexpressibles and drawers off, leaving them in a heap at his feet.

Tamsin's mouth went dry and tight at the sight. His arms and torso were sculpted, as if from warm golden marble. His skin was pale and tawny, his chest lightly sprinkled with hair, as sandy blond as his head. It glinted in the moonlight, leading her eyes down to where the hair trailed lower past his waist. She could feel heat flush up her neck and across her face. And lower, where the hot pulse of bliss stirred restively.

He didn't seem to mind her stare. He reached to light a candle on the small table next to the bed. "I want to see you."

"I want to see you, too," she agreed quietly.

Simon went momentarily still, looking down at her. Then he kissed her again, lightly tracing the indentations of her dimples with his tongue, before he followed the angled line of her jaw up to her ear. "With my body I thee worship," he whispered against her ear.

Tamsin's heart expanded and filled with something deeper and more profound, something more exalted than mere physical bliss, and she kissed him back with all the love and heart-wrenching, bittersweet happiness she felt. But kisses alone, no matter how glorious, were not enough.

She ran her hands down his smooth chest and then lower, curiously seeking the firm length of his cock.

"Oh, God, yes. That is indeed the way of it," he bit off, the words deep and guttural with gratification.

He kissed her more deeply as her hand settled firmly about him, hungrily delving into her mouth with his tongue, until she felt the urgent press of his pelvis against hers, and he pushed her legs wide with his knees.

Then he replaced her hand with his own, and she felt the blunt push of his body as he guided his cock into her quivering flesh.

Tamsin felt stretched and pressed, but interestingly, surprisingly so. Glorying in the curious sensation of her body stretching to accommodate his, she pulled up her knees to give herself more room, to feel the exquisite pressure more deeply within her. The glorious, slippery sensation strengthened and then receded. She tried to get closer, arching her pelvis toward him, and he nudged his hips against her again, and lowered his head to her breast, suckling her in time with the pulse of his body into her center.

Tamsin felt the erotic cadence catch hold inside her, urging her hips to move in time to meet his. She closed her eyes and concentrated on the rhythm, and the wonderful, powerful sensations skating under her sensitized skin. Her palms tingled with the need to touch him, and she ran her hands up the living sculpture of his sleek, powerful arms, kneading the sinuous muscles there, before riding upward around his neck, over his wide shoulders, and down onto the contoured plain of his chest. She danced her inquisitive fingers across his curiously flat nipples, and he made an inarticulate sound nearer to pleasure than pain.

Tamsin opened her eyes to see him rising above her, his teeth gritted and bared in something too much like anguish. "Simon?" She whispered her question.

"Do that again."

"This?" She ran her hands across his chest again, slower this time, her fingers tracing over his nipples in imitation of the way he had touched hers. "Do you like that?"

"Yes. Like that." He rose higher upon his knees, pulling her tight against him before he let go of her hips, and molded his hands to cup her breasts. He flicked the tight, rosy peaks with his clever thumbs.

A carnal sound of encouragement and need broke from her mouth on a cry. Her eyes crashed shut as she felt the first wave of pleasure push deep into her belly.

In response he ran his hands down over her hips and around to her bottom. He traced the curve of the taut globes with his palms, kneading her flesh as he rose upon his knees and pulled her up high against him. She felt a jolt of such intense, joyous pleasure streak through her, and something inside, some last vestige of restraint came untethered and ran riot—a heady, insistent, intoxicating mixture of pain and pleasure that rose higher with each escalating thrust.

His body surged into her, stronger and stronger, feeding the need, stoking the fiery heat that built where their bodies touched.

Tamsin felt herself slipping away, losing herself to the inexorable whirl of sensations. She clutched at the sheets, fisting up the smooth, fine linen, trying to anchor herself against the relentless onslaught of pressure and pleasure.

Oh, she wanted. She wanted, she wanted.

She planted her feet flat against the sheet and angled her body higher, trying desperately to appease the furious, needy ache, but he was rocking into her now with such force that she slipped, her feet sliding out from under her.

Simon reached away and grabbed a pillow from the headboard and stuffed it under her bottom, leveraging her up. But it wasn't enough—he was too tall and the feeling was slipping away.

She made a sound of frustrated anguish and pushed her thighs higher, clutching at him in desperation, and he made an echoing sound of frustration very near to a curse, and shoved the pillow away. Then he drove the breath from her lungs with the simple efficacy of lifting her legs flat against his chest.

The sharp, aching pleasure bolted back through her. She heard a high, keening moan and knew it came from her, that it was a sound of approval as much as distress, because it felt so good, too good—a pleasure so intense it was almost pain.

But Simon was relentless. He leaned into the strength of her legs and she watched him, rising above her with such grace and beauty that her heart constricted. She felt him, apart from her and yet in her all at the same time, and she knew in that instant what it meant to be undone—to let go of every last tie to reality, and give way to the glorious upending emotion that shot through her.

She closed her eyes and felt him stroke his hand down her belly, into the thatch of curls shielding the place where they were joined. He teased his fingers through the hair, then slipped his fingers lower, ever so slightly lower, to the sensitive flesh below.

Tamsin cried out and bucked up hard. It was too much and not enough all at the same time. She felt her head begin to thrash against the sheets, from side to side. But Simon wouldn't let up. He pulled her tight against him, holding her hips still as he surged inside her. He held her just so, so that something changed and sharpened, and it felt good, so good. She felt like she was going to break into a hundred pieces of bliss.

And then she did. And he pulled her to his mouth and kissed her just as she screamed.

Heat and joy and peace and relief cascaded through her body in rushing, tumbling waves, leaving the glorious serene warmth behind.

And then, in the next second, it was he who tensed, and with a sound that was both joy and anguish, thrust himself into her, one last time.

Tamsin felt strange and weightless, as if she couldn't feel the bed beneath her. As if all the feeling had drained from her body, leaving her pleasantly, gloriously numb. She watched with a sort of detached amusement as Simon let go of her and sat back on his heels, slipping away from her body.

He looked as dazed and disoriented and ridiculously happy as he had that first evening upon the sofa. She felt her lips curve into a broad smile, heard the puff of laughter that blew across her lips.

"My darling, Tamsin, Are you laughing at me?"

She heard the wicked amusement in his voice. "No, I am laughing with you. Sharing your marvelous sunny outlook on life."

"You look rather sunny yourself." He reached out to stroke her thigh as he collapsed down alongside her, and then scooped his hand around her belly to pull her snugly against his chest, before he pulled a thick eiderdown over them. "Seems a shame to cover it all up. But it's powerful cold night, my curious, determined Miss T," he whispered against her hair. "Happy Christmas, Tamsin."

Tamsin smiled in wonder at the strange scratchy feeling of his chest against her back and closed her eyes in contentment. "Happy Christmas, Simon." She felt so happy, so safe in his arms that she wanted to stay and savor the moment for just a while longer.

"I meant what I said—or rather what I wanted to say before."

"Hmm?" She was too content to think of what he had said.

"That I've warmed to the idea. Of marriage. To you." He hugged her tighter, as if she might not realize that he was talking about her. As if she might not know that he was proposing to her.

She turned so she might see his face in the silver moonlight. "But Simon, you said—"

"I said a lot of things I didn't mean. I spouted a load of nonsense to keep people—to keep you—from finding out who I really am. But you found out anyway."

"I did." She took his dear, familiar, beautiful face between her hands. "You really are the most remarkable man. And I love you."

His smile was a benediction. "And I love you. So very much. Enough to share this house with you." The crinkled twinkle in his eyes told her he was teasing.

She kissed him. "You don't need to bribe me with the house—access to the neighbors would have done it."

Simon kissed her back. "I'll take that as a yes."

"No." But she smiled and kissed him again to lessen the sting of her—temporary—refusal. "Not yet. Not until I set things right."

"Tamsin, things are already right," he insisted. "This"—he kissed her to make his point—"is right. It's Christmas—make me happy by giving me the gift of marriage."

319

"But as things lie, I've already given us the gift of scandal, which I find I don't want anymore."

"What are you hatching in that clever, deliciously governess-y mind of yours?"

"Don't worry, Simon, I'll arrange everything. I have a plan."

CHAPTER 23

Tamsin arrived quietly at her aunt's house on Manchester Square to find the salon empty but for a single person—her mother seated rather forlornly on a chair facing the frozen white garden. "Mama."

Mama turned her head sharply, but sat gaping at her daughter for some moments before she could speak. "You've come back."

"Yes." Tamsin tried to smile at her to show her she was well, and that all would be right now that she knew what she wanted. "Of course I came back."

"I didn't think you would." Her mother shook her head. "I didn't think you *could*."

"Mama." Tamsin reached for her poor mother's hand.

Her mother stood, snatching her hand away, knocking over the chair. "How could you? How could you have done this to me? I was worried sick. Couldn't sleep for wondering what had happened, what evil thing might have befallen you."

"Mama." Tamsin tried to have patience with her mother's wild imaginings and righted the chair.

"Don't you dare *Mama* me! I've been waiting for two days for your return. Listening every moment for your footfall upon the stair. Days. I'd given up hope." The pain and terror in her mother's voice were real. "I've had to write your father that you were lost to us forever."

Tamsin felt suitably chastened. "But I'm not lost. I'm here. Nothing evil has befallen me."

"And why not?" her mother demanded. "What else but the most horrible scandal, or the most terrible accident could keep you from your family? From your home?"

"Mama, I can explain."

"Damned if you can, Tamsin. You've finally achieved your object. There is nothing I can do for you now."

Tamsin refused to be defeated. Not when she knew how the story was supposed to end. "Certainly there is. It can be just like before. What was it you said—it's only a scandal if you act like it's a scandal?"

"But it *is* a scandal!" her mother wailed. "How could it not be? How could I keep this from anyone? You've been gone days, Tamsin. I had to leave the house on Hill Street—you knew the lease was up—but I could not leave London not knowing… I had to write your poor father, and he was so concerned that he felt he had to put in for leave to support me. He is at this moment making his way from Portsmouth Port to collect me, as I felt myself too weak to go home on my own, for what was I to tell your sisters when I got there?"

The pain she had quite purposefully inflicted upon her family weighed heavily upon Tamsin's conscience. But she knew she could make it right, if only she could make her mama listen. "You can tell them that I am fine and safe and home."

Mama was as stubborn as Tamsin was determined. "I still don't know what I am to tell them of your shame."

"Tell them I feel no shame, and that in recompense, you may add my portion to theirs, if you like."

"May?" Mama drew herself up. "If I like? Of course your portion will be divvied up between your sisters. Of course! I won't bother to ask you what you expect to live on—clearly my sister has offered you a place here—a position I had planned to secure for your sister Anne, who has none of your advantages of beauty. What's to become of poor Anne now—or any of your poor sisters —I've no idea."

Tamsin softened her voice to show she understood the error of her ways. "You may still offer Anne the position, Mama, for I shall not be staying here and imposing upon Aunt Dahlia. I've made other plans. Other arrangements."

"What sort of plan?" Mama's brow beetled in confusion. "Where have you been?"

Tamsin decided to ease her mother into the truth slowly. "I went away to Hampstead to visit a friend—a friend who needed my comfort. So naturally I had to abandon London to help them."

Her mother was not born yesterday—she took a long moment to consider her words. "It's a good story, I'll give you that."

"Thank you." Tamsin's relief began to transform itself into surety. "Would you like to know how the story ends?"

"Only if it ends in marriage."

"It does," Tamsin assured her. "If you'll help me?"

"I don't know if I can," her mother sighed. "What is it you hoped to accomplish with all this? Who is it you want?"

"I want"—Tamsin said the words slowly, testing them to make sure they were true—"to marry Simon Cathcart."

Her mother closed her eyes as if the very idea pained her. "But he has no money."

"Turns out he has," Tamsin was happy to report. "Enough to marry. He owns a lovely house on Hampstead Heath."

"But he's simpleton, an idiot," Mama insisted. "Everyone says so. So what if he has some grace and favor house on Hampstead Heath along with half the army? He doesn't *do* anything.

Tamsin felt righteous ire rise hot in her chest. "Don't say such a thing! He's not an idiot. He's an author—a very good one. He's been secretly writing books—writing beautiful, truthful stories that people love. He is not poor. I daresay Papa will like him."

Her mother fell back into her chair as if she had been pushed. "Why did you tell me he had no money?" she breathed. "Why did you not let me marry you to him from the first?"

"Because I didn't know. Because I was blind. I thought I knew what I wanted, and I just couldn't see that it was him." The truth of her words was liberating. "I am sorry, Mama. I am sorry for all the trouble I put you through. But I had to find my own way."

Her mother looked beyond astonished. "I am sorry, too. " Her admission came on a heavy, weary sigh. "Sorry I did not listen to you. Sorry I tried to—"

"Put me beyond the reach of Cousin Edward," Tamsin finished for her. "I know."

She had an admission herself. "I wish I had talked to you. I wish I hadn't let myself feel so desperate."

"Desperate," Mama echoed.

They'd both been desperate in their different ways, hadn't they?

"So what is to happen now?" Mama asked.

"I'm not sure," Tamsin admitted. "Simon and I had hoped—"

"Your pardon, Miss Tamsin." Aunt Dahlia's housekeeper stood at the door bearing a silver salver. "Letter has come for you. From Allingham House."

That would be Lady Evangeline writing to tell her that their friendship must be at an end—that her disappearance and sham elopement had put her so far beyond the pale that not even Lady Evangeline's friendship or patronage could help her now.

Tamsin broke the seal and opened the page. And was completely astonished.

"Tamsin?" Mama came to her side. "What does it say?"

"It says we've been invited. Most particularly, by Lady Evangeline herself. To Allingham House, for a betrothal ball."

Mama sat heavily, as if her legs had given way. "Dare you go?"

"Oh, yes." Tamsin felt entirely sure. "I have an entirely new plan." A plan to turn her scandal into a romance worthy of one of Simon's heroines.

Into the romance of the season.

CHAPTER 24

This time, it was Mama who was nearly shaking with nerves when they alighted from the hired carriage to attend Lady Evangeline's betrothal party at Allingham House. Tamsin was too determined for nerves. And because she knew of all the people in London and Society, Lady Evangeline alone would recognize her ruination for what it truly was—victory.

And romance—the true chance for the intellectual life she had once envisioned for herself but now saw with Simon by her side. If she got it just right.

"Are you quite sure?" Mama asked.

Tamsin smiled, as serene as a swan. "I am."

"And are you quite sure we're going to be admitted?" her mother asked with a nervous glance at the very imposing door. "Despite your plan, you are still a ruined women."

"I am." Tamsin was undaunted. "Lady Evangeline wrote me our invitation herself. I have it here."

Mama seemed to take some comfort in her surety. "I do hope you know what you're about."

"I don't," Tamsin laughed. "But I'm hoping that doesn't matter."

Mama took her hand. "I hope so, too."

Thankfully, they were admitted without incident. In fact, the dignified *major domo* of Allingham House went so far as to welcome her by name. "Miss Lesley, Lady Evangeline bids you welcome. She'll be very gratified to know you've been able to attend."

"Thank you." Tamsin gave over her evening cloak and took a deep, strengthening breath as she revealed the wine-red evening gown she had chosen—if she was going to be called a scarlet woman, she was going to look the part. She would be herself without hiding.

"Are you sure you don't want to stay a part of this world?" Mama whispered.

"Quite sure." There was nothing she wanted from Society save for Lady Evangeline's friendship. And Simon.

Dear, kind, unsimple Simon.

Mama gave her hand another encouraging squeeze before they had to pick up their skirts and mount the tall stairs up to the ballroom of Allingham House.

They were left alone to take a slow promenade of the holly-bedecked ballroom. While no one was openly friendly, they were not openly snubbed—her friendship with Lady Evangeline had been noted.

After their leisurely circuit of the dance floor, they passed the time visiting the refreshment table, where Tamsin fortified her nerves with an early glass of French champagne. But the bubbles provided only temporary respite.

Because behind her mama breathed, "Tamsin."

So she turned.

And there he was.

So tall. So handsome. So...everything.

Everything she wanted.

Everything she had missed so terribly.

He was at the arm of his aunt, the Countess Cathcart, who was one of the diamond-clad luminaries attending the most important social event of the season. But she was nothing next to the heroes of the peace: her husband, the illustrious diplomat, Earl Cathcart, and the warrior of the battlefield, the Duke of Wellington. And Lieutenant-Colonel Simon Cathcart, their brilliant negotiator, their strong right arm, resplendent in his regimentals. He looked more than handsome—he looked to be a man in full possession of himself. A man to be admired.

So naturally, he was surrounded by young ladies and their mamas who pushed their daughters forward in the hopes of catching the tall officer's glad eye.

Oh, how she had missed his sunny, happy smile. Even though she knew now his smile had been a sort of mask—a mask that both revealed and hid his true self.

But the time had come. Tamsin swallowed the fear that scored her throat like acid, and stepped within the circle surrounding him.

Several of the mothers, no doubt having heard that she was beyond the pale, pulled their daughters away from her.

But Tamsin didn't mind—she smiled and thanked them for clearing a path.

Until there she was in front of him. "Colonel Cathcart."

For the longest, most fraught moment, he said nothing. And then only, "Is that you, my dear Miss Lesley?"

Hope made her giddy—victory, happiness and joy were within her reach. "It is. Colonel Cathcart, I wonder if I may be so bold as to ask you to dance with me."

While the others gasped at her audacity, Simon did not.

He bowed to his aunt, the countess, and bowed to the phalanx of ladies assembled around her, and then held out his hand to Tamsin. "I should be delighted, Miss Lesley. It's been an age since we last danced."

The breath she had not been aware she was holding whooshed back into her lungs. "Too long."

"Most exactly."

A path seemed to clear before them—people backing away while craning to see what was going on. And what was going on was that Simon was holding her hand, and conducting her out to the dance floor as if he were a king escorting a queen to her throne.

And so when he stopped and turned to take his place in the set, she bowed to him, in a low, deeply respectful curtsey.

He took her hand to lead her up. "Well done, Miss T. That has nicely put the cat amongst the pigeons."

Tamsin wasn't sure she liked the allusion. "Are you one of the pigeons?"

"No. I'm one of the cats," he declared. "A rather untamed one, what?" And then he smiled and tossed her the same sort of naughty, unrepentant wink he had given her that very first night.

And just like that, he opened all the possibilities. "I think I am glad to hear that."

"I am just glad that you're here, not hiding away," he told her.

She gave him what she hoped was a saucy smile. "I might say the same."

"A hit, Miss T. Acknowledged." He sketched an elegant bow. "Your aim is as good as a gunner."

"Thank you."

They went apart from each other in the dance, casting off to weave down along the line until they were at the end.

"And I come back to my heroine, hoping that she has decided upon her story."

"She has." Tamsin had her answer ready. "She has come to rescue you."

His smile was all in the mischief at the corners of his eyes. "From...?"

"From your lair in the library," she offered. "Or your hidey hole on the Heath. Or whatever else it is you might need rescuing from."

He nodded, as if acknowledging her right. "And you, my dear Miss T? You no longer require rescuing?"

"Oh, I do. I need rescuing from myself."

His smile spread across his face like sunshine. "Right ho!" He laced his fingers with hers and held on. "A mutual rescue, what?"

"Indeed. Exceptionally mutual, I hope."

"Indeed." He stopped and raised her hand to kiss it, and caused all sorts of havoc on the dance floor in the process. But he did not seem to notice—his eyes were only for her. "And how are we to accomplish this, my dear Tamsin? You know I've no head for *arranging.*"

Tamsin knew she was grinning like a madwoman, but she didn't care. "Well, normally I would ask you to take me into a darkened room…"

"But?" He tugged their enmeshed hands to his chest, bringing her closer. "This seems like a reasonable arrangement to me."

"But I'm done with darkened rooms and running away," she pledged. "And what I want to do needs to be done in the light."

"Now, now," he chided. "Not all of it, my dear, Tamsin." He kissed her hand again, but led her away toward somewhere they might have more privacy. "Save a thought for what we still might do in the dark."

"Still?" That sounded promising. "We might if you'll have me."

"Only if I can have all of you. Mind, body, heart and soul. Because you already have mine."

"You may, all and forever." She had to close her eyes to keep the hot tears of joy burning behind her lids from leaking down her cheeks. But then she couldn't see him, so near and so dear. So handsome and so unique.

"Is that a proposal?" he teased her.

"Yes." This she knew. "I promised that if you were ever made to propose, I would refuse. So I must be the one proposing. Will you have me to wife, Simon Cathcart?"

He pulled an unhappy face. "I'm afraid my proper name is longer than that. Simon Edmund James Aloysius—"

"Aha! The S.E. of Essie Greenock!"

"Well done, Tamsin. All points to army."

"But Aloysius? I don't know if I can marry an Aloysius. What sort of name is Aloysius?"

"A fourth sort of name. And exactly the sort of fourth name a fellow like me gets saddled with. But don't try to get me off tack, my dear Miss T—"

"Not if you marry me—then I'll be Mrs. C."

"Done." He put his arms around her and held her as if he would never let her go. "But I'll need a full, formal proposal to be set forth, so there is no misunderstanding what it is you want of me, my love. I'm rather fond of orders, don't you know."

"No orders. What I want from you is just that—your love. Now and forever.

"Done."

And he kissed her. Right there on the side of the dance floor, in the middle of the set. The sort of long, deep, unbridled kiss that ought only to take place in darkened rooms, or frozen lakes, or torch-lit orangeries, and not in the middle of a dance floor at someone else's betrothal party.

Lady Evangeline might forgive the lapse, but only for a moment.

So Tamsin pulled away. "Will you marry me, Simon, and make me the happiest woman alive?"

"I think I must. Because you've ruined me for anyone else, my darling lass."

She did cry then, because she had never been so happy or so lucky. Or so very well loved. "Take me home, Simon."

And he did. From that day forward, and forever after. Always.

EPILOGUE

"Just one ball," Tamsin cajoled. "One last ball and then you'll never have to endure another again. I promise."

Simon looked unmoved—he kept his head down, writing at his desk.

Tamsin tried again. "I should very much like to attend Evangeline and Henry's wedding celebration, and I should very much like to attend it with you."

With her husband.

Simon set down his pen. "I'll go on one condition—that you promise to wear your spectacles. You must know I can't resist them."

"Done."

Tamsin did as her darling husband asked, though she disobliged him by sitting too far away from him in the carriage to take the hand he offered her—too much agreeable compliance would go to his head.

And she had plans for their slow return ride back up Hampstead Hill. Plans her darling husband was sure to approve—once he knew of them. He liked her *arrangements*.

But all the arranging was worth it when she could stand side by side with her handsome husband, and accept the smiles and congratulations that came now that their marriage had turned them from a scandal to a romance. Just like in Simon's books.

The thought put a warm smile on her face. As did the knowledge that she had done the impossible and made everyone happy—mama had been able to return home to Somerset vindicated by Tamsin's marriage.

So, too, did the fact that she was able to greet her hostess as a true friend. More than a friend—a confidant. "Evangeline!"

Evangeline gave her a warm hug. She looked every inch a diamond of the first water—the diamond of their season. "Thank you for coming, *Mrs. Cathcart!*"

The appellation made her smile more, if possible. "I am still not accustomed to being called by my married name. It all happened in such a whirlwind."

A whirlwind of snow and ice and love. They had married by special license while the Christmas snow was still on the ground.

But Evangeline already knew that—her friend was happy to take the credit for the marriage. "I imagine so! Considering not so long ago, you wanted a peaceful, man-free existence."

"I thought I did. Until I didn't." Simon had changed her mind on that, hadn't he?

"So you love him then?"

Tamsin had no hesitation. "I do. More than I thought was possible. Simon is my perfect match." The perfect gentleman wallflower. And Tamsin was happy to thank her friend for her part in the arrangement. "Thank you for kicking him awake that fateful night. Otherwise, I might never have known him."

It was strange to think that even with all her planning and arranging—and what had Evangeline called it, *machinating*—her fate had hinged on a chance friendship. A friendship that led to the library, and masculine wallflowers, and Simon.

The perfect ending to any story.

And while she and Evangeline talked and shared their good

333

fortune, something else caught her eye—that calm, happy, sleepy look her husband sent her from across the room. Whatever lovely thing Evangeline was saying was forgotten.

"...I shall ask you and Simon for supper."

"We would love to join you." Tamsin recalled herself enough to assure her friend. "Though right now I must leave you, for I can see my husband sending me a look across the room. If you'll excuse me..."

Evangeline understood. "Best go to him then."

And she did. "Longing for the library, my love?"

"Indeed, I am—my own library, what?"

"Then let us go there at once."

"Right ho," he whispered. "Though you made me come a very long way for such a short stay."

"That's because the stay wasn't the point." She let him wrap her in her cloak. "The carriage ride is."

His eyes lit with a spark strong enough to start a bonfire. "Right ho, Mrs. Cathcart. I do like the way you think."

"Excellent. Because I've made arrangements."

"Have you?" His smile spread across his mouth with all the warmth of a summer sunrise. "You may be surprised to find so have I, Mrs. Cathcart. So have I."

Tamsin reached for his hand. "Then let us go at once, and find the way of it."

And they did.

They took their time, climbing slowly back to their love nest high on Hampstead Hill, where they rested peacefully in each others arms.

The good had been rewarded, and the evil punished, and even if they were one in the same, they lived happily ever after.

The End

ABOUT JESS MICHAELS

USA Today Bestselling author Jess Michaels likes geeky stuff, Vanilla Coke Zero, anything coconut, cheese, fluffy cats, smooth cats, any cats, many dogs and people who care about the welfare of their fellow humans. She is lucky enough to be married to her favorite person in the world and lives in the heart of Dallas, TX where she's trying to eat all the amazing food in the city.

When she's not obsessively checking her steps on Fitbit or trying out new flavors of Greek yogurt, she writes historical romances with smoking hot alpha males and sassy ladies who do anything but wait to get what they want. She has written for numerous publishers and is now fully indie and loving every moment of it (well, almost every moment).

Jess loves to hear from fans! So please feel free to contact her in any of the following ways (or carrier pigeon):

www.AuthorJessMichaels.com
Email: Jess@AuthorJessMichaels.com

Jess Michaels raffles a gift certificate EVERY month to members of her newsletter, so sign up on her website:
http://www.AuthorJessMichaels.com/

facebook.com/JessMichaelsBks
twitter.com/JessMichaelsBks
instagram.com/JessMichaelsBks

ALSO BY JESS MICHAELS

THE SCANDAL SHEET

One wicked little paper, six stories of the scandals within.

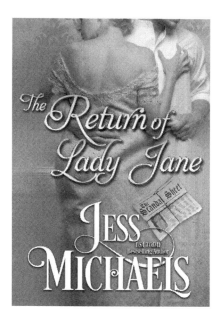

The Return of Lady Jane
Stealing the Duke
Lady No Says Yes
My Fair Viscount
Guarding the Countess
The House of Pleasure (coming November 2019)

THE 1797 CLUB

For information about the series,
go to www.1797club.com to join the club!

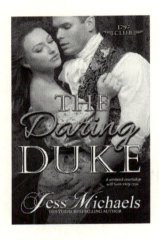

The Daring Duke

Her Favorite Duke

The Broken Duke

The Silent Duke

The Duke of Nothing

The Undercover Duke

The Duke of Hearts

The Duke Who Lied

The Duke of Desire

The Last Duke

SEASONS

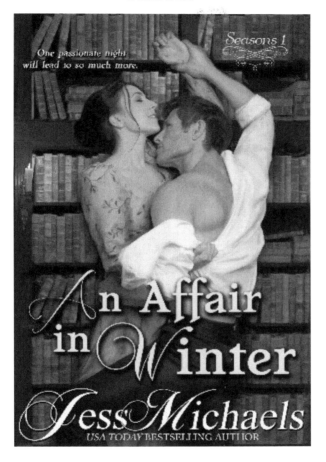

An Affair in Winter
A Spring Deception
One Summer of Surrender
Adored in Autumn

THE WICKED WOODLEYS

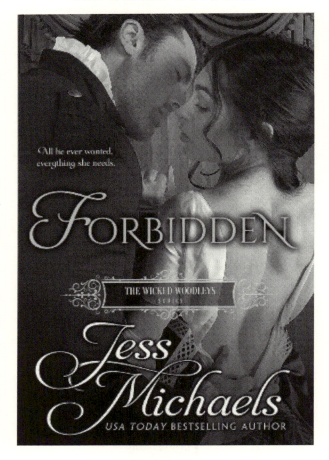

Forbidden
Deceived
Tempted
Ruined
Seduced

THE NOTORIOUS FLYNNS

The Other Duke
The Scoundrel's Lover
The Widow Wager
No Gentleman for Georgina
A Marquis for Mary

THE LADIES BOOK OF PLEASURES

A Matter of Sin
A Moment of Passion
A Measure of Deceit

THE PLEASURE WARS SERIES

Taken By the Duke
Pleasuring The Lady
Beauty and the Earl
Beautiful Distraction

ABOUT ELIZABETH ESSEX

Elizabeth Essex is the award-winning author of the critically acclaimed historical romance, including Reckless Brides, and her new Highland Brides series. Her books have been nominated for numerous awards, including the Gayle Wilson Award of Excellence, the Romantic Times Reviewers' Choice Award and Seal of Excellence Award, and RWA's prestigious RITA Award. The Reckless Brides Series has also made Top-Ten lists from Romantic Times, The Romance Reviews and Affaire de Coeur Magazine, and Desert Isle Keeper status at All About Romance. Her fifth book, A BREATH OF SCANDAL, was awarded Best Historical in the Reader's Crown 2013. MAD, PLAID AND DANGEROUS TO MARRY is her eighteenth book.

When not rereading Jane Austen, mucking about in her garden, or simply messing about with boats, Elizabeth can be always be found with her laptop, making up stories about heroes and heroines who live far more exciting lives than she. It wasn't always so. Long before she ever set pen to paper, Elizabeth graduated from Hollins College with a BA in Classics and Art History, and then earned her MA in Nautical Archaeology from Texas A&M University. While she loved the life of an underwater archaeologist, she has found her true calling writing lush, lyrical historical romance full of passion, daring and adventure.

Elizabeth lives in Texas with her husband, the indispensable Mr.

Essex, and her active and exuberant family in an old house filled to the brim with books.

ALSO BY ELIZABETH ESSEX

HIGHLAND BRIDES

Mad for Love
Mad About the Marquess
A Fine Madness
Mad, Plaid and Dangerous to Marry
Mad Dogs and Englishwomen (Coming soon!)

DARTMOUTH BRIDES

The Pursuit of Pleasure
A Sense of Sin
The Danger of Desire

THE KENT BROTHERS CHRONICLES

Between the Devil and the Deep Blue Sea

ANTHOLOGIES

Vexed (featuring *Between the Devil and the Deep Blue Sea*)
Tempted at Christmas (featuring *A Merry Devil*)
Dashing All the Way (featuring *Up on the Rooftops*)
Christmas Brides (featuring *The Scandal Before Christmas*)
A Christmas Brothel (featuring *The Ship Captain's Tale*)

For news and up-to-date information on Elizabeth's books, please sign up for her newsletter at elizabethessex.com.